Rafe took a deep breath. "Julie, marry me."

That got her attention. "Are you out of your mind?"

"Yes. It doesn't have to be a forever thing. It doesn't have to be a romantic thing. But let's get married so that the babies will have the best start we can give them."

She raised her brows. "Marrying you is a best start?"

"Yes. I know you don't have a whole lot of reasons to trust me right now, but we need to do this for the children."

"Not really. And don't start with the father's-last-name machismo. Jenkins is a fine name, a better name in this town than Callahan."

The Cowboy's Baby Surprise

NEW YORK TIMES BESTSELLING AUTHOR

TINA LEONARD
&
BRENDA HARLEN

**Previously published as *His Valentine Triplets*
and *Double Duty for the Cowboy***

ISBN-13: 978-1-335-61742-2

The Cowboy's Baby Surprise

Copyright © 2021 by Harlequin Books S.A.

His Valentine Triplets
First published in 2012. This edition published in 2021.
Copyright © 2012 by Tina Leonard

Double Duty for the Cowboy
First published in 2019. This edition published in 2021.
Copyright © 2019 by Brenda Harlen

Recycling programs
for this product may
not exist in your area.

This edition published by arrangement with Harlequin Books S.A.

For questions and comments about the quality of this book, please contact us at CustomerService@Harlequin.com.

Harlequin Enterprises ULC
22 Adelaide St. West, 40th Floor
Toronto, Ontario M5H 4E3, Canada
www.Harlequin.com

Printed in U.S.A.

CONTENTS

Tina Leonard is a *New York Times* bestselling and award-winning author of more than fifty projects, including several popular miniseries for Harlequin. Known for bad-boy heroes and smart, adventurous heroines, her books have made the *USA TODAY*, Waldenbooks, Ingram and Nielsen BookScan bestseller lists. Born on a military base, Tina lived in many states before eventually marrying the boy who did her crayon printing for her in the first grade. You can visit her at tinaleonard.com and follow her on Facebook and Twitter.

Books by Tina Leonard

Harlequin American Romance

Bridesmaids Creek

The Rebel Cowboy's Quadruplets
The SEAL's Holiday Babies
The Twins' Rodeo Rider

Callahan Cowboys

A Callahan Wedding
The Renegade Cowboy Returns
The Cowboy Soldier's Sons
Christmas in Texas
A Callahan Outlaw's Twins
His Callahan Bride's Baby
Branded by a Callahan
Callahan Cowboy Triplets
A Callahan Christmas Miracle

Visit the Author Profile page at Harlequin.com for more titles.

His Valentine Triplets

TINA LEONARD

There are so many people I can never thank enough for the success in my writing career, but at the top of the list are my patient editor, Kathleen Scheibling; the magical cast of dozens at Harlequin who unstintingly shape the final product; my family, who are simply my rock; and the readers, who have my sincere thanks for supporting my work with such amazing generosity and enthusiasm. Thank you.

Chapter 1

"Rafe is too smart for his own good."
—Molly Callahan, recognizing the seeds of mayhem
in her too-bright toddler

As Augusts in New Mexico went, it was a hot one. Rafe Callahan stared at Judge Julie Jenkins in her black robe in the Diablo courtroom and felt a bit of an itch. Was it the heat, or was he just thinking about what they'd done in July when his steer had gotten tangled in her fence?

"Counsel," Julie snapped to his brother, Sam. "Why should I recuse myself from hearing *State* v. *Callahan?* Have you any substantive reason to assume that I could not hear proceedings in this matter fairly?"

"Judge Jenkins," Sam said deferentially, "as you know, your father, Bode Jenkins, has brought suit against our ranch, invoking the law of eminent domain."

"Not my father," Julie said, her tone stiff. "The State handles matters of eminent domain."

Yeah, Rafe thought, *and everyone but Julie seems to understand that her father is in it up to his neck with every government official and thief in the local and state governments. Good ol' Dad can never do anything wrong in his little girl's eyes, and vice versa.*

Julie's gaze flashed to him, then away. *Guilt.* It was written all over her beautiful face. He knew what was under that prim black robe, and it was the stuff of dreams, a body made for the gods. He'd been lucky enough to find the chink in her sturdy armor—a testament to the fact that she couldn't resist him, Rafe thought smugly.

He'd made her guilty. Julie knew very well that their night together meant she should step down from this case.

"Mr. Callahan," Julie said to Sam, after sending another defensive glare Rafe's way, "it seems to me that you have no good reason why I shouldn't hear *State* v. *Rancho Diablo.*"

Sam, the crack-the-whip attorney assigned to saving the Callahan family fortunes, looked down at his notes, marshaling his thoughts. It was important that Julie not be the judge hearing this case, Rafe knew—as did all six Callahan brothers—because she was completely partial to her father. What good daughter would not be? But Julie seemed to have it in her mind that the case was purely New Mexico versus the Callahans, not Jenkins versus Callahans, Hatfield and McCoy style.

Ah, but he knew how to bring little Miss Straitlaced to heel. He hated to do it. She'd been a sweet love that one night, and a virgin, which wasn't so much a shock as it had been a pleasure he'd remember forever. He got warm all over, and stiff where he shouldn't be at the moment. There was something about those brown eyes and midnight hair that just undid him, never mind that she had enough sass in her to send up fireworks.

But this was war, unfortunately, and the Callahans needed all the help they could get to draw level with Bode Jenkins and his bag of crafty tricks. Rafe stood, and with Julie's gaze clapped on him warily, leaned over to whisper to Sam. He could feel her eyes on him, as well as those of his brothers, his aunt Fiona and uncle Burke's, and half the town, who'd come to hear today's proceedings. Julie wouldn't want to be embarrassed in front of the people who'd helped raise her after her mother died. But it had to be done.

So he whispered some nonsense in Sam's ear about the price of pork bellies, all the while knowing that Julie thought he was telling Sam about their passion-filled sexcapade.

"Now act surprised," he said to Sam, and his brother pasted a dramatic and appropriately shocked expression on his face.

Julie said quickly, "Would counsel step up, please?"

Sam went to Julie, as did the lawyer for the State, a slick Bode yes-man if Rafe had ever seen one.

"I'll consider recusing myself," Rafe heard Julie say, her tone soft yet tinged with anger. His ear stretched out a foot trying to hear every word. "But I'm not happy that you've indicated I don't hear cases completely fairly. I've never been asked to recuse myself before, and I feel this is another case of Callahan manipulation, for which they are famous."

Her accusing stare landed on Rafe, and he couldn't

help himself. He grinned. She stiffened, so cute in her judge getup, but completely naked to his eyes. It was as if she knew it.

After a long glare his way, during which time he noted her pink cheeks, and her full lips pressed flat with annoyance, she said, "Court will adjourn while I consider the motion. We will resume in one hour. And Mr. Callahan," she said, her voice tight as she addressed Rafe, "I'd like to speak with you in my chambers, please. Counsel will not be required."

"You've done it now," Sam said in a low voice. "She's going to eat you alive, scales and all. It's your fault, too, for sitting there smirking at her."

"I can't help it," Rafe said. "She just looks so stiff and formal in that robe. I remember tacking her hair to her desk in biology class, and chasing her on the playground. It's hard for me to take her seriously."

"She's going to teach you the meaning of respect, dude. Good luck. I'm off to get a hot dog." Sam sauntered away, his conscience clear, unconcerned about his brother's impending misfortune.

Rafe sighed and approached the chamber of doom. "Judge?"

"Come in, please, Mr. Callahan, and close the door."

She sounded like a vinegary old schoolteacher. Rafe sat down, and tried to arrange his face into the most respectful expression he possessed.

"Mr. Callahan," Julie began, and he automatically said, "You can call me Rafe. I'm not a formal guy."

She nodded. "As you wish. And you can call me Judge Jenkins."

He nodded, reminding himself not to grin at her prissy tone. The fact was, Julie was in command of their futures at Rancho Diablo. If they could get her to recuse herself, they could probably get a more impartial judge to hear their case. This thought alone kept Rafe from smiling. He even tried his damnedest not to stare at Julie's legs, shapely stems skimmed by the black robe, and elongated by high-heeled black pumps. Very severe, and very sexy. She wore her ebony hair in a no-nonsense upsweep, which made her look like a dark-eyed, exotic princess. She wore a lipstick that was a shade off red, and he wanted to kiss her lips until there was no lipstick left on her.

But he couldn't. So he waited for her ire to recede.

"Mr. Callahan," she began again, "you may be under the misapprehension that because we have had an engagement of a personal nature—"

"Sex," he said.

Her full lips pursed for a moment. "You may be under a misapprehension that I will tolerate disrespect in my court."

"No, Judge. I have the utmost respect for you."

Her big brown eyes blinked. "Then quit smiling at me in the courtroom, please. You look like a wolf, which you may not be aware of, and it comes across as if you take this proceeding lightly."

"I do not." Rafe shook his head. "Trust me when I tell you that this proceeding is life-and-death to me."

She nodded. "See that you try to maintain a more serious composure in the courtroom."

"I will." He nodded in turn, his expression as earnest as he could make it. "And you're wrong, Julie. Just because I let you seduce me in a field doesn't mean I don't respect you."

She gasped. "I did not seduce you!"

He shrugged. "You're a powerful woman, Julie. Not only are you beautiful and smart, you're sexy as hell. I couldn't resist you." He shook his head regretfully. "Ever since then, I've wondered if holding you in my arms was a dream."

She glared at him. "You can be certain that I didn't seduce you. You—you…" She seemed at a loss for words for once. "You seduced *me!*" she said in a whispered hiss. "This is what I'm talking about, Rafe. You Callahans always manage to twist things around!"

"Oh, Judge, it's every man's dream to be seduced by a gorgeous woman. Don't burst my bubble." Rafe smiled his most charming smile. "I wish I could seduce you, but I'm pretty sure you're impervious to men."

She blinked. "That didn't sound very nice."

"Maybe you're just impervious to me." He sat on her desk and swung a leg, considering his words. "That's probably it."

"I don't even know how that happened that night. But," Julie said, her voice low, "I'd appreciate you not bringing it up again, and particularly not in the courthouse."

"But was it good for you?" Rafe asked. "That's a worry that's kept me up at night."

Julie drew back. He gave her a forlorn look. "Good for me?" she repeated.

He nodded. "Did I make you feel good?"

She hesitated. "I guess so. I mean, considering it was you, I guess it felt as good as it could have."

He tried not to laugh. She was lying like a rug, and in her own judge chambers, just down the hall from where she made people take oaths to tell the truth. "Ah,

Julie," he said, "there are nights when I wake up in a sweat thinking about how sweet you are."

She appeared confused. Probably no one had ever said that to her before. But he knew she was sweet. He took her hand and tugged her close to him. "Seduce me again, Julie."

"No," she said. "You're bad news, Rafe Callahan. My dad always says that, and it's true. You're really, really bad, and I should never have—"

He touched his lips to hers, stopping her words. "So why did you?"

"I don't know," she said, not pulling away from him. "I have no idea why I even let you talk to me, Rafe. I shouldn't have done it, though, and I can tell you it will never happen again."

"I know." Rafe framed her face with his hands. "And it makes me so damn sad I just don't know what to do." He kissed her gently, then with more thoroughness as he felt some of the stiffness go out of her. "We geeks never get the beautiful girls."

She blinked, pulling back. "Geeks?"

"Yeah. You know, those of us who think too much, when we should be men of action." He moved his hands down her shoulders, down her arms, and began kissing along her neck. God, she smelled good. He had a stiff one of epic proportions sitting in his jeans, and the call of the wild firing his blood. "I'm guilty of thinking too much, when I should be going after what I want."

He circled her waist, holding her to him, and kissed the hollow of her throat.

"Rafe—"

"Mmm?"

"Is this about the court case?"

He pulled back a moment. "Is what about the court case?"

"This."

He looked into her dark eyes, completely confused. His mind was totally fogged by Julie, her sweet perfume, her sexy mouth—and then he realized what she was asking. "God, no, love. I compartmentalize much better than that." He couldn't help the grin that split his face. "I may be a thinker, but I'm not that good, sweetie. This is all about trying to get under the robe of the most beautiful girl in Diablo."

Julie seemed to consider his words. Rafe was pretty certain he should strike while the iron was hot. Clearly, she was of two minds about letting him kiss her, and the fact was, he wasn't about to let Julie out of his grasp. He remembered far too well how wonderful it had felt to be inside her. So he did what any normal, red-blooded man would do when faced with an uncertain female: he staked his flag on Venus. Pushing up Julie's robe and dress and everything else that was in his way, he slid off the desk and kissed her soft tummy. She gasped, and he ran his hands under her buttocks.

"What are these?" he asked, staring at the darling little pink straps holding up her stockings. Julie looked like a Victorian saloon girl, and he was pretty certain he was so hard right now diamonds couldn't chip him.

"Garters," Julie said. "And a thong."

"Pretty," Rafe said, and moved the thong so that he could kiss her the way he wanted to. Gently, he licked and kissed and tasted her, and when her knees were about to buckle, he pushed her into her desk chair where he could kiss her to his heart's content. He'd waited a long time for this moment, and when he could tell she was about to rip his hair out by the roots, he licked inside her, taking great pleasure in her gasping cries as she climaxed.

He wanted to just sit and look at her for a second, all disheveled in her black robe, but she shocked him by grabbing his belt. "Wait," he said, "just a minute, Julie. I don't want you to do anything you don't—"

She cut off his words with urgent kisses. Okay, he wanted her to do everything. She was pulling at him, trading places with him, and the next thing Rafe knew, he was sitting in the tall-backed black leather chair and Julie was sliding down him, clutching his shoulders as if she was afraid he was going to disappear.

What could he do but give her exactly what she wanted? "Hang on," he said, crushing her bare buttocks in his hands so that he could hold her tightly to him. He thought he was going to black out from the pleasure. Julie gasped against his neck, then tore off the judge's robe and threw it on the floor.

"Let me help you." Rafe undid the frilly white blouse she had on, tossing it away. That left a sweet ivory bra, but he was a pro with bras, and he had that hanging over a law book before Julie could realize that she now was seated on him wearing nothing but a soft peach skirt, pink garters and black heels. *I'm living a dream,* Rafe thought, taking in Julie's breasts, which were beautiful, shapely, peach-nippled. He wanted to grab them, but his hands were full of her soft buttocks and he had her right where he wanted her, so when she rose on a thrust and wrapped her arms around his neck, and her breasts engulfed his face, he was profoundly grateful. He sucked in a nipple before it could get away, and

Julie stiffened on him, giving him a very pleasurable jolt where it counted.

"Oh, Rafe," she murmured. "Oh, God, don't stop."

He didn't. He suckled, and thrust, and touched, and invaded. And when Julie tightened up on him, giving a tiny muffled shriek of pleasure as she came, Rafe held on for just a moment longer, making sure he'd never forget this moment, before letting himself surrender to the magic of Julie.

He was pretty certain he'd rested his case, and that the jury had found him more than irresistible.

Ten minutes later, Rafe tried to help Julie dress.

"I've got it, thanks." She swept his hands away, fixing her robe and her skirt. He could tell she didn't want to meet his gaze, so he pushed his white shirt into his dress jeans and straightened his tie.

Tidied up, Julie regained her professional demeanor. "This is awkward."

"Not really." Rafe stole another kiss, which he noticed she didn't return. Well, of course, she needed time to process how much she wanted him. He grinned. "See you in court."

Julie didn't smile. "Remember, please. Respect, Mr. Callahan."

"Oh, I do, Judge." Taking her hand, he raised it to his lips. "I respect the hell out of you."

She jerked away. Rafe saluted her and went to the door. Then he turned, catching her eyeing his butt just before she realized he'd found her staring. "Next time, this is going to happen in a bed."

Her cheeks pinked. "There won't be a next time."

He smiled at her. "The thing is, as good as it is between us in all these hot locations you pick out, Julie, I could make you feel so much better in a private place where I can spend hours giving you pleasure you'd never forget."

She gasped. "Go!"

He nodded, drinking in her straight posture with appreciation. She was a darling little thing, so prim and bad by turns. My God, he loved a woman with sass, one who said no but begged so prettily, too. He didn't tell her that her hair was slightly mussed—actually, she looked like a Barbie doll that had gotten caught in a windstorm—and he didn't tell her that her lipstick was shot. Nor did he tell her that somehow she'd forgotten to put her bra back on. It was still draped over a law book in the corner of her office.

"Thank you, Julie," he said softly, meaning every word, and then he left her chambers and returned to sit beside Sam.

"Where the hell have you been?" his brother demanded. "I brought you a hot dog."

"Thanks. I'm starved."

"So, did she read you the riot act?"

"Pretty much." Rafe bit into the cold hot dog, moaning with satisfaction.

"Did you apologize for pissing her off?"

"I did. I apologized the only way I know how. Is this soda for me?"

Sam nodded. "And did she accept your apology?"

"She did. She accepted everything." Rafe chewed his hot dog happily, feeling like a new man, thanks to his encounter with Julie. "She's a very generous woman."

"I'll say she's generous if she accepted your dopey

apology." Sam sighed. "I hope you didn't do anything to change her mind about recusing herself."

Rafe froze. "Uh…"

Julie swept into the courtroom. Everyone rose as the bailiff instructed, then seated themselves again. Rafe swept his food out of sight.

"She doesn't look happy," Sam said.

No, but she does look satisfied. His little judge was going to flip when she realized she'd forgotten to put on lipstick. Her hair was pretty much blown out of its 'do. She looked gorgeous to him, but flustered, and Rafe grinned, thinking that next time he wasn't kissing Julie Jenkins until she begged him to.

He snapped himself out of his sexual reverie, realizing that her gaze was on him, and she did, in fact, look annoyed again. It was the smile, he remembered, and he put on his most serious expression.

She didn't seem impressed.

But she had been a few moments ago, and that had to speak well for the future. He hoped so, anyway. *Next time, I'm going to figure out how those little garter things work, and spend about an hour kissing the judge where I know she likes being kissed the most.*

"Though there is no fundamental reason for me to recuse myself," Julie said, "I will do as the defendants have requested. Let the record reflect that I do so with a good deal of misgiving for the request that was made of this court." She pinned Rafe and Sam with a mutinous glare. "Court adjourned."

"She's really ticked," Sam observed. "This will not be good for our neighborly relations."

Rafe watched Julie sweep from the courtroom on a

cloud of displeasure and irritation—with maybe a little embarrassment thrown in. He watched her go, fascinated by the woman he loved wrapped in a real good snit. What Julie didn't know was that he loved her all the more for her spiciness and warmth, and now that she was good and mad at him, he was dedicated to getting her out of that black robe again. He had a one-track mind when he wanted something, and he wanted Judge Julie Jenkins badly.

They said the best sex was makeup sex—and if that was true, then he was all for making up as soon as humanly possible.

"That was ugly," Sam said as he and Rafe walked out into the sunlight. People left the courthouse and were milling around, chatting over what had happened in Julie's court.

"Not ugly," Rafe said, thinking about how beautiful she was. "The Callahans are free to fight another day."

His brother shoved his briefcase into the front seat of his truck. "I'd like to know what Judge Julie was thinking that made her do a turnaround like that. She is not an easy judge to sway. Frankly, I was expecting a lot more fight. And what the hell was all that 'act surprised about pork bellies' crap? We don't do pork at Rancho Diablo."

Rafe shook his head. "It doesn't matter now." He got in the passenger seat and pondered how he might ever put his plan of The Seduction of Julie into place. As Sam had said, she was not an easy woman to sway—and she seemed to hold him in as much esteem as a rattlesnake.

If he didn't know better, he would think she hadn't enjoyed his lovemaking.

But he did know better. Judge Julie didn't have a faking bone in her body, and the woman put on no grand act. He'd be forever thankful for his steer getting tangled in her fence in the first place. Okay, maybe making love in a field on a blanket he'd grabbed from his truck wasn't a woman's idea of My First Time, but by golly, he'd waited for years to hold Julie Jenkins, and he'd made the most of it. He'd had her sighing and moaning like crazy, a yearning cat under his fingertips. Today, he'd tried to make her second time something she'd remember with a heaping helping of must-have-more. "I'd just put it up to the fact that she'd heard of your reputation, bro, and went down before the fight."

Sam shook his head. "There's something funny about Judge Julie calling uncle that easily. Bode's hired one of the best teams of lawyers around."

Rafe clapped his brother on the back. "No one's as good as a Callahan."

And it's true, Rafe thought. *I've had it from Judge Julie's own lips. Maybe not in those exact words. Maybe not in any words at all. But I know Julie Jenkins digs her some Callahan cowboy.*

For a week, all was silent. Rafe saw his brothers at mealtimes and at work, and everybody seemed preoccupied. He wrote it off to the heat. Jonas was moody, but what the heck. When one was a retired surgeon turned rancher, perhaps one got moody. Jonas had always been a brooding cuss, anyway, and as far as Rafe could tell, his oldest brother had been eyeing Sabrina McKinley for the past couple of years, and nothing had changed. If there was one thing guaranteed to put a man off-kilter, it was the unrequited desire for the love of a good woman. It could kill a guy. "Or at least the lust for a good woman," Rafe amended out loud, earning a glance from Sam, who was studying a mass of papers almost as thick as the Bible. Rafe went back to considering the sales figures for Rancho Diablo, but his mind wasn't on it. *Sam works too hard. He's been trying to save this ranch for nearly three years now, and I don't think he's even looked at a woman in all that time. Callahans should have it easier getting sex than we do.*

"The problem," Rafe said out loud, "is that we all work too hard. And we're picky."

"What, ass?" Sam said. "Do you mind taking your braying elsewhere? These briefs are eating me, and I can't think with you chattering like a teenage girl."

His brother definitely needed a woman. "You know, Sam," Rafe said, "since I'm the thinker of the family, I've been thinking. And I think it's time we got you out of the house."

Sam glared at him. "Thank you, Sophocles, for that bit of news I can't use."

"Dude, this lawsuit has sucked you dry."

"You have a solution?" Sam shrugged. "I'm not giving up on Rancho Diablo, no matter what barrel Bode Jenkins thinks he's got us over."

"Yeah." Rafe considered his brother. "Nothing seems to be working, does it? Aunt Fiona's Plan has gone off the rails. We've had weddings and babies out the wazoo around here, and our brothers have populated a small town all by themselves, and still we can't convince the courts that we should have our own zip code free of Jenkins."

"Do you mind, Hippocrates? Can I get back to this?" Sam waved some documents.

Rafe grunted. "I'm just saying maybe you ought to get some fresh air. Or get lucky, alternatively, if that's in the range of your possibilities."

Sam laughed, and it wasn't a pretty sound. "And when, pray tell, was the last time a woman opened her door for you, Einstein?"

Rafe couldn't brag. It would make Sam feel bad. He probably felt that they were brothers in bachelorhood. Of the six Callahan boys, only Sam, Rafe and Jonas were unmarried. No woman was going to throw her cap at Jonas, because he was about as much fun as a wart. Sam had an easygoing style, when he let himself hang loose, which wasn't often.

Of the three of them would-be champions to Fiona's Plan to get all the Callahans married—and then award Rancho Diablo to the brother with the largest family—Rafe figured he had the best chance. *I have the highest IQ, I have the best hair, I fly the family plane and girls love geeky guys like me.* "If you knew anything at all about Hippocrates, brother, you would know that he believed the body must be treated as a whole and not just a series of parts. Therefore, with your mind in overload over Rancho Diablo's attempt to free itself from Bode Jenkins, you're under too much stress. We've got to find you a woman."

"Excuse me," Sam said, "but I didn't hear you tell me when you last saw a woman naked and welcoming you."

Rafe didn't reply. He didn't want Sam to feel bad, and he would never let the cat out of the bag about the judge. Especially since Sam was pitting his wits against Julie's father.

"That's what I thought, genius." Sam went back to glaring at the mountain of paper in front of him.

"Never say I didn't try to help," Rafe stated, and leaned back to continue studying ranch paperwork.

The bunkhouse door blew open with the speed of a rocket, crashing against the wall. Rafe's jaw sagged as Bode Jenkins barreled into the room.

The old rancher was holding a rifle in his hands, pointing it at him.

"Jesus, Bode," Sam said. "Put that popgun down before someone gets hurt."

"I'm going to *kill* him," Bode said, glaring at Rafe. "You dirty, thieving dog!"

"Are you talking to me?" Rafe stood, pushing Sam behind him. "What the hell, Bode?"

Fiona burst in behind their neighbor and faced him, before kicking him a smart one on the shin. "Bode, give me that gun, and cool your head. Whatever's gotten up your nose now, it isn't worth doing time in jail."

Burke appeared and snatched the gun from Bode, who seemed to give it up without much fight. All the other Callahans filed in, glaring at the rancher, then glancing around the room to make certain everyone was in one piece.

"Do you mind telling us what's going on?" Jonas demanded.

"I'll tell you," Bode said, his voice quavering. The man's face was red, pinched with fury as he glared at Rafe.

"No, you won't." Julie winked and shoved a few Callahans out of the way so she could reach her father. "Dad, you're going to give yourself a heart attack. Calm down."

Rafe blinked at Julie, who was stunning in a summery sundress and sandals, with her inky hair swept up in a ponytail. There was just something about her that hit him like a fist to the solar plexus every time he saw her. He liked her in her judge's robe, he liked her in a dress, and he loved her naked in the moonlight.

But something had her wound up tight. More than the court case. "What's up?" he asked her. "What's got Bode steamed this time?"

That got Julie's laserlike attention. She practically stabbed him with her eyes as she sent him a particularly poisonous glare. "Now is *not* a good time for you to be speaking disrespectfully to my father. I just saved you from being shot, Mr. Callahan, so if you don't mind, zip your lips."

Well, wasn't that a big dose of judgelike attitude? He grinned at Julie. She liked him, he could tell. No woman was that starchy around a man unless he rattled her love cage. He couldn't wipe the smile off his face.

"Bode, the next time you come running onto our property like a madman—and may I remind you this is not the first time you've acted crazy…" Fiona began.

Bode pinwheeled his arms with frustration. "You Callahans make me crazy. Why can't you just git? This is my land, my property, but you're like fleas. You multiply like fleas—"

His face turned redder, as if he'd just thought of something horrific. He glared at all of them, reserving his most potent fury for Rafe. "You—"

"Dad," Julie said, "we're leaving right now. Come on. There's nothing here we want."

Rafe watched her go, tugging her protesting father along with her. Of course there was plenty here Bode wanted. He wanted the ranch, he wanted their home, he wanted the Diablos and the rumored silver mine—

Bode whirled, punching his finger toward Rafe as he escaped his daughter's clutches. "You're not winning," he told him. "You haven't won."

Julie dragged her dad from the bunkhouse.

"Damn," Rafe said, "I believe Bode's finally gone over the edge." He sank onto the leather sofa. His brothers and Fiona and Burke gathered around. "I thought he had a caretaker over there to keep an eye on him."

"Seton's busy, I think," Fiona said. "She's been over here helping Sabrina with some things for me." Their aunt shrugged. "Seton does have time off, and she chooses to be here with her sister. That has nothing to do with Bode's visit, because he seemed mostly upset with you." Fiona looked at Rafe. "Didn't he say he was going to kill you?"

Rafe shrugged in turn. "I took that 'you' in the global sense, as in all of us. I don't think he meant me personally. If he wants to kill anyone, it would probably be Sam, who is beating him all to hell in court."

"Oh." Fiona nodded.

"I swear," Rafe said. "I didn't do anything to the old man. We all agreed we'd abide by the law, and the decision of the courts, and I'm cool with that." He held up two fingers in a V. "Peace, brothers. It's all chill in the house of Callahan."

Jonas snorted. "Yo, thinker, don't do anything stupid. The man is tense, and next time we might not be around to save you."

"Save me?" Rafe shook his head. "He's crazy. Everyone knows it."

"Everyone may know it, but that won't save you if Bode decides to get crazy on you."

Burke looked at Fiona. "Actually, that's the most

upset I've ever seen our neighbor. Thankfully, his firearm wasn't loaded, although they say there's really no
such thing as an unloaded gun."

"He *is* crazy," Fiona agreed, "but he'd been quiet for
a while. Which made me nervous in a different way.
But now I'm really nervous." She looked around the
room at all the brothers. "Now is as good a time as any
to tell them," she said to Burke, and Rafe thought, *oh,
that didn't sound good.*

"It's up to you," Burke said, moving his hands to
her shoulders.

Fiona looked down, allowing Burke to massage her
shoulders, which was strange, for this independent
woman rarely accepted anyone's comfort. Rafe could
tell his little aunt was struggling to put her thoughts
in order. Bode's untimely visit had put speed to something that had been on her mind. Rafe waited, feeling
tense himself now.

"Burke and I believe that Bode's ill feelings in this
suit have largely been directed at me. I've been a thorn
in his side for quite some time," she said.

The room was so silent Rafe thought he could hear
Sam's heart beating beside him, which was really annoying. *It should be my heart I hear beating. Sam's
always been one for attention. It's why he's a lawyer.*

"Remember the Plan I put forth to all of you? How
I put Rancho Diablo in trust for whichever of you married and had the largest family?"

They all nodded. A couple of his brothers looked
pretty proud, because they figured they were in the lead.
Rafe snorted. It didn't matter. They'd decided among
themselves that, whoever won it, they were going to
divide ranch ownership between them equally, in spite

of Fiona's Plan. And once he got started making a family—when he finally decided to settle down— Rafe would make all his brothers look like beginners, anyway. There was such a thing as proper planning, which all men of deep thought knew. Strategy. Chess players understood the importance of strategy, for example.

"Well, after a great deal of thought, worry, prayer and yes, even strategic plotting, Burke and I have decided," Aunt Fiona said, taking a deep breath, "to move back to Ireland."

Chapter 2

"Now see what you've done, brain man," Sam said beside him, and Rafe turned.

"What?" he demanded. "What did I do?"

"You've upset Fiona." Sam shook his head. "None of this would have happened if you hadn't ticked off Bode and his precious pumpkin, Julie. By the way, did you get my play on words? Brain man? Like the movie *Rain Man?*"

"Yeah, a laugh riot." Rafe turned to face his aunt. "Okay, before everything gets really out of hand, I suggest we discuss topics of concern that affect the ranch and its future." He went to Fiona and patted her on the back. "Let's meet in the library in thirty minutes, which will give everyone time to finish what he was doing just as our neighbor had another of his dramatic fits."

The brothers went off in separate directions, muttering and murmuring. Rafe looked down at Fiona. "It's going to be all right. You can't let Bode upset you every time he decides to be a clown. Because he does it so often."

She stared up at him, her eyes bright. "I've made a lot of mistakes, I know, in my raising of you boys and the management of this ranch. But I cannot let something bad happen to any of you." Fat tears plopped down Fiona's wrinkled cheeks.

He hugged her. "We're grown men, Aunt. You don't have to worry about us anymore."

"That's not what that rifle said." She sniffled.

"Yeah, but we all know Bode's a terrible shot."

"Eventually even a bad shot finds a mark."

That might be true. Rafe pondered the wisdom in his aunt's words as he held her to him. He looked at Burke over Fiona's head. The only father figure most of the brothers remembered shrugged helplessly.

"All right, no more tears. We'll get this figured out." Rafe patted Fiona on the back and let Burke lead her away.

She was shaken, of course. They all were. Except him, for some reason. *Staring down the barrel of that gun didn't upset me like it should have.*

Bode was just superhot under the collar because the Callahans made his precious lamb recuse herself from the lawsuit. He'd expected Judge Julie to be his ace in the hole.

Ha.

"Crazy old man," Rafe muttered under his breath.

But an annoyed Jenkins was not to be treated lightly. Rafe remembered the time Julie had been teed off with him, and his brothers had let her into the bunkhouse where he'd been sleeping off a bender, and she'd drawn about fifty tiny red hearts all over his face with indelible marker. It had taken a week for those suckers to wear off. He'd been the laughingstock of Diablo.

He still had a bone to pick with her about that.

She hadn't looked too happy with her father's attempt to put a piece of lead in him today, but it wasn't because she cared what happened to Rafe. All Julie cared about was her old man.

"Which means," Rafe muttered as he left the bunkhouse to head to the family council, "that the next time we make love, I'm going to have to make certain that the folks all the way over in Texas hear my darling little judge banging her gavel as I completely disorder her sweet little court."

"You realize he's an ass," Julie Jenkins snapped to Seton McKinley thirty minutes later, after she'd remanded an exhausted Bode back into Seton's care.

The blonde and beautiful care provider blinked at her. "Your father?"

"No," Bode interrupted, impatient for the story delay. "Rafe Callahan. He's an ass. An eight-point horned ass."

Julie sighed. "Dad, calm down. Put all this behind you. Most importantly, it's against the law to go waving rifles at people and threatening them. I know you don't realize this, but you jeopardize my career when you lose control."

"I would never do that."

Bode looked at her with big eyes. Julie sighed again, realizing only too well how much the Callahans got under her father's skin. "Dad, you did. I could be in trouble for not calling the sheriff out on you."

"This is what I'm talking about." Bode waved a hand at her and Seton. "The Callahans are always at the root of every problem."

"Usually I agree with you wholeheartedly." Most especially, she would agree with him that Rafe was something of a rascal. No sooner had his longhorn gotten caught on her land then Rafe had shone all his legendary Callahan charm on her. And she, like a weak, silly princess in a fairy tale, had let him wake her up from her self-imposed sleep, and then made certain she'd not had a night since when her dreams weren't interrupted by his devilishly handsome, always grinning face. She didn't even want to think about what he'd done to her last week in her own chambers—and yet she hadn't had five minutes where she didn't remember his mouth all over her body, tasting her hungrily as if he'd never had a meal so good. It sent shivers shooting all over her just thinking about it.

"This time, I can't agree with you. You're at the root of this problem." Julie settled a red-and-black plaid blanket over her father and left him to Seton, who seemed to have decent luck soothing Bode. Once again the situation was equally split, with blame for both sides. Her father was angry that the Callahans had asked her to recuse herself, and the Callahans were doing what they had to do to keep their ranch. It was all pointless. In the end, Bode would get Rancho Diablo. Her father always got what he wanted.

She should have taken herself off the case long ago. But she'd wanted to stay in control as long as possible to make certain the Callahans didn't pull any of their numerous tricks on her father.

Callahans were famous for practical jokes on people they considered friends, and dirty tricks on those they didn't.

She had to protect her dad.

"I gave him a shot of brandy, and he went right to sleep." Seton walked into the kitchen and handed a glass to Julie.

"Oh, no, thank you." She waved away the crystal glass and reached for water.

"I'm not sure what set him off," Seton said. "I'm sorry I wasn't here when he got emotional."

Julie shook her head and began unloading the dishwasher. "Trust me, there wasn't anything you could have done. When Dad gets his mind made up, off he goes. Wild horses couldn't hold him back."

"Do you know what was bothering him?"

Julie didn't turn around. "The Callahans. They always bother him," she said simply, but she knew the truth wasn't simple at all. "Don't worry about it, Seton. Dad gets worked up about once a month. It always blows over."

"All right. Let me know if you need anything."

She nodded, and heard Seton leave the kitchen after a moment. Julie kept straightening, her mind not really on the task. After she finished the dishes, she closed the dishwasher and went out to the den to look at the black-and-white photos on the mantel. Almost every picture was of her and Bode. Riding horses. Swinging on the porch swing. Hunting deer. Skiing in Albuquerque. She'd framed them all in black frames so they matched, a chronology of their years together. Just the two of them—except one photo.

That picture was of her, Bode and her mother. The three of them, a family, before Janet Jenkins had passed away from cancer. Bode had been a different person before her mother died. He was pretty focused now on wheeling and dealing, the thrill of the hunt.

Julie didn't think her father had ever mentioned the Callahans except in passing before he'd become a widower. His hatred of that family knew no bounds now.

Of course, the Callahans stirred the pot like mad. Fiona was no wimp at plotting herself, and seemed to take particular delight in keeping Bode wound up.

Julie had gotten revenge once, but even when drawing hearts all over Rafe's face, she'd known she was totally attracted to him. Like his twin, Creed, he was lean and tall, with dark hair and a chiseled face. Creed's nose looked a bit broken, but Rafe's certainly wasn't, despite the fact he'd rodeoed and been in numerous fights. He was totally, hauntingly masculine. Julie couldn't touch his skin and not know he was totally delicious.

But she'd never dreamed she'd slip under his spell and willingly shed her dress and her inhibitions for him—cross line, father and court to experience the wonder of making love with Rafe Callahan.

"He's still a jackass," she muttered. Rafe did not like her. She was pretty certain their day in court had been a game, a Callahan hookup, for which the cowboys were famous. She looked at the picture of herself as a small child held by her mother, and knew there were some things she couldn't even tell her father. He was just too mentally fragile these days—and some things were too terrible to confess.

Especially when they had to do with Callahans.

Unfortunately, she was pretty certain she was under the spell of a certain black-haired, crazy cowboy.

* * *

"There is no reason for us to pay any more attention to Bode than we have before," Rafe said. He looked at Fiona, who was seated next to Burke in the upstairs library. Each brother had joined in the family council to discuss the next move, and Fiona's startling pronouncement.

Rafe took a sip of brandy from a crystal glass. "The strain of the suit is no doubt taking a toll on everyone, but there's no reason for you to feel that you're the problem, Aunt Fiona." He shrugged. "Bode's just getting himself caught in his own game, and it's making him a little nutty."

"That's right," Jonas said. "There's no reason for you to go back to Ireland, when we need you here."

"I second that," Pete said. "Who would watch my three bundles of joy? Jackie needs help now more than ever."

"I third that," Creed said. "I've got my hands full with *kinder* now that Aberdeen's expecting again. Her sister Diane living on the ranch with Sidney means three more toddlers on top of that. Who has the energy to keep up with all these children besides you, Aunt Fiona?"

She gave them all a leery glance. "Do not try to entice me with babies."

"But that was The Plan all along, wasn't it?" Judah grinned. "The Plan was to get us married and in the family way as quickly as possible. You wanted babies, and we complied."

"And have been having a lot of fun doing it," Pete said, and everyone booed him.

"It's true, though." Creed glanced around at his

unwed brothers with a big grin. "The fifty percent of you who haven't joined in Fiona's Grand Plan don't know what you're missing out on."

Rafe rolled his eyes. "Dirty diapers? Sleepless nights? Pint-size potties?"

Creed raised his glass. "Nightly lovemaking that you don't have to go hunting for."

"Afternoon quickies on call," Pete said with a smile.

"Booty that has your name on it," Judah said with a big grin, "and furthermore, has her name on yours, as much as you can stand it."

Rafe blinked. "Jeez. Is it all about sex with you knuckleheads?"

"Yes," his three married brothers said in unison, and Rafe sighed.

He knew exactly how they felt. If he could go home to Julie every night, he'd beg her to cook naked for him. He'd make certain she had see-through baby doll nighties that he could tear off her every night, a different one for every day of the month. He'd—

Damn. They're getting to me. My own brothers.

He looked at everyone staring at him, and swallowed hard. *Creeps.*

"Anyway, what I was saying before I was so rudely interrupted," Rafe said with a glare for the married side of the room, "is that if you leave, Aunt Fiona, you cede the field to Jenkins."

"Which is a bad idea," Judah said, "because you've been running Rancho Diablo for over twenty years. There's no reason for you to let him run you off."

"And besides," Pete chimed in, "someone's got to marry off the rest of our brothers. We don't need half of us causing trouble in our bachelor phases."

"Jonas, Sam and Rafe." Creed shook his head. "My twin, Rafe, and Jonas, the eldest of the bunch, and Sam, the youngest of the bunch. I'd say we still need you, Aunt Fiona."

"Don't coddle me," she said. "Don't try to lure me with babies and matchmaking and spitting in Bode's eye. I know what's best, and what's best is that Burke and I leave you men to unite against a common foe."

They all stared at their tiny, determined matriarch.

"Damn," Rafe said, "that's pretty strategic thinking, Aunt."

She nodded. "One of my better plots, I must say."

He glanced around the large library. His brothers lounged in various positions, some looking lazy (but always ready for action), some rumpled (hard workers), and Jonas, who looked cranky, as always.

Rafe loved his brothers. They were a tight-knit band.

"But what if we don't unite?" he asked. "What if we turn on each other?"

"Would you?" Fiona asked, looking at him.

"Hell, I don't know. There's a ranch at stake." He shrugged. "Without your hand on the reins, we might go running wild through the New Mexico desert."

"I doubt it." Fiona's voice was crisp. "Anyway, today's flare-up has convinced Burke and me of what we'd been discussing since Bode launched his grab for your land. We think you are better off without me here to rile him. I've divided the ranch up into six equal parts. For the three of you who are married, I've put your portion in your name. For those of you who are not married, your portion is in trust, which you will receive upon my death or your marriage, whichever comes first. Without me here, I'd say it won't be marriage."

She nodded and took Burke's hand. "It has been an honor to raise you. We love you like our own sons. We always did. There are a lot of questions you may one day want to ask, and when you're ready, we'll answer them for you. And remember that everything you think you know isn't always what is. Take good care of each other, and most importantly, be brothers."

Fiona and Burke made their way from the library. Rafe tried not to gawk at the departing figures of their aunt and uncle. "I think she's serious."

Sam nodded. "She really believes she's the source of Bode's anger. I say we just kill him."

They all snorted at him.

"She can't go back to Ireland," Jonas said. "We need her here. She belongs here. Burke belongs here. They haven't been back to Ireland in over twenty-some years. What are they going to do there?"

The brothers turned to stare at him.

"That is the most emotion I think I've ever heard you spew," Rafe said. "I feel like I'm in the presence of the angel of human psyche."

"There's probably no such thing," Sam said, "but that *was* pretty heavy, Jonas, for a tight-ass like you."

Jonas threw a tissue box at them. "Go ahead, bawl your brains out. We all want to."

"I'm not crying." Rafe took a deep breath, not about to let himself get drizzly, although he did feel like a water balloon in danger of being punctured. Fiona's decision had left him pretty torn up. "I'm going to convince Fiona she's worried over nothing. I'm—"

They heard a door slam. The brothers glanced at each other.

"Must be going out to check on the horses," Creed offered.

"Or to change her holiday lights. It's about time for her to take down the Fourth of July décor-anza." Pete nodded. "She left them extra long because all the little girlies liked them so much. She said her great-nieces should always have sparkly decorations to look at."

Fiona was famous far and wide for her lighting displays. Rancho Diablo always looked like a fairyland, sometimes draped with white lights, sometimes colored—but always beautiful. "I want to wring Bode's scrawny chicken neck," Rafe said.

"I do, too," Judah said, "but that'll just land us in jail."

"Miserable old fart." Rafe couldn't believe what had happened. His luscious Julie had to know that her father was beginning to go around the bend. Not that she would ever admit to such a failing in him, locked in her ivory tower of daddy-knows-best. "Maybe Bode has terminal dumb-ass disea…" Rafe stopped, listening to a sound that had caught his attention. "Was that a motor? A vehicular motor? Visitors, perhaps?"

Or Bode serving up more trouble.

The brothers looked at each other, then jumped to the many windows of the library to study the driveway in the dimming evening light.

"*That* is a taxi," Jonas said, "and if I'm not mistaken, our aunt and uncle just bailed on us."

Chapter 3

"I'm not sure what any of this means," Sam said to Rafe a week later. They were all busy trying to adjust to Fiona and Burke's sudden departure. He waved a bunch of legal documents. "It seems our aunt was keeping a lot of secrets."

Rafe gazed out toward the horizon of Rancho Diablo. The two of them were in Fiona's library, Sam having called him there to vent his frustration with their aunt's dispensation of the ranch. "You'll figure it all out."

"I wish I'd known half the stuff before we got knee-deep in battling Bode. Did you know that originally this land was owned by a tribe? Our father bought it from them."

Rafe shrugged. "That explains the yearly visit from the chief, maybe."

"Yeah, it sure does. The tribe retained the mineral rights to the property."

Sam sure had his full attention now. Rafe turned away from the window to goggle at his brother. "All mineral rights?"

"Oil, gas, silver—you name it, it's not Rancho Diablo's."

Rafe couldn't help grinning.

"What's so damn funny, Einstein?" Sam snapped.

"Bode doesn't know." Rafe laughed out loud.

After a moment, the thundercloud lifted from Sam's brow. "That's right, he doesn't. And he can't sue a tribe for their mineral rights. Well, I guess he could, but he wouldn't win. This is a signed and properly executed document."

They both sank onto a leather sofa and chuckled some more. Jonas poked his head in, favoring each of them with a grumpy gaze.

"Don't you two ever do any work?" he snapped.

"Listen, Oscar the Grouch, close the door," Sam told his elder brother.

Jonas obliged, though not happily. "Why are you two lounging when there's work to be done?"

Sam handed him the sheaf of papers. Jonas gave it a cursory glance and handed the stack back. "I don't have time to read a wad of papers as thick as your head. That's your job, Counselor."

"Well, if you would read," Sam said, "and if you could read, as your medical degree claims you can, according to these papers, Rancho Diablo Holdings owns no mineral rights. They are instead owned by the tribe of Indians from which Chief Running Bear hails." Sam grinned, waving the papers. "An interesting turn of events, don't you think?"

Jonas stared at his brothers with obvious disbelief. "All mineral rights?"

"Yep. All we own is the land and the bunkhouses and the main house. Actually, if you think about it," Sam said, waxing enthusiastic about the topic, "no one really owns the houses, either. The banks do, and even once they're paid off, the government can still come along and decide to kick you out. They either want the land for building, or they decide you owe back taxes on the property, and poof! There goes your domicile." Sam shrugged. "The value is in the mineral rights, I'd say, and those, brothers, we do not own."

"And we never did," Rafe said, glancing at the papers. "These documents were executed the year before you were born, Sam."

"Yeah, I noticed that." He frowned a bit. "But let's not go there for the moment."

"Holy Christmas," Jonas said, "that means Bode's lawsuit is basically nullified."

"In large part, if not in total," Sam agreed. "Lovely day, don't you think?"

"Fiona knew this," Jonas said. "She had to know the mineral rights weren't ours, and that we couldn't give them over even if Bode won his case."

"Maybe she didn't," Rafe said, wanting to defend their small, spare aunt. "Even Sam said he didn't really understand the papers."

"I understand them perfectly," Sam said, "and I can't find any documents that state otherwise, which might indicate a later sale from the tribe to Rancho Diablo Holdings. So what that tells me—"

"Is that Fiona probably never saw those documents," Rafe said stubbornly. "They were signed before she came. When our parents were alive."

Sam pursed his lips. Jonas sighed and looked out the same window that Rafe had been gazing from. Rafe knew his brothers thought Fiona had withheld the information on purpose.

"She hardly had time to go digging through every document pertaining to the ranch. Overnight, she became guardian to six boys in a foreign country," he pointed out. It made him slightly angry that his brothers seemed to think Fiona might have been deceptive about what she knew about their property. She was the executor of their estate. "It doesn't make sense."

"She became guardian overnight to five boys," Sam said, bringing up a point that Rafe had chosen to gloss over. "I came later."

Rafe saw no reason to chase that particular ghost right now. He waved a dismissive hand. "You're a Callahan. Let's not dig up every screaming specter in this house right now."

"What I'm saying is that Fiona knows who my parents are," Sam said, and Rafe and Jonas stared at him in shock.

In all the years they'd been a family, this was the most they'd discussed Sam's abrupt arrival. They wouldn't have even known about it, but Jonas had been old enough to remember that Sam had come later— after the accident that had claimed their parents. Rafe wished Fiona hadn't left, and that all this discussion of documents had never arisen. Nothing good could come of the past interrupting the present. He looked at Sam's strained face and felt sorry for his brother.

"I'm just saying this because Fiona knows who my parents are, and she knew about the mineral rights. I know that," Sam said, "because Chief Running Bear doesn't swing by every Christmas Eve just to share toddies with our aunt in the basement."

"Well, he probably does," Jonas said, "if I know Fiona."

Rafe sighed. "This is ridiculous. Just call her and ask. Or go down to the county courthouse and sift through some records. There's no point in getting all wild and woolly about stuff that doesn't matter." He felt ornery at this point. It was too hard seeing Sam suffer. "There'd be no reason for her to keep this from us," he said, refusing to believe that their aunt could be quite so manipulative. "If she'd known, she would have revealed it in court so Bode would shove off."

Jonas shook his head. "She might be protecting the tribe."

"Or she didn't know!" Rafe insisted.

"Or, and this is the most likely scenario," Sam said, "this was the perfect way to get right up Bode's nose."

Rafe blinked. "You mean to let him sue us for practically no reason?"

Sam shrugged. "Everyone's been talking for years about the rumored silver mine on our property. We know there's nothing here, but Bode would believe the gossip. More important than land would be a silver mine. Treasure seekers have always tilted at windmills."

"Bah," Rafe said impatiently. "So what. I'll tell him myself." He was getting more ruffled by the moment, which made sense, since he was enamored of making love with Bode's daughter.

"You can't tell him," Jonas said, his tone forceful

and big-brother-like for a change. "None of us in this room is going to say a word to our brothers or anyone, until we find out why Fiona didn't want it known that the mineral rights had been sold. I'm pretty certain it's bad to withhold pertinent information in a court case, and we can't get our aunt in trouble."

"Not in this case," Sam said. "Fiona and Burke are just going to say that the document was executed before they arrived, and they had no knowledge of its existence. And you," he said to Rafe, "may I suggest you curtail your activities with a certain judge? Try not to annoy her or her father? We need time to figure everything out, before we hurt our case or our aunt. And I don't trust you to keep your mouth shut if you're in the throes of pleasure."

Rafe crammed his hands in his pockets so he wouldn't take a swing at his brother, and told himself that the family that kept secrets together stayed together.

He could keep a secret.

He could stay away from Julie.

No, I can't.

I'm sitting on a powder keg. And when it blows, I'm probably going straight to hell.

Life didn't seem to be getting any better when Rafe opened the door to his room in the bunkhouse and found the judge sitting on his bed. "What the hell?" he asked, trying to be nonchalant and not quite making it. She looked delicious, and as heat flooded his groin he realized he'd never been cut out for a monklike existence. "Get out," he said. "If you've come to mess up my face with a permanent marker again, I should warn you I don't fall for the same tricks twice." He waved his hat at her. "Anyway, let's go out in the main room."

"I have to see you privately," Julie said, and Rafe sighed.

If it was up to him, he'd love to see the good judge very privately. But he wasn't going to break with the rules set forth by his brothers, even if the rules were unfair as hell. He looked at Julie's clouds of luscious dark hair and beautiful tilted brows and delectable full lips and made himself sound stern. "Julie, you need to go."

"Rafe, I'm not going."

"Then *I'll* go." He turned to leave, and it was harder than leaving behind part of his own body. He told himself he was truly a man of steel for his virtuousness.

"Rafe," Julie said, standing up, "we have to talk."

But his brothers had warned him, and somewhere in his mind, he figured they were probably right. "You'll find me on the couch if you want to tal—"

Her hand on his arm stopped him. "Rafe."

Well, technically, they were in a doorway; they weren't really alone, right? "Yes?"

"If I have to have this discussion with you via a court order, I will."

He grunted. "So your father sent you."

"No one sent me. I'm here because I need to talk to you." She looked at him closely. "The last two times I've seen you, you've done your best to seduce me, and unfortunately, I've let you. Now you're acting like you don't even want to look at me…" Her voice drifted off. "It *was* all about the lawsuit."

He blinked. "What was?"

"Seducing me in chambers. You just wanted to convince me—compromise me—into recusing myself."

"Well," he said, wishing he could kiss her, but knowing he couldn't without risking his brothers' wrath, "it's an interesting premise, but no."

She pulled away from him, standing a prim and proper three feet away, no longer in the doorway but outside in the den. Rafe knew it was for the best, though he could tell by the hurt look on Julie's face that she completely had the wrong impression.

But how could he tell her that if it was up to him, he'd toss her into his bed right now and ravish her until next week?

He couldn't. And the curse of it was he'd never had Julie in a bed. Never had her with hours to spare.

Always quickies. "Damn."

"What?" Julie stared at him, her pretty face wreathed with suspicion.

"Nothing," Rafe said with a sigh. "Anyway, what did you want to tell me?"

She took a long look at him. "I wanted to tell you I heard through the grapevine that your Aunt Fiona and Uncle Burke have left."

He shrugged. "It's true. What of it?"

"What does this mean for the lawsuit?"

He shrugged again, not interested in discussing it. "Ask your father."

"I…we don't discuss it much," Julie said, and Rafe snorted.

"Right. You were the judge in charge of hearing the case."

"And since I'm off the case," Julie said with heat, "we have not discussed it, or your family. I am not the judge, and therefore I am not privy to details!"

She was so cute when she got snippy.

"You're a jerk," she said, when he made no reply, and she flounced out the door, her white sundress practically blinding him as he tried to stare through it. He remembered her delightful derriere, and he wanted her. She made him crazy in ways he'd never been crazy before.

"I am a jerk," he said, and turning, bumped into Sam.

"I won't argue with that," his brother said gleefully. "I heard the whole thing, and you have very little understanding of how to treat a woman, bro."

"What the hell does that mean?" Rafe snapped, his patience addled by being so near Julie and unable to possess her. "You told me to stay away from her until this whole thing blows up or over."

"True," he conceded, "but she didn't wear that darling little dress to talk about cases, dummy. She came wearing that hot number hoping you'd take it off of her." His grin was wide. "Boy, are you dumb."

Sam continued on, and Rafe sighed before heading out to the barn.

He wasn't dumb. He was playing it safe, and right now, that seemed like the smart thing to do.

And maybe the only thing to do.

Rafe Callahan was an ass, Julie fumed as she stalked to her truck. She got inside and resisted the urge to peel out of the Rancho Diablo driveway. It would solve nothing, and it served no purpose for him to think he'd won.

That's what this was all about. From time immemorial, women had been played by Romeos, and she was no different. The Callahans were great tricksters, fond of practical jokes and mayhem. They loved one-upping anyone who tried to outdo them.

Her father was right: Callahans were trouble. And

she should have known better than to think there was anything real going on between her and Rafe.

"An ass," she muttered. "A big, braying ass."

Her heart jumped and fluttered as she thought about how wonderfully he kissed, and she wiped at a tear that slid down her cheek. One tear, that was all she'd spare for that tall, dark, handsome Romeo.

He wasn't worth her time.

Unfortunately, she still had to talk to him. The problem now was telling him what she had to tell him without killing him.

This time, she wouldn't settle for permanent marker hearts all over his face.

A branding iron would be much better, but unfortunately, she didn't have one of those. "Oh, heck," Julie said to herself. "This is not going to be good."

Chapter 4

"So," Jonas said, rattling pots and pans in the kitchen as Sam walked in. "We're going to need to organize KP duties. I think an org chart might be necessary. We'll divide up days of the week for cooking, cleaning—"

"Whoa," Rafe said, "I'm not eating your cooking."

"Excellent," Jonas said. "You can have my days."

"All right," Rafe said, as Sam entered the kitchen and poked his head in the fridge. "You can do my cleanup."

"Why can't we just eat out?" Sam asked, his face mournful as he considered the fridge. "Frankly, I don't think the three of us are qualified to take care of ourselves."

It was probably true. Creed, Pete and Judah had wives and families who could take care of them. Rafe figured Jonas and Sam were pretty useless at providing for themselves, and he didn't particularly want to be shackled with babying them. Sabrina lived upstairs at the main house, but she definitely could fend for herself. Rafe grimaced. He could take care of himself, too, but someone was going to have to take care of his boob brothers. Sam was busy with the court case and probably couldn't subsist on hamburgers from Banger's Bait and Tackle, not if they wanted him firing on all cylinders legally. And Jonas didn't have the sense to come in out of the rain. Rafe sighed as he looked at his helpless brothers. "We could hire a cook."

"For the three of us?" Jonas looked outraged. "Doesn't that seem wasteful?"

"It seems practical," Rafe snapped. "I make good food, but I'm not cooking for you babies."

They both looked at him with regret in their eyes. Rafe realized that a trap had been sprung on him. "You two discussed this. You planned this pity party! You want me to do the woman's work—"

"Don't let a female hear you talking that way," Sam interrupted with a glance toward the ceiling, as if he suspected Sabrina might be lurking upstairs. "You'll get your head handed to you."

"I don't care." He shot his brothers a sour look. "What a pair of wienies."

"If you cook," Jonas said, "I'll do the grocery shopping."

"And I'll do cleanup," Sam said. "Sort of. We'll eat off paper plates and use paper napkins. No more niceties like cloth napkins, which Fiona used to spoil us with." A woeful sigh escaped him.

"And what about clean sheets in the bunkhouse?" Rafe asked. "Basic hygiene? We haven't taken care of ourselves our whole lives."

"No time like the present," Sam said, injecting cheer into his tone.

Rafe wasn't buying it. "We need a housekeeper. Jonas, you're going to have to open the purse strings."

"I can't," he stated. "Remember, we said we were going to be cautious with our resources until the lawsuit gets dismissed."

Crap, Rafe thought. "If I cook it, you eat it, no whining. And I never, ever do cleanup." The very fact that his brothers had shanghaied him into this, when he needed to be thinking about Julie and her long, beautiful legs, teed him off greatly. "I do not have time to be Rachael Ray for you lazy bums. But I will, as long as all I ever hear from you is 'mmm-mmm good.'"

"Deal," Jonas and Sam both said, and Rafe stalked out of the kitchen, wondering why today was his day to have everyone lined up against him.

He poked his head back inside the kitchen. "Starting tomorrow."

His brothers nodded eagerly.

"By the way," Jonas said, "congratulations."

Rafe blinked. "On what? Being a patsy?"

Jonas stared at him for a long moment. "Yeah. Sort of."

"Great. Thanks." Rafe left again, wondering why Jonas had looked so surprised. "Jerk," he muttered under his breath, though he loved his older brother. The word *jerk* made him think about Julie calling him that, walking away from him in her pretty white dress, and he decided maybe thinking about her was just too hard.

To hell with his brothers. They were weird, anyway, even for Callahans.

He was the last normal one left on the range.

* * *

Five minutes later, Rafe stared at Julie's latest handiwork in the bunkhouse. As pranks went, it was a doozy. He appreciated the size and scope of her one-upmanship. He hadn't wanted to pay attention to her, so she clearly had decided there were better ways to get a man's attention.

She'd put a sign on his bedroom door in the bunkhouse. It had a stork carrying a blue-swaddled bundle of joy.

His breath stung in his chest. "'Congratulations,'" he read aloud, "'baby Jenkins arrives in May. Julie.'"

Rafe was reeling. There'd been no warning. No clue.

Except from Jonas, but whoever paid attention to him? "My world has gone mad," Rafe muttered, and tore the stork off his door.

He was not having a baby. This was some mad attempt by Julie to rattle him, like the time she'd doodled on his face. Only this would last longer than a week. His brothers would be in top form over this joke. Everyone knew that Callahans were supposed to marry and populate. She was adding fuel to the fire.

But the sign said May. That was pretty darn definitive, and judges were typically pretty careful with details. Rafe tried to take another gulp of air and decided he might be having a wee panic attack. He needed a shot of something stiffening, like perhaps whiskey.

He hit the bar, and didn't bother with a glass, just let the liquor burn down his throat from the bottle. After capping it, he wiped his brow and concentrated on the pain.

"I had no other way to tell you," Julie said, stepping out of his room. Rafe's throat went dry as a bone, no longer moist from the alcoholic drenching. "It takes a lot to get your attention, cowboy."

"There's no way," he told her. "I used a condom when we were in the field. Mind you, it wasn't the newest, but latex lasts forever. It's nuclear material. So you must be mistaken, Julie. Condoms are safe."

"I don't remember hearing the sound of foil tearing open in my office."

This was true. "I figured you were on the pill or something by then," he said, and Julie looked outraged.

"Excuse me if I never considered us an ongoing thing."

He blinked. "And now?"

"Now you know." She walked past him, obviously about to leave. "That's all I owe you, Rafe."

"Who else knows?" he asked, wondering if he needed to talk to Bode.

"You and whoever saw this sign."

"Did Jonas know you were waiting in my room?" Rafe's head was spinning. "I mean, he told me congratulations."

She smiled. "I asked him not to."

Great. Everyone loved pulling the wool over good ol' Rafe's eyes, he thought bitterly. "Well, things will have to change. You, me, everything."

"Probably," she said, and walked out the door.

As if he was supposed to know what to make of that. Rafe hurried after her. Julie got in her truck, gunning it, sending up plumes of driveway dust, and the little judge went off without even a glance at him.

Not even caring that she'd totally kicked his ass in a major way.

"I'm going to be a dad," Rafe said. "More importantly, I'm also going to be a husband, whether that little judge and I ever see eye to eye on the subject or not."

"Talk to yourself often?" Sam asked, wandering by with a smirk on his face. "Dad?"

"Only when I want to," Rafe said, and headed off to ponder what the hell had just happened to him.

"You'd best find a bunker," Jonas told Rafe an hour later when he found him staring up at the ceiling, his gaze fixed on the plaster as he lay on the leather sofa. "Bode's going to tear you limb from limb when he hears the not-so-good news. Jeez, Rafe, what were you thinking?"

"I wasn't."

"Obviously. This throws a wrench into everything."

"Tell me about it," Rafe said. "Great sex goes out the window once the little woman's got a bun in the oven. And I never got to have great sex with her." He moaned piteously.

"Ugh," Jonas said under his breath to Sam, who leaned over the sofa to punch his brother in the chest with a grin. "Do something with him, will you? Explain to him how neatly, with one fell swoop, he's destroyed our court case you've slaved over for three years."

"Idiot," Sam told Rafe. "You're supposed to be the smart one. Turns out you're the dumbest of all." He laughed, enjoying his brother's plight.

"It's not funny," Rafe said. "Now she hates me."

"Now we all hate you, dummy." Jonas sank onto the sofa, staring at the fireplace. "I was hoping it wasn't true. I was hoping you weren't as dumb as you look. Once again, however, you prove yourself."

Rafe waved a hand in the air. "Try being me for a

change. The most beautiful woman in the world is having your baby. She doesn't want you. Life is ugly from where I'm lying."

"Please don't let me ever be that pitiful," Jonas said aloud. "If I ever get like him, Sam, you're in charge of shooting me."

Sam took a seat in a wingback chair. "It's just that he's been convinced for so long that he was so much smarter than everyone. Bulletproof, like Superman. Only now you're Superwienie," he told Rafe. "This is going to complicate the hell out of things, especially when Bode comes to kill you."

"I know," Rafe said. "I think I better go talk to him."

"No!" Sam and Jonas exclaimed.

"Don't set a foot on that property, Rafe." Jonas's tone was grim. "Don't go see Julie. Don't upset Bode. We'll try to hide you as best we can, but we're not the Secret Service. We're not nannies, damn it."

"Be careful," Rafe said. "I'm the cook. Mind your manners or you'll be eating Rice Krispies for days."

Sam shook his head. "Look, Plato, Jonas is right. You're going to have to lie low. If you think Bode wanted to put lead in you for picking on his little girl when we made her recuse, he's going to send out a team of snipers to take you out once he finds out you've knocked up his little lambkins."

"I think he should leave town," Jonas said, as if Rafe wasn't there. "He could hit the rodeo circuit. The boys'd cover for him. He could fly the plane up to Alaska and do something productive for a change."

"Fly fishing's productive?" Rafe asked. "I'm not going anywhere except over to Julie's."

"No!" Sam said. "Look, freak, you're in big trouble,

even if you're too dumb to know it. God, all kinds of IQ and not a grain of street smarts."

"I'm going to handle this like a man." Rafe jack-knifed to a sitting position. "I'm not going to run like a cowardly dog."

"You're going to go until this clears over." Jonas glanced at his watch. "Right now, only the three of us and Julie knows. But she can't keep her secret long. So pick a place and get gone. We don't have time to baby you to death."

"You could go to Ireland to check on Fiona and Burke," Sam said.

"Hell, I don't care if he goes to Mars," Jonas said with a growl. "I just want him where he can't cause more trouble."

"The tribe might hide him," Sam suggested, and Rafe jumped to his feet.

"I'm going," he said, mashing his hat onto his head.

"Where?" his brothers demanded.

"To Julie's. Where else?" Rafe strode out the door.

"Just a warning," Seton McKinley said, as she helped Julie carry some groceries into the house. "Word around Rancho Diablo is that when a Callahan decides he wants a woman, he's pretty unshakable in his determination."

"It won't matter to me." Julie set the grocery bags on the counter in the big, white kitchen. "You just take care of Dad, and I'll handle Rafe Callahan. And if you tell a single soul, even Sabrina—"

"I won't." Seton pushed food around in the fridge. "Don't say I didn't tell you, though. How do you think your father would like spaghetti for dinner? Or I could grill some hamburgers."

Julie glanced upward. "Did you hear something?"

"No." Seton looked at her. "But your father is napping, so it's probably just a creak in the ceiling."

Julie frowned. "Maybe I should check on him."

"I will." Seton left the kitchen, and Julie sank into a chair.

She was going to have to tell her father. It was probably going to kill him. The worst thing she could ever imagine was becoming pregnant by her father's worst enemy.

"I am a horrible daughter," she murmured out loud.

"He's fine," Seton said, coming back into the kitchen. "Are you all right?" She looked at her, concerned.

"I'm fine. I think." Julie felt cold, almost sick with nerves.

"You don't look fine. You look like you just ate a bad oyster." She put away the groceries Julie had left unattended. "It's going to be all right, Julie."

"You don't know Dad. The shock could—"

"Nope," Seton said, interrupting her worrying. "He's a tough guy, Julie. Nothing can kill him."

"You didn't see him after my mother died. His skin turned gray," Julie said quietly. "I thought I was going to lose him. And he's not as young as he used to be."

Seton sat down across from her. "So what are you going to do?"

Julie didn't answer. She thought about her dad, and how he would take the news. He was a proud man. Of course he would feel that the Callahans had won, that they'd done this on purpose. That there'd been a plan to get her pregnant, so that Bode would drop the suit. Everyone knew Fiona had a Grand Plan to get her nephews wives and lots of babies so community sentiment—and pressure—would be on their side. Fiona wanted Bode to look like a bad guy, an evil man.

He wasn't.

"I thought I just heard something," Seton said, glancing at the ceiling as Julie had. "Like a thump."

She shook her head. "I'm going to go take a nap."

"Good." Seton rose. "I'll start dinner. Don't worry so much, Julie. It isn't good for the baby."

Julie blinked. "Don't talk to me about babies. Not today. Maybe tomorrow."

She went upstairs, remembering the shock on Rafe's face. He'd seemed thunderstruck, although not angry, not upset, not unhappy. Just thunderstruck. As she'd been, when she went to the doctor's complaining of some nausea, and discovered she was pregnant.

She'd never even thought about becoming a mother. And now she was going to be one.

Closing her bedroom door behind her, she walked straight into her bathroom. Pulled her hair down, looked at her pale face. Seton was right; she did look as if she'd eaten something bad.

A nap would soothe her. She went to crawl into her four-poster bed with the white lace hangings—and stopped dead in her tracks seeing the long, lean cowboy lounging in her bed, sound asleep.

"Oh, for a good indelible marker right now," Julie said, and whapped Rafe with a pillow.

Chapter 5

Rafe put his hands up to protect himself from the pillow assailing him.

"Have you no respect? No fear of my father?" Julie demanded. "No shame, Rafe Callahan, at stealing into my bedroom and falling asleep in my bed?"

He was relieved when she quit whaling him. "Let's see. No, I have no fear of your father, thanks for asking. Shame? Nope, I'm pretty low on that, too. After all, you've stolen into *my* bedroom, Julie Jenkins."

"Get out or I'll scream."

"Nah," he said, loving the sudden high color in her cheeks. "You're not a screamer, love, except maybe in bed. We'll have to investigate that. I kind of think you are." He smiled at her, knowing he was making her madder.

"You're a rat." She stared at him, highly annoyed, but

not throwing his boots at him. They lay on the floor at her feet, right where he'd dropped them as he got into the marshmallow-soft bed, and he took that as an excellent sign.

"You're a cad, a bad man, a—"

"I get the picture." Rafe held up a hand. "You don't like me. And yet you do. What a complete conundrum for you, a quandary, even."

Julie began smacking him with the pillow again. "I don't even know what you're saying half the time," she complained. "I think you make stuff up—" she hit him again, harder, though the goose down wasn't making much impact "—because you have a big stupid head and think you're smart, and—"

He grabbed her wrist and pulled her into the bed. She fell with an ungraceful *oomph!* and he buried his lips in her hair. "I told you I'd eventually get you into a bed, Julie Jenkins."

"Not *my* bed," she said, trying to hop out, but he held her fast to him.

"Go to sleep. We have a lot to talk about, and we can't talk when you're cranky and worked up like this, darling."

She kicked back and caught him a smart one on the shin.

"That's going to leave a big bruise," he said, rueful but not letting go. "I hope you locked the bedroom door."

"I did not," she said, her voice tight as a guitar string. "When my father finds you in here, he's going to—"

"Shh." Rafe ran a hand through her long hair, as he'd wanted to do for so long. "You need your beauty sleep, lamb chop." He felt safe teasing her because she'd dropped her pillow and was lying fairly still now. Tense, but still.

She talked a hard game, but she was a softie for him.

"You fall asleep in my bed again, Callahan, and you won't ever wake up."

He laughed, pulled her tightly against him so her derriere was right where he wanted it, and promptly dozed off.

When Julie awakened from the best rest she'd had since learning she was pregnant, she was shocked—then annoyed—to find herself alone in her bed. *Typical. Sneak into my bed and then sneak back out.*

Something was going to have to be done about the father of her child. "He can't be an arrogant male 24/7," she muttered, smoothing her hair to go downstairs. If he thought he was just going to move in and take over her life now that they were expecting a child together, he had a surprise coming.

"Seton," she said as she walked into the kitchen, "that smells delicious."

"Thank you," Seton said.

"Do we have a large nail?"

Spoon in hand, Seton turned to her. "How large? To hang a big picture?"

"To nail a window shut."

Seton's eyes widened. "The thumping noise we heard was your window?"

"It was boots hitting the floor after a big cowboy climbed through my window. Apparently he doesn't use front doors." Julie smiled. "I'd like to teach him that climbing trees to sneak in windows is dangerous."

Seton put down her spoon. "I'll go get a hammer and the largest nail I can find in the toolshed."

"Thank you." Julie began humming as she went to her office to study some law books for existing statutes on a new case she was hearing.

The nerve of that man to think he's above the law—

Although Rafe did have a point: Like everyone else, she treated the bunkhouse as if it had a Welcome, We're Open sign on it.

No more, she resolved. She'd paid the last visit to Rafe that she ever would—and they were never, ever sleeping together again.

"I think," Jonas said as the three brothers ate a few pre-made burgers they threw on the grill that night, "we're screwed, thanks to you, Romeo."

"It looks grim," Rafe admitted, though he didn't feel grim. Knowing he was going to be a father made his heart sing with joy. If there was ever a time to praise the joys of condomless sex, this was it. His brothers could rib him all they liked, but Julie was his.

And all thanks to his good ol' sex appeal and charm.

"I just wonder when she's going to tell Bode." Sam threw his burned bun in the trash with disgust and stared up at the velvety sky. "You're still alive, so he hasn't heard. Doesn't your gut cramp just a little, knowing you're soon to be a dead man?"

Rafe shrugged. "He's a bad shot. Besides, Julie talks a tough game, but she wouldn't let anything happen to me. She's really into me."

"Oh, for crying out loud." Jonas shook his head and sank onto the redwood bench near the grill. "Did you ever once think about the ranch? Or just yourself?"

"At the moment that it all occurred," Rafe said, "I was pretty much just thinking about how good it felt, and how long I'd waited, and how lucky I was, and—"

"Would you shut up?" Sam glared at him. "You're nauseating."

"Why?" Rafe glanced around at his brothers. "I'm crazy about the woman. I have been for years. Sure, Bode's going to be a little wound up when she tells him, but it's nothing we can't handle."

"We?" Jonas stared at him. "We?"

"We, the ranch. Isn't that what you're all worried about?"

His brothers looked at him.

Sam sighed. "No common sense at all." He poured a half gallon of ketchup on his bun to drown the charred edges, and took a bite. "Are you going to marry Julie or not?"

"Marry her?" Rafe blinked. "I never thought about it."

Jonas spewed out his beer. "Do you want your ass kicked? Of course you're going to marry her!"

"I mean," Rafe said patiently, "she wouldn't marry me. She's going to have to understand that, as the father, I have certain rights. I will be staying with her every night, for example. It's my right to protect her and my baby, and provide for them financially." He shrugged. "Marriage is like a mirage to me right now. Far in the distance, pretty much just a figment of imagination where Julie is concerned. I'm lucky if she talks to me."

He was sad about that. Secretly, he wasn't certain how long he could keep up Robin Hooding through her window. Breaking down her walls. Scaling her tower and all that rot. "It's hard romancing a woman," Rafe said, "especially one who's as independent as Julie."

"If Aunt Fiona was here, she'd whip you into shape, you sad sack," Sam said. "I'm almost embarrassed you're my brother. And you're older than me. You should be setting a good example."

Rafe wasn't certain what his brothers wanted from him. They didn't realize that to get Julie to acknowledge him, he needed a dark room and thirty minutes. The woman had never said hi to him on the Diablo streets. She'd cross the road to avoid him. "You don't understand. As far as Julie is concerned, the Callahans are rodents."

They sat at the picnic table, considering that.

"I'm doing the best I can," Rafe assured his brothers.

"Do better," Jonas said. "This isn't even about the ranch. It's about your future child, who's going to wonder why his daddy lives on the next ranch over and didn't marry his mother."

Rafe sat very still, his mind envisioning the scenario.

"I could sue for custody," he said, and Sam let out a hiss.

"She's a well-respected judge, dummy. No other judge in this county or beyond is going to take her child from her and give her to you, a guy who has no common sense." Sam drank from his beer bottle and regarded him. "I don't know how you'll get out of this mess."

Rafe shook his head. "Me, neither."

"You really don't have a plan, do you?" Jonas asked.

"If I had a plan, I'd be over there eating real food with my woman instead of sitting here listening to you two wheeze." Rafe got up and threw his untouched burger into the trash. "It would be so much easier if women just did what we wanted them to do."

"Sounds like a real romantic guy," Sam said, and Jonas said, "Sounds like a guy who's going to get a woman real mad." They went off, leaving Rafe sitting at the picnic table.

He looked up at the New Mexico night sky and thought about teaching the constellations to his son. Playing football, riding rodeo. Looking for the Diablos.

Julie can't leave me out of her life. Somehow, our two lives have got to meet in the middle.

He just didn't know how they could.

A week later, Rafe found himself dragged off by Seton and Sabrina McKinley for a private chat in the north barn. Being surrounded by beautiful blondes was not a bad thing, but since he had a not-too-chatty raven-haired beauty on the brain, he wasn't in the mood to be corralled.

Still, he sank onto a hay bale and tried to look attentive. "So, what can I help you ladies with?" he asked.

Seton gave him a once-over. "It's more like what we can help you with."

Sabrina nodded. "We debated whether we wanted to have this conversation with you. We feel like traitors. So please keep our visit to yourself."

"Who are we hiding from?" Rafe asked. "You guys live upstairs, when you're not over at Bode's. It's hard to hide anything around Rancho Diablo."

"We don't want you telling Julie that we talked to you." Sabrina looked at him. "She's not too happy with you right now."

"She'll get over it," Rafe said. "She'll have to."

"She's nailed her bedroom windows shut." Seton gave him a sidelong glance. "I don't think she plans to get happy with you anytime soon."

Rafe leaned back on the hay bale and tried to act as if he wasn't concerned. He was, but man law required saving face. "So what's up?"

"Since your aunt Fiona left, we've been in a small situation. You're the one we chose to talk to about it. Fiona always said we could trust you," Seton said, "and that you were the smart one who could think your way out of any box."

"It's true," Rafe said with a deliberate lack of humility for the praise. "I like puzzles."

Seton perched on an old cracked leather chair and stared at him. Her sister parked nearby against a saddle rack. "So, the first thing you should know is that your aunt hired us to do some work for her."

Rafe waved a hand. "Yes, cooking and cleaning is very important at the ranch."

Sabrina rolled her eyes. "I told you he could be a wee bit dense for a smart guy."

Seton nodded. "Dense is perhaps too mild a word. Look, cowboy, I'm a private investigator and Sabrina is an investigative reporter."

"When she's not telling fortunes." Rafe smirked. "Wasn't that how you came to Rancho Diablo in the first place? To warn us that our ranch was in trouble? If I recall correctly, your sister was posing as a gypsy from the circus."

"Which your aunt hired her to do. Pay attention, Rafe. I can't be gone too long from Mr. Jenkins. He doesn't know I'm here." Seton looked irritated, so Rafe sat up and tried harder to focus.

"Okay, so what does all that have to do with me?"

"Your aunt hired us to spy on Bode," Sabrina said. "Now that she's gone, we don't know who to report to."

"We don't feel our services are needed any longer," Seton said, "given the new relationship between you and the Jenkinses."

"Ah," Rafe said, the light beginning to dawn. "Because Julie's pregnant, you feel a conflict of interest."

"Yes." Seton nodded. "There's a baby to consider. We can't spy on the grandfather of the child you're expecting."

Rafe blinked. "So all the information you were giving my aunt on Bode's comings and goings…"

"Is now terminated." Seton stood. "It's not right for us to live there and spy for you when there's a baby who might be harmed by something we report."

"Well," Rafe said, "I see your point. You realize Bode is a bad man, and my aunt hiring you, while perhaps sneaky, was a very clever plan."

"But we have to think about the baby," Sabrina pointed out, "so you're on your own."

Rafe sighed. "Did you ever tell my aunt anything pertinent?"

"Practically his every move, though I don't know how it was all that useful. I think Fiona just liked knowing she was putting one over on Bode," Seton said. "But Julie's become one of my dearest friends."

"Very unprofessional of you, but understandable." Rafe liked Julie, too. It would be easy to like her, even if he didn't lust for her as he did.

"Clown," Seton retorted. "I'm being professional by telling you that there's a conflict of interest."

Rafe nodded. "Sorry. You're right. Okay, from now

on, we Callahans are on our own. We always have been, you know, so it's no big deal. Your services have been greatly appreciated." He cleared his throat, trying to look like a man who knew how to think his way out of a box, as his aunt had bragged. "So, does this mean you are moving out and living with Bode and Julie? Because obviously Sabrina can't live here and you, Seton, live there. Who knows who could trust whom?"

The sisters looked uncomfortable for a moment.

"We're hoping you'll trust us to remain living as we are," Sabrina admitted. "I like living here. Seton likes living at Bode's."

"He's a crusty old man, but I don't mind him." Seton shrugged.

"Hardly private investigator work," Rafe observed. "More like caretaker and cook." He looked at Sabrina. "Why are you still living with us? Fiona had you helping with correspondence and her duties. She's not here any longer." Rafe was truly curious. "I guess if you two aren't going to be moles any longer, then you have no reason to live at Rancho Diablo, Sabrina."

He was just musing out loud, thinking about this new gnarl in the Callahan affairs and how Jonas would feel if Sabrina decided to depart, so he was surprised when Seton said, "I told you he'd say that," to her sister.

"It's okay," Sabrina replied quickly. "He's right. I'll go."

Rafe sat up, realizing he might have just stepped in a big one. Jonas had a thing for the little gypsy faker. Jonas had never said as much, but it didn't take a man of huge IQ to see that Rafe's oldest brother seemed to lose a little focus when she was nearby. In fact, Jonas hadn't taken a woman out since he'd come back to the ranch, Rafe realized with some alarm. "There's no rush, of course. My aunt would—"

"I'll be staying with my sister," Sabrina said. "If your aunt ever returns, I'll be happy to come back to work for her."

Seton got up from the leather chair. "I feel much better now that we've talked. Thanks for listening to us, Rafe. We were starting to feel caught in the middle."

Sabrina nodded. "It's so important to have a clear conscience. I'll move my things out from the main house. And, Rafe, thanks for everything."

He blinked, watching the sisters leave the barn. "Oh, this is great," he muttered. "Jonas is going to kill me. And I don't think Sam's going to be too happy, either."

So much for getting out of boxes.

Two hours later, Rafe was clearly the bad guy in the Bait and Tackle. He could barely enjoy the delicious burger placed in front of him, since his two brothers appeared ready to cram it up his nose. His fine aquiline nose. Rafe sighed, hating being the bad guy lately. It seemed he was wearing the black hat quite often now.

"You did what?" Jonas demanded. "Who gave you the right to do anything without a family council?"

Sam's face wore outrage in its normally easygoing creases. "I'm the lawyer in the family. I get a vote on what's legal, right and proper when it comes to all things Callahan. How dare you kick out those beautiful women?"

"To be fair, Seton didn't live here," Rafe pointed out.

"But she was here every day because her sister lived here, goose," Sam said. "And now we're just a trio of unhappy bachelors with nothing in the fridge and no hot chicks upstairs."

"You had no right." Jonas frowned, his black brows drawing level with each other. "What made you think you were the head of the household?"

Rafe held up a hand. "I didn't know they'd been spying for Fiona. They indicated that they'd become uncomfortable with the situation now that Julie's having a baby—"

"Which is your goof-up, not ours," Sam said. "It shouldn't cost us women on the premises just because you can't read the directions on a box of condoms."

"Holy cow," Rafe said. "They wanted to go!"

"Because you weren't quick enough to figure out how to invite them to live with us, instead of Bode." Jonas shook his head. "You go over there and get them back."

"They won't come." Rafe stared miserably at his plate. "Seton is still employed by Bode and Julie. Julie will need more help now that she's expecting a baby. Sabrina didn't want to live with us because she had no real employment now that Fiona's gone."

"We need our adventurous aunt back." Jonas pushed his plate away and drank his beer.

"I couldn't agree more," Rafe said.

"What we need are jobs for ladies." Sam looked as if a lightbulb had parked over his head.

"Sabrina isn't going to be our cook," Rafe said morosely. "She has a real career. She doesn't want to take care of us."

Jonas drummed his fingers on the table. "Trust you to go and mess up everything that was working just fine."

"Yeah," Sam said. "If you'd just marry the woman, everybody could settle down again. We told you to marry her, but no, you had to go cost us ladies. Now when will we see them? Think Bode's going to let us in on Saturday nights? I think not." He slugged down more beer. "Get that judge to the altar, Rafe, for the love of Mike."

Rafe's jaw dropped. The music in the bar was loud, but didn't drown out the rushing in his ears. "I can't do that."

"Why not?" Jonas demanded. "It's what big boys do when their pants don't stay zipped."

"She hates me," Rafe said. It tore him up to have to say it. "She nailed her bedroom windows shut, she hates me so much."

Sam shook his head. "Just because you've made a bumpy bed doesn't mean we all should have to lie in it."

Rafe threw his napkin on the table along with some money. "Not to be an ass, but you guys were barking up the wrong trees with Sabrina and Seton, anyway."

He stalked out of the bar, not feeling good about his bitter words, but tired of being the bad guy. His brothers didn't understand.

He'd marry Julie in a heartbeat—even though she'd rather cut out his heart than have him.

Chapter 6

On the fifteenth of October, Rafe couldn't take it another day. He showed up on Julie's doorstep with roses, knowing very well he wasn't going to get past Bode.

He didn't. In fact, he didn't get past Seton and Sabrina, who stared out at him and his pink roses as if he were some kind of interplanetary being.

"Julie doesn't want to see you," Seton said.

"Come on, ladies. I need to see her." He gave them his most winning smile.

In the background, he heard Bode roar, "Who the hell is bothering me?"

"He doesn't like visitors," Sabrina said. "You know that."

"I don't particularly care what Bode likes. I need to see Julie." Rafe frowned at Sabrina. "And you need to come back home."

Long blond hair waved as she shook her head. "Rancho Diablo isn't my home, Rafe."

"You lived there for over a year," he pointed out. "It's more your home than this is."

"I've been scoping out some new journalism opportunities." She blinked at him, quite serious about her announcement. "I've got a few hot leads on some jobs, so I don't plan on being here much longer. Why wouldn't I want to be with my sister, though?"

Jonas was going to have his head if Sabrina went off and he never saw her again. Rafe saw that quick action and a silver tongue were needed. At the moment, he seemed to possess neither. He looked at Seton with a pleading expression. "Can you talk some sense into her? She belongs at the ranch with us. We have more than half a dozen toddlers running around who depend on a consistent environment."

Seton shook her head. "My sister is quite sensible." She took the flowers from his hands. "I'll give these to Julie," she said, and shut the door in his face.

He stared at the closed white door. Then he trotted around the house to stare up at Julie's window. Taking a chance, he hurled a few pebbles at the glass.

Julie's face appeared for a moment, then disappeared. Rafe waited a few minutes, then sighed and went to his truck. This was not good.

At least Bode hadn't tried to shoot him.

But Julie hadn't invited Rafe in, and that was going to have to be fixed. Soon.

"He went away more peacefully than I expected." Julie put the roses in a vase and carried them to Seton's room.

"Why are you giving those to me?" she demanded.

"Because I don't want my father to see them. I haven't told him yet about the baby. I have to choose the appropriate time."

Sabrina and Seton stared at her. Julie sighed. "It's difficult. He hasn't been feeling well. I don't want him to have a heart attack or something."

Actually, she knew full-blown war would break out once she confessed. It was so hard to bring that down on Rafe's head. But she was starting to swell, and surely it couldn't be much longer before her father noticed.

The next hearing for the court case wasn't scheduled for another month. She had to do something between now and then.

And she couldn't avoid Rafe forever.

"Is there anything we can do?" Sabrina asked.

Julie shook her head. Sabrina had once posed as a fortune teller with the circus, but there were times when she was eerily prescient. Julie didn't want to talk about Rafe anymore in case Sabrina chimed in with something she didn't want to hear. Having lived with the Callahans, Sabrina knew them better than Julie did. "I don't think there's anything anyone can do. I'm just waiting for the right moment."

"There's no such thing as a right moment," Sabrina said cheerily. "All moments are what we make of them."

Julie sighed. "I knew you'd have some piece of advice that would make me feel guilty." She did feel a little guilty—okay, a lot guilty. Guilty about her father, and guilty about Rafe, and even about this baby, who would grow up in this weird existence between two families who couldn't stand each other. "Thanks for everything, girls," she said. "I appreciate all you're doing for my father and me."

She went out to take a walk in the late October sun, soaking up the last bits of autumn before the season began to change. Halloween would be upon them soon enough. The little girls at Rancho Diablo would be old enough to trick-or-treat now, but Fiona had never allowed trick-or-treating. She'd always given a little Halloween party, complete with a friendly scarecrow the girls could admire, and pumpkin-colored cupcakes—organic and gluten-free, of course. The girls had been so little, still babies, and Fiona didn't want anything scary around them. Her boys, Fiona said, had been afraid of everything when they were young.

Julie smiled, and then gasped when she realized Rafe was standing at the end of her field. He waved, and she decided she couldn't run off again. "Hi, Rafe."

He didn't look at her stomach, which Julie appreciated, because she felt self-conscious enough in the leggings and oversize orange top she wore.

"Hi, Julie. You look well."

She thought if anyone looked well, it was Rafe. The man was gorgeous. But it wasn't simply that; he was kind, too. She checked out his dark blue eyes and wide chest, broad shoulders and dark hair. Nerves prickled her scalp. It was just all too much to take in at once. "How's the family?"

"Fine. Growing. Busy." He shrugged. "How do you feel?"

"Never better." It was true. Thankfully, pregnancy seemed to agree with her.

"I assume you haven't told your father, since he hasn't come waving his shotgun."

Julie didn't particularly appreciate the reference and frowned to let him know it. "I'm waiting for the right moment."

"Good luck with that."

There wasn't really anything left to say, Julie decided. They were just too far apart, on everything. "I've got to go back in. What are you doing out here, anyway?"

"Checking out trenches. And these fences. One got cut, so we had to repair it." He looked at her, one brow slightly raised.

"You think my father did it."

Rafe shrugged again. "Don't know why he would."

Anger flared inside her. "Still, you're thinking that he might destroy your property—"

"Don't put words in my mouth. There are three women in that house at all times with your father. I'm not sure when he'd have a chance to get into mischief." Rafe shook his head. "My brothers raised hell on me when Sabrina left. I don't want any more trouble between the houses of Callahan and Jenkins."

"There wouldn't be trouble," Julie snapped, "if you and your brothers weren't always looking for it."

Rafe didn't say anything. His gaze was so clear, so honest, that Julie knew she'd taken offense too quickly. He was trying to be nice. "I'm sorry."

He shook his head. "No worries. Hey, I'm going to get back to work, Julie. But it was great seeing you. Let me know if you need anything. Anything at all."

His gaze jumped for a fraction of a second to her stomach, then he turned back to the four-wheeler he was driving.

"Rafe," she called.

He turned. "Yeah?"

"I am sorry."

"For what?"

She didn't know how to put it in words. "For everything. The awkwardness. The pregnancy. Just…everything."

"The pregnancy is just as much my fault," he said.

"I could have remanded you into custody for disrespect in my courtroom," Julie said, grasping at straws. Anything to try to make it easier to say what she had to. "Instead I…"

"You what?"

She shook her head. "I wanted you," she said simply.

His eyes went wide.

"I mean, you didn't hear me saying no, did you?"

Rafe shook his head.

"Well," Julie said, feeling as if it was time to be honest and face facts for everyone's sake, "it takes two to tango. I should have told you I didn't have birth control. Now you're stuck in a terrible situation, and I think…"

He waited, his hands jammed in his jeans pockets.

"I don't see how this'll ever get better," Julie admitted.

Rafe reached out and stroked one finger down her cheek. "It has to, for the baby."

Then he got in his four-wheeler and drove away.

Julie took a deep breath and wished her conscience felt clear.

It didn't.

Rafe was surprised to see his brother Judah riding toward him as he drove the four-wheeler home. "Hey. How are the kiddoes?"

"The twins are keeping me up at night." Judah grinned, looking happy about it. "Got a minute?"

"I've got minutes," Rafe said. "Hell, I've got hours."

Judah tied his horse in front of the house and hopped in the four-wheeler. "Let's take a drive."

"Why not? Give me the coordinates, amigo."

Judah pointed to the south of Rancho Diablo. "Head that way."

Rafe did, glancing over at his brother, who was a happy man since Darla had tied him down. "Marriage seems to agree with you."

"It would agree with you, too, if you decide to try it."

Rafe sighed. "I guess you've heard the good news, then."

"Yeah, but I'm keeping my lips zipped. This doesn't need to go past the Callahan family until you tell Bode."

Rafe's jaw sagged for a moment. "Me tell Bode?"

"You think Julie's going to?"

Rafe blinked. "I don't think that's my place."

"It probably wasn't your place to knock her up, either, but you did. Apparently with typical Callahan speed. Keep going toward the canyons."

Rafe shook his head and decided maybe his brother had lost his mind just a little to baby brain. What else could explain the outlandish notion that he should beard Bode in his den and give away Julie's secret? Judah must have forgotten how recently Bode had been aiming a shotgun at his dear brother.

"Here," Judah said, and Rafe stopped the four-wheeler. "We'll walk the rest of the way."

"Far?" Rafe asked, and Judah said, "Whine much?"

Rafe sighed. "Only when everybody's having a pound-on-Rafe day."

Judah didn't reply. Rafe followed his brother, beginning to wonder what the hunt was all about. It wasn't like Judah to wander too far from Darla, and as far as Rafe knew, the foremen, Jagger Knight and Johnny Donovan, kept watch on land this far from the house.

"I thought it was time to tell you about this," Judah said, leading him under a small outcropping and into a deeply set-back cavern.

Rafe blinked in the darkness. "How'd you ever find this? We've ridden every inch of this land and I've never seen it."

"The way it's tucked back in the cliffs hides it pretty well."

As his eyes adjusted, Rafe was astonished by the size of the cave. It was big enough to fit a lot of people into, and even horses if necessary. "I've ridden past this a hundred times over the years."

"Come on back here." Judah waved a hand to draw him farther into the cave. "See this?"

Rafe eyed the shaft and basic pulley and cart. "What the hell is it? Something to do with smugglers?"

Judah shrugged. "Maybe once upon a time. I'm not sure now."

Rafe speared him with a stare. "How long have you known?"

"A few months."

"Why haven't you told anyone?" Rafe looked at symbols smeared on the wall, and a hand-loomed Native American rug on the floor nearby, almost a temple of sorts. Or a resting place. "Why are you telling *me*?"

"Fiona didn't want anyone to know." Judah looked at him. "After she left, I wondered why I was keeping a secret of something that might affect the court case."

Rafe swept his gaze around the cave. "You think this is the rumored silver mine?"

Judah picked up some silver pieces off a low flat rock. "A few months ago, there was a different pile of coins here."

"Coins?" Rafe looked at the silver. "Silver bars?"

"Someone is paying someone for something."

"And someone is hanging out on our land." Rafe glanced around. "Smugglers."

"I'm not so sure." His brother sat down on the rock. "Fiona kept a lot of secrets, bro."

"We're not going to go through that again, are we?" Rafe was impatient with the thought that their aunt was always up to her elbows in plots. *She probably was,* he thought, *but I'm not selling her out.* "Fiona had nothing but our best interests at heart. The most I'll believe is that maybe there are poor people who come through here that she was trying to help." He looked at Judah. "Don't you imagine that was the case?"

He shrugged. "I've thought about it for many moons now, and lots of scenarios come to mind."

"Why haven't you told Jonas? Or Sam, if you're worried about the case?"

"Because you're the smart one in the family," Judah said. "You're supposed to know stuff. I'm just passing the knowledge off to you."

Rafe sighed, glanced at the blue marks on the wall. "You read Navajo?"

"Is that what that is?"

"What the hell did you think it was? Martian?"

"You're the one who studied Latin, and as I recall, some Sanskrit. Which, might I add, I thought was pretty useless at the time."

"German, Flemish and some Mandarin," Rafe murmured. "It's helpful in the military to know how to say more than 'Yes, sir!'"

"Whatever," Judah said. "So what does it say, Einstein?"

"It says," Rafe said, "that Fiona's friend Chief Running Bear uses this cave."

Judah blinked. "Really?"

"No, dummy. It's an educated guess." Rafe went over and looked at the coins, the rock, the rug, the writing on the wall. "And my highly attuned sense of discernment tells me more than one person uses this cave."

"How do you do that?" Judah demanded.

"Counting shoe marks. There's a pair of cowboy boots, a pair of ladies' boots, which is strange, and something softer, like a moccasin. Those are popular these days in the fashion mags, you know. But I would guess also with anyone who doesn't want to leave a dedicated shoe tread." He looked at Judah. "Someone else found this cave."

"Fiona told me that Johnny Donovan and his bride had found it, but Fiona swore them to secrecy. It happened last Christmas, when they were out chasing Bleu through the storm."

"How far back in the cave have you gone? How deep is this shaft?"

"Too scared to find out. Until today, I was out here by myself." Judah shrugged. "And Fiona seemed to want to keep it secret, so I didn't bother."

"Let's go back there." Rafe was really curious.

"Let's not." Judah looked at him. "Not without our brothers, candles, rope…"

Rafe peered into the darkness. "What if we've found

the silver mine? It means Bode has a bigger reason for trying to get our land."

"Again, we don't own the mineral rights," Judah reminded him.

"But Bode doesn't know," Rafe said thoughtfully.

"And Bode doesn't know you knocked up his daughter. Life's weird that way."

Rafe ignored him. "Fiona and the chief were fast buddies and met once a year."

"Or more, if they met here. I'd say they did."

"I'd guess they did, too," Rafe said. "Check this out." He lifted the flat rock and pulled a plastic bag out from underneath. Inside were several photos.

"Strange," Judah murmured. "Baby pictures."

"Yeah," Rafe said. "All the newborn Callahans' first baby pictures."

The brothers stared at each other for a long time.

"My God, she was strange, wasn't she?" Judah said.

Rafe put the photos back in the bag and inserted it under the rock. "Fiona isn't strange. She's the most wonderful guardian we could ever have had."

"And we all kept her secrets. We never questioned her. We just let her lead us around."

"Because we love her," Rafe said. "Don't get freaky because of a few baby pictures under a rock. Jeez." But even he couldn't think of a reason for his aunt to be in this cave storing pictures. "God knows what else she's probably hiding in here."

"That's it. She's using this as a satellite storage facility." Judah snapped his fingers. "Like she uses the basement."

"You mean that long gravelike scar in the basement floor?"

"Not necessarily a grave," Judah said, "but something."

"I don't think I want to know." But he had an eerie feeling about what Judah was planning to say.

"You're going to have to dig up whatever she's hiding in the basement."

"No," Rafe said, "I'm leaving sleeping whatevers alone. You want to know, you dig."

"We could just ask her."

They pondered that for a few moments.

"We could, but she's not ready to tell us," Rafe said, and Judah nodded.

"Are you going to tell the others?" Judah asked.

"I need to reflect on what all this means." He glanced around the cave. "It might be best to keep it away from Sam, since he's the legal beagle on the case. We don't want to prejudice him from being honest. Now that we suspect this is some kind of mine, he'd have to admit it in documents. And we don't know that this is a silver mine. It could just be, like you said, a storage facility."

Judah frowned. "I think you should call Fiona."

"I might." Rafe looked around one last time, eyeing the pile of silver. "Or I might just go find the chief."

Judah stared at him. "That's why we let you be the brains of the outfit."

"Why?"

"Because you're so smart sometimes you're stupid." Judah looked at his brother with admiration. "Only you would suggest hunting down a man, who probably doesn't want to talk to you, about a cave on your own land."

"They own the mineral rights, don't they?"

"True."

"So," Rafe said, "I'm sure we're going to get the yearly visit from him on Christmas Eve, just like our aunt always did, to discuss business."

Judah considered that. "How are you going to find him?"

"Like this." Rafe picked up a piece of blue clay and wrote on the flat rock. "Chief Running Bear, looking forward to seeing you on Christmas Eve. R. Callahan." He grinned at his brother. "Looks like a holiday invitation to me."

Judah followed his brother out into the late twilight. "Too bad you're not so smart about your love life, bro."

"Yeah," Rafe said. *But Julie admitted she wanted me, and that means everything is going to start going my way, eventually.*

At least he hoped so.

Chapter 7

"Dad," Julie said, walking into Bode's study, "how are you feeling?"

He nodded at his only child. "Fine, girl. How are *you* feeling?"

Julie went to sit by her father so they could look out the windows together. Her dad loved to sit and stare at the landscape. His study happened to face the Callahan spread, which she herself could have done without viewing.

It reminded her of Rafe, and she didn't want to think about him. Even though she did all the time.

"Tomorrow's Halloween," she said, not that it mattered. They didn't celebrate the holidays, not like the Callahans did. Fiona always strung lights like mad, and had the house festooned for every holiday, even a whisper of a holiday. Some she made up, or at least Julie thought she did. Saints' birthdays, holidays in foreign countries—Fiona liked to celebrate everything.

"Are we passing out candy?" Bode asked, and Julie smiled.

"Not this year, but maybe next."

Bode sat up in his worn wingback chair and looked at her. "Oh? Will we have something to celebrate? I'm not much for kids ringing the doorbell, you know. Any kids ringing the bell around here will likely be that crop of Callahans that's sprouted up next door."

Julie sighed. "Dad, I'm having a baby."

Bode stared at her. "You're what?"

"I'm having a baby." She took a deep breath. "In May."

Bode blinked. "That can't be possible." He looked worried.

She shook her head. "I'm afraid it is, Dad." And then, because she knew what the next question would be— the normal question any parent would ask—she went ahead and answered it.

"Rafe Callahan is the father."

Bode's face turned red. He stared at her, uncomprehending, or perhaps just disbelieving. Then he shot from his chair and paced the room before coming back to stand in front of her.

"I'll *kill* him!"

She held up a hand. "No, you won't."

"I will!"

"Dad, listen." Julie tugged her father's hand, guiding him to sit back down. She was terrified she'd give him a heart attack, or worse, a stroke. "Calm down. Rafe didn't do anything to me that I didn't want." It was so painful to admit that to her father. She felt like such a traitor. But the truth was, Rafe *hadn't* done anything that she hadn't loved every moment of.

"You hate the Callahans," Bode said, his hands trembling.

"*You* hate the Callahans, Dad. *I* barely know them."

"Obviously you know them better than I thought you did! Unless—"

"No." Julie shook her head, putting an end to what she knew her father was thinking. "I was a completely willing participant with Rafe."

Her father turned his face away and sank back in his chair. "He seduced you. He messed with your mind. It's because of the court case, because you were the judge. I know the Callahans better than you do, Julie. If it hadn't been for the lawsuit, he'd never have looked twice at you."

Her father's words cut at her like knives. "Regardless of how it came to be, I'm having a baby with Rafe Callahan. I'm going to be a mother, and I have to act like a mother. Which means I can't spend time worrying about feuds. I have to do what's best for my child."

Bode looked at her suspiciously. "What exactly does that mean?"

"It means, Dad," Julie said softly, her hand covering his, "I'm moving out."

His eyes bugged. "That snake is going to cost me my only daughter? The comfort in my old age?"

Julie shook her head. "I'll still be living in Diablo. I just won't be under your roof. You have an excellent caregiver, and frankly, Dad, you don't need me. I blinded myself into thinking that you did, but right now—"

"He needs you more?" Bode's voice was a sneer. "I

would have saved you the pain if I could have. If you think that by moving out of here, that man'll start coming around, you're wrong."

Julie stood. "It doesn't matter. It's past time for me to be on my own."

Bode's eyes went wide. "You'll need help with the baby."

"Plenty of women have a baby without help." Julie crossed to the door. "I'm a judge, Dad. I think I can make proper arrangements for my baby when the time comes."

Tears began to slide down Bode's cheeks. Julie steeled herself against her father's newest ploy. It was heartfelt emotion, she knew, but she was also completely aware that her father had always played to her affection for him. "Please don't leave me, Julie. You're all I've had after your mother died."

She went back to him and kissed his cheek, giving him a hug he gratefully returned. "It'll be all right, Dad. You'll see how much you enjoy having the house to yourself after I've moved out. I'm buying a place in town, and you can visit often, too."

"Buying a place! You've already made plans?" Bode sat up, worried. "Don't you realize how that'll look once people realize that scoundrel won't marry you?"

"*I* won't marry *him*," Julie said. "And I'm not worried what people think about me."

Bode looked at her, his gaze shrewd. "Has he asked you?"

"Rafe made some noise about us being together. I wasn't paying attention. Marriage is so far from my mind I can't even bring myself to think about it."

Bode sniffed. "Good. You can do better than a Callahan."

Julie turned at the door. "Maybe I can and maybe I can't, and maybe I don't even care. But, Dad, he's the father of my child, and from this moment forward, I don't want to hear one negative thing about Rafe. Or any of the Callahans. Can you understand my feelings?"

Her father shrugged. "Not really. Pitiful genes for the baby, I'd say." He frowned. "This isn't going to change my mind about getting their land. You don't remember what it was like when they first came here, Julie. It was quiet out here, peaceful. Suddenly the Callahans came, and a bunch of brats, and everybody liked them, wanted to be their friend. Suddenly you couldn't go anywhere without hearing Callahan this, Callahan that. And then those damn Callahans went and died, and left the brats here. I thought the county would have to be called. Your mother wouldn't hear of that, though. She was always going over there helping Fiona. Worked herself to the bone, in my opinion. And why?" Bode shook his head. "No reason at all, to my mind."

"Dad, Fiona was new to this country. I'm sure there was a lot she needed help with."

"If your mother had stayed home with me, where she belonged, she'd probably still be here. The Callahans destroy everything they touch."

"Dad," Julie said softly, "I'm so sorry for what you've gone through. But surely you know it wasn't the Callahans' fault."

He closed his eyes. "I know what I know. Go. I need to nap."

Her father's skin was pale. He looked lifeless in his chair, his hands dangling over the sides. Julie's heart broke, knowing how much she'd hurt him. "I love you, Dad."

He didn't say anything. Tears jumped into her eyes. She left his study and went to find Seton.

"Can you check on him in a little bit? He's had a bit of a surprise." Julie picked up her keys and her purse. "I've got a doctor's appointment, so I'll be out for a while."

Seton looked at her, her blue eyes wide. She set down the bread she'd been kneading, and wiped off her hands. "You told him, didn't you?"

Julie nodded.

"Was he very upset?" Seton handed her a glass of water she didn't want. Julie took a sip, surprised by how dry her mouth was.

"It wasn't the happiest day of his life."

"Not even to know he's going to be a grandfather?" Seton was incredulous.

"No," Julie said, her voice breaking a little. "He never said anything about the baby."

"He'll come around," Seton said, but she didn't sound certain. Julie nodded, put the glass down and left.

There wasn't any reason to think that Bode would ever forgive the Callahans.

Or her, for that matter.

Julie wasn't comforted to see Rafe waiting by her truck. It was unfortunate that he made her heart pound and her breath catch in her chest. After the discussion with her father, she had the strangest urge to throw herself into Rafe's arms and have a small meltdown.

She was a Jenkins. She didn't do meltdowns.

"Now's not a good time," she told Rafe, who shrugged.

"Probably never going to be a good time," he replied. "I get that you don't want me sneaking in to see you. That leaves me hanging around, hoping you'll make a run to the grocery store. You look great, by the way."

Julie slung her handbag into the truck. "Thanks. You don't look so bad yourself, which I'm sure you know."

Snarky. She was being rude and snarky, and Rafe had no idea why she was all wound up. "Look, I'm not having the best day," she confessed. "So I'm not up for small talk."

"That's all right." He gave her the winning smile that never failed to make her heart flip over—when it wasn't making her mad. "I'll buy you a hamburger."

"No." She got in her truck. "I don't want you to buy me anything."

He leaned against her window so she couldn't shut it. Too near, too much chest, too much handsome male staring in at her. Julie felt hot, even though it was late October.

"We need to talk." Rafe shrugged. "Sooner rather than later."

He was right. Julie sighed. "I'm really busy these days."

"Tell me about it. Bribing Seton to give me your schedule today was not easy. She says you're always going ninety to nothing." He frowned. "I hope that's not unhealthy for you."

"Don't concern yourself with my health," Julie snapped. "You should be more worried about yours. I just told my father that he's expecting a grandchild. Let's just say he's not a happy person right now."

"Hot damn," Rafe said, his tone awestruck. "It's a wonder he's not out here with a shotgun."

"He doesn't know you're here." Julie put the keys into the ignition, a trickle of unease sliding through her. "If he did, there would be all kinds of uproar. I'd appreciate it if you wouldn't deliberately antagonize my father, Rafe. He has health issues."

She frowned when Rafe laughed out loud. "Sorry, sweetie. There's nothing wrong with that old man except that he's mean and stubborn as hell. He's kept you tied to him like a nanny all your life so he won't be lonely." Rafe leaned in and brushed her lips gently with his. "Don't worry about me, lamb chop. I'm not afraid of your old man, who is arguably the worst shot in the county."

Julie sucked in a breath. "You're contemptible."

"Ah, but we're not in court, are we? It's just me and you, sugar." He went around the front of the truck, which Julie thought was brave of him—or arrogant, since she could pleasantly run him over right now. When he got in the passenger side and grinned at her, she wished she had the desire to throw him out.

She didn't.

"You can't go with me. Get out," she said, but her voice sounded unconvincing even to her. "I'm going to the gynecologist, and no man wants to go there."

"I do." Rafe perked up. "It'll be good for me to be around other pregnant females."

Julie shook her head. "There is always a pregnant female at your ranch."

"But I don't pay attention to them. Their moods are not my concern." He tweaked a lock of Julie's hair. "Your moods are much more interesting. Right now, you seem all bothered to me. The way you marched out to the truck made me think that all's not well in the house of Jenkins. Now you tell me your father knows about the baby, and therefore his new relationship to me, and I wonder to myself, has that got my little judge's robe in a twist?"

She frowned at his question. "You sound so happy about it, but no, I'm not in a mood because of my father."

She was, but family was family. Rafe was the enemy. He didn't need to know anything about her father. "I'm not happy that you're in my truck," she said. "Can you blame me? You're nothing but trouble."

"You have been talking to your father. You know, doll," Rafe said, leaning back and pushing his hat down over his eyes, "for the sake of the baby, you're going to have quit letting your father fill your head with fantastically evil fairy tales about the other side of the family. You might even start thinking of us as the good guys."

"I don't think so," Julie said, feeling snippy. "I'll drop you off in town. If you even darken the door of my doctor's office, I'll tell them to call the sheriff."

"Sheriff Cartwright thinks highly of me." Rafe sounded unconcerned, and possibly sleepy. "He'd be amazed that you'd made such a catch, Julie Jenkins."

She rolled her eyes, started the truck and rumbled down the drive. "I wouldn't catch you if you were a catch, Rafe Callahan. My father says you're all a bunch of thieves."

Rafe chuckled under his hat. It annoyed her, and she was in no mood to be more annoyed than she was.

On the other hand, she wondered if maybe once Rafe saw the baby on the monitor, he might realize this was a real person, a child, something that was going to change his life forever.

Maybe he'd leave her alone.

"You know," she said, her tone casual, "maybe you should come in while I'm at the doctor's."

He ripped the hat off his face. "You mean, to the appointment?"

"I'm having a sonogram. We'll probably be able to see something that looks like a baby by now. Most of the time, the sonogram just looks like black-and-white lines and holes to me." She beamed at him. "I don't know for certain, but maybe you could hear the heartbeat, too."

Rafe seemed relieved. "That would be cool." He gave her a careful look, then sat back. "Why'd you change your mind?"

"Can't a girl do that?"

He snorted. "Yeah. All the time. In your case, Judge, no. Never. Not without reason."

"Oh," Julie said airily, "suspicious Callahan."

"Suspicious Jenkins."

They left it at that.

Twenty minutes later, Julie wanted to scream.

In fact, she did let out a hysterical squeal of denial. "That's not possible!"

The doctor looked more closely, as did a nurse and a technician. "Definitely triplets. See? There's one, two, three…"

Rafe was sitting as close to the screen and her as he possibly could. "That doesn't sound right. My twin, Creed, had only one baby with his wife. Multiples don't always run in our family. Pete's the only one fortunate enough to have three, but he's the responsible brother."

The doctor looked at Rafe as if he were daft—or in denial—and he figured he was. He swallowed hard. "I don't see three babies."

"I don't, either." For once they agreed. Julie was afraid she was going to hyperventilate.

"Absolutely certain on this one," the doctor said, and the technician nodded. "It's too soon to tell the genders, and we might have difficulty doing that, anyway. Depends on how they situate themselves in the—"

"Stop." Julie sat up, wiped the lotion off her stomach. "I'll come back another day. I had a hamburger, and maybe that—"

"Calm down, love. We haven't eaten yet." Rafe pushed her down on the table with a gentle hand, and Julie surprised herself by lying back. "Take a deep breath. Think of this as the happiest day of your life."

The medical personnel in the room were studiously trying to listen, but the endearment and the concern Rafe was showering her with had them somewhat agog. At first, perhaps they'd assumed she'd brought Rafe along for moral support. Maybe as a birthing coach. Although that would have been stretching it, considering the long-standing lawsuit that everyone in town had been following for years.

But now…now everyone would know Rafe was the father.

Julie jumped off the table. "I'm getting dressed. Rafe, you wait out in the waiting room. Better yet, don't wait at all." She forced back tears.

Everyone cleared out of the room with sympathetic glances.

"She'll calm down in a bit," Julie heard the doctor say to Rafe once the door closed. "Often mothers get a bit emotional upon seeing their firstborn in utero. And multiples are always a shocker."

Julie pressed her hand to her stomach. Three babies! The Callahan curse! She flung the door open to find Rafe standing on the other side.

"I thought I'd wait to see if you needed anything—"

She pulled him inside the room. "If I didn't know better, I'd say you made triplets on purpose!"

"No." He shook his head, but his deep blue eyes twinkled. "If I could train my sperm that well, love, I'd have gone for four. I need four to take over the ranch. My brothers are ahead of me. Pete, you might recall, has trips. I definitely would have gone for the big win."

She smacked him on the chest.

Rafe grunted and rubbed at his pectorals, which she knew were rock-hard, amazing and wonderful.

"That's dumb," Julie said. "None of you are going to have a ranch to take over."

He pulled her into his arms. "Now, Judge, this is not the time to be all competitive. You just won the grand prize. Go ahead and cry, gorgeous. You deserve a weep."

She started to push off his nicely warm, comforting chest, and then thought *maybe this once I will be a little silly and cry.*

"Judges don't cry," she said, and he handed her a tissue.

"Did your daddy tell you that?" Rafe rubbed her back, comforting her.

"No, but he always said boys didn't, and neither should I."

"Julie Jenkins, it's time for you to quit letting Daddy run your life."

"I know," she said, with a last sniffle. "And he's going to be so sad."

"Nah, he's tough. He'll get over it. And it'll be good for him." Rafe held her away from him, stared down into her face. "You ever stop to think that if you give the old man some independence, he might find a woman and settle down? And then the whole county could relax?"

"That's awful." Julie let Rafe crush her back against his chest. She thought she could hide there for a few more minutes. What could it hurt? No one saw her being emotional. "Know any ladies his age?"

Rafe laughed. "Let's go get that hamburger. You're eating for four now."

"Don't remind me."

Yet Julie went with Rafe, trying to decide if maybe he wasn't as bad as she'd always thought he was.

He probably was. But it was time to find out.

Chapter 8

A week later, Rafe was still overwhelmed. He had too much on his plate to brag. He wanted to boast like mad, but figured it was Julie's right to put the word about, let everyone know that the Callahans had struck again.

He hadn't even told his brothers.

"It's almost miraculous," he muttered to Bleu, as he tossed hay into the feed box. "Except for Creed, who's a bit slow anyway, we've all gone multiple."

Bleu snorted, the equivalent of an equine shrug.

"You don't care now, but wait until there's three little boys tugging at your mane, wanting a ride."

Bleu looked as if he was certain he wouldn't put up with those kinds of shenanigans. Rafe laughed and went on down the wide aisle, checking the horses they'd put in the barn. As Novembers went, it wasn't that cold yet. Soon enough it would be. He liked knowing the horses were snug in the barns at night.

He'd like knowing that Julie was safe and snug in his room at night.

Ever since his lady had found out he'd knocked her up in a trophy-winning way, she'd been a little uncommunicative.

"I'm just about ready to deliver myself to Julie in a giant tub of chocolate ice cream," he told Bleu, coming back to gaze at Rancho Diablo's favorite horse.

"Hello?"

Rafe turned to look in the direction of the female voice. "Hi," he said, shocked to see Julie standing in his barn. "Long time no see."

Her brows rose. "A week?"

He cast a quick glance at her tummy, which was rounding nicely with his offspring. "You look great."

"I look plump. I think it's subconscious. As soon as I heard 'triplets,' I started eating a lot more."

Rafe nodded. "I'd eat more, except I'm responsible for the grub around here now. One thing I've noticed is that if I cook it, I don't want to eat it. At least not much of it."

She hesitated. "I want to show you something."

He wanted to see anything she wanted to show him. "Let me wash up."

Rafe made fast work of that, then joined Julie as she led him to her truck. "Taking a drive, are we?"

"We are."

There were a thousand questions he wanted to ask. Had she told Bode—or anyone? Rafe didn't have a pound of lead in him, so he figured Julie had been as silent as he had. Seton and Sabrina never came around anymore, so he wasn't certain what was going on at Chez Jenkins.

"You know," Rafe said, deciding other subjects were safest, "my brothers are none too happy that Seton and Sabrina moved to your house."

"Oh, don't worry." Julie turned down a drive in town. "Sabrina's not with us anymore."

He blinked. "Where is she?"

"She took a job up north, I think." Julie's brow furrowed. "Wait, I remember. She's in Washington, D.C."

Jonas was going to be furious. "Doing what?"

"She got a job. I'm not certain what she's doing. Seton says her sister writes for newspapers."

Ha. If Julie knew that Sabrina had been a plant to spy on Bode, she'd flip. For that matter, Seton was also a plant, and a more serious one, because she wasn't just an investigative journalist hired by Fiona, she was actually a private investigator.

Not that she'd been worth beans, Rafe thought. She was more loyal to Julie these days. "Does Seton ever date anyone?" he asked, making his tone casual.

"Why would you want to know that?" Julie sent a glance his way that he felt despite the approaching evening hours.

"I don't know. Just wondered. Not sure why a young, beautiful girl like that would want to coop herself up with an old man."

"It may shock you, Rafe Callahan, but not everyone thinks my father is running the evil empire."

Rafe held up a placating hand. "Hey, let's not go over that again. I'm all for getting along with the in-laws and the out-laws."

Julie stopped in front of a small, two-story white

house in a cul-de-sac one street off the main town drag. "Here we are."

"Where?" he asked, getting out, since Julie was.

"Home sweet home." She beamed, then put a hand on her stomach without realizing she did it, which Rafe thought was cute and very mamalike of her. "This is my new house."

Rafe turned to look at the small place surrounded by a few split-level adobes. "Someone didn't care for the tried-and-true Southwestern style?"

"I guess not. It's all right, though. It has everything I require. Come on in." She pulled out a key and unlocked the door.

Rafe followed her inside. "It's been redone. That's nice."

She nodded. "It has so much of what I need for raising three children."

He turned to her, wanting to tread carefully. "You didn't want to live with Bode anymore?"

"Weren't you the one who said I needed to let him do his own thing?" Julie shrugged. "It was time for me to have my own place."

He nodded. "Julie, I—"

The words wouldn't come to him. He wasn't certain how to express what he wanted to say. Congratulations were in order, he could see that. Any man knew that when a woman purchased her first digs, she was standing on her own two feet. A house purchase was a serious thing.

But didn't they need to live together as a family?

Quite obviously, that thought had never occurred to Julie.

"It's nice, Julie," he said, as she waved him into the kitchen. "Real nice."

"I've already gone grocery shopping to fill up the cabinets." Julie smiled, pleased, and continued the tour. "Laundry room with a sink off the kitchen. I figure the extra sink will be handy." She was like a girl, showing him all the treasures of her new house. "Four bedrooms upstairs, and an office down. Or I could switch it, and have a master down and an office up. While the babies are small, we're all going to sleep upstairs."

He swallowed hard, barely able to think. "This is great."

"You really think so?"

He wasn't about to deny the delight in her voice. It was a huge step for her to get away from her father. "I do," Rafe said with conviction. "Congratulations. This house ought to be a wonderful home for you and the boys."

She looked at him, one slim brow rising. "Boys?"

"The babies."

"They're girls, Rafe."

Silence fell in the kitchen.

"All of them?" he finally asked, and Julie laughed.

"I don't know. The doctor can't tell yet. It's too early to know."

"So they could be boys," Rafe said.

Julie grabbed some cookies from the cupboard and put them on a plate. "You sound like my father. He was always disappointed I wasn't a boy."

"No, he wasn't," Rafe said, following her as she went upstairs. "I have it on good authority from Fiona that you were the apple of your daddy's eye."

"Yes, but he would have preferred a boy. And I don't want you doing that to our girls."

"Not me," Rafe said, noticing that the "master" bedroom was about the same size as a tack room at Rancho Diablo, and not a very large one at that. He'd be lucky if he and Julie both had enough closet space in here. "Hey, girls are great. I'm all about girls. If we're having girls, I say break out the pink."

Julie laughed. "My girls will wear blue. And whatever other color they like."

"Works for me," Rafe said swiftly. "Break out the blue."

She looked around the room, ignoring his noble attempt to be easygoing. "The movers come tomorrow."

"Need some help? You don't want to overdo things."

"No," Julie said, "I've got Seton and some friends helping me."

"Friends?" An unbidden, unwanted spark of jealousy shot through Rafe. "Like, guys?"

"Yes," Julie said. "All your brothers, if you must know."

His jaw sagged. "I thought you said *friends*."

She came to stand in front of him. "I'm trying, Rafe. I have no desire to let the past stand between my kids and their family. So I invited your brothers."

"What about me?"

"I need some space from the men in my life. I hope you can understand that."

"I don't know," Rafe began.

"I brought you here tonight, didn't I? You're the first person who's seen my house, except Seton."

"Well," Rafe said, slightly mollified, "I'm still very good with carrying and unpacking boxes."

"Thank you," Julie said, "but no."

"All right," Rafe said. "But I'm not used to being left out."

She laughed and went down the stairs. He followed, watching her sweet derriere sway, while automatically cataloging all the changes that needed to be made to the house to make it baby-safe.

Baby gate at the top of the staircase. Plug covers to keep little fingers out. Et cetera, et cetera.

He figured she probably wouldn't appreciate him interjecting his opinions. Maybe if he kept his mouth shut, Julie would invite him back.

Basically, he needed to prove to her that he wasn't going to over-own her like Bode had. It wasn't going to be easy to achieve some distance, when all his senses were screaming to possess her.

But he had to give her space. Otherwise, he was never going to get her into a real bed.

And that would be a shame.

Rafe sat outside admiring the night sky, and thinking how much a full moon agreed with Julie, who was in full nesting mode, when a shadow at his elbow made him sit up.

"You wanted to see me?" a male voice asked, and Rafe jumped to his feet.

"See who?" He peered into the darkness and saw nothing but an outline.

The figure came closer. In the light from the house windows, he recognized the chief.

"Why would you think I want to see you?"

"Got your message." Chief Running Bear grinned.

"No point in waiting until December twenty-fourth, is there?"

"Any time is good with me."

"What can I do for you?" the older man asked.

Rafe narrowed his eyes. "Why did you meet my aunt every year? What's going on in the basement?"

The chief shrugged. He wore jeans, a flannel shirt, boots and a hat, looking much like anyone else in the town. "That's between me and your aunt."

"My aunt is gone."

His companion nodded. "I know."

"So I need to know what she was working on down there."

The chief gave him a long look. "If she'd wanted you to know, she would have told you."

"Not necessarily. Fiona kept a lot of secrets."

The chief shrugged again. "What else?"

Clearly, the man wasn't going to talk about Fiona. Rafe sighed. "Does your tribe own Rancho Diablo's mineral rights?"

He inclined his head. "It was our land before we sold it to your parents."

Rafe thought about that for a moment. "You know Bode Jenkins has filed all kinds of suits to get our land taken from us."

The chief shrugged again. "It won't happen. This land is yours. As part Native Americans, you are entitled to this ranch."

Rafe shook his head. "We're full Irish. Our parents were straight off the boat. So were our aunt and uncle."

"Your mother, Molly, was Irish, your father, Jeremiah, full Navajo." The chief looked at Rafe. "The land will always be your family's. This is Diablo land. Shall we walk?"

Rafe figured the chief didn't want to be seen by anyone. He fell into step with his visitor, wondering why Fiona had never told them of their true heritage. "So this whole plot of my aunt's to give the ranch to the person with the most children was just an excuse to get us married."

"Once the lawsuit happened, we knew that the land had to be safeguarded. The only way to do that was to split it up among you. Extracting anything from six brothers, their wives and children, and their estates, would be a difficult thing. Your aunt did want you settled down, but you would have all gotten your portions in due time, anyway."

Rafe shook his head. "Such a complicated way to do business."

"I liked her idea. Family is a good thing."

"Maybe." Rafe thought about Julie and how he was ever going to get her to agree to become one big happy family with him. "So you own the mineral rights, which Bode doesn't know, and so he can't get those. We have the land in our possession, and he can't get that. Shouldn't we just tell him?"

"No," the chief said. "He believes everything can be solved if he just greases the right palm with silver."

"Speaking of silver," Rafe said, "is that a real silver mine?"

The chief nodded. "It is. It's not a working mine anymore. It could be, but it's so small it would only be worth mining silver for jewelry. What was most valuable was dug out long ago."

Rafe nodded. "So why are you hanging out in the cave now?"

"Storage. It's an excellent storage facility." His broad face creased with wrinkles and a smile. "No one would ever find anything in there."

"Fiona used it."

The chief nodded. "It's safe."

Rafe wondered how safe. He'd seen many footprints in the cave. "We found photos of all the Callahan babies. What was that about?"

His question earned him a shrewd look from the chief. "That you must ask your aunt."

Rafe grunted. "I intend to. I'm planning to head over to Ireland to see my cagey aunt and tell her there wasn't any reason for her to leave. She didn't have to go, and she knew it. And I know it now."

"She felt like the family was better off without her. She'd served you well."

"We're better off *with* her." Rafe was certain about that. "Unless she doesn't want to live in New Mexico."

Impenetrable brown eyes met his. "It was home."

"She shouldn't have left."

"Fiona did not want Mr. Jenkins focusing on her any longer. He can't get over the fact that he believes his wife died because she was taking care of Fiona and your family too much. Mrs. Jenkins was ill, though. She wanted to do what she did for Fiona. Mr. Jenkins doesn't like to accept the things he knows to be true. He's angry."

"You're telling me," Rafe said, but he felt a twinge of sadness for the bitter old man.

"He's not going to like you for taking his only child away from him," the chief pointed out. "Have you considered that your children will likely not have a willing grandfather?"

Rafe squinted at him. "How do you know about my children?"

"I knew long before I heard it in town." The tall, still-vital elderly man smiled. "You know, your parents wanted one thing—a large family."

Rafe stopped walking to stare at him.

"I knew your parents," Chief Running Bear said, "and I know their children, and I will know their grandchildren." He nodded. "This has been a good talk. We'll talk again one day."

"Wait," Rafe said, but then realized the chief was walking away, not listening anymore. Rafe had a thousand questions to ask, more about his family, his parents, his heritage. But just then a sharp whistle rent the air, and a black Diablo mustang ran toward the chief, who launched himself at a dead run onto the horse's back. "Holy smokes," Rafe said, "I thought I was a good rider."

He watched until man and horse disappeared into the night, and then he turned toward home, wondering if he was any closer to knowing what he had to know.

Rafe walked into the upstairs library, surprised to find Jonas and Sam there already, toasting each other in front of a small fire. They had a couple snifters of brandy, which was a bigger surprise, because typically they relaxed with a beer. "Family meeting been called that I should know about?" Rafe asked.

"We're celebrating." Jonas swirled his snifter. "Come in and join us in the festivities."

Rafe wasn't feeling all that celebratory after his chat

with Chief Running Bear. While he'd been digging up the family ghosts, his brothers had been indulging themselves. But he took the snifter Sam handed him, and sat down near the fire. He felt cold, chilled.

It was all the talk of the past that had him feeling as if he was stuck in a meat locker.

"So what are we celebrating? The full moon? A new lady?" Rafe gulped some brandy, knowing he was putting off the inevitable. He was going to have to tell his brothers what he'd learned—and it was going to change them as much as it had changed him.

"Lots." Sam grinned. "First, your hot judge has got herself some new digs."

"Don't I know it." Rafe set the brandy down, deciding he needed a clear head.

"It's a start, getting her away from Bode. You're smarter than you look, bro." Jonas grinned.

"I had nothing to do with it."

"You had everything to do with it," Sam said. "You got her pregnant, and that alone deserves some kind of trophy. I didn't think anyone would ever get Julie away from Daddy."

"Don't make it sound like she's some kind of silly girl whose father makes all the decisions for her." Rafe felt cranky hearing his woman discussed in such a cavalier manner. "Anyway, what else are we toasting?"

"Jonas finally put in an offer on the Dark Diablo Ranch." Sam's face was gleeful. "Combined, we'll have fifteen thousand acres."

Rafe's jaw sagged. "Why?"

Jonas shrugged. "If I've learned one thing from Bode, it's that land is power. With land, you're safe. You have a place to call your own. And, basically, I was tired of putting up with him. We'll just move ranch operations over there if he bugs us too much, and put a monster hotel right here to drive him nuts. Maybe a high school. Something with lots of lights and noise to keep the old geezer up at night."

Rafe blinked. "Do you think we might have discussed this?"

"It's my money," Jonas said. "All you boys go on and have babies by the truckload. I'm happy to be King Jonas. Everything I touch turns to land."

Rafe glanced at Sam, who shrugged. "What's gotten up your nose, Jonas?" Rafe pressed.

Their oldest brother leaned back in his chair, savoring his brandy. "All the years of Bode yapping at us. I just want to be free. I want more of what matters most."

He was really going to freak when he learned that Sabrina had moved to Washington, D.C. Rafe took another swig of brandy, coughing as it went down the wrong way.

"Easy," Sam said, "it's brandy, not water. Meant to be rolled across the tongue, not slung down your hatch."

Rafe sighed. "Here's the thing. While you two have been sitting up here in your ivory tower feeling good about life, I've been down on the ground taking in the lay of the land."

"Here comes Mr. Sunshine. Brace yourself," Jonas said, pouring Sam some more brandy.

Rafe took that comment in without a word. "First, the gossip. Sabrina's picked up stakes and gone to Washington, D.C."

Jonas stared at him. "What the hell are you talking about? She would never leave her sister."

"She did." Rafe nodded. "She got a job, and that was that."

"Washington, D.C.?" Jonas asked, his tone incredulous. Rafe felt sorry for him.

"Yes. That's the gossip." Knowing that he'd poleaxed Jonas for the moment, he went on. "And I just had the most interesting discussion with our friend Chief Running Bear."

"What?" Sam sat up. "How did that happen?"

Rafe didn't mention that he'd left a message in the cave for Fiona's friend. "It just happened. Just now, as I was standing outside."

Jonas glowered at him, still not happy about the Sabrina bulletin. "And?"

Rafe shrugged. "He doesn't say much. I got the feeling he's keeping a lot of Fiona's secrets. However, he did mention that we're not full Irish, like we thought we were. We're half Navajo, courtesy of our father. Fiona is our mother's sister, but we were always told she was our father's sister."

Sam and Jonas stared at him, taking in the ramifications of his announcement.

"I suppose," Rafe said, "it would explain why we all have blue eyes and black hair."

"That doesn't make sense," Sam said. "Fiona said she came from Ireland to take care of us because she was our father's sister. Fiona is completely Irish. Therefore, our father couldn't have been Native American."

"Did she say it, or is that how we remember it?" Rafe thought about this angle for a moment. "Where are our aunts and uncles, grandparents? Any relatives?"

"Why didn't you ask the chief?" Jonas demanded.

"I was in such shock I didn't get everything out I

wanted to know. And frankly, we could ask questions for twenty-four hours, and we wouldn't know everything." Rafe gulped some more brandy, welcoming the fire as it burned down his throat. "I was more focused on Rancho Diablo and the Bode issue."

"You realize I'm the only one here who probably isn't related to the rest of you. God only knows where Fiona got me," Sam said.

"From under a rock," Jonas said, not cheery now that he'd learned Sabrina had left. "Finish the story," he said to Rafe.

"Chief Running Bear said Fiona left to protect us. He said that the land will always be ours. His tribe does own the mineral rights. Bode can never really get our land away from us, considering that the mineral rights and the land are split. And I suppose, with the tribe being involved, the government won't take any land away from them. I mean, obviously." Rafe shrugged. "So we're home free on that issue, since we may be part Navajo."

"Bode doesn't know any of this," Sam said.

"No." Rafe nodded. "And now that you know, you'll have to declare it."

"I need to see documents first," Sam said. "Easy enough to look up land ownership and mineral rights through court records."

Rafe nodded again. "We wouldn't need the Dark Diablo property, Jonas. Unless you want it."

His brother shook his head and didn't reply.

Sam walked over to the fireplace. "And it wasn't necessary for Fiona to leave—"

"Except she was afraid Bode was so mad at her he might hurt one of us," Rafe reminded him.

"But it's dumb," Sam went on, "that we don't just tell Bode to stick it in his ear—"

"Easy," Rafe said. "I'm trying to marry his daughter."

His brothers stared at him. "You are?" Jonas demanded.

"I thought Julie wouldn't have anything to do with you," Sam said.

"She's having my babies," Rafe said. "She's going to have to get with the program sooner or later."

"Babies?" Sam exclaimed.

"Triplets," Rafe said, practically boasting. "Let it never be said that the Callahan men don't shoot straight as an arrow."

Jonas shook his head. "Disgusting. Meantime, you and your blabbermouth ran off Sabrina."

"I didn't do it," Rafe said defensively. "Sabrina wanted a real job. She wasn't working for Fiona anymore. You're going to have to deal with the fact that your little gypsy wasn't really a fortune teller, Jonas. She's a career woman who couldn't sit around here waiting for you to decide to get off your sawhorse and ask her out."

Jonas blinked. "This isn't Six Brides for Six Brothers, as much as Fiona might have wanted it to be, Rafe, and as happily as you're falling in with The Plan."

"At least Seton's still around." Sam sipped his brandy. "Maybe that means Sabrina will be home for Christmas, Jonas. Anyway," he said, raising his glass to Rafe, "congratulations, bro. Excellent shooting. They say the smart ones have little to no common sense, and I guess you proved the theorem."

Rafe wasn't sure what Sam was driving at. Sam

wasn't a mathematician, he was a damn fine lawyer. And if Rafe knew one thing about math, it was that a theorem proved was a theorem true. He wasn't certain, but he thought Sam had just claimed that he'd done something dumb by getting Julie pregnant. Then again, what the hell did Sam know about geometry and math in general? Or even women?

He looked at his brothers, realizing how stuck they were. Neither one would go after the lady he wanted. They'd sit here all day, claiming they weren't interested. Locked in their towers, as usual. *I'm not stuck, though. I've got my woman. And she knows exactly how I feel about her.*

Well, maybe not exactly.

After Julie moved into her new house tomorrow, maybe Rafe would tell her.

Chapter 9

"Where've you been?" Bode demanded of Julie as she returned home from showing her new house to Rafe. She was all wrapped up in dreams and thoughts of the future. It shouldn't have mattered, but she'd been proud to show her place to Rafe. She wanted him to see where his children would be raised. That was fair, wasn't it?

Despite the past, she meant for him to be a welcome part of his children's lives.

"I told you, Dad. I went by my new house."

He shook his head, agitated. "You didn't tell me."

Julie turned to look at her father more closely. His tone was more querulous than usual. "I didn't tell you, specifically. I asked Seton to tell you."

Bode frowned. "Seton's not here."

"She's not?" Julie stared at her dad, wondering how long he'd been alone. "Do you know where she is?"

"I don't know. She said she was giving notice." Bode's frown grew deeper. "She said she was moving to Washington to be with Sabrina."

Julie's mouth dropped open. "Dad! Why didn't you call me on my cell?"

"Would it have made a difference? You're leaving, too." Bode sat back, a stubborn, unhappy lump in his chair.

"I…" Julie glanced at her father. "I'm not leaving. I'm moving fifteen minutes away."

"Same as leaving." Bode looked out the window. "Anyway, she just up and left. I guess you'll be doing that tomorrow."

"You can come to the new house and help me unpack boxes." Julie refused to allow her father to dim her happiness. "You know, Dad, you don't really want to live in a house with a bunch of children. You think it wouldn't be that bad, but you're used to peace and quiet."

Bode stiffened. "Children? As in future children?"

"No," Julie said, keeping her voice calm, "children as in I'm having triplets."

A red wash flooded Bode's face. He bounded from his chair, leaping to his feet so fast and hard that he knocked over the end table. "Damn those Callahans! Nothing but trouble, every last one of them!"

"Dad!" Julie frowned at him. "Calm down!"

Her father's head swung around. "How can I calm down, knowing that those Callahans, those damn Callahans, who've taken everything I have in life, have stolen my daughter?"

"Hardly stolen." Julie shook her head. "You need to stop looking at the Callahans as competition. They're not. As far as I can tell, they're barely aware that we're over here."

A sharp bark of laughter escaped Bode. "Aware enough to put a bull's-eye on my daughter!"

Julie crossed her arms. "I'd appreciate it if you never say another cross or unkind word about the father of my children. I mean it, Dad. Please."

He frowned, sweeping her with a disbelieving gaze. "What's happened to you? What's made you change? It's like a spell's been cast on you."

Julie's expression matched her father's. "What do you mean?"

"It means," Bode said, his tone furious and betrayed, "that once upon a time, you knew what it meant to honor your father. Now all you do is talk about that Callahan like he's some kind of prince."

"There are no princes and no villains. I'm simply accepting my life as it is." Julie gave her father a pleading smile. "Dad, let's not fight. We're going to have three beautiful babies. That should put back a whole lot of what you feel has been stolen from you."

"See? See?" Bode wheeled his arms. "*What I feel has been stolen from me?* Like I'm making the whole thing up." Bode stared at her, disbelieving.

"There are two sides to every story. I've been a judge long enough to know that." Julie turned to leave his study.

"You used to know which was the right side," Bode said, his tone filled with bitterness. "Before you got your head turned."

"I have a lot to do. If you want to come to the house tomorrow, you're very welcome. If not, it's your choice."

Julie left her father, not feeling good about it, but not

knowing how to fix it, either. He simply didn't realize she just couldn't go on living in the past.

His past.

"Not my past," Julie whispered, putting a hand to her stomach for just a moment to feel the babies there, "and certainly not yours."

She could only think of her children's futures.

The next day, Julie was aware of Rafe hanging back, watching his brothers unload everything. Her father had elected not to come, and if he couldn't be pleasant, then it was for the best.

The other man in her life, who also seemed unhappy, clearly wanted to be a participant in the move. Julie fought off the guilt, telling herself that both men were going to have to learn that not everything could go their way all the time.

"Don't mind him," Sam said, walking by with a flowered ottoman. "Rafe's a suffering succotash if there ever was one."

"He's so pitiful," Julie said. "Maybe I should—"

"Nope." Sam jerked his head toward the house. "Show me where this flowery thing goes."

She followed him into the house, and pointed to the den. "Right there, please."

Sam grinned. "It'll serve Rafe right to have to put his feet on this." He looked at the huge, tufted pink-yellow-and-blue ottoman with glee. "Rafe deserves every bit of this girlie stuff."

Julie blinked. "You don't think he'll like it?"

Sam chuckled. "He'll feel right at home."

Julie didn't think Sam was being quite honest. Maybe

the things she'd bought were a little on the feminine side, but did it matter? It was her home, her first home.

"Your dad decide not to come?" Sam asked, heading back out for more items.

The other brothers kept up a steady stream, carrying things from the van they'd rented, and the Callahan women and some of Julie's friends unpacked, refusing to allow her to lift so much as a cup.

"My father is at home, upset that his little girl grew up." Julie smiled when Sam glanced back at her. "He's also in a bit of a mood because Seton left."

Sam gave her a sharp glance. "What do you mean, left?"

"Just left. No notice, no nothing. No goodbye." Julie was still annoyed—and hurt—about that. She'd considered Seton a true friend.

"I don't believe it," Sam said. He thought about it, then shook his head. "Nope. She wouldn't do that."

A tiny trickle of unease flowed over Julie. "Well, she did."

Sam pulled a pie table from the truck. "Now here is piece of furniture just made for a man to sit a beer on."

"Stop." She put a hand out to impede Sam's progress. "First of all, I'm aware that you're having a giggle at my expense. You think my stuff is too feminine for Rafe. It doesn't matter. Your brother doesn't live here, and isn't going to be moving in," Julie said, her tone stern.

"Yes, ma'am," Sam said, having the decency to look a little respectful.

"Rafe never implied he'd want to live here, and I'm looking forward to life on my own."

"Yes'm." Sam gazed at her, his blue eyes twinkling. "Second, what do you think happened to Seton?"

"Me? I'm just a lawyer. How would I know?"

Julie gave him a look that spoke volumes about his innocence ploy. "Counselor, I'm not in the mood for word games. I'm a pregnant lady with mood swings. Let's respect that."

"Yes, ma'am!" Sam grinned hugely.

"So what do you think happened to Seton?"

The smile slipped from his face. "My guess? Your father's throwing a hissy fit because you moved out. He fired Seton and told her to go without saying goodbye to you." Sam shrugged. "That's my guess, based on years of watching Bode get what he wants."

Julie's face burned with anger. "Put the table down," she said, her tone soft but sharp, "and go."

"Julie—"

"Go," she said, and turned away.

She heard the pie table being set gently on the ground, heard boots walking away. She was so mad she was shaking. Of course, she'd asked him, practically forced him to tell her what he thought.

Yet she hadn't expected Sam to have such a vile opinion of her father.

And if Sam had that kind of totally wrong take on him, likely all the Callahans felt the same way. Including Rafe.

What had she expected?

She glanced down the street, seeing Rafe leaning against his truck. Sam had gone straight to his brother, no doubt filling him in on her "mood swing."

But what Sam had accused her father of was so dark, so manipulative, that she could barely imagine him thinking it. Her dad would never have dismissed

Seton—fired her—just to try to make Julie regret moving out, to try one last thing to keep her tied to him.

He wouldn't have done it.

Julie went back inside to unpack.

By nightfall, after everyone had left, Rafe decided the time had to be right to take Julie a housewarming gift—namely, himself. He rang the doorbell, holding the set of rubber-tipped cooking spoons he'd bought her, arranged nicely in a clay pot of beautiful Native American design. He was pretty proud of himself for shopping for something practical, when he'd really wanted to buy her a see-through nightie.

Spoons first, then nighties, he told himself. *Play it cool.*

Julie opened the door and stared out, not exactly smiling at the sight of him.

"Hello, Julie," Rafe said. He extended the pot. "Brought you a housewarming gift."

She glanced at the spoons. "This isn't a good time."

He didn't know what to say to that.

Julie decided to jump into deep water. "I'm sure you know about the conversation Sam and I had."

Rafe looked at her, thinking she was beautiful even when clearly annoyed. Being attracted to your woman even when she was mad was a good thing; if a man could stand his woman in a mood, their relationship was sure to be a go. "He didn't mention anything to me. Sam's the baby of the family. He teases a lot, but he's harmless."

She shook her head. Rafe thought she looked tired, which was reasonable, given her long day, but it also alarmed him. Her blue dress stretched over her stomach, which, he noted, was filling out nicely to accommodate his boys. "You look hot, Julie. Sexy hot. Drive-me-crazy hot."

She gave him a wry look. "That line shouldn't work, but I'm afraid it does. Come in, you silver-tongued devil."

"I'm serious," Rafe said, slipping in the door before she could change her mind. "You can't let Sam get to you. He doesn't mean anything he says."

"He does when he's in court."

"Yeah." Rafe removed his hat and tossed it on a flowered mushroom-type footstool near the sofa. "But when he's not in barrister mode, we barely pay attention to him. Trust me, he's like your favorite farting grandfather. You just don't know what he's going to say or do, so you just ignore it and hope everyone else does, too."

He could see that Julie was trying not to smile. "This is serious, Rafe."

"All right." He seated himself next to the hat on the floral tuffet, even though he wasn't certain if men were supposed to sit on such things. Maybe they were meant only for ladies, hence the puffs and fringe and ribbons. "Tell me what's on your mind. But can you come a little closer while you unload? If this Venus flytrap swallows me, I'll need you to pull me back out."

"What is it with this ottoman?" Julie didn't step closer. "Sam had the same reaction."

Rafe patted the sides. "It's like a pregnant cupcake. Didn't Jeannie have something like this in her bottle?" He bounced a little, testing it. "Not like my leather sofa at home, which is substantial and manly."

Julie laughed. "It does look a little like something

out of *I Dream of Jeannie.* Get off. I'm sending it back tomorrow."

"No, you're not. I like it. I really do." Rafe didn't like it at all, but he didn't want to hurt Julie's feelings. If his pumpkin liked it, then he'd learn to love it. "You realize my boys are going to use this as a launch pad."

"My girls will sit on it and look pretty," Julie retorted.

Rafe shrugged. "So, Judge, what did Sam do to get himself kicked out?"

Julie took her attention from the ottoman, putting it back on him, where he liked it. He sat up, enjoying having her dark eyes looking into his. "I told him that Seton had left my father's employment unexpectedly, without even a goodbye to me."

Julie put her hands on her hips, which he watched with interest. His buttercup was spreading out in that area, developing a goddess body. Rafe got an erection just thinking about how her curves were blossoming. "Doesn't sound like Seton."

"Exactly. And Sam's theory is that my father fired her."

Rafe's gaze left Julie's hips unwillingly and settled on her face, which wasn't exactly a hardship. She was so beautiful, he thought. He couldn't wait to kiss her mouth again—he never got to kiss her long enough to suit him. "Did you ask your father if that's true?"

"No. I didn't think that far. Sam's reasoning is that Dad did it so I'd be guilted into staying in his house."

Rafe blinked, thinking it was entirely plausible the old man had done exactly that, but realizing this was a moment for great diplomacy. Boot-scooting around the facts, as it were. "Sam talks a lot. He's a lawyer." Rafe shrugged. "What does that have to do with you being mad at me right now?"

"I'm pretty sure you feel the same way about my father," Julie said.

"Ah…" Rafe hesitated. "It doesn't matter what I think. Sam cares what happened to Seton because I think he's got a thing for her. I'm just trying to stay out of trouble with you, Judge."

Her lips pursed. "My father wouldn't have fired Seton. He liked her a lot."

Rafe put up his hands. "Don't ask me. Ask your dad what happened to her. In the meantime, give me something to unpack. I don't want you lifting a finger, gorgeous."

Julie stared at him. "Rafe, this isn't going to work."

He put on his best innocent face. "What isn't?"

"Your family, my family. In-laws and out-laws."

"I don't care if it does. I care about you, and my children, and that's all I have to care about." He got off the stuffed, frilly footstool and went to her, enveloping her in his arms, even though he worried he might be moving too fast for her. "I don't care what Sam or your father says. I don't care where Seton is, or anybody else, at the moment. All I care about is you."

Julie gazed up at him. "That might be a good idea."

"That's right. You listen to me, and everything will be fine."

She put her head on his chest, which he liked very much. He held her close, enjoying her being a little more relaxed than usual.

"You know, you have a tendency to talk a little like a male chauvinist at times," Julie said.

He chuckled. "I'm certain the best judge in the county can keep me in my place."

"You remember that."

Rafe wondered if it was too soon to try to sneak a kiss. He decided it was. "So, friends?"

She looked up at him. "Until you annoy me."

"Sounds like marriage to me," Rafe said, and kissed her on her forehead. "Give me something to unpack."

"You can put your spoons in the kitchen." Julie handed him the pot he'd given her. "Why spoons?"

Rafe took his gift into the kitchen. "I sure wasn't bringing you a knife set, sweetie."

"You're smart," Julie said, and Rafe smiled.

"That's what they tell me, Your Honor. That's what they tell me."

When Rafe finally ended up in a bed with Julie, it didn't happen the way he thought it would.

"No," he said, steering her away from unpacking in her room, "you're not doing a thing. You sit on that bed and see how well I take direction."

"I don't want you unpacking my personal things," Julie protested. "That would feel so strange."

"Tough." He held up a blue nightgown. "This is pretty."

"Closet," Julie said with a sigh.

Rafe dutifully trooped into the closet and hung it. Returning to the box, he pulled out a sheer white nightie. "I like this one better."

"It's going to be a slow process if you inspect all my undergarments," she said.

"I'm not in a hurry." Rafe handed her some nighties. "As intriguing as unpacking Victoria's Secret is, you handle this stuff, and I'll go do the dishes and pots. I don't want you lifting heavy things."

"You won't know how I want my kitchen set up. And I'm very particular about my kitchen."

Rafe ran his finger down Julie's nose. "You're particular about your nighties, too. Some might say you have a bossy streak, Julie Jenkins."

"They would not. I'm particular, which is different from bossy."

Rafe smiled. "I like a woman with opinions."

"I don't care what you like," Julie retorted.

"I tell you what I don't like," Rafe said, glancing toward the stairwell, "I don't like that staircase. It scares me. You're getting quite, um, stately. What if you fell? What if one of my babies falls?"

Julie looked at him. "My father's house was a two-story. Your house has several stories."

"Three," he said absently.

"And more than one staircase."

"Front, back and secret." He shrugged. "This one's steep. I don't like it."

Julie's dark brows rose. "Rafe, it has a handrail."

"Yeah." He scratched at his stubble, wondering why his little darling hadn't had the common sense to purchase an adobe one-story. The thought of little feet trying to negotiate that bear of a staircase bothered him. "All right, I'm going down to do the kitchen. You do your bedroom. I figure if we get these two rooms more settled, you're good to go until the ladies come back tomorrow to help."

"They were mostly interested in setting up the nursery. And they unpacked the living room, laundry room, craft room, all those things that take hours. But the nursery got the most attention."

Rafe's head whipped around from the box he'd been perusing. "I didn't see a nursery."

Julie waved a hand. "Open that door across the hall."

He walked to the door with a giant Pooh bear stuck on it. "I would have preferred a cowboy or a football player, but Pooh it is," he muttered, and opened the door.

He was shocked to see three white cribs set up with mobiles hanging over them. A white rocker sat in a corner, and a giant woven circle rug graced the wooden floor. "Wow. This is something else."

Julie came to stand beside him. "Makes it real, doesn't it?"

"Yeah." His heart was banging around inside his chest. "Scary real."

"That's the first time I've heard you admit you're scared."

"Spitless, at the moment." Rafe turned to look at her. "When are these babies due?"

"May." Julie smiled. "It's not even Thanksgiving. We have a while to adjust."

Rafe thought he was having his first panic attack. "Let's let you lie down for a moment," he told Julie. "You look a little pale."

"*I* look pale?" Julie stared up at him. "You look pale, Rafe. Like you've seen a ghost jumping around in your—"

"You definitely need to lie down." He stumbled toward Julie's bed, collapsing on it as manfully as he could. "You'll feel better in a moment, I'm certain. And I'll get you a cold drink of water, which will help."

She put a hand on his brow. He liked the way her skin

felt cool and calming against his. His pulse was going faster than he'd ever felt it. "Funny how this dizzy spell just all of a sudden came over you, isn't it?" he asked.

"It sure is." Julie sank down next to him, running her hand over his face. "One of us feels kind of clammy."

"Yeah," Rafe said, "although I've never understood what clammy means. What is clammy? Have you ever thought about what a strange word that is? I could understand it if people said sweaty, or 'your skin is moist.' But what is clammy, anyway? Where did that come from?"

"Dear heaven," he heard Julie murmur, "I actually let you get me pregnant."

Rafe waved an expansive hand in the air. "That was easy. Callahan sperm can swim through a maze to find the perfect egg."

Rafe thought she said something about someone being an overly arrogant ass, but he wasn't certain. Her bed was so soft, and Julie felt so clammy—whatever that meant, but she'd said it, so it had to mean something—that he thought the best thing for her to do was rest. He decided to join her in a small nap until she started feeling better.

I have to look out for her. She's such a delicate little tulip.

I'll protect her from everything.

Chapter 10

"Then he fell asleep." Julie looked at the two tall, strong, handsome men sitting at her kitchen table the next morning, gazing at her with sympathetic, dark-denim eyes just like Rafe's. "Or fainted."

"Did anyone ever mention that Rafe is the odd one of us?" Sam asked, seeming almost pleased that his brother had a weak spot. "He faints when he sees blood, particularly his own. I'm pretty sure baby poop and spit-up are going to be way beyond his powers to stay upright."

Julie nodded. "That just may be true. However, I'm still annoyed with you, so tell me again why you're here?"

Sam glanced at Jonas. "To apologize. I shouldn't have said what I did."

Julie placed a cup of coffee in front of each of them. "You shouldn't think it, either."

"That's true." Jonas gave Sam a warning glare as he sipped his coffee. "Julie's part of our family now. Since Rafe can't take care of her, we'll have to look out for her. In the future, guard your tongue."

Sam appeared chastened.

"Now, look," Julie said, sitting back down. "I don't need anyone taking care of me. Your brother needs more help than I do. Frankly, I'm just focused on trying to get along with my children's family."

"Despite the lawsuit." Sam nodded. "We're all for that. We're all about the joys of being uncles."

"The lawsuit has nothing to do with me," Julie said coolly. "I'm not the judge hearing it, so I don't care."

"And you've got your hands full with your pregnancy," Jonas said, his tone kind. "I'm sorry our brother went lights-out on you. He's an excellent pilot, but he may not be that great a birth coach."

"I haven't asked him to be a birth coach." Julie frowned. "I wouldn't want Rafe anywhere around me while I'm giving birth."

"Oh," Sam said, "that'll kill him."

She thought about the big cowboy still flung across her sheets. Rafe had fallen like a giant oak across the width of the queen-size bed. The bed had protested the weight falling on it, and Julie had been relieved when it didn't collapse. She'd briefly considered pulling off Rafe's boots, then decided not to. He had to be uncomfortable, and yet he seemed perfectly happy.

She'd left him there, listening to him snore while she unpacked more clothes. After about twenty minutes, she'd decided she needed a nap, too, and had crawled up alongside him. He'd immediately snuggled into her back, cupping her stomach with his big hand.

Truthfully, she'd enjoyed the intimacy.

"So, what brought you here so early in the morning, anyway?" Julie asked, telling herself that thinking about Rafe was unproductive. It would take a forklift to get him out of her bed, and so it was best to let him sleep off whatever had hit him.

"We saw the lights on, and Rafe's truck, and decided to make sure our brother wasn't annoying you." Jonas smiled. "Since he wasn't supposed to be here yesterday."

Julie nodded. "I might have been a bit hard on him. But this house means a lot to me, and I want it to feel completely my own."

"Understandable," Sam said jovially. "We wouldn't want him, either."

"True," Jonas said, "except he's a decent cook, so we let him come around."

She knew they were teasing her. Still, it was difficult understanding the byplay of brothers, since she'd been an only child. And she wasn't used to such a large family. It had surprised her when the doorbell had rung at nine o'clock in the morning.

Then it came to her: the Callahans were treating her like part of their family. Despite the lawsuit, despite her father, and no matter what happened between her and Rafe, they were going to include her.

Julie liked the feeling of security that knowledge gave her. "Does he always sleep like a dead man?"

Jonas nodded and got to his feet. "We all do. We can drag him off with us, if you like."

She considered that. "That's all right," she said. "I'll kick him out when he wakes up."

Sam got up, too. "Thanks for the joe. And let us know if you change your mind about Rafe. We're used to dragging one or the other of us out of strange places."

She smiled as they went out her door. "Thanks for checking on me."

They tipped their hats and departed.

Julie glanced around the living room of her new house. After a moment, she went back upstairs and looked at the man engulfing her bed.

Then she got back in with him. His arm instantly covered her, tugging her close.

It was the best thing she'd ever felt.

"No, no, no," Rafe said an hour later as he sprang off the bed. "Didn't I tell you? If you feed them, they keep coming around. You'll never get rid of them."

Julie smiled as he stretched and tried to work a kink out of his back. "I had to feed your brothers. They said you weren't there to do it."

"Helpless. I have to do everything for them."

Julie nodded. "I know."

He threw her a suspicious glance as he rubbed his stubble. "Are you feeling better?"

"Wonderful. You?"

"That bed may be smaller than I like, but it's comfy." Rafe patted it. "However, I think I pulled a muscle in my back."

"Unpacking nightgowns is tough work." Julie got up from the bed. "I'm kicking you out now."

"That's okay. I need to go supervise the Rancho Diablo affairs, or nothing will be done right. In the mean-time, you go downstairs, sit on that flower thing and rest."

"I'll do that," Julie said, and Rafe glared at her.

"I'm serious. Moving is hard work."

"I know. It nearly killed you." Julie patted his shoulder. "Be careful of the staircase. That might kill you, too."

"You laugh," Rafe said, his boots clomping as he walked down the stairs, "but phobias have always been good to me."

Julie giggled. "I'm sure."

"Well, remember, there's your chair." He pointed at the flowered ottoman. "I don't want to see you any-where but on that when I return with your dinner. You're having organic salad, fruit, and a steak to put good red blood cells in my boys."

"That's not quite the way it works. And you don't have to bring me anything," Julie said, ignoring his confident insistence that he was having males, unlike his brothers.

Rafe stuffed his hat down on his head. "I have to look out for you."

"I've taken care of myself for nearly thirty years."

"And look what happened the first time a real man looked at you." Rafe brushed Julie's hand across his lips. "You let him seduce you in a field."

She withered him with a stare. "That's all right. I'm keeping him at arm's length now."

"Yes." Rafe ran a gentle palm down her cheek. "That's got to change."

Julie closed the door after he went down the steps. She leaned against it for just a moment, her eyes clos-ing. Rafe was a lot of man to "keep at arm's length."

Did she want to anymore?

* * *

Julie knew she couldn't put off visiting her father any longer. So at lunch, she swung by Banger's, grabbed her father a burger and went by to see how he was doing.

It was almost as if he knew she was coming. He sat in the darkness of his study, his face arranged woefully.

"Turn on some lights," Julie said, flipping on a few lamps. She handed him the hamburger bag. He set it on the table beside him while she sat on a chair nearby.

"You're going to have to get over all this, Dad."

He looked at her. "My only daughter running to my greatest enemy. How do you expect me to get over it?"

"I don't know, but you'll have to." Julie frowned. "I know it's hard, Dad, but I've got children to think of. I can't live in the past."

"The past." Bode snorted. "It's not the past. It's the right now. It's the future."

"It can't be for me."

Her father looked at her. "You probably want me to drop the lawsuit."

Julie sighed. "It's not my business what you do. Rafe and I have never discussed it, anyway."

"It's why he got you pregnant."

She shook her head. "That's not what happened."

"You can't deny the coincidence of it. The man never asked you out before, and suddenly, you're having his children. It makes me look like an old man who got bested in court and in my own home." He shook his head. "Never in all my years did I think you'd be my weak link."

"I'm sorry you feel that way."

Her father looked at her in a way he never had. "I

don't think you are. I think he's turned your head. I believe you honestly think he'll ask you to marry him."

Julie glanced out the window, seeing the afternoon sun beaming despite November's early herald of winter. "I don't think of marrying Rafe."

"Well, that's something. Pregnant but not married. Your mother must be turning in her grave."

Julie got up. "Dad, I'll be back later in the week. If you want to see my new house, come anytime."

Bode shook his head. "There was no need for you to buy a house. I'm sure he told you that you needed to get away from me. Driving in those spikes, the way the Callahans always do."

"Perhaps you've misjudged them."

"Maybe you don't know them like I do."

"It doesn't matter now." Julie picked up her purse and walked to the study door. "I love my new house, Dad. Maybe you wouldn't be so afraid if you saw that I'm not that far away."

"That's not what I'm afraid of." Bode looked at her. "I'm afraid that you've been the victim of the Callahan plots. They're great pranksters, you know. Always looking for the setup."

Her father was going to be destroyed by bitterness, but there was nothing she could do if that was the path he chose. "Dad," Julie said suddenly, "did you fire Seton?"

He stared at her, his white brows beetled over his eyes. "Who says I did?"

"No one. I just wondered," Julie said. There was no reason to bring Sam's wild guess into it.

Her father shrugged. "Yeah. I fired her."

Julie held in a gasp. She stared at him. "Why?"

"Because she was a private investigator."

"No, she wasn't. She was a home care provider."

Bode laughed. "That was the story."

A chill passed over Julie. "What story?"

"The one the Callahans gave her to feed us. So you hired her." Bode smirked. "She was a plant, courtesy of Fiona."

Ice jumped into Julie's veins. "That can't be true."

Bode shrugged. "Papers are on the desk."

"You had her investigated?" Julie stared at the papers with some horror.

"Anyone who's hiring a home health care provider has them checked out. She's a private investigator, and her sister is an investigative reporter. They were hired by Fiona to dig up dirt on me."

Julie felt all the blood rush from her face. She'd thought Seton was a friend! She'd trusted her!

She'd trusted Rafe. And begun to trust the Callahans.

"The lawsuit," she murmured. "It was all about the lawsuit."

"It really wasn't that hard to figure out," Bode said. "They're Corinne Abernathy's nieces. And Corinne, of course, is one of Fiona Callahan's best friends. So in the end, Fiona tried to pull a fast one on me, but once again I was too smart for her."

Julie felt ill. "Oh, no," she murmured, thinking how Rafe must have laughed at her. The whole time she'd been falling in love with him, he'd been plotting against her. He'd known about his aunt's devious mission to best Bode. They'd influenced Julie to recuse herself. She'd gotten pregnant by Rafe.

She'd fallen for him—so easily.

Chapter 11

Rafe balanced a picnic basket and a bottle of nonalcoholic champagne as he rang Julie's doorbell around six that evening. The champagne to celebrate her new home and independence—and the picnic basket because he was dying to see her again. What lady could resist the charm of a red-and-white-checked picnic basket?

He had delicacies in the basket a master chef would appreciate, all for his lovely judge.

Julie opened the door wearing a scowl, which did not bode well for him. Rafe went into charming mode.

"Dinner is served, madam. Steak grilled to perfection, baby peas, French bread, mushrooms sautéed in—"

"I'll be dining alone. Thank you." Julie took the basket from him. "I won't need the bubbly."

She started to close the door.

"Hey!" Rafe saw his picnic basket disappearing and held the door open. "Julie, what the heck?"

"The heck is that you're a snake."

"Oh. Are we back to that?" He inched the door open a little more—gingerly, so she wouldn't notice—in order to gain a better look at his turtledove. She didn't disappoint, as usual. A teal-colored dress slid nicely over her breasts and hugged her tummy, which was getting quite bodacious, if he did say so himself. "You're too pretty to hold a grudge."

"You're still a snake. Let me shut the door."

Rafe sighed. "Have you been talking to your father?"

She gave him a long stare. Rafe felt his romantic evening slipping away.

"I don't have to talk to anyone to know that you're a member of the serpent clan."

"Oh. You *have* been talking to your father." Rafe shook his head. "What lies did he tell you this time?"

"No lies. Just facts." Julie frowned. "I'm fully capable of making my own judgments."

"I know." Rafe nodded. "Don't I at least deserve a trial?"

"All right." Julie set the picnic basket down on her dining room table and returned to the doorway, fixing him with a distinct glower. "Your aunt hired Seton and Sabrina McKinley to spy on my family."

Rafe nodded. "You know, I think you have that right."

She put a hand on a shapely hip. "You think?"

"Well, it's not like Fiona keeps us informed about all her doings. I do recall her saying something to that effect, but it was several months ago. And I don't think they ever told her much. I couldn't swear to that, because I don't know." He shrugged. "Anyway, after Fiona left, they decided all their loyalties had to be with your family, since that's where Seton was employed. So Sabrina moved out."

"Your aunt is exactly what my father always said she was. Trouble," Julie stated.

"Oh, come on, everyone loves Fiona. Anyway, she was only protecting us."

"From what?" Julie demanded. "My poor old father?"

That got Rafe's attention. "Julie, let's not paint Daddy with a romantic brush. He's no saint."

"Well, he doesn't plant spies!"

"Sure he does. More stuff has gone missing around our property than we can keep up with. Not to mention how many times he's shown up at a family function with a firearm. Which, I might add, you never even bothered to call the law about, Judge."

She sucked in a breath. "Rafe Callahan, you're as bad as your aunt."

The conversation was not going his way. Any hope he'd had of getting back into that cozy bed upstairs with Julie was just about obliterated. War was being declared here, and Rafe decided that if he was going to be branded a rat, he might as well go out rat-style. "What was Fiona supposed to do? Let your father steal our property for no reason? Bode has no right to it, none. He's been a crook and a cheat for so many years, he's forgotten how to play a straight hand. And you've looked the other way, Judge. You've enabled him. Which I can't really understand, because you're such an independent woman. But all this daddy-knows-best crap's hurt a lot of people even more than us."

Julie burst into tears.

"Julie—" Rafe began, only to eat his words from the force of the door slamming in his face.

"Damn," he said, "so much for getting along with the in-laws and the out-laws. Damn, damn, damn."

Romantic dinner shot, he got in his truck and drove to town to nurse a beer in Banger's.

And try to figure out how he was going to fix the problem with the judge. She didn't trust him at all.

He really couldn't blame her.

"I could have told you not to mess with a pregnant woman." Sam waved a longneck at him and grinned. "And let's not forget your *turtledove* has a bit of the temper in her."

"Yeah." Rafe stared at his beer. "But I shouldn't have laid it on quite as thick as I did."

"True," Jonas said, "but better to have these little pourparlers in the beginning of the relationship rather than later. Clears the air."

"Whatever," Rafe said. "She acts like her father is some kind of white knight or something. Saint Bode. I was trying so hard to be restrained. I didn't bring up all the evils her father has committed over the years. I didn't ask her what made him decide one day that he had to have what was ours. No, I stuck to the facts. Merely, that he's a weasel."

Sam laughed. "Good money says you don't ever get a foot back in her house."

"Better money says he never gets her to the altar," Jonas said, his tone morose. "The first Callahan not to get his woman wed. Hope you're not setting a trend. We wouldn't want our reputation sullied in this town."

Rafe grunted. "Appreciate the rich sympathy from

you two. Anyway, Julie going on about Fiona made me lose my customary cool. If you put Fiona and Bode side by side, everybody knows who'd be voted Sly Dog of the Year."

"It only matters how Julie sees it," Jonas says, "because she's carrying your progeny. Therefore, you have to dance to her tune."

"Apparently I don't have a proper ear for tunes," Rafe said.

"Or know how to dance," Sam added agreeably. "The judge is going to sue you for all kinds of custody, probably. The Jenkins are a litigious bunch, you know."

He did know. "Bode's determined to hang on."

"Yep," Jonas said, "but I would think that for someone who's supposed to have an Einsteinian IQ, you'd play your cards a little better."

"You'd think so," Rafe said, getting up and tossing some money on the table, "but unfortunately, not so much. I want to show you something."

"We don't want to go to Julie's," Sam said. "We don't want her mad at us. I barely wormed back into her good graces. As an uncle, it's important to be on her good side. I don't want your bad rep rubbing off on me."

Rafe grimaced. "For a lawyer, you sure do have a fear of confrontation. Come on."

Jonas and Sam stared at the cave Rafe took them to, clearly as surprised as he'd been by its existence.

"How could we never have seen this?" Jonas asked. "As kids we spent our time looking for nooks and crannies in the canyon."

Rafe shook his head. "You'd have to be positioned

just right to see it. The placement in the canyon obscures it."

"But it's been found before." Sam walked over to look at the blue clay writing on the wall.

"I would guess this is Running Bear's home away from home." Rafe looked around, still amazed by the size of the cave. "It can't really be called a cave. It's sort of a mine shaft."

"A mine for what?" Jonas asked, going to inspect a rudimentary cart. "This has been here a long time."

"This is the legendary silver mine." Rafe nodded at his brothers' surprise. "Yes, there really was one on our property all along. It isn't in service, and we don't own it, but it's here."

"Wow," Sam said, going to stare down the shaft. "Probably lucky we didn't find this when we were kids. We'd likely have fallen down it."

"Probably." Rafe shrugged. "The chief says he and Fiona use this place as storage now."

"Storage?" Jonas looked at him. "For what?"

"Papers. Documents. Things they wouldn't want a thief to find. Presumably whatever they discuss every year, which I would assume pertains to the mineral rights agreements and the land." Rafe looked at Jonas. "If you get serious about buying that spread you're going to call Dark Diablo, be sure to lock in the mineral rights."

"Already done when I made the offer." Jonas sat on the flat rock and looked around. "What's the sign say?"

"I forgot to ask him." Rafe had been too surprised to ask about a lot of things. "I've called this council to share a couple of thoughts that have been on my mind." He raised a hand at Jonas, who'd started to speak. "I know. You're going to say that we can't have a council without the others. But it's the three of us who are still living at Rancho Diablo, so I want to share my thoughts with you first."

Sam and Jonas glanced at each other, then shrugged. Rafe continued. "One of us has to go see Fiona and Burke. It's time they come home. The winds of change have already blown up all over Rancho Diablo, and whether or not Fiona's here to egg Bode on doesn't matter. He hasn't calmed down in her absence."

"Well, hell. No, he hasn't." Jonas laughed. "You knocked up his daughter and she moved out. He found out his caregivers were spies planted by our aunt. What's the old man got to be zen about?"

"Still," Rafe said, "nothing would have changed if Fiona had been here. All this would have happened."

"True," Sam said. "You'd best go, Rafe. You can fly the plane and sweet-talk the stubborn aunt."

Rafe pondered that for a moment. "I'm not going. I've got a pregnant woman to romance."

"We'll settle that later. Anything else on your pea brain?" Jonas asked.

"Yeah. Now that I've shown you this, there's something we have to do." Rafe stood and turned off the flashlight.

"No ghost stories," Sam said. "Remember, Jonas scares easily."

"No ghost stories to be told yet," Rafe said. "We're going to go digging for one."

Twenty minutes later, after a fast four-wheel drive ride home, Rafe led his brothers to the basement. He stood over the long scar in the ground that had fascinated them as kids.

"I'm not digging that up," Sam said. His face looked pale in the dim light.

Jonas took a step back from where they'd always imagined a coffin had been buried. "I'm not touching it."

"What a bunch of wienies." Rafe sighed. "One of you babies ought to raise his hand to throw the first spade."

"Nope." Sam shook his head. "Nothing good lies hidden under a house, bro. Mainly family skeletons and things you don't want to bring up from the ground. I say we all go upstairs to the library and have a shot of whiskey. I need it."

There were too many secrets long buried at Rancho Diablo. "Come on. What's the worst it could be?"

"What do you really want to know about Fiona, Rafe?" Jonas demanded. "What we dig up can't ever be reburied. Is that a price we want to pay?"

"You act like she buried bodies down here." Rafe wasn't going to admit to feeling a chill running down his own spine. "We *have* to know."

Jonas handed him the shovel. "So dig."

"Something's here." Still, Rafe was reluctant to find what their aunt had hidden. "We should have made her tell us long ago."

"As if she would have," Sam said.

"She might've, if we'd asked." Jonas nudged Rafe. "Want me to mark an X so you can get started?"

"No." Rafe took a deep breath. "If spirits strike me, tell Julie she was the only woman I ever loved."

"Yeah, right. She'll believe that," Sam said.

"Christmas is going to arrive before you break ground." Jonas nudged him again. "If you don't want to do it, Rafe, let's hire someone."

Sam laughed. "Hire someone to dig up ground under our own house?"

"You can laugh, but it's not going to be me doing the shoveling." Jonas shrugged. "She didn't bury her cookbooks down here, that's for sure."

Rafe clenched the shovel. "Never let it be said that Rafe Callahan was afraid to spit in the face of the dev—"

"Hello!" someone called down the basement stairs, and they all jumped a foot.

"Holy crap!" Rafe glanced at his brothers. "It's Pete. Do we tell him what we're doing?"

"Anybody down there?" Pete trotted down the stairs, with Creed and Judah close behind. He peered at them in the dim light. "What the hell are you doing? Conducting a séance?"

Rafe sighed. "We're digging up the dead."

"Bad idea," Judah said. "I vote no."

Creed shook his head. "Nothing good can come of this. Fiona told me once that it was just an old sewer pipe that she and Burke had covered over. Trust me, you do not want to hit a sewer pipe."

Rafe blinked. "He has a point."

"Go on, Rafe," Pete said. "You're the thinker in the family. Figure out the best place to start, and go for it. Pick the head or the feet." He grinned at his brother.

"It's not a body." Rafe felt himself breaking a bit of a sweat just thinking about all his brothers' advice, which ranged from "just do it" to "let sleeping dogs lie." "Hell, what have I got to lose?"

"That's right," Sam said. "Keep thinking those snively thoughts, and then just whale away on that dirt."

Rafe took a deep breath. "Stand back," he said, and with a great thrust he tore into the dirt scar, then jumped back.

Chapter 12

"Damn," Sam said, "that was anticlimactic. I was half expecting an oil gusher. Weren't you expecting something dramatic like that?" he asked Jonas.

"At least a banshee to come screaming out of the hole," Jonas agreed. "Keep digging, Rafe."

"Why is it always 'keep digging, Rafe'? You guys are capable of a little dirty work, too." Rafe went for another shovelful, feeling more confident now that the ground had been disturbed. Over and over he thrust, building up a nice pile of dirt beside the hole.

"I bet it's nothing," Creed said. "Probably just dirt that wasn't filled in properly when the house was built."

When the shovel made a sudden thud on impact, Rafe froze.

"Uh-oh," Pete said, "that sounded like wood."

"A wood box," Judah said. "That can't be good. Rather coffinlike, wouldn't you say?"

"That's it," Sam said. "Just fill in the hole, put it all back, and let's remember that we love our wily aunt and would never tell anyone that she kept coffins in the basement." He mopped at his brow. "I feel like I'm watching an old movie. Remember that one with the two crazy little aunts who kept bodies in the basement? I always knew Fiona reminded me of someone." He looked around at his brothers. "I need a whiskey something fierce. Anybody care to join me?"

Rafe leaned the shovel against the wall. "This time I agree with Sam. We fill it in and leave it."

"Now?" Jonas demanded. "Right when we're having our finest Indiana Jones moment?" Squatting, Jonas brushed at the dirt with his palm. Plain pine wood appeared under his fingers, and Jonas wiped his hands and stood. "You know, I think I'll throw my vote in with these other two chickens."

"I'm good with that," Pete said. "I'm pretty sure nothing underground needs to come out."

"We'll just ask her," Judah said, pushing some dirt back into the hole with his boot. "Did any of you geniuses ever think of that?"

"I did, but no one ever listens to me." Rafe filled the hole in, then smoothed it over. "Listen, there's only one solution to this tangle. You guys finish up, okay? I've got something to do."

He heard murmurs of protest as he left, but uncovering the wooden footlocker thing had cleared his brain. They'd spent too much time living in the past.

It was time to think only of the future—whether Julie agreed or not.

* * *

Rafe banged on her door twenty minutes later, making enough racket to raise the county. "Julie! We've got to talk!"

The door was opened by a small elderly woman whose blue eyes sparkled behind polka-dotted glasses. "Hello, Rafe."

"Hello, Mrs. Abernathy."

Two more faces appeared behind her. "And Mrs. Waters, Mrs. Night." Rafe took off his hat. "Is there a Books'n'Bingo Society meeting I'm interrupting?"

"Not today." Corinne Abernathy opened the door. "Julie's asleep. She told us not to let you in. So you'll tell her that the door was open and you thought it was all right to pop in for a quick visit."

"Thanks." Rafe nodded. "What's going on?"

"She's been put on complete bed rest." Nadine Waters smiled at him. "Don't worry. It's pretty normal with triplets."

Rafe gulped, his heart rate jumping. "She was fine when I last saw her."

"Yes," Mavis Night said, "but she started having some cramps. The doctor gave her a shot and told her she's to stay absolutely still for the next three months."

Rafe blinked. "Are the babies all right?"

"They're fine," Corinne said, "as long as she does what she's told."

Rafe looked at Corinne. "I'm surprised Julie would let you in, considering what happened with Sabrina and Seton."

"Don't you worry about my nieces," Corinne said airily. "Julie knows her father can be a pip."

"I don't think she knows that," Rafe said. "We'd been discussing her father, and—"

"I know all about it," Corinne said, brushing his words away. "Fiona had a right to protect her family, and Seton and Sabrina were only doing their jobs. They didn't know Julie then." She smiled at him. "Julie forgives easily."

"She doesn't forgive me," Rafe said, pretty torn up about it.

The ladies all smiled. "Probably not," Corinne said. "Julie's asked us to be her daily help. Not all at once, of course. One of us will be here every day. You'll have plenty of time to consider how you're going to get your family under one roof."

"Any advice?" Rafe was open to suggestions that might help.

"We don't do advice," Mavis said.

Rafe looked at them. "Can I see her?"

"We wouldn't advise it at the moment," Nadine said. "That's the only advice we have."

Rafe shook his head. "If you don't mind, I'm going to go up there and talk to her. I'll say you three were in the garden and had no idea I had come in the door. Deal?"

Corinne nodded. "Five minutes only. This is a serious situation."

"I know. Thanks." He went upstairs to Julie's room, slowly opening the door. "Julie?"

"Go away." She tossed a pillow his direction. "You and your family are bad news."

"Probably." Rafe approached the bed, noting her tired face and pale skin. "How do you feel?"

"Scared."

He pulled a chair up next to the bed so he could sit for a second. "I saw the ladies in the garden, but they—"

"I heard the whole thing. There's no rug on the stairs and sound travels, particularly your deep voice."

"I had to see you." Rafe picked up her hand, which felt cold to him. "Julie, I'm sorry about everything."

"It doesn't matter, does it?" She turned her gaze away.

Rafe took a deep breath. "Julie, marry me."

That got her attention. "Are you crazy?"

"Yes. Julie, listen. It doesn't have to be a forever thing. It doesn't have to be a romantic thing. But let's get married so that the babies will have the best start we can give them."

She raised her brows. "Marrying you is the best start?"

"Yes. I know you don't have a whole lot of reason to trust me right now, but we need to do this for the children."

"Not really. And don't start with the father's-last-name machismo. Jenkins is a fine last name, a better last name in this town than Callahan."

"Julie, think about it." He placed his hand over his heart. "I promise to give you a divorce as soon as you want it."

"I don't want to get married."

"I know. But just consider it. We can have the judge come marry us here."

Julie shook her head slowly. "Even if I wanted to marry you, which I don't, no woman wants to get married in her nightgown, Rafe."

Even if Julie got dressed, she wouldn't want to be married in her bedroom. This was a problem, because there was no way of getting her up and down those steep stairs. "I have to go," he said. "I know this wasn't the most romantic proposal, but it comes from my heart."

"You just want Rancho Diablo. And to stick your finger in my father's eye."

"No," Rafe said, "trust me, I could not care less about any of that. The ranch—heaven only knows what will happen with that. I don't even care anymore. I care about you and these children, and that's my job."

He got up to leave. Julie's eyes followed him as he went to the door. "Julie Jenkins, you're never going to believe this, but I've loved you ever since you drew those fifty red hearts on my face in indelible ink."

A brief smile tried to flit across her face, but she wouldn't let it. "You're right, I don't believe you."

"It's true."

"What's gotten into you?" Julie asked.

Rafe thought about the box he'd unearthed. He thought about his brothers, and their aunt, and realized it was all too complicated to explain right now. "Nothing, except I realized I couldn't live in the past. There's nothing back there that matters. So I'm hanging my hat on the future."

It was true, whether Julie wanted to believe it or not. He put his hat on and departed, leaving his heart in her hands.

Julie was astounded by Rafe's proposal. As she listened to his boots clomping down the steep wooden staircase, she thought about everything he'd said. Did she want to marry him?

"Not exactly," she murmured. "Not just because I'm pregnant."

Her father would be furious. He'd probably have a stroke.

But a lot of what Rafe said made sense.

Secretly, Julie knew the truth of what was in her heart, what she wouldn't tell a soul.

She got out of bed and went to the window, pushing it open to look down at Rafe, who was walking to his truck. "Hey!"

He glanced up at the window, did a double take when he saw her standing there. "Get back in bed, damn it!"

He disappeared, and a moment later she heard his boots thundering on the stairs before he burst into her room. She dived into the sheets, covering herself up to her neck.

"Have you ever heard of a cell phone?" he demanded. "I have one in my pocket at all times. Don't get out of this bed again unless it's necessary."

"It was necessary. Don't tell me what to do."

He glared at her, and she glared back.

"Well, I won't say I didn't enjoy the sight of you in your nightie bellowing at me from the window," Rafe said. "I just prefer that the whole neighborhood doesn't enjoy said experience."

"Anyway," Julie said, ignoring him, "I accept your proposal. Not that I forgive you in the least for what you and your family did to mine, but I accept your proposal, considering my children."

"You do?" Rafe sounded shocked, and Julie felt smug that she'd surprised him so much.

"On one condition," she said.

"Anything. Name it."

"Two, actually."

"Whatever. The moon and the stars. Just get on with it."

Julie smiled. "You put the divorce agreement in writing. Have Sam draw up the papers stating that you promise to divorce me without any Callahan shenanigans as soon as I pick a date after the births."

"Why Sam?"

"I'm well aware that Sam is a fine lawyer," Julie said. "I know that if he draws up the papers, they'll be airtight."

"Great," Rafe said. "You trust my brother, but not me."

"Sam's ethical, even if he is a Callahan. I'm hiring him to do this job, and I know he'll do it right. Plus, as your brother, he'll pound you if you try to weasel out of the divorce."

"All right," Rafe said, not sounding happy about it. "What else?"

"I'm not getting married in my bed."

His brows rose. "I can't do much about doctor's orders, Julie."

"You'll figure something out." She smiled. "Aren't you supposed to be the genius in your family?"

"Yeah, but…" He glanced at her stomach, then outside her room. "Why'd you buy a two-story?"

"I wanted this house, Rafe."

He put his hands up at her cool tone. "All right. Let me think for a moment. A small adjustment to your house would have to be made."

"Small? How small?"

"I don't know. I'm going to have to think. You've presented me with a Gordian knot. And yet I've always loved a puzzle, my bountifully plump turtledove."

Rafe glanced at her. "I accept all the terms. Do we have a deal?"

After a long moment, Julie nodded.

"Good." Rafe bounded over to the bed and gave her a nice juicy kiss on the mouth before she could gather her wits to protest. "One week from now, you will be Mrs. Rafe Callahan. Doesn't that have a nice ring to it?"

Julie looked at him. "I'll always be Judge Jenkins, Rafe."

"Sounds good to me."

He strode from the room. Julie watched him go, a little startled that he'd given in so easily. She sank back on her pillows. It was the right thing to do, the practical thing to do. Everyone would be astonished, and happy for her—except her father. She couldn't think about that right now. Rafe had come to her, smelling faintly of earth, and with a dark smear of mud across one cheek, and she'd known that his proposal had been born of the moment. Something had been bothering him.

Both of them knew that the past would always be between them. There was no changing that.

The hardest part of being in love was falling in love with the absolutely most wrong man for her. And yet she'd always had a thing for Rafe Callahan.

She'd have to give him up as soon as the babies were born, though. There was no way to make the past right, because it was too deep, too strong.

May seemed a long way off.

The next day, Rafe came into Julie's room looking like a man with a lot of secrets.

"Why are you grinning at me?" Julie asked, her radar

already up. "That's how you used to smirk at me in court, and it never failed to annoy me."

"That's okay." Rafe pulled the wooden chair next to her bed and handed her a box. "I can put up with my little woman's moods."

Julie glared at him. "What's this?" she asked, her gaze moving from his handsome face—which she could have looked at for hours, not that she'd ever admit that—to the gold-wrapped box.

"A small token of my affection." Rafe continued smiling at her as if he'd won bingo. "Very small. But expressive."

"I don't want anything from you."

"Not true. You want my name, which I'm giving you gladly."

"No," she said. "Let me remind you I'm keeping my name. Your name is for my children."

"*Our* children. Open."

She was excited to have a gift, though she wouldn't swell his head by telling him. "There's nothing in here."

"There's not?" Rafe peered into the box, pretending to be surprised. "Makes sense, doesn't it?"

"I'm not sure," Julie said, becoming aware that Rafe was having a small laugh at her expense. "Perhaps to you."

He kissed her hand. "I must say I adore you, Julie Jenkins. I love it when you try to act all stiff and schoolteachery, and then go little girl on me."

"You're an ass," Julie said, setting the box on her bedside table.

He handed her another box, this one more delicate than the other. "An even smaller token of my affection."

Julie looked at him. "Why do you go to all this trouble?"

"Because you're so cute when you're annoyed. I always thought that when we were in court. I could sit there for hours watching you purse your lips as you deliberated."

"All right, cowboy, enough with the flattery." She tore into the box, finding a jeweler's box inside. "Now you're just being cruel. This is a Callahan prank, right?"

"You'll have to open it to find out."

He was incorrigible. Still, Julie opened the box. She gasped at the heart-shaped diamond ring nestled in velvet. "Oh, my goodness!"

"Yeah," Rafe said, "that's what I said when I saw the price tag."

She stared at the ring, practically afraid to touch it. "It's…ostentatious, don't you think?"

Rafe grinned. "Yep. Just like my lady."

Julie raised a brow. "How do you figure?"

He leaned back in the wooden chair, pleased with himself. "Well, three babies right off the bat impressed me. So I told the jeweler to make it three carats, one for each baby. If you can't find a stone that size in that shape, then make a diamond band for it."

Julie shook her head. "This is too much."

"Don't you like the ring?" Rafe looked worried.

"I do. What woman wouldn't?" She closed the lid, fighting temptation. "But we're not really going to be married, except on paper. And we're getting divorced. I don't need a ring like this, Rafe."

He patted her hand. "I never realized you're a thinker, too." He smiled at her, his eyes kind. "This will be good for our children."

Julie was dying to try on the ring. "It's a lot of money to spend—"

He pulled the ring from the box and slid it on her finger. Checking it from every angle, he seemed to decide it suited him. Then he pressed her hand to his lips, making her heart jump like crazy. "Don't worry, angel cake. It's not real. A pretend ring for a fake marriage. Pretty smart, huh?"

"Oh," Julie said. "I see." Her heart sank to her stomach. "Yes. It is smart."

"Now." Rafe got to his feet and pulled out a tape measure. "I've been working on the problem of getting you downstairs to your living room for our wedding. That's where you want to be married, isn't it?"

"If it could be managed," Julie said.

"I can do anything," Rafe boasted, and she sat back to admire her pretend ring.

"Thank you, Rafe." Trust him to think of a pretend symbol for their temporary marriage. She wished she felt relieved when she thought of being a temporary wife to him, but somehow she didn't. "I do like the ring."

He smiled. "Enough to let me sleep in that bed with you?"

"No," Julie said. "Nice try, though."

He went off whistling, and closed her door. She heard him moving around on the landing, muttering to himself. It sounded as if he was measuring something, because she heard a metal tape extend, then snap shut. Occasionally, she thought she heard a disgruntled curse or two. Then the tape measure snapped shut a final time. "I'll be going now, beautiful!" Rafe called. "Try not to miss me too much!"

"I won't!"

The front door slammed, and Julie took off the ring, inspecting it from every angle. It was the most stunning thing she'd ever seen. The diamond was so big she'd feel flashy wearing it—and yet it was so pretty, with the heart shape, that she couldn't help admiring it.

It was fake. "Fine with me," she said. "I wouldn't have expected anything else from a Callahan."

She looked in the band, found "950 plat" inscribed there, and gasped. The ring was in no way fake—it was platinum, which meant the diamond was real, too. And expensive.

That was the problem with Rafe. She never knew when he was serious, or when he was just being a Callahan.

He didn't want her to feel forced or rushed into something she didn't want, obviously, given the elaborate presentation he'd gone through, first with the empty "joke" box and then the "fake" ring.

Yet Julie knew one serious thing about Rafe now: he was very intent on marrying her.

It was the children he wanted.

She slipped the ring back on, wondering if it was all right to be falling just a little bit in love with a Callahan, in spite of knowing how much it would hurt later on when it all ended.

It was too late now to wonder about that. She'd just have to keep pretending.

Chapter 13

When Rafe arrived the next day, he brought backup. The only way to keep his easily alarmed fiancée from figuring out what he was up to was to keep her mind on other things.

Therefore, he pressed his five brothers into service. Sam and Jonas would help him with the installation. Pete, Judah and Creed would entertain Julie with tales of his heroic exploits.

It would take some finesse, but finesse he and his brothers had in spades.

"What's he doing out there?" Rafe heard Julie ask.

He looked at his brothers. "You see what I'm up against. She's such a distrustful lady. We'll have to make quick work of this if I'm going to marry her in five days."

"No pressure or anything," Sam said.

Rafe handed Jonas a piece of mahogany. "I figure this has got to be strong enough to hold a man who weighs two hundred pounds, just for safety's sake."

Julie's squeal of protest could be heard in the next state. "Creed, shut that door!" Rafe yelled.

"Whew," he muttered when the door was closed. "Remind me not to mention weight around the judge again."

Sam laughed. "Never mention it around any woman you're trying to sleep with."

"Yeah, well." Rafe let that go. Julie didn't seem in any mood to let him into her bed. He really couldn't blame her. Unless he played his cards very well, the doghouse was going to be his abode for the duration of their short marriage. "Now, for the motor."

Judah poked his head into the hall. "She's trying to come out."

"She has to stay in bed. Doc's orders."

Sam and Jonas looked worried. Judah's expression was one of panic.

"The judge says you better not be messing up her beautiful house," Judah told him.

Rafe sighed. "How does she expect me to get her downstairs? Shove her out the window onto a trampoline?"

Another shriek pierced the air.

"Damn," Jonas said, "didn't you tell her what you were installing?"

"No," Rafe said. "The chariot is none of her business."

"You're a thickheaded prince." Sam grinned. "I'll never follow your example."

"Good idea." To Judah, Rafe said, "Did you give her the chocolates?"

"Forgot about that!" Judah slammed the door.

"If everyone would just follow orders, this would be a piece of cake." Rafe eyed the pine banister, satisfied that in about ten minutes the hideous old pine would be replaced by the purposeful and stronger new mahogany.

"So when are you going to tell her about the chief and the mineral rights?" Sam asked.

"I'm not. That's your job. File it." Rafe measured carefully. He was pretty proud of thinking how to best get his angel down these hideous stairs, and at the moment that was all he intended to worry about. "Now, roll that Oriental rug down the stairs, Jonas. Let's see if it's long enough to cover this ugly staircase."

The rug fit the wooden stairs like a dream. "Like *Architectural Digest*," Rafe said, proud of himself. "Let's fasten the brass attachments, and that's stage one complete."

"There's not a woman on the planet who likes it when a man butts his nose into her decorating," Jonas said.

"She assigned me the job of getting her downstairs safely, and that's what I'm going to do." He looked at the wall, measuring the handrail again for the hundredth time. "All right, Sam, let's unscrew this ugly thing and put this beauty on."

Pete poked his head out. "Julie says you'd better not make so much as a mark on her *beautiful* house."

"I'm not." Rafe didn't even look up from his measuring. "Tell Rapunzel she either goes down the stairs my way or marries me in her bed. Her choice."

Judah stuck his head out. "Julie says she's changed her mind about marrying you, if you're doing something to her staircase. She says it's the reason she bought this house."

"Lovely," Rafe muttered. "Shut the door."

They did, and he pulled the handrail off the wall. "Like a dream," he said, "which is what proper measuring does for a project. Now, the new one."

"It's a vast improvement," Jonas said, holding the long piece of rounded mahogany, while Sam and Rafe each fitted an end. With the first *zzz!* of the electric screwdriver, a shriek curdled Rafe's bravado.

"Damn, she sounds bloodthirsty, bro," Jonas said. "The judge is going to have your head."

"It's all right. I've had nightmares about my munchkins falling down this staircase. Everybody knows stairs and kids go together. This one's going to be as safe as I can make it, regardless of little mama in there."

Jonas and Sam looked at him.

"You may not stay married long with that attitude," Sam said.

"I probably won't stay married long, anyway, but that's a problem for another day. This is rock solid." He looked with satisfaction at the beautiful rug on the stairs and the wonderful hand-carved handrail he'd bought from an artisan. "Now, let's get to the fancy part. We don't have much longer before she tears down that door."

Jonas and Sam sprang into action faster than he'd ever seen them move. It was now or never for his grand plan.

This was the only way to get his bride to the altar to say I do.

He pulled out the pieces of the magic chariot and began.

* * *

"If we were in court," Julie said, "I'd hold all three of you in contempt."

"We know," Judah said. "Trust me, we're nervous as hell, Your Honor."

"I'm going to that door." Julie glared at Creed and Pete. "I'm going *out* that door. You will not stop me."

"It's not a good idea, Judge," Pete said, looking rather sickly for a man who was once considered one of the hottest bachelors in town.

"It's like Christmas. No peeking," Creed said, sounding worried. "Let's look at that fake ring our brother bought you. Does it fit? Can he get anything right?"

"Don't worry about my ring. Out of my way." Julie rose from the bed, glad she'd put on a pretty dress before Rafe had shown up with his crew.

They parted before her like a little boy's wet hair under a wide-toothed comb. She flung open the door.

Her jaw dropped.

Rafe looked up at her, his expression proud.

She stared at the chair attached to the wall. "What is *that?*"

"This," Rafe said, "is the first automated chair genie in Diablo. I promised I'd get you downstairs for our wedding. And I always keep my promises."

Julie blinked. Looked back at the new rug, which she had to admit was lovely, and the new rail, a thing of beauty—and the awful chair thing. "When I said I wanted you to get me downstairs for the wedding, Rafe," she said, "I was sort of hoping you'd carry me."

His eyes went wide. His gaze bounced to her stomach and back to her face. "Carry you?"

"Down the stairs and back up." Julie looked at the

motorized chair lift and wanted to cry. It was practical. She knew it made sense. In fact, it was a great idea. Rafe couldn't carry her down the stairs. Especially not these stairs, which were pretty steep.

It was so practical it made her mad.

She burst into tears, and the brothers scattered. She'd never seen five men run down a flight of stairs so fast; it sounded like thunder on the rug-covered steps. They hit the front door without looking back.

"Everything all right up there?" Corinne Abernathy asked. Her doughy face and polka-dotted glasses appeared at the bottom of the stairwell. "I almost have your dinner ready, Julie. Oh, look. Isn't that lovely? Now I have a way to get up the stairs without worrying about falling. You'll have to show me how to work that contraption, Rafe."

Corinne went back into the kitchen, and Julie went to bed.

"Julie," Rafe said, going to her bedside, and she waved a tissue at him.

"You always go overboard," she told him. "That's the problem. It can't ever be a small ring, or that you simply carry me. You have to do everything huge."

"Well, yeah. And may I remind you that you're the one who's having triplets. That's not exactly small, you know." He got into bed beside her, pulling off his boots and letting them fall to the floor before he collapsed on her white comforter. "Did I ever tell you that this is the softest bed in the world?"

"How would you know?" Julie blew her nose ungracefully.

"Just a hunch." He turned his head and smiled at her. "Tell the truth. You love the chariot. See, it's a *chair-*

iot so you'll know it's romantic. I don't want you to feel like it didn't come straight from my heart."

"You're an idiot," Julie said, blowing her nose again, "and I don't love it. But it is a good idea. Let the record reflect I admit that with prejudice. I do not want that thing in my darling little house."

"Duly noted."

"Still," Julie said, "I see the practicality of it."

"That's my girl." He sounded distinctly sleepy. Julie realized he'd worn himself out putting the "chair-iot" in. She scooched down on her pillow and closed her eyes, wondering how many men would think of such a gadget for their pregnant fiancée.

Probably not many.

Rafe was smart, and she admired that about him.

He was a rascal, and in spite of herself, she admired that, too.

"Thank you, Rafe," she said, but he was already sound asleep.

Julie smiled, and snuggled up to her cowboy while he was too unconscious to know that she was giving in—just a little.

Rafe got up carefully so he wouldn't wake Julie. She slept like a woman expecting triplets should—hard. And she was a bed hog. Another thing he'd learned about his quickly growing lady.

He went out to the hallway, examined his handiwork and decided to take it for a spin to the bottom of the staircase. Then he rode it back up, listening for any squeak or sound that might indicate it needed an adjustment.

"Perfect," he murmured. "If only women were as easy as gadgets."

"I heard that!"

Rafe grinned at Julie's voice and went down to find Corinne in the kitchen. "When you're ready, I'll show you how to use the chariot, Corinne."

She waved a potholder at him and handed him a sack. "There's your dinner. Your brothers said you do all the cooking now."

"It's true. Mostly chops and stuff. They don't complain." They didn't dare.

"How are you doing now that your aunt is gone? We miss Fiona so much."

Rafe shrugged. "It's not easy. We miss her and Burke, too."

"We need a new president of the Books'n'Bingo Society. But we don't want to elect just anyone. Fiona was always so full of energy."

Rafe nodded. "I know. Maybe we'll hear from her soon."

"In the meantime, what are you going to do about Julie's father?"

Rafe frowned. "Do about him?"

Corinne gazed at him, her blue eyes huge. "Every girl wants her father to walk her down the aisle."

"Oh." Rafe stared at Corinne. "Ah, that would be Julie's department, wouldn't it? I don't dare interfere with whatever those two have decided."

"He's difficult. Horrible, even. But he is her father. He'll be your father-in-law, and grandfather to your children." Corinne smiled gently at him. "You're such a clever young man, Rafe. Your mother was always so proud of you. I'm sure you'll think of something."

"My mother?" Rafe was startled.

"Well, yes." Corinne looked surprised. "She did live here, you know. She used to bring you boys into town."

This was the first time he could recall anyone talking about his parents. They'd been gone before he'd been old enough to realize that his was not a normal family. When he'd asked about a mother and father, first the brothers had been told they'd gone away. Later, that they'd gone to heaven.

"Well," Corinne said, patting him on the arm, "you think about it. Families come in all shapes and sizes, you know. And life is shorter than we think it is. It's best to start a marriage off on the best foot possible."

Rafe nodded. Then he left, not wanting to think anymore about Bode. The man was a troublemaker. Even Julie couldn't manage him.

Inviting him to the wedding would be inviting disaster.

Nothing was getting in the way of Rafe getting Julie to say I do. There was too much at stake.

It was a miracle she'd agreed to marry him, even for a short while.

No one could blame Rafe if he didn't ask Bode for his daughter's hand in marriage. The man was evil, he'd made Fiona's life a nightmare and nearly got their ranch.

Not a chance in hell will I invite him—not even for Julie.

Chapter 14

Rafe was taking over her life.

He had to, because, he said, she needed to focus on her pregnancy and nothing else. She'd endured him sending someone to the house to take her blood, draw up the license—all doable, Rafe said, because of her position as a well-respected judge—and she was pretty certain he'd redecorated her entire downstairs. Every day for the past week, Julie had heard all types of noises coming from the living room, no matter how quiet everyone tried to be.

Now it was the big day.

He'd had his sisters-in-law Jackie and Darla come fit her in a gown they'd brought from their wedding shop.

"It's a caftan," Julie said, and Darla laughed.

"But a lovely caftan." Jackie smiled at Julie. "You're lucky the doctor says you can stand for the five minutes it takes to say I do. Otherwise, Rafe would haul Judge Pearson upstairs to get you married."

"I know." Julie didn't exactly appreciate the knowledge that, where once she'd had a lot of power—even over the Callahans—now she was helpless as a baby. "He's annoying."

"He's amazing." Jackie checked the dress for fit one last time. "You're going to be a beautiful bride. Welcome to the family."

Jackie and Darla hugged her, and Julie felt that she had new sisters who understood her predicament. "Whoever heard of a Thanksgiving wedding?" she muttered.

"That's the wedding march," Jackie said. "Let's get you seated on this chariot thing. My daughters are going to scatter rose petals as you come down the, ah, wall. I hope you don't mind."

Julie felt tears prickle her eyes. "What a darling idea. Thank you."

"Thank Rafe. He thinks of everything. He drove us nuts trying to make everything perfect," Jackie said.

Darla nodded. "He's crazy about you, Julie." She placed a bouquet of white roses and pink ribbons in Julie's hand. "You're marrying a great guy."

Julie blinked, about to say *Rafe's not crazy about me,* but they were hustling her into the chair, and Julie was trying to look beautiful and not huge and stressed, so she forgot to argue. The little girls began tossing petals when Jackie told them to, and then, like magic, Julie began to move down the wall. Guests snapped pictures, and tears jumped into Julie's eyes, and when she saw Rafe standing at the bottom of the stairs, so handsome and tall in his tux, she nearly began weeping in earnest.

But then she saw her living room and gasped. It had been transformed into a fairyland of wedding magic. Julie could hardly believe all the flowers and ribbons that had been artfully placed around the fireplace. "It's so beautiful," she said, and Rafe squeezed her hand.

"The Books'n'Bingo Society has been hard at work. I'm no good with flowers." He smiled down at her. "You're gorgeous."

"I'm not," she said, thinking *but* you *are*.

Then she saw her father standing next to the judge. Another gasp escaped her. "How did you get my dad to come?" she asked softly.

Rafe took her hand, helping her to stand up. "I told him I'd beat him to a pulp if he let you down."

Julie looked up at Rafe, not certain if he was serious this time or not. "Did you really?"

"He's here, isn't he?"

Rafe wasn't smiling. Julie had a funny feeling he might be telling the truth. "Thank you, Rafe."

He shrugged. "Don't thank me. I didn't do that out of the kindness of my heart, trust me. I did it for you."

She felt a little forgiveness slide into her soul. Even if his family had planted spies at her house, it seemed as if Rafe was trying to go forward with a clean slate. She wanted so badly to trust him, to put the past behind them.

But then she looked at her father's face—not happy, and certainly resentful—and Julie knew Rafe probably *had* threatened her father if he didn't show up today.

Bode would say that Rafe made him come, not from sentimental reasons, but to lord over him that he was stealing his daughter from him, in front of the fifty guests packed into her living room.

Julie held in a sigh, and let Rafe walk her to the altar.

* * *

The I do's were said within five minutes, Julie was allowed to see the lovely table the Books'n'Bingo Society ladies had set up with a wedding cake and cookies for the guests, and she cut the cake with Rafe.

Then she was hustled back up the stairs on her chair. Rafe walked beside her, and the guests threw paper hearts as they went.

"All right, Mrs. Callahan, back in bed you go. Can I help you out of that dress?"

Julie grimaced. "I think I can manage. And please don't call me that."

Rafe kissed her on the nose and unzipped her dress before she realized his hand had searched out her zipper. "I deserve to get as much mileage out of your new name as possible, since I had to call you Judge Jenkins for so long."

"I don't feel like being teased about it, Rafe." She didn't feel married. The babies were moving around like mad inside her—so active it felt as if her stomach were a jungle gym. "Arghh, I think my children know they didn't get a piece of wedding cake." She got into bed, moving slowly.

"Do you want some cake?" Rafe asked.

"No, thank you. They don't need sugar. Until you've had some of Corinne's cake, you don't know what high octane is. Her cake is the stuff of sugar heaven, and my babies would be bouncing around all day."

He looked at her as she pulled the pins out of her hair. "You're the most beautiful bride I've ever seen. And I've seen a lot lately."

An unwilling smile crossed Julie's face. "Go enjoy the guests. I'm going to nap."

"I'd rather enjoy you."

"Well, I don't see that happening in your near future." The words came out more snarky than she intended, and Julie instantly looked at Rafe. "I didn't mean that quite the way it sounded."

"Talk about dashing a guy's hopes." He kissed her and went down the stairs whistling the wedding march. Julie sighed, slightly resentful that her party was downstairs and she was up here. Still, it had been a lovely wedding—except for her father.

He was never going to understand. But she was doing what she had to do.

"The last guest is gone." Rafe fell into bed next to Julie, still wearing his tux. "There's a boatload of gifts stacked in one of the bedrooms. My brothers said they were developing great glutes from going up and down the stairs storing your gifts."

"Our gifts," Julie said sleepily, glad Rafe was in bed with her. "No one should have given us anything, considering that was a faux wedding."

"All right, faux bride. I worked my tail off on our wedding. I don't want to hear anything about fakery." Rafe patted her hand, and then his palm stole over to her abdomen. "You'll probably want to keep me before this is all over."

"Whoever heard of a Thanksgiving wedding?" Julie murmured yet again. "It can't be lucky."

"That reminds me. The ladies left a turkey and a potato casserole in the fridge for you." He opened his eyes and looked at her. "Hungry?"

Julie shook her head. "Tell me how you got my father here, Rafe. I want to know the story."

Rafe sighed. "Must we talk about warlocks when we could be discussing your handsome prince?"

"Yes."

"All right." He shrugged. "My brothers and I rounded him up. Just like you would a bull. We penned him in his house, gave him his options, and then I assured him that if he so much as made you cry at your wedding, I'd give him a thrashing he'd never forget."

Julie couldn't help feeling sorry for her elderly father. "Rafe, he's old and not in good health."

Rafe waved a hand. "Julie, I promise you, he's mean as a snake and going to live forever drinking the nectar of bitterness. He's fine."

She pursed her lips, imagining her small, wiry father being set on by six beefy Callahans. "Do you always have to get your way?"

"Yeah." Rafe picked up her hand, kissing her fingertips one by one without opening his eyes. "Remember that."

She pulled her hand away. "Not a day goes by that I don't."

"Good. Now go to sleep. Tell my children to sleep. Let's all wake up tomorrow and eat turkey and stuffing."

He was snoring a moment later. Julie glanced over at her new husband. He hadn't kissed her like a real bride usually was kissed, nor told her he loved her.

"I've got myself in a real pickle," Julie muttered.

"Did you say pickle?" Rafe demanded groggily. "You want pickles and ice cream?"

Julie flopped a pillow over Rafe's handsome face. Snores burst from underneath, and she shook her head.

I'm married.

What am I going to do with him?

* * *

From the day she got married, Julie's life changed. When she said she felt awkward about Corinne helping in the house so much because her nieces had been spying on her, Rafe said spying was an art form, and wondered if Corinne could teach him the skill.

Julie had thrown her knitting at him. Mavis had been teaching her to knit. Knitting was not meant for impatient judges, but Rafe said she should probably make him a pair of socks as a wedding gift. He'd said it in a smug tone, as if he didn't think she could do it, so Julie set her mind to learning to knit—though she assured him she'd rather stab him with her shiny new knitting needles.

He didn't spend much time with her during the day, but every night, he rubbed her stomach before falling asleep. Julie told him her stomach was not a pumpkin to be manhandled, and Rafe said that anything that large ought to be given a blue ribbon at the state fair.

She'd seriously thought about using her knitting needles as weapons then, eyeing them on her bedside table with relish.

On Christmas Eve, Rafe brought her a plate of turkey and a present.

She looked at him, already leery of the grin he wore.

"It's a book," she guessed.

"But what kind?" he asked. "Open it."

She did, not impressed with the baby name book. "I don't want to think about names."

"That's fine," Rafe said. "We can just use family names for my sons. Like Rafael Peter, or Jonas Creed—"

"Did I not tell you?" Julie asked, keeping her tone light.

"Tell me what?" Rafe looked at her, his handsome face wreathed with concern.

"You're having daughters, cowboy. Three of them."

Rafe's expression was comical. He sank onto the bed, staring at her. "Girls?"

Julie nodded. "Mmm."

"All of them?"

"Every one." She patted his hand. "Just for you."

Rafe laughed out loud. "That's awesome."

She looked at him, fully expecting a completely different reaction. "It is?"

He hopped over the bed and took her face in his hands, giving her the kind of kiss she'd hoped he'd give her when they got married. "Julie Jenkins, that's a jackpot. Three stars, all the way across. Triple judges."

"You're weird," Julie said, pulling back from him. "I thought you'd be disappointed."

"My sweet lamb chop. Nothing about you disappoints me." He kissed her hand, then her stomach, then kissed her lips, so deeply her ears rang. "Julie, you were keeping that a secret, weren't you?"

She sniffed. "Just hoping to take you down a peg or two."

He rubbed his palms together. "This is going to be great. You realize what this means, don't you?"

He was just too happy for his own good. "What does it mean?"

"It means," Rafe said, "we'll have three candidates for FFA Sweetheart."

She blinked. "They might be tomboys. They might be cheerleaders."

"I get three little Julies," Rafe said, ignoring her trying to burst his bubble, as he usually did. "Jackpot!"

He went off whistling again, and Julie flounced against the pillows. It was just too easy to fall in love with him. She was falling hard, too hard.

And it was much too late to stop now.

May births meant a May divorce.

Julie picked up her knitting—the sock had become a sleeve—and ignored the baby name book.

It would serve him right to have to pick out the girl names. Maybe he'd realize that life with four women wasn't going to be a matter to whistle about all the time.

"I feel like an incubator," she groused, "thanks to that Christmas turkey!"

On Christmas Day, Rafe brought her a giant slice of tenderloin, brown rice, sweet potato pie and no fudge, which she knew very well had been made by Nadine Waters and passed out to all her friends. The Callahans would have received a pound of the luscious dark fudge sprinkled with pecans.

Rafe fell into the wooden chair across from her bed after delivering the Christmas tray. "You said the babies couldn't have sugar. Nadine's fudge is all sugar."

"True." Julie was big as a house now, and a piece of fudge was uppermost in her mind. Could it hurt to add to the weight at this point? "But I know how good it is, so if you don't bring me a piece, I'll probably make you wear your Christmas present."

He raised a brow. "The sweater?"

"Don't sound so snide." She pointed to the knitted pile, which was a horrible, misshapen beginner's attempt. "Once you put it on, you'll love it."

"I absolutely will." A shadow crossed his face from

out of nowhere. "This is such a strange Christmas without Fiona."

Julie put her fork down, surprised. Rafe never had down moments. "I'm so sorry," she said, before she realized she probably shouldn't be sorry at all. Since Fiona had left, her father had calmed down quite a bit. He was still ornery—especially since the marriage—but he wasn't running around all the time mad as a hornet.

Rafe shrugged. "We didn't have a Christmas party this year. We've had those since before we could remember. It's part of the Callahan tradition. My brothers and I had to put up the Christmas lights this year, and I can't tell you what a chore that is. I always knew Fiona did the work of ten people, but I don't think I realized I couldn't keep up with her."

"It's because you're running two households." Julie felt guilty about that.

He'd fallen asleep, his head rolled back against the wall. Here he was, day after day, taking care of her, feeding her, amusing her.

All because she'd secretly always had a thing for Rafe Callahan, and couldn't keep her dress down around him.

It felt vaguely dishonest. And when he'd talked about how much he missed Fiona, and how different their Christmas was with her gone, pain flashed through Julie. Fiona had left because of Bode.

Bode wasn't even speaking to Julie.

Something had to give.

There was no way a real marriage could be built on such a shaky foundation.

Chapter 15

Rafe woke up, his neck seriously crinked from falling asleep in the wooden chair in Julie's room. "I'm replacing this damn chair, Julie. It's killing me."

And something came over his turtledove. It was as if fire shot from her pretty brunette head. "You're not changing another thing in my house," she snapped. "In fact, I don't want you staying here anymore, Rafe."

He looked at her. "Of course I'm staying with you. You're my wife. Why wouldn't I stay with my family?"

Julie glared at him like an avenging princess. "Your family is at Rancho Diablo."

"It's Christmas, Julie. You don't want to kick Santa Claus out." He was dying to show her what he'd done downstairs. And what he'd done to the girls' nursery.

He was pretty certain he'd mastered the art of pleasing a woman by decorating. "Besides, I want my Christmas sweater."

"I haven't finished it. And I'm not going to."

Julie sounded mad about something, real mad. Rafe went through the files in his brain quickly. He'd come in, they'd made small talk, he'd fallen asleep... "Oh," he said, grinning, "you think I forgot your Christmas present. You greedy little girl."

Fire did spark from her eyes. "I don't want a present, I want you to go back where you belong."

Now Rafe was really confused. His lady never turned down a present. "Chocolates?"

"No."

Well, hell, if chocolate candy wasn't going to soothe her, he really was in the soup. "You know, this wooden chair isn't so bad—"

"Go."

Maybe it was a hormone thing. Could be a holiday thing, Rafe mused. Some folks got moody around this time of year. And it couldn't be easy being cooped up in here when she'd probably rather be running around town doing her judge thing and spreading holiday cheer. He scratched at his head. "Will you call me if you need something?"

"I'll call my father."

"Oh." Rafe stepped back. "Uh, did he come by?"

"No," Julie said, and Rafe said, "Oh."

So she was having misgivings because of the holidays. He understood. Julie had been through a lot in a short amount of time. "All right. I'm going. But just remember, it's Christmas, and you could have had Santa."

She waved at him, not falling for it.

So he left, pretty certain everybody loved Santa—except his wife.

"And then I was out, just like that." Rafe flung himself on the sofa in the library, feeling depressed. Sam and Jonas sat commiserating with him, even though he refused the brandy they offered him.

"Well, you got a lot done in a short amount of time. Think of it that way," Sam said.

"Why?" Rafe felt as if his relationship with Julie was moving at turtle speed.

"One day we were digging up the basement, and suddenly you ran out to shanghai Julie. I mean, think about it." Sam shrugged. "Whatever ghost you stirred up, at least you got yourself a bride."

"Yeah." Rafe was puzzled by Julie's about-face. "I think Bode's at the bottom of this."

"Bode's at the bottom of everything," Jonas said, tranquil for the moment as he sipped his brandy. "Did you ever tell her about the mineral rights? The tribe? She's not going to like you too much when she finds out you weren't honest with her."

Rafe winced. "I've made it a policy not to discuss Rancho Diablo with Julie. Why should I? We're still being sued by her father."

"I was wondering how that was working." Sam shook his head. "I foresee troubled waters ahead for you, bro. I do see your side, in fact I'm impressed by your ability to compartmentalize." He poured himself more brandy, and then a snifter for Rafe. "I just don't think your wife's going to be all that impressed."

"Yeah, well." Rafe took the snifter, sipped, then sighed. "She claims she's not really my wife."

Jonas and Sam stared at him.

"I think that's a first in our family," Sam said.

"You're telling me." Rafe was pretty hurt by that. All the Callahan brides had seemed happy to be at the altar with his brothers.

"You and Julie did start from a different place." Jonas nodded at him. "It'll probably all work out eventually. Right now, Julie's got all kinds of things happening to her."

"Yeah." Rafe knew that. It didn't make it easier.

"And while we're on this subject," Sam said, "there's something I've been meaning to mention."

Jonas and Rafe looked at him. Sam cleared his throat.

"My suggestion, acting as legal counsel for Rancho Diablo, is that we countersue Bode."

"Nuts," Rafe said. "That won't go over well with my wife." He could think of nothing worse.

"What are you thinking, Sam?" Jonas asked.

"Bode's got a team of lawyers who spend their lives drawing this thing out. It's motion after motion. The problem is that, even with me heading up our legal team, it's running into some stiff money. As you know, Bode will never be convinced that he didn't best Fiona financially. He thinks he caught her square in his net."

"Are we planning to reveal that the mineral rights are not part of our ranch?" Jonas asked.

"If Rafe hasn't told Julie—"

"I haven't," Rafe snapped at Sam. "The last thing I want to do is remind my wife why she hates me so much."

"Then I suggest at the first of the year we drop the

bomb on Bode," Sam said. "To try to convince him that we're tired of monkeying around with him, and hopefully, to get this suit wound up."

Rafe blinked. "On what grounds?"

"Harassment, for starters. Think of how many times he's come over here threatening us," Sam stated. "We should file that his claims are unsubstantiated, and that the State can't take property that is a family dwelling. Many dwellings now, in fact. The State never wanted this ranch until Bode egged his buddies on to take it." Sam drew a deep breath. "Contrary to his lawsuit trying to take our ranch, I suggest we sue for his. I discovered, for one thing, that his fence line is ten feet over on our side."

"Crap," Rafe said. Sam was really sharpening the ax.

"Aerial snapshots also reveal that his livestock regularly encroach on our land. They're clearly marked, and we don't have the type of steers he has, anyway." Sam held up some photographs. "We'll also claim that since he hasn't paid his taxes for the past five years, his property should go into default."

Rafe sat up. "Sam, you have to be wrong about that."

"Nope." His brother shook his head. "Discovered it when I was looking through some tax liens."

"I wouldn't think anyone could file a lawsuit against someone's property if they're in arrears on their own taxes. He can't have a lawsuit pending if he's currently in debt to Uncle Sam, can he?" Jonas asked.

"He can if his lawyers don't know, and if his daughter's a well-respected judge," Sam said.

"Oh, no," Rafe moaned. "You're sticking pins in my marriage."

"We have to do whatever it takes to save Rancho Diablo," Jonas said. "We fight fire with fire."

"I just don't believe Julie would be that unethical," Rafe argued, "even for her father's sake."

"I didn't say she knew he was behind in his taxes." Sam held up some papers. "I didn't get these from Seton, by the way."

"You did!" Jonas said. "What the hell?"

"I didn't," Sam insisted. "I don't know where she is right now. Which is your fault," he told Rafe.

"Not really," Rafe said. "Continue."

"These are his tax bills, and what he's behind on." Sam shrugged. "According to tax lawyers I consulted, anyone who's that far behind on taxes and hasn't lost their property has friends in high places. I say we force the issue."

"This is bad." Rafe took a giant swig of his brandy and coughed when it went down the wrong way. "I think I'm going to have to recuse myself from this conversation."

"You can't," Jonas said. "You're one-sixth of the ranch. You're married now, and have three kids on the way. That means your part of the ranch will come out of trust and be fully yours."

"She's never going to forgive me." Rafe looked from Sam to Jonas. "Do we have to do this? Can we wait until after the babies are born? I mean, you don't know the little judge. She's going to throw me out for good."

"When's the due date?" Sam demanded.

"I think May. I don't know. By the size of her, I'd say tomorrow." He groaned. "My angel is going to roast me alive."

"I heard she got rid of Corinne and Nadine and Mavis," Sam said.

"What?" Rafe shot straight up. "How do you know this?"

"I have my sources," Sam said, his face serious.

Rafe was astounded. "She didn't say a word to me. Did they tell you why she did that?"

Sam nodded. "Corinne said that Julie was uncomfortable having them around because Seton and Sabrina are Corinne's nieces. And they were all Fiona's best friends."

"I don't know how she thinks she's going to take care of herself," Rafe said, not liking that decisions were being made without him concerning the welfare of his children.

"She hired a girl from the county to help her." Sam shook his head. "Only at night, though."

Rafe's blood pressure felt as if it might shoot through his head. "I'll be glad when the babies are born."

Jonas frowned. "What does the doc say?"

"That if she doesn't stay still, he's going to give her some kind of IV to keep the babies in." Rafe gulped. "I don't want to talk about this anymore. I'm caught square in the middle."

"Yeah," Sam said, "you'd best figure out a way to get your wife on your side."

"Right," Rafe said, "and chickens are going to fly out of my butt." He took his snifter and went to the kitchen to dig around for some of Nadine's fudge.

Julie was sitting at home by herself, wanting fudge.

He wanted his family.

She'd thrown him out.

He had three daughters on the way who deserved their rightful heritage.

"Crap." Rafe put the fudge down and stared out the window. "It's going to get ugly around here fast."

On Valentine's Day, Bode handed his daughter three pink teddy bears. "You look well, daughter."

Julie took the bears. "Nice of you to finally visit, Dad."

"Well, a father worries about his girl, you know." Bode looked at her. "I miss you being in my house, Julie, but I shouldn't have thrown such a tantrum about it. I hope you can forgive me."

She was glad he was here to put the angry words behind them. "There was really nothing to forgive. So much happened so fast that everyone was a little unsettled."

"Yes." Bode nodded. "I'm afraid I didn't act my best when I found out Seton was a plant. I'd grown very fond of her. No one likes to find out that someone they care about doesn't care about them in return."

"No, they don't," Julie murmured.

"Of course, I was also upset that you'd decided to move out. I knew that as soon as you did, Callahan would start hanging around, twisting your mind with lies about me."

"He didn't, Dad." Julie could say that with complete honesty. "We rarely talked about you."

"Well, the Callahans are more subtle than that," Bode said. "He got you pregnant, and that was how he beat me."

Julie looked at her father. "That thought never crossed Rafe's mind."

He laughed. "Trust me, it would cross any man's mind. You're a rare jewel, Julie, a prize. Any man who got you away from me was going to feel like he'd won the jackpot."

Rafe had called their daughters a jackpot. Julie's skin chilled. "I haven't seen Rafe in a month and a half."

Bode looked at her, not registering surprise. "Is that so?"

She sighed. "Who have you had watching my house?" Just from his tone, and his sudden visit, she knew someone had reported to her father that Rafe hadn't been around. What he didn't know was that she'd kicked Rafe out. Rafe called every day, and every day she told him she didn't want to see him.

She'd been shocked that he'd stayed away. It would be different after his daughters were born. He probably had an army of lawyers teed up, waiting to help him claim custodial rights.

The thought made her mad. "Dad, you need to stay out of my business. Rafe needs to stay out of my business. I love you both, but my life is my life."

"You don't love him," Bode said. "Honey, you don't know what love is. Love is what your mother and I had."

Julie nodded. "I know you loved Mom, Dad."

"I still love her. And I'd have her today if the Callahans—"

"Dad!" Julie couldn't go on hearing another poisonous word. She felt as if she were caught in a tunnel that never seemed to end. "Listen, Dad, I really need to rest. Do you mind going now? It's been great seeing you, but I'm not supposed to have visitors."

Bode jumped to his feet. "Do you need anything?"

Rafe, Julie wanted to say. "No, thanks."

"I'll let myself out."

"Thank you. And take the spy off my house. Rafe's a part of my life you'll have to accept."

Her father gave her a long look.

"If I find out that you don't remove them, you won't see your granddaughters," Julie told him.

She shut her eyes, relieved when she heard the front door close. It was never going to end. Her father's suffering was a terminal thing, something he'd had for so long he couldn't let it go.

Pain sliced across Julie's abdomen, making her gasp.

She waited for the cramping to go away, closing her eyes and willing herself to relax.

The pangs got worse.

An hour later, realizing the pain was becoming more intense, Julie picked up the phone.

Chapter 16

The astonishing thing to Rafe was that three little humans could come out of his beautiful wife. He couldn't believe his eyes as one, two, three daughters were taken from his wife's stomach in an emergency cesarean procedure.

He wasn't allowed to do much. He could watch, and comfort Julie. The babies were born early enough to still be considered high risk, so they were whisked away.

But they were healthy, and viable, and Rafe thanked God for that. "You're amazing," he told his wife.

She didn't say anything. He reached for her hand, heartened that she seemed to accept his fingers holding hers. Her skin was so cold it scared him. "I think she's cold," he told the delivering doctor and anesthesiologist and the army of nurses doing their jobs.

He himself felt warm as toast. Too warm, in fact.

"We're taking good care of her, Mr. Callahan," he was advised, and Rafe focused on holding Julie's hand. He'd never felt so helpless in his life.

What could he do for her?

Did she even want his help? She'd called him to take her to the doctor, and then the hospital, so he tried to take comfort from that. But it was hard when she'd been distant since around Christmas.

Maybe now that their daughters were born, everything would be different. He prayed so.

"Hey, gorgeous," he said softly, "how are you feeling?"

Julie didn't answer. She turned to look at him, her steady gaze melting him. Then she closed her big brown eyes in exhaustion.

Rafe reminded himself to not ask any more stupid questions.

When Julie awakened the next day, her life went into overdrive. The nurses wanted her to try to express breast milk. This was harder than it sounded, because she was sore from the stitches in her abdomen, and more tired than she'd ever been. Rafe left the room in a hurry every time nurses came in after that, the breast milk thing obviously throwing him for a loop.

She worried constantly about the babies. "They weren't supposed to come so early," she told a nurse.

"Happy Valentine's Day," the nurse responded cheerfully. "There are roses outside your door, which are about to be delivered. Your husband's quite the romantic."

"I know." Julie wrinkled her nose. She didn't want roses from Rafe. At the moment, she didn't know what she wanted, but it wasn't romance.

"He keeps going down to the nursery and staring at them. And asking what their names are." The nurse smiled. "He doesn't like that their bassinets say Jenkins/Callahan #1, #2, #3."

Julie shook her head. "We haven't discussed names."

The nurse looked at her. "You have a lactation consultant coming this afternoon to help you learn some techniques for breast-feeding triplets. And do you want a baby name book?"

"No, thank you." Julie was too tired to think about names right now. She felt guilty about it, but Rafe was the father. He deserved some share in the naming of their daughters.

The fact that she'd kept him away from her for the past six weeks had postponed the discussion. Or debate, as the case usually went. "I gained sixty pounds," she told the nurse.

The small, dark-haired woman laughed. "Count yourself lucky."

"He keeps calling me gorgeous. I don't feel gorgeous. I feel enormous."

"Don't burst his bubble." The nurse left the room, and Rafe arrived just as the flowers were being carried in.

Three bouquets of lovely pink roses. Julie looked at him. "This wasn't necessary."

Rafe pulled a chair close to her bed. "It was. And I've been snapping photos of our daughters. They look a little scary right now, very extraterrestrial, with all the tubes and stuff. But they look healthy to me." He smiled, his face tired. "Can I get you anything?"

"No, thanks." Julie sneaked a look at him, wondering how the most handsome, rugged man in Diablo had ended up at her bedside, when she was the most rumpled, overweight woman in town. "Perhaps a new body."

He patted her hand. "I bet you'll feel better in a few months. It probably takes a while for everything to acclimatize."

Julie sniffed. "I guess so. Rafe, listen. I want to apologize for—"

He squeezed her fingers, then kissed them. "Don't apologize for anything. Just rest."

"But I want you to know that you can see your daughters whenever you like. I shouldn't have kicked you out before." Julie looked at her hand, which was held in Rafe's. She'd missed him so much. "The whole situation has been so confusing."

"It doesn't matter. We have our daughters, and that's going to be our focus from now on."

Julie didn't know what to say. He didn't really understand that with the birth of the babies, the divorce could be filed anytime. The small connection holding them together was over.

"You're thinking too hard, Judge," Rafe said. "I'm ordering you to rest. Or name your daughters. One or the other, but stop sitting there borrowing trouble. I can feel the vibes."

Julie looked at him. "Naming is your job."

He shook his head. "Nope. I want no part of it. Whatever I pick they'll hate later on, and blame it on me."

Julie smiled. "So you want me to be the bad guy?"

"You have more experience with what girls like," he said.

"I wouldn't necessarily agree," Julie said, glancing around at the beautiful roses in her room. "I'll do first names, you do middle names."

"I'll try." He sounded doubtful. "I don't even name the horses at our ranch."

"Well, this time you can't pass the buck." Julie thought about her mother, and said, "Janet."

"I like that." Rafe looked at her. "Let's see. We have, in order of appearance, Fiona, Molly and Elizabeth. Those are Jackie and Pete's. Then we have Joy Patrice, who is Creed and Aberdeen's little one, and the new one she's expecting around the middle of March. Creed hits singles," Rafe said, bragging just a touch. "That baby will be named Grace Marie, according to Aberdeen. Of course, we must count in Aberdeen's sister Diane's young'uns, who live at the ranch, which are Ashley, Suzanne and Lincoln Rose." Rafe squinted. "And Judah and Darla's are Jennifer Belle and Molly Mavis. That last one is named for my mother, and then Darla's mother is Mavis Night. Mavis had Darla very late in life—almost a miracle, she always said. Unlike Corinne, whose daughter was born much earlier. She married early, and moved up north. Corinne was enjoying having her nieces, Seton and Sabrina, around, not that she got to see them much because they were always helping out at your place." Rafe puzzled over all the names he'd mentioned, looking at Julie. "That's a lot of females in our town, isn't it?"

The mention of Seton and Sabrina had put a scowl on her face. In fact, all the names he'd just thrown out annoyed Julie. It was typical in the small town of Diablo to know everybody's business and think of everyone as family, but she didn't like it.

In fact, she was jealous. She frowned, looking at her big husband. She was so jealous she wanted to crab all over Rafe, who was staring at her innocently, unaware that he'd just stirred up a cauldron of anxiety inside her.

She wasn't supposed to be jealous. She was supposed to be mad at him for hiring plants. Not that he'd done it himself, but he'd probably been aware of his aunt's perfidy. Julie pressed her lips together. "Now that you've gone through the roll call, did you think of anything?"

"I'm working on it," he said. "I don't think as quickly as you do."

"If I'd been thinking quickly, I would never have allowed you to—"

Rafe blinked as she cut off her words. "Allowed me to what?"

She shook her head. "Don't mind me. All kinds of toads are trying to fly out of my mouth today."

"You're angry with me." Rafe nodded. "I can understand that. But, Julie, they're beautiful little girls. We can't let bitterness color our lives with them in it."

"I know." Julie was ashamed. "I'm sorry. I've been having a lot of negative thoughts lately."

"Go ahead. Spill to Rafe. I'm the thinker of the family, you know."

She rolled her eyes. "I'm not proud of the way I've been thinking. I'm jealous."

"Of what?"

She wasn't going to feed his ego by telling him that she didn't really want the divorce, when she knew he did. It was a practical solution for two people who would never have gotten together if not for a pregnancy. "I've gained so much weight I couldn't wear the magic wedding dress that the other Callahan brides wore."

Rafe looked shocked. "Julie Jenkins Callahan, that doesn't sound like you at all."

She sank against her pillow. "I know. And yet I am jealous. We didn't get married at the ranch, either, like the other brides."

"Holy smokes," Rafe said. "Is that what's been bugging you?"

"Among a few other things," Julie admitted.

"Well, we don't live at Rancho Diablo like everyone else does, either," Rafe pointed out. "You bought a house in town. Is that going to bother you, too?"

Julie considered that. She thought about her daughters living so far away from their cousins and aunts and uncles, and nodded, a little embarrassed. "I think it does."

Rafe shook his head. "Let's go back to naming our daughters, shall we?"

Julie looked at him. "All right," she said, her voice small. "Rafe, by the way, this summer I plan on getting back to hearing cases."

He stared at her for a long time. Then he said, "Whatever you think is best," and left the room.

Julie gazed at the roses after he was gone, wishing she was better at saying what she really felt.

"I think," Sam said, "that what Julie was trying to tell you is that she doesn't feel married to you. She doesn't feel part of the family. So she's going on with her life, making the plans she needs to make."

Rafe had been poleaxed by everything his wife had told him. "I don't even know her."

"That's probably true," Sam said cheerfully. "You'd best get a move on, bro."

"Like I know how." Rafe was honestly perplexed. "I think it's too late."

"Maybe. But you can't fail the Callahans now. All of us have caught our women, and are pretty happy about it."

"You don't have a woman," Rafe said, irritated.

"I was speaking in the familial possessive."

"Whatever," Rafe said.

"My point is, you're going to have to try harder," Sam said. "Truthfully, we don't think you've been giving it your best effort."

"We?"

"The family."

"Ah, yes. The familial plural." Rafe stared at his tiny babies through the glass of the preemie nursery, his heart sick and sore. "I'd do anything for them."

"Of course you would." Sam clapped him on the back. "So marry their mother again."

Rafe's jaw clenched. "That is not the answer."

"Sure it is. What Julie was trying to tell you, dunderhead—though she may not have realized she was saying this—is that she feels like you two got married under the gun. For these babies. And you'd already baked in the divorce. Now she wants to know that you want to marry her for her." Sam looked pleased with himself. "And you're supposed to be the thinker in the family. Ha!"

Sam went off down the hall to see Julie. Rafe turned to look at his lovely daughters who he thought were tough little nuts, like their mother. They wailed for the nurses, and got their share of attention, and then sometimes they lay quite still, doing their baby thing. He was proud of them, so proud he didn't know what to do. "One of you is named Janet," he whispered, "because

Julie loved her mother. And you'll love your mother, because she's special."

He heard a camera click at his elbow. Part of him wasn't surprised to see Chief Running Bear taking a few fast snaps. "Fancy meeting you here," Rafe murmured.

"Not really," Running Bear said. He grinned, looking pleased.

"What's with all the baby photos?" Rafe asked. "I found the pictures under the rock in the cave, so I know you're collecting them."

"Not really." Running Bear snapped a few more, then nodded at Rafe. "You have been blessed. These babies keep your family heritage alive."

"Isn't that what babies do?" Rafe asked.

The chief ignored him. "Six brothers, all girl children. It's a good sign."

"Wait," Rafe said, grabbing the man's arm as he prepared to depart. "A good sign for what?"

"A good life." Running Bear nodded, and when Rafe released him, went silently down the hall.

Rafe looked back at his daughters. "All right, good signs," he said. "Good sign number one, you're Janet. Good sign number two, your name is Julianne. And good sign number three, your name is Judith, because three *J*'s will likely really drive your mom nuts, and because it's a jackpot. Three *J*'s in a row." He wished he could kiss their small fuzzy heads, but that wouldn't be allowed for weeks. "I have to go explain to your mother now why I picked the first names and she's going to have to do the middle names. I deviated from my assignment."

Rafe walked into his wife's room, astonished to find

Bode sitting by her bed. "Jenkins," he said, not happy to see his father-in-law.

"Callahan," Bode growled.

"Not now, you two," Julie said.

"I'll go," Rafe said.

"You do that," Bode said.

Julie clapped her hands to demand their attention. "There is going to be order in my family whether either of you like it or not. This ceases today." Her eyes flashed at both of them. "Family dinners are not going to be things of misery. Family occasions are not going to be had with each of you in a separate corner. So shake right now."

They ignored her.

"Shake," Julie said, "or I'll kick both of you out and nobody will be holding any babies."

Rafe and Bode shook hands in the fastest timing Rafe could manage. They glared at each other, although Rafe tried to temper his glare slightly for Julie's sake.

"I'm going," Bode stated. To Rafe he said, "You do anything to upset my daughter, and I'll—"

"You'll do nothing," Rafe snapped. "That's for damn sure."

Bode left. Julie burst into tears.

"Cripes," Rafe said, sinking onto the chair next to her bed. He was still steaming. "Don't cry, Julie. It's going to take some time for our family to connect." It would take a hundred years, but he wasn't going to say that to her. Right now, she might take his head off.

"Hey," he said, trying to curry favor with his wife, "I named the babies. Janet, Julianne and Judith—*J*'s all the way across. Jackpot."

Julie pointed to the door. "Out."

His heart dropped. "Why? What did I say?"

"Rafe Callahan, this has been nothing but a game for you, nothing but a gamble. You wanted me off your family's court case in the beginning, and—"

"*My* family's court case?" Rafe interrupted. "Your father sued *us*." He didn't want to think about Sam's plan. "And the whole thing was dumb, anyway, because we don't own the mineral rights to Rancho Diablo."

She stopped crying, staring at him over her tissue. "What?"

He shrugged. "We don't."

"Who does?"

"A Navajo chief. His tribe, actually." Rafe looked at her. "What your father wants with more land is beyond me. He's five years behind paying the taxes on his own land."

Her jaw dropped. "Get out. Get out. Get out!"

Rafe jumped up. "Julie, we have to put this behind us once and for all, if we're ever going to be a family. You have to know the truth—"

She pointed at the door. Rafe's shoulders drooped and he slunk out.

In the hall, Jonas waved a bouquet of flowers at him.

"I just heard the sound of a marriage blowing up," his brother said. "And right after Valentine's Day, too." He shook his head. "Are you sure you're the smart one in the family?"

Jonas went into Julie's room, which Rafe thought was brave, considering she probably didn't want to see any Callahans at the moment.

She certainly didn't want to see him.

Utterly deflated, Rafe headed home.

Chapter 17

"I don't know what happened," Rafe told his sister-in-law Jackie. He was paying a call on her at the bridal shop she co-owned with Darla. It was a handy thing to have two sisters-in-law in the bridal business, he decided. "It's like my mouth left my face and started quacking. I think it was seeing Bode. The shock of him sitting there just got me angry."

Jackie nodded. "I understand. But you're going to have to put Julie first. Being a mom of triplets is hard, Rafe. Everything is times three. Take it from me."

"You and Pete seemed to take everything in stride."

"Trust me, there were times I told him to go put his head in the horses' trough." Jackie shook her head. "You guys just saw the happy side. We kept the darker days to ourselves." She smiled at him. "In six months, everything is going to look different, Rafe. Don't give up hope."

"Six months!" He didn't think he could wait that long for things to straighten out for him and Julie. "Isn't there a shortcut?"

Jackie laughed. "I don't think so. Not from where you two are starting. Anyway, babies tend to put relationships in a different gear."

"It seems I've been waiting forever," Rafe said. He felt as if hope was sifting away for him and Julie.

"And you love her," Jackie said.

"And I love her," Rafe repeated. He looked at his sister-in-law, who was smiling at him. "I really do."

"I know you do." She handed him a box of hand-me-down baby clothes. "Give these to Julie, please, and see if she can use them. I found that what my babies used the most were little nighties and onesies in the beginning."

"Thanks. Hey, Jackie?"

"Yes?" She smiled at him.

"Do you know whatever happened to that magic wedding gown thing? It wouldn't still be at your shop, would it?" He was hoping the darn thing hadn't gone with Sabrina when she'd left town. Julie had seemed really interested in wearing the gown, which had shocked him.

"It's here." Jackie's brows rose. "You're not needing it, are you?"

"I'm not sure. Can I see it?" Rafe asked on a whim.

She went into the back, bringing out a heavy clear sack encasing a long, beautiful white gown. He could see sequins and beads and all kinds of sparkly things on the fabric.

"Very different from what we had to fit her in for her wedding," Jackie said with a laugh. "Most of the Callahan brides managed to get into the dress before we got too huge to fit."

"Yeah." Rafe looked at the dress through the bag, trying to decide why it would matter to Julie. "Isn't a dress a dress, though?"

Jackie smiled. "Not to a woman."

"I guess." He didn't think Julie could have been more beautiful than the day he'd married her. "She doesn't seem like she'd be the sentimental type, though. Rather, all-business and judgelike."

"She feels like she's outside the family circle." Jackie hung the dress on a hook at the wrap stand. "You can take it with you if you like."

She went off to help some customers who walked in. Rafe looked at the gown for a while, thinking he might not ever understand women.

Then he grabbed the dress and headed out.

For Julie, he'd do anything.

At the end of March, Rafe and Julie were finally allowed to take the triplets home. Julie let him help her with the three car seats, let him drive them home, let him carry the babies upstairs. He was proud to see that the names he'd selected had been painted over each daughter's crib.

He was pretty certain Julie would want him to leave. Things were so awkward and uncomfortable between them. She looked stronger, she looked beautiful—if a little tired—and the last thing he wanted to do was upset her.

So he went to the front door. "If there's anything you need, feel free to call, Julie."

She looked at him, surprised. "Where are you going?"

"Home?"

"Oh." She looked down for a moment. Then she took a deep breath. "I do want you to be part of our girls' lives, Rafe."

"I want that, too," he said quickly, thinking nothing had been right or easy between them since the babies had been born on Valentine's Day.

"This house is big enough for both of us," Julie said.

He looked at the babies in their carriers, still soothed by the car ride home. "You're going to need lots of help, I'm sure."

She didn't say anything. Rafe swallowed, trying again. "I'm happy to stay and help if you want me to."

"If that's what you want." Her chin lifted. "But only if it's what you want."

"It sounds like a good idea to me." Rafe wasn't sure what more he should be saying or doing. He felt like a fish on the end of a line, dangling. "Just tell me what *you* want." *Because all I want is you.*

She shrugged. "Let's take it a step at a time."

He nodded. Baby steps were fine with him.

Julie and Rafe began a merry-go-round of diapers and feeding and burping and soothing crying infants. He suffered more than Julie did, because she was patient. His daughters' wailing unnerved him, because in his world, if something cried, that was bad, and it needed to be fixed. Half the time he couldn't fix what the problem was—only Julie could. And then there was the random occasion when even Julie couldn't fix the problem. On those nights, he would take whatever daughter was expressing her opinions, and put her on his chest, rocking her until she felt comforted.

"The doctor said it might be gas," Julie stated, and while Rafe was pretty certain that anything as beautiful as his daughters could not possibly have gas, he still encouraged them to toot, and praised them when they did.

"Do you think that's normal parenting?" Julie asked him.

"Ladies are self-conscious about breaking wind," Rafe said. "I want mine to know that the family that breaks wind together, stays together."

Julie winced and went back upstairs. "Well, it's true," Rafe told Julianne. "You just send that gas right out the back of your little diaper. Daddy's got a catcher's mitt, sweetie."

He spent a lot of time rocking his daughters. In fact, he spent so much time doing it that he ordered an extra rocker, this one with a cushioned back and arms. "Now this is a chair," he told Julie, when she came down to look at it. "I had to move your flowered pincushion into the dining room, though."

Julie glanced at the ottoman she'd loved, and went back upstairs.

"We exist on two levels," Rafe told Sam, who was visiting. "She's mostly upstairs, me mostly downstairs. I have a big-screen TV, though, so it's working for us."

"Congratulations, I guess." Sam looked at him. "Which baby is this?"

"This pink-faced doll is Judith." Rafe grinned. "She tends to be the noisiest because she was born last. She thinks she has to stand up for herself, so she's the squeakiest wheel."

"You know," Sam said, "perhaps the reason the two of you exist on two levels is because Julie's figured out that you're a bit odd."

"Nah," Rafe said. "I'm the only normal one in the family."

"Which family?" Sam asked.

"The Callahan family." Rafe looked surprised. "Why are you asking that dumb question? Julie and these babies are all Callahans. Unless you've heard differently."

"No," Sam said hurriedly.

Rafe looked at his brother. "Tell me before I wring your neck. I've been lifting babies for a couple of weeks and am therefore packing extra muscle. And, I might add, am a little edgy from lack of sleep."

"Sheesh," Sam said. "It's just that you might want to know that I filed a motion for countersuit today."

"Great," Rafe said. "That ought to put the finishing touches on my failing marriage. The nuclear option usually wipes out everything in its path, doesn't it?"

"Think of the future, Rafe. We have a ton of children at Rancho Diablo now to consider. You don't want the ranch taken away from your daughters, do you? This is the way to stop Bode."

It was also a fast way to stop Julie from thinking of him as a husband. Yet it couldn't be helped. "Judith, if I give you to Uncle Sam here, would you please spit up on him for Daddy?"

Sam hopped up. "I'd go upstairs to say hi to Julie, but perhaps today is not the best time."

"I'm pretty sure you're right." Rafe didn't know what he was going to do about his wife. He was no closer to being with her than he had been. Hell, he was no closer to being a husband than he'd ever been. "Sam, listen, I need you to do me a favor."

"Anything," Sam said, but when Rafe told him what he wanted, his brother's face went white as a sheet.

Julie loved her daughters. She would never have imagined she could love anything as much as she did them. Except Rafe. She shouldn't love him, maybe, but she did, even though it hurt her father. There was a lot of pain on both sides. Although she'd almost relented and asked Nadine, Corinne and Mavis to help a couple of hours every day, she wanted Rafe to have time with his daughters.

First, he began by helping her at night.

Then she noticed some of his clothes were hanging in a guest room closet. His shampoo, toothbrush, et cetera, showed up in the adjoining bath.

This all seemed reasonable to her. There were times when neither of them got more than an hour of sleep at a time. Grabbing a shower whenever possible was paramount.

He slept downstairs on the sofa. This made sense, because if either of them could catch some sleep, it was best to do it. Never did they both sleep at the same time, even with the Books'n'Bingo Society's help.

Julie learned to nurse double football style—and Rafe learned that she wanted privacy during that time. It was too embarrassing, feeling as if she was exposed completely—which she was. There was simply no delicate way to feed two infants at the same time.

Although Rafe said it was probably the most beautiful thing a man could ever see, he would dutifully take whichever baby wasn't nursing, and go downstairs with her and a bottle. At night, he brought Julie dinner that someone made, or takeout.

He said he'd given up cooking at the ranch starting on Valentine's Day, the babies' birthday. Apparently, Sam and Jonas were eating a lot of Rice Krispies and takeout from Banger's Bait and Tackle.

Julie had just put the babies down and was ready to try to nap herself when she heard Rafe on the stairs. She sat up and tried to look not exhausted.

"Can I come in?" he asked.

She frowned.

Husbands didn't usually have to ask. She hadn't realized there were such clearly defined lines in their living situation. "Of course."

He peeked around the corner. "Everybody decent?"

"Yes." Julie gazed at him. "Just us girls in our gowns."

He didn't look directly at her. "Nadine's here. She's wondering whether, if we take all three babies downstairs, you might be able to nap more than fifteen minutes. She says we can bottle-feed them."

Julie nodded. "That would be wonderful."

"Uh…" He looked at her directly this time. "Corinne is also downstairs. She's wondering if it's all right if she helps."

"I already told her she was welcome anytime." Julie felt bad that she'd asked the three elderly ladies to stop coming by several months ago. Corinne had known nothing of her nieces' employment by Fiona. "Why is she asking?"

"She's just making certain you don't mind her helping out." Rafe looked sheepish. "She wants to do the right thing."

"I'd love to have her." Julie smiled at Rafe. "If the babies are going to be in such good hands downstairs, maybe you should come upstairs and take a nap, too."

He rubbed at his face. "I might sneak into my room and grab a couple of winks. I'm not as tired as you are, but I definitely feel like…" He looked at Julie. She raised her eyebrows and waited.

Rafe hesitated. "You were saying I should nap, too?"

"Mmm-hmm." She patted the bed next to her.

"Oh." He gave her a careful stare. "Are you sure?"

"Absolutely."

After a moment, Rafe grabbed Judith up, carrying her downstairs with almost indecent speed. Julie jumped from the bed quickly and ran into her bathroom to swish mouthwash and splash her face, brush her hair.

When Rafe came back, she was back in bed, waiting.

"I don't know if this is a good idea," he said. "You need sleep, and I—"

She patted the mattress again.

"Well, never let it be said that a woman had to ask me twice to get into her bed. A wife's wish is her husband's command," Rafe said, diving in beside her.

The bed squeaked under his weight.

"Shh," Julie said, laughing. "The ladies are going to think my bed is possessed."

Rafe sprawled on the pillow next to hers. "I can do an excellent impression of a haunting if given the chance."

"Today, just a nap," Julie said. "Hold me, cowboy, if you want to."

Rafe wrapped his arms around her, and Julie fell asleep, feeling as if she'd finally made a wise decision.

* * *

Five hours later Julie woke up. Rafe was long gone, because "his" side of the bed was cold. She smiled to herself. The most wonderful feeling had stolen over her as they'd slept in each other's arms.

For the first time, she began to believe that their marriage might survive.

She wanted that, she realized, more than anything.

After a fast shower, she went downstairs. Rafe was alone, the ladies gone.

"Why didn't you wake me up?" Julie asked.

He shrugged from the recliner. "They're asleep. No need to wake Mom unless the princesses are demanding dinner. How did you sleep?"

"Like a baby." Julie smiled at him, then surprised both him and herself by crawling up into his lap and resting her head on his shoulder. "I never did thank you for everything you did while I was bed-bound."

"I didn't do much." He rubbed her back, his hand moving in slow circles across her shoulders. It felt so wonderful to be in his arms.

"You arranged a wedding. You decorated the nursery."

"I didn't do it all. The ladies did a lot of that. I merely instructed on function. And wrote checks."

Julie smiled. "You picked out baby names."

"That was the hard part. Imagine choosing things you know your daughters are going to complain about."

"They won't." Julie looked at the babies sleeping in the playpen they used as a makeshift downstairs crib, and smiled. "The doctor says they're growing fast. And that given time, maybe all the little kinks will lessen."

"Soccer will help the lungs develop," Rafe said, his voice sleepy. "Riding horses will develop strong bodies."

Julie smiled. "Is that what happened to you?"

"Not so much. Fiona gave us all the ranch chores to do." Rafe laughed softly. "That grows a boy into a man quick. But my little angels aren't going to be allowed to do ranch chores."

"They have to," Julie said. "Otherwise, they won't be independent."

He nuzzled her neck. "How did *you* get so independent?"

Julie opened her mouth to say she'd always been that way. Losing her mother at a young age had forced her to stand on her own two feet. "I don't know that I am, anymore. I've become pretty dependent on you."

"That'll change when you go back to being a judge."

Julie thought for a moment about what she wanted Rafe to know. "What I meant was, I've come to a place where I really enjoy being with you."

He turned her chin so that he could look into her eyes. "I enjoy being with you, too."

"I'd like our marriage to work, Rafe. If that's what you want," Julie said, her heart practically in her hands.

He kissed her on the lips. "It is what I want. I was hoping you'd decide to keep me at some point."

"Let's keep it open a little while longer," Julie said, thinking that things had been going almost too smoothly in the past few weeks. "I feel like good things are happening. But I'm still afraid."

He ran a hand down her shoulder-length dark hair. "Don't be afraid of me, sweetheart. I'm easy."

She was afraid, because it was so hard to blend their families. "I'm glad you're here," she said softly, and Rafe brushed a soft kiss against her lips.

"I'm not going anywhere, unless you say so."

They sat like that, holding each other, for a long time, until their daughters woke up. But even when they had to let each other go, Julie could have sworn she could still feel Rafe touching her, stroking her skin, making her feel he loved her.

Hope began to build inside her heart.

Chapter 18

Rafe was pretty certain his wife's change of heart where he was concerned was due to the babies. He wasn't complaining.

He sat in the barn, staring at Bleu, who seemed interested in chatting with him today. "Life is good," he told the big horse. "It's all going to work out."

He had a lot of plans.

Jonas came into the barn, putting a few bridles he'd repaired on their hooks. "Still talking to yourself? We've noticed you do that a lot."

"It's all right," Rafe said. "I'm damn good company."

Jonas laughed. "Did you hear Creed's baby was born last night?"

Rafe sat up. "No. How is Aberdeen? Did everything go all right?"

"Everything's fine. Creed's bragging that Aberdeen

gave birth naturally. I guess he's hoping that'll mean his baby is getting the best possible start in life."

Rafe grinned. "That's awesome. I'll have to go by the hospital."

"How's your crowd?"

Rafe's grin stretched wider. "We're all fine."

"We?" His brother looked at him. "You're part of the family now?"

"It's looking better." Rafe had a lot of hope for himself and Julie. He was positive that they belonged together forever. There just couldn't be any other way. Certainly no woman was made for him like Julie was. He adored her, from her delicate toes to her mass of midnight hair. "We're getting the hang of things."

"That's good to hear." Jonas shrugged. "Since you reneged on your chef duties, Sam and I have reshuffled things a bit."

"I guess you two are batching these days, huh?" Rafe asked, not feeling sorry for his brothers at all. "I guess you could always try to find a woman who might have you."

"Nope." Jonas shook his head. "I see what you and all my brothers are going through, and I get real content with my bachelorhood. You guys are not exactly poster dads for married life."

"You're jealous." Rafe grinned. "Anyway, try it, you might like it."

"No, Fiona's hex will pass me by. Thanks."

"It wasn't a hex, it was a blessing."

Jonas laughed. "Whatever. I'll believe that when Julie decides to keep you." He left, whistling a tune from *Seven Brides for Seven Brothers*.

Rafe thought his eldest brother might possibly be

annoying in a league of his own. "Sourpuss," he muttered. Of course Julie was going to keep him. And he was most definitely going to keep Julie.

It was too beautiful a May morning to pay attention to his brother's dark moods. Rafe decided to ride Bleu to clear his head.

Jonas had made him nervous. He'd go home and find his wife, and he'd tell her. He'd tell her that he loved her, and how much she meant to him, and surely everything would start coming together.

When Rafe walked into the house that night, it was dark. He didn't hear the sounds of babies crying, or Julie singing, or the Books'n'Bingo Society ladies chattering. It was strange.

"Julie?" he called. "I'm home."

She came down the stairs, pale as a ghost.

"What's wrong?" he asked. "Are you all right?"

"First," Julie said, "I want you to take this stupid chair off the rail."

"Okay," Rafe said. "That can be easily done." He watched his wife carefully. Now that she came closer to him, Rafe realized she looked angry, really angry. "What happened?"

"You happened," Julie said, her voice tight. "Your family happened."

He hesitated, his heart sinking. "Tell me what's going on. All I know is that Aberdeen and Creed had their baby today, baby Grace Marie. A whopping seven-pounder with blue eyes, her mom's chocolate-brown hair and her dad's full set of lungs."

That seemed to stop her for a moment, but then Julie

speared him with another deliberate look. "My father got the papers today."

"What papers?" Rafe felt his heart rate jack up. If Bode was involved in whatever had upset Julie, things did not look bright for the home team.

"The countersuit. Your family suing my father for his ranch. I remember you saying something about my dad owing five years of back taxes." Julie crossed her arms. "Too good an opportunity to pass up, was it?"

Rafe shook his head. "Don't talk to me about any of that. I didn't know the papers were actually filed."

"But you knew they would be. You knew it was your brother's plan." Her eyes blazed. "You're a scoundrel, Rafe Callahan."

"Julie." Rafe rubbed the back of his neck. "The legal thing is going to drag on for years, as long as your father wants it to. You can't keep getting all ginned up every time there's a twist or turn in the proceedings."

"As long as my father wants it to?"

Rafe nodded. "Well, hell, yeah. You wouldn't expect us not to defend ourselves, would you? And while we're on the topic, may I remind you that you're a Callahan now. Those are Callahan children, Julie. Whether you accept it or not, you're playing for Team Callahan. You need to think about your daughters' futures." He shrugged. "You're my wife."

"I'm my father's daughter."

"But this is your family now. I'm your family, and the girls are your family. I don't really see a conflict."

"The conflict," Julie said, her tone furious, "is that you just can't leave my father alone. You're not going to leave him with any pride."

Rafe shrugged again. "If that's the cost of getting him out of our hair, so be it. His pride is little concern to me. I'm not playing for pride, Julie. I'm playing for my family. Of which you are the most important part."

She turned away. "I don't know what to say to you, Rafe."

"Where are the babies?"

"At my father's." Julie turned back around. "I'm going home."

"The hell you are." Rafe frowned at her. "Julie Callahan, you go get my children right now and bring them back here where they belong. I don't know what poison your father's whispered in your ear, and I don't care. But you and my daughters are going to stay right here in this house that you bought, because you wanted to be free of your father. And quit wearing me out with this mean-to-Daddy routine. Somebody needs to straighten that old cuss out. It's unfortunate that it has to be us, but we'll do it."

"I know you will," Julie snapped, "and that's the problem."

"Would you prefer if we rolled over?"

She didn't answer.

Rafe looked at her for a long time. "All right, Julie," he said softly, "you win. You go get my daughters, and you bring them back here where all their things are. I'll go. And I won't be back." He took a deep breath. "I concede that you were right all along. Next month is June, a perfect month for a divorce. So file."

He left, his heart shredded to ribbons.

But there really wasn't anything he could do. Julie had made her decision long ago.

* * *

Julie was astonished when Rafe walked out. She wanted so much to think she'd made the right decision. After her father's visit, when he'd told her about the countersuit, she'd realized Rafe had been keeping things from her once again. Important things. And she'd known then that, in his mind, she was very separate from whatever happened at the Callahans' ranch. Whatever they were going to do to her father, he would never share with her. This was the second time he hadn't warned her of what was coming.

It was almost as if she existed on the periphery of his mind. Love could not exist unless both partners shared everything.

And he'd walked out. She'd wanted to go away for a few days to her father's, keep an eye on him. She was really afraid he was going to have a heart attack or a stroke with this latest ploy by the Callahans.

She felt so torn, so caught in the middle.

But she'd never expected Rafe to just leave. It seemed as if he'd given up, almost as if he'd known he would. Planned it.

They'd agreed to stay together until after the babies were born. And he'd kept to that part of the bargain.

Julie wondered how long he'd known that there was going to be this dastardly countersuit. It really was a trick to beat all tricks.

The Callahans were, as her dad had always said, capable of anything.

Cold fear stole over her. She was worried for her father.

Yet she was absolutely terrified her marriage was over.

And she didn't see any way to put trust back between her and Rafe. Maybe because it had never existed at all.

Two days later, Sam and Jonas looked at their brother as he sat perched on a fence rail, staring out onto Julie's father's land.

"Wanna grab some grub?" Jonas asked him.

"I don't feel like eating. Thanks." His wife and daughters were in that house, having "gone home," as Julie put it. He missed them. He supposed he'd miss them a lot more in the coming years.

Sam cleared his throat. "You've been up there all morning. You can't stay there all day."

Rafe shrugged. "I'll come in eventually."

Jonas sighed. "Why don't you just go ring the doorbell and ask to see your babies? Julie won't keep them from you."

That wasn't possible. Bode wasn't going to want him showing up to stick his finger in his eye. That's how the old man would feel—and Rafe couldn't blame him.

There was really nothing he could do.

"Nah," Rafe said. "Sometimes it's best to let sleeping dogs lie very still in their own corner."

"You know it had to be done." Sam's voice carried conviction. "There was no other way to stop him."

"You're the family legal beagle. You're heading up the team of lawyers that's going to save this ranch." Rafe shrugged. "I'm fully confident that you're the only man who can do it. So whatever happens, happens."

Jonas leaned his elbows on the wood rail. "Did you tell her you didn't know when it was getting filed?"

He shook his head. "It wouldn't have mattered. It's still *Callahans* v. *Jenkins*. It always will be."

"Look," Sam said, pointing.

Rafe turned toward the south. And there, highlighted by the dusky canyons, the black Diablo mustangs ran, hooves flying and manes straight out like flags. The hair rose on Rafe's arms. Besides his daughters, the Diablos were the most beautiful things he could ever imagine seeing on this earth. "I'll never cease to be amazed by those mustangs."

His brothers shook their heads. Behind him, Bleu nickered, recognizing kindred spirits at play. They all watched for another five minutes until the dust dissipated and the thunder of hooves could no longer be heard. Then Rafe got down from the rail, and without another look back at the house where his wife and daughters were, he rode to the barn and unsaddled Bleu.

"You want to run with those Diablos," he said to Bleu. "I want my daughters and wife back. We don't always get what we want, old friend."

Bleu snorted. Rafe patted the animal's neck and handed him over to a groom.

They'd always believed—probably because Fiona had told them—that the Diablos running was a mystical portent of things to come. A magical, unexplainable hand of future over Rancho Diablo. The Diablos were one with the land, and the spirits that had guided them there.

Rafe wasn't certain if he still believed his aunt's fairy tales anymore.

Chapter 19

Julie was in the kitchen warming milk for the babies when she heard thunder. "Rain," she murmured. "Your first rain, babies." She'd decided to begin utilizing soy formula and weaning the babies off nursing. They were getting bigger and stronger faster than she'd expected, and the doctor seemed pleased—surprised, even—by their progress. "It's your father's DNA," she murmured, picking up little Janet. "All those brawny Callahan genes are going to help you catch up fast."

She'd just settled in when the doorbell rang. Since her father was upstairs, Julie called, "Come in!"

Her eyes went wide when Seton McKinley walked into the house. "Seton!"

The blonde P.I. smiled. "Am I catching you at a bad time?"

Julie wasn't certain. She should be mad at Seton,

shouldn't she? Yet she'd had a lot of time to think. Seton had been good to Bode, and to Julie. Rafe had said that Seton and Sabrina hadn't shared anything about their family after Fiona had left. Didn't that mean Seton was honorable?

Still, she looked at her old friend cautiously. "It's not a bad time. What are you doing back in town?"

Seton looked at her. "I never apologized to you, Julie. I feel I owe you and your father an apology."

"You don't," Julie said quickly. "I don't want an apology."

"I need to offer you one. I should've quit as soon as Fiona left. Instead, I stayed on." Seton smiled at her, then at the baby. "I got too close to your family, I'm afraid."

"Thank you," Julie murmured. "We enjoyed you being with us."

"I hope you can forgive me, Julie."

"It's in the past," she said quickly.

"Thank you. That means a lot to me."

"So," Julie said, not knowing where to take the conversation next. Little Janet was busy taking her bottle, completely unworried about her mother's tenseness. "What are you doing now?"

"I've been working in D.C. But I'm planning to stay here this summer with Aunt Corinne." Seton walked to the door, about to depart. "It's good to see you again, Julie. You look well. Tell your father I said hello."

"Wait." Julie cleared her throat. "I'm certain that this is confidential. I'm aware that what you do is client sensitive. But I have to know something. Did you ever report anything to Rafe? Did he ever ask you anything about our family?"

Seton shook her head. "The brothers weren't really aware of what was going on. Fiona and Burke were in charge at the time. I understand everything's changed now."

Julie's brow wrinkled. Janet had finished drinking, so she put her to her shoulder to work out a burp. "What's changed?"

"Sam's heading most everything now, along with Jonas. I think they're making joint decisions. The other brothers are too busy with their families. At least that's what I heard from Aunt Corinne."

Julie frowned. "What about Rafe?"

"Rafe doesn't do anything except work."

"What does that mean?" Julie felt a strange tickling sensation in her conscience.

"According to my aunt, he's not involved in ranch decisions."

Julie blinked. "I don't understand."

Seton shrugged. "I'm sure it's complicated. Goodbye, Julie. It was nice seeing you."

"Good to see you, too," she said. "Will you mind if I don't walk you to the door?"

"I know my way." Seton left, and Julie sank back in the chair, rubbing little Janet's back.

How could Rafe not be involved in ranch decisions? All the brothers shared everything equally. Fiona's big idea of giving the ranch to the brother with the largest family had started things off with a bang. But if Rafe had known all along that he'd be asking for a divorce, that would make him ineligible, according to Fiona's rules.

Had he not cared? "Maybe it didn't matter," she told Janet. "Maybe Fiona changed the rules."

He wouldn't give up his share of the ranch because of Julie. But if he was no longer making executive decisions about the ranch and the running of it, when she knew darn well he'd been "the thinker" and a chief decision maker, something had changed. Drastically.

"I don't understand your father," she told baby Janet. She listened for her other daughters, who were upstairs sleeping, but no sounds filtered to her.

The doorbell rang, startling her. "Come in," Julie called, wondering if Seton had returned.

The door opened and Sam poked his head inside. "I should have called first, I know. But I'm afraid of waking babies. Around the Callahan ranch, a ringing telephone has been known to upset a baby or two. And new moms don't like that."

Julie was astonished. This was the first Callahan who'd ever come to this house, unless she counted the time Rafe had sneaked in through her window. She didn't.

"If my father sees you, it won't be a telephone that upsets the babies," she told Sam.

He grinned. "Brave of me, isn't it?"

"Or crazy." She looked at him. "Seton was just here."

His dark blue eyes went wide. "Seton?"

Julie wondered if Rafe was correct about Sam having a thing for the private investigator. "Just missed her."

"What's she doing in town?"

"Visiting her aunt, I think. What are you doing here?" Julie worked up a glare, but it was hard. Sam was one of her favorite Callahans, if she could bridge family loyalty enough to have a favorite.

"I need you to sign some papers." He held up his briefcase. "Can I come in?"

"Yes." Julie nodded. "But please keep your voice down. I don't want my dad to know you're here."

"Sneaking me in like a thief?" Sam grinned.

"Or a lawyer." Julie looked at him as he dug around in his briefcase. Her heart suddenly sank. "You've brought divorce papers, haven't you?"

He stared at her. "Divorce papers?"

Julie nodded. She felt tears burn at the back of her eyes, told herself she wasn't about to cry. Not over her marriage.

Yes, she was. As soon as Sam left, she was going to bawl like Janet and Julianne and Judith. Rafe's jackpots. "Arghh," she said, "Rafe told me to file. He got tired of waiting for me to do it, didn't he? So he did it."

"Jeez," Sam said, "I don't do family law. My specialty is property and otherwise. You'll have to ask Rafe about all that."

Julie's breath came back into her lungs with a whoosh. "Oh." She wanted to say thank heaven, but bit the words back. Sam was already looking at her as if she had two heads. "What do you need me to sign, then?"

He gave her another assessing glance, then spread some papers out on the coffee table. "These documents pertain to Rafe's sixth of the ranch, which will now be held in trust for Janet, Julianne and Judith. They will now be the sole owners, split three ways, of course, of that portion of Rancho Diablo. You and Rafe, naturally, will be executors until the girls are of age." Sam looked carefully at the papers. "Actually, you'll be joint executors until the girls are forty years old. Rafe felt it was a lot of ranch and business for the girls to undertake when they're twenty-one."

Julie stared at Sam. "I don't understand."

"Well," he said, looking at her, "Rafe's sixth of the ranch is his daughters', once you sign these papers."

"Why?" Julie asked, completely confused. She hadn't ever considered the ranch in relation to her daughters. Her father had always wanted Rancho Diablo—but now Rafe was handing his share of it over to her daughters.

Just like that.

"Why would he do that?" she asked, growing more nervous. She was trying to think fast, but her brain seemed slushy. A divorce between them would mean perhaps some of the ranch might be awarded to Julie. Their daughters would receive monthly support. But a full sixth of the property was a lot of wealth.

It was worth millions.

Julie stared at Sam. "What's going on?"

"Rafe recused himself. That's what he said," Sam told her. "He said you'd recused yourself from the case, and so was he. And he instructed me to draw up these papers." Sam shrugged. "He loves those little girls."

"I know." Julie stared at the papers. "But he hates my father. He's been fighting for years to keep Rancho Diablo away from my family."

Sam waved his hand with a grin. "Bode'll be long gone before the little ladies hit forty. Trust me, Rafe's not stupid." His brother laughed. "Anyway, sign these papers, will you? Before Bode catches me down here? I'm a lawyer. I do my fighting in court, Judge."

"Believe me, I know, Counselor." Julie gave him a wry glare, not altogether pleased that Sam had teased her about Bode passing away. She bit her lip, considering the papers. "I don't know if I want to sign these papers."

She wasn't certain she wanted anything of Rafe's.

Not like this.

"Hey, if we call your father down here, he'll tell you to sign these papers jiffy-quick," Sam said, completely unbothered by the idea.

"I don't need my father to make decisions for me, thank you," Julie retorted.

Sam smiled. "Now, sister-in-law, don't get all irritated. Rafe's doing a good thing for his girls. You should be making that pen fly like lightning."

She wrinkled her nose. "I have to think."

"You won't get more through a divorce," Sam told her, and Julie gasped.

"I don't want more, you ape!" She glared at him. "I don't even want the divorce!"

She clapped a hand over her mouth as Sam smiled at her.

"So that's the way it is, is it?"

Julie looked at him. "Maybe."

He got to his feet, beaming. "Send those papers over to me when you've signed them. Or I can come get them if you send up a smoke signal."

"I'll call you, Counselor, when I've had sufficient time to consider executing these documents."

"Thank you, Your Honor. I'd be real happy to tell my client everything is wrapped up." He bent down to kiss little Janet on her head. "You sweet thing. So good and quiet. I guess the apple does fall far from the tree on occasion, doesn't it?"

"Sam," Julie said, ignoring his teasing, "is Rafe all right?"

Sam looked at her. "He'll be fine."

She nodded. "Thanks."

Sam patted her on the shoulder, then departed.

Julie stared at the front door for a few moments, her head whirling. Then she looked at the documents.

They were dated February 14.

Valentine's Day. The babies' birthday.

Julie blinked. "Oh, Janet," she murmured. "I completely underestimated your father."

Rafe had taken himself out of the picture a long time ago when it came to ranch affairs. He'd put her and the girls first. She'd accused him of plotting against her and her family. No wonder he'd given up.

She had to fix this somehow.

"Somehow," she whispered to her daughter. "Somehow."

It was going to take a miracle.

Chapter 20

After a long few moments thinking about everything she'd just learned, Julie took Janet upstairs. "Dad," she said, putting Janet carefully in her portable bassinet and picking up Julianne. "Seton just came by. She said to tell you hello."

"I don't care." Bode glared at her from his chair. "She need not bother coming by to see me."

"She came to apologize." Julie held Julianne to her shoulder, enjoying the feel of her baby. Julianne gave her the strength she needed to do what had to be done.

"She can't be sorry enough for what she did."

"You know, Dad, Seton didn't have to stay here after Fiona left. Seton's apparently a pretty good P.I. She had people lined up to hire her. She stayed here with us because she'd become fond of you."

"I don't care," he said. "A person gets one shot with me. Once I learn I can't trust them, that's it."

Julie shook her head, thinking about Rafe. "It doesn't always work that way, Dad. Sometimes things aren't exactly the way we see them."

"They are from where I sit. My eyesight's fine." He glared at her. "You've let that Callahan make you all wishy-washy. You used to know exactly where your loyalty belonged."

Julie looked at her father. "Dad, listen. Rafe signed over his portion of the ranch to his daughters."

"So?" Bode's brows knitted in a frown. "That doesn't mean anything to me except that he's a sneaky snake. He's just trying to look like a good guy. One-sixth of that ranch is a pittance compared to what I will get."

Julie took a deep breath. "I'm not going to be able to go on with your feud anymore. I've lived it most all of my life. I'm sorry, but as much as I love you, I've got to put my family first."

Bode stared at her. "Don't fall for his tricks, Julie."

She stepped back. "I don't think I am. I know I'm not. Dad, he doesn't want anything from me. He's trying to give me what I never asked for. I don't want their ranch! I never did. Never will." Her eyes filled with tears. "That probably sounds crazy to you. But I don't think I really ever wanted anything but him."

Bode's jaw sagged. "You don't mean that. You can't."

She nodded. "I do. And when I found out I was pregnant, I was happy. I was afraid that what I'd done would hurt you, but I was happy to be pregnant with Rafe's children." Julie wiped her eyes with Julianne's burp cloth. "Dad, try to understand. Rafe is the husband I chose." She kissed Julianne's downy head, then went to kiss her father's cheek. "I love you, Dad. But if you can't accept my decision, and my new life, you should know you probably won't see much of us. I can't go on grieving for Mom with you."

Bode sucked in a breath. He didn't say anything. Julie waited, but he never spoke, and so after a few moments, she left the room.

Then she packed up her daughters. She signed the papers Sam had left, and, her heart free for the first time in years, drove to Rancho Diablo.

Rafe was astonished when the van he'd bought for Julie to transport the babies pulled up in the drive at Rancho Diablo. He was shocked when she got out and began unloading baby paraphernalia.

He hurried to the van. "Hi, Julie."

"Hello, Rafe." She handed him the signed papers. "I'll get them notarized when I have time. Until then, there you are." She looked at him. "Are you certain you want to give up your ranch?"

He shrugged. "I had to recuse myself, Julie. Same as you did."

She looked into his eyes. "Why?"

"You come first. You and the girls." He looked sad. "It's always going to be that way, no matter what happens between you and me."

"Oh," Julie said. "Rafe, I am so sorry about everything."

"Don't be," he said. "Not everybody gets a happy ending." He poked his head inside the van and looked at the three babies in their car seats. "Except you angels. You get happy endings. Daddy will make certain of that."

They were asleep, so they didn't care about his promise. Rafe didn't mind. Any father would want his daughters to be happy. These were his tiny treasures, Rafe thought. He didn't need the ranch.

"Rafe," Julie said, and he straightened up to face her. "Yeah?"

She took a deep breath. "Are you going to divorce me?"

His shoulders seemed to slump; his face fell. "If you want me to."

"No, I mean, do you want a divorce?" Julie asked quickly.

"Oh, hell, no. Why would I?" Rafe looked toward his daughters, then back at her. "I never wanted a divorce. It sounded like a good idea at the time, to keep you from panicking. I knew that the pregnancy and then everything else that was happening really bothered you. So I thought it was best to give you the option, so we could get married. But no, I never wanted a divorce."

She nodded. "I don't, either."

He perked up. "You don't?"

"No." Julie shook her head. "In fact, I hope you'll come back home."

"You do?" His expression changed, a smile lighting his face.

"We took a vote," she said, waving a hand to include their daughters. "It was unanimous."

"That's awesome," Rafe said. He kissed her on the lips, then went around to jump in the passenger seat. "How well does this van accelerate?"

Julie laughed and handed him the keys. "Why don't you drive us home, cowboy?"

Rafe smiled at his wife. "Drive the four most beautiful ladies in the state home? That's an offer I can't refuse."

They drove away from Rancho Diablo, and the babies napped in their carriers, comforted by the drive.

"Angels," Rafe said.

"Not always," Julie said, laughing. "But most of the time."

"I have something for you." Rafe helped her carry the babies inside and settle them in their cribs. Then he pulled her to "his" room and opened the closet door.

The magic wedding dress twinkled at Julie. She recognized it immediately. Her gaze shot to Rafe. "Why is this here?"

He shrugged. "You said something about wanting to wear it. And get married at the ranch. And since we had to hurry before—"

Julie squealed and jumped into his arms. "I love you, Rafe Callahan. I'm so happy you're willing to marry me again."

"Well," he said, laughing, "I wasn't sure you'd like the idea. But I guess that's a yes. And I love you, too, little judge. It's an honor to get to marry you twice."

She kissed him on the lips, overjoyed that he understood how she'd felt. "You don't think it's silly?"

He shook his head. "I think it's smart. A second chance to lock you down? I'd be a fool to pass that up."

"How did you get this dress without me knowing?"

She got down from Rafe's arms and held the wedding gown up to herself, surprised that she felt some kind of electricity run across her skin. It was the stories, of course—romantic nonsense. But she looked at her handsome husband and smiled.

Rafe shrugged. "I told the babies to keep my secret, and they said they would."

Julie held the dress up again. "I can't wait. I felt so frumpy the first time we said I do. I want to be beautiful for you."

"You were beautiful." Rafe winked. "I wanted to undress you and get you into bed as soon as we said I do."

Julie looked at him, then hung the magic wedding dress in the closet. "You know," she said, "while the babies are napping…"

Rafe scooped her into his arms and carried her across the hall to the bed that would now be theirs. "Let the honeymoon begin."

"I remember you boasting that you'd get me in a bed eventually," Julie said, as her husband laid her gently on the sheets. His gaze simmered, promising everything she'd dreamed of.

"I said that," Rafe said, joining his wife in the bed, "and I always keep my promises."

"Although once under the stars and once in my office showed creativity," Julie stated, and Rafe laughed.

"Three's the charm," he said, and proceeded to make love to his wife the way he'd never been able to before, holding her close while the babies slept in their cribs, completely unaware that their parents were now truly husband and wife.

Forever.

Epilogue

Rafe and Julie's wedding day in September was beautiful, with clear blue skies. It was perfect weather for an outdoor wedding—everything Julie had ever hoped for as she prepared to marry the man she loved.

"You're gorgeous," Rafe told her. "I can't wait to get that gown off you, though."

Julie looked down at the magic wedding gown. "This dress is supposed to make certain I know who my perfect husband is. I think it works, too."

Rafe looked devilishly handsome in his black tux. "I don't believe in magic."

She looked at him. "You're the most superstitious man I know."

"All I know is that I'm pretty certain your bikini is going to be more magical than a wedding gown. I'm counting the hours until we get to Tahiti."

"Tahiti!"

Rafe looked at her. "A nice, quiet hut just for the two of us. I don't want any interruptions while I'm alone with my bride."

Julie couldn't wait, either. She'd count the hours until she got her big, strong husband in her arms. "You've thought of everything."

"That's why they call me the thinker." Rafe grinned.

The wedding march began to play. Julie looked at Rafe. "This is it, husband. Speak now or forever hold your peace."

Rafe took her arm to walk her to the altar on Rancho Diablo land. "The only thing I need to say is I love you." He kissed her, and the wedding guests clapped, loving the fact that Rafe clearly intended to romance his wife on the way to the altar.

"I love you, Rafe Callahan. I never thought today would happen, but I'm so glad it is. Thank you." She could feel her eyes twinkling with unshed tears of joy.

"No tears, or your dad'll come after me," Rafe said, glancing toward Bode. "He already looks fit to be tied."

"He promised to be good for one day." Julie looked up at her big, strong husband, thinking that she was the most blessed woman on earth. "Just today, mind you, and then he plans to fight fire with fire, he said."

Rafe shrugged. "Makes no difference to me." He glanced over to where the ladies of the Books'n'Bingo Society were fussing over Janet, Julianne and Judith—his three special-delivery valentines. "I'm living for the future these days."

"Me, too," Julie said, stepping up to the rose-festooned altar. This was heaven, all she'd ever dreamed of, all she'd ever wanted. After all the years of loving him from afar, finally Rafe Callahan would be her husband in name as well as spirit.

He looked down at her, smiling, and then sweetly kissed her lips before the priest had a chance to begin the service. The guests laughed again, enjoying their happiness, and Julie smiled. This was the start of their new lives together, a marriage reborn.

And then, like a benediction, the sound of hooves came to them. On the horizon, black shadow horses ran through the canyons, heralding blessed days ahead.

"Magic," Julie whispered to Rafe, and he nodded, holding her close.

True magic, the kind that would last forever.

Rancho Diablo magic.

* * * * *

Brenda Harlen is a former attorney who once had the privilege of appearing before the Supreme Court of Canada. The practice of law taught her a lot about the world and reinforced her determination to become a writer—because in fiction, she could promise a happy ending! Now she is an award-winning, RITA® Award–nominated nationally bestselling author of more than thirty titles for Harlequin. You can keep up-to-date with Brenda on Facebook and Twitter, or through her website, brendaharlen.com.

Books by Brenda Harlen

Harlequin Special Edition

Match Made in Haven

The Sheriff's Nine-Month Surprise
Her Seven-Day Fiancé
Six Weeks to Catch a Cowboy
Claiming the Cowboy's Heart
Double Duty for the Cowboy
One Night with the Cowboy

Those Engaging Garretts!

The Single Dad's Second Chance
A Wife for One Year
The Daddy Wish
A Forever Kind of Family
The Bachelor Takes a Bride
Two Doctors & a Baby

Visit the Author Profile page at
Harlequin.com for more titles.

Double Duty
for the Cowboy

BRENDA HARLEN

For my readers—
because I would never have made it to
this milestone book (#50) without you!

Prologue

It had been a fairly quiet week in Haven, and Connor Neal was grateful that trend seemed to be continuing on this Friday night of the last long weekend of summer. Sometimes the presence of law enforcement was enough to deter trouble, so the deputy had parked his patrol car in front of Diggers' Bar & Grill and strolled along Main Street.

There was a crowd gathered outside Mann's Theater, moviegoers waiting for the early show to let out so they could find their seats for the late viewing. Construction workers were sawing and hammering inside The Stagecoach Inn, preparing the old building for its grand reopening early in the New Year. Half a dozen vehicles were parked by The Trading Post; several people lingered over coffee and conversation at The Daily Grind.

He waved at Glenn Davis, as the owner of the hardware store locked up, then resumed his journey. Making his way back toward Diggers', he heard the unmistakable sound of retching. Apparently, patrol tonight was going to include chauffeur service for at least one inebriated resident, which was preferable to letting a drunk navigate the streets. He only hoped that whoever would be getting into the backseat of his car for the ride home had thoroughly emptied their stomach first.

He followed the sound around to the side of the building, where he discovered a nicely shaped derriere in a short navy skirt, beneath the hem of which stretched long, shapely legs. He felt a familiar tug low in his belly that immediately identified the owner of those sexy legs—it was the same reaction he had whenever he was in close proximity to Regan Channing.

She braced a hand on the brick and slowly straightened up, and he could see that she wore a tailored shirt in a lighter shade of blue with the skirt, and her long blond hair was tied back in a loose ponytail. She turned around then, and her eyes—an intriguing mix of green and gray—widened with surprise.

Her face was pale and drawn, her cheekbones sharply defined, her lips full and perfectly shaped. It didn't seem to matter that she'd been throwing up in the bushes, Regan Channing was still—to Connor's mind—the prettiest girl in all of Haven, Nevada.

She pulled a tissue out of her handbag and wiped her mouth.

He gave her a moment to compose herself before he said, "Are you okay?"

"No." She shook her head, those gorgeous eyes filling with tears. "But thanks for asking."

He waited a beat, but apparently she didn't intend to

say anything more on the subject. He took the initiative again. "Can I give you a ride home?"

"No need," she said. "I've got my car."

"Maybe so, but I don't think you should be driving."

"I'm feeling a lot better now—really," she told him.

"I'm glad," he said. "But I can't let you get behind the wheel in your condition."

"My condition?" she echoed, visibly shaken by his remark. "How do you know—" she cut herself off, shaking her head again. "You don't know. You think I've been drinking."

"It's the usual reason for someone throwing up outside the town's favorite watering hole," he noted.

Regan nodded, acknowledging the validity of his point. "But I'm not drunk... I'm pregnant."

Chapter 1

Six-and-a-half months later

Regan shifted carefully in the bed.

She felt as if every muscle in her body had been stretched and strained, but maybe that was normal after twenty-two hours of labor had finally resulted in the birth of her twin baby girls. Despite her aches, the new mom felt a smile tug at her lips when she looked at the bassinet beside her hospital bed and saw Piper and Poppy snuggled close together, as they'd been in her womb.

The nurse had advocated for "cobedding," suggesting that it might help the newborns sleep better and longer. Regan didn't know if the close proximity was responsible for their slumber now or if they were just exhausted from the whole birthing ordeal, but she was grateful that they were sleeping soundly.

And they weren't the only ones, she realized, when she saw a familiar figure slumped in a chair in the corner. "Connor?"

He was immediately awake, leaning forward to ask, "What do you need?"

She just shook her head. "What time is it?"

He glanced at his watch. "A few minutes after eleven."

Which meant that she'd been out for less than two hours. Still, she felt a little better now than when she'd closed her eyes. Not exactly rested and refreshed, but better.

Her husband hadn't left her side for a moment during her labor, which made her wonder, "Why are you still here?"

Thick, dark brows rose over warm brown eyes. "Where did you think I'd be?"

"Home," she suggested. "Where you could get some real sleep in a real bed."

He shrugged, his broad shoulders straining the seams of the Columbia Law sweatshirt—a Christmas gift from his brother—that he'd tugged over his head when she'd awakened him to say that her water had broken. "I didn't want to leave you."

Her throat tightened with emotion and she silently cursed the hormones that had kept her strapped into an emotional roller coaster for the past eight months. Since that long ago night when she'd first told Connor about her pregnancy, he'd been there for her, every step of the way. He'd held her hand at the first prenatal appointment—where they'd both been shocked to learn that she was going to have twins; he'd coached her through every contraction as she worked to bring their babies into the world; he'd even cut the umbilical cords—an act that somehow bonded them even more closely than the platinum bands they'd exchanged six months earlier.

"I think you couldn't stand to let the girls out of your sight," she teased now.

"That might be true, too." He covered her hand with his, squeezing gently. "Because they're every bit as beautiful as their mama."

She lifted her other hand to brush her hair away from her face. "I'd be afraid to even look in a mirror right now," she confided, all too aware that she hadn't washed her hair or even showered after sweating through the arduous labor.

"You're beautiful," Connor said again, and sounded as if he meant it.

She glanced away, uncertain how to respond. Over the past few months, there had been hints of something growing between them—aside from the girth of her belly—tempting Regan to hope that the marriage they'd entered into for the sake of their babies might someday become more.

Then a movement in the bassinet caught her eye. "It looks like Poppy's waking up."

He followed the direction of her gaze and smiled at the big yawn on the little girl's face. "Are you sure that's not Piper?"

"No," she admitted.

Although the twins weren't genetically identical, it wasn't easy to tell them apart. Poppy's hair was a shade darker than her sister's, and Piper had a half-moon-shaped birthmark beside her belly button, but of course, they were swaddled in blankets with caps on their heads, so neither telltale feature was visible right now.

He chuckled softly.

"Do you think she's hungry?" Regan asked worriedly.

The nurse had encouraged her to feed on demand, which meant putting the babies to her breast whenever they were awake and hungry. But her milk hadn't come in yet, so naturally Regan worried that her babies were always hungry because they weren't getting any sustenance.

"Let me change her diaper and then we'll see," Connor suggested.

She appreciated that he didn't balk at doing the messy jobs. Of course, parenthood was brand new to both of them, and changing diapers was still more of a novelty than a chore. With two infants, she suspected that would change quickly. The doting daddy might be ducking out of diaper changes before the week was out, but for now, she was grateful for the offer because it meant that her weary and aching body didn't have to get out of bed.

"She's so tiny," he said again, as he carefully lifted one of the pink-blanketed bundles out of the bassinet.

They were the first words he'd spoken when newborn Piper had been placed in his hands, his voice thick with a combination of reverence and fear.

"Not according to Dr. Amaro," she reminded him.

In fact, the doctor had remarked that the babies were good sizes for twins born two weeks early. Piper had weighed in at five pounds, eight ounces and measured eighteen and a half inches; Poppy had tipped the scale at five pounds, ten ounces and stretched out to an even eighteen inches. Still, she'd recommended that the new mom spend several days in the hospital with her babies to ensure they were feeding and growing before they went home.

But Regan agreed with Connor that the baby did look tiny, especially cradled as she was now in her daddy's big hands.

"And you were right," he said, as he unsnapped the baby's onesie to access her diaper. "This is Poppy."

Which only meant that the newborn didn't have a birthmark, not that her mother was particularly astute or intuitive.

Throughout her pregnancy, Regan had often felt out of her element and completely overwhelmed by the prospect of motherhood. When she was younger, several of her friends had earned money by babysitting, but Regan had never done so. She liked kids well enough; she just didn't have any experience with them.

She'd quickly taken to her niece—the daughter of her younger brother, Spencer. But Dani had been almost four years old the first time Regan met her, a little girl already walking and talking. A baby was a completely different puzzle—not just smaller but so much more fragile, unable to communicate except through cries that might mean she was hungry or wet or unhappy or any number of other things. And even after months spent preparing for the birth of her babies, Regan didn't feel prepared.

Thankfully, Connor didn't seem to suffer from the same worries and doubts. He warmed the wipe between his palms before folding back the wet diaper to gently clean the baby's skin.

"Did you borrow that plastic baby from our prenatal classes to practice on?" she wondered aloud.

He chuckled as he slid a clean diaper beneath Poppy's bottom. "No."

"Then how do you seem to know what you're doing already?"

"My brother's eight years younger than me," he reminded her. "And I changed enough of Deacon's diapers way back when to remember the basics of how it's done."

There was a photo in Brielle's baby album of Regan holding her infant sister in her lap and a bottle in the baby's mouth, but she didn't have any recollection of the event. She'd certainly never been responsible for taking care of her younger siblings. Instead, the routine child-care tasks had fallen to the family housekeeper, Celeste, because both Margaret and Ben Channing had spent most of their waking hours at Blake Mining.

But Connor's mom hadn't had the help of a live-in cook and housekeeper. If even half the stories that circulated around town were true, Faith Parrish worked three part-time jobs to pay the bills, often leaving her youngest son in the care of his big brother. Deacon's father had been in the picture for half a dozen years or so, but the general consensus in town was that he'd done nothing to help out at home and Faith was better off when he left. But everything Regan thought she knew about Connor's childhood was based on hearsay and innuendo, because even after six months of marriage, her husband remained tight-lipped about his family history.

Which didn't prevent her from asking: "Your father didn't help out much, did he?"

"Stepfather," he corrected automatically. "And no. He was always too busy."

"Doing what?" she asked, having heard that a serious fall had left the man with a back injury and unable to work.

"Watching TV and drinking beer," Connor said bluntly, as he slathered petroleum jelly on Poppy's bottom to protect her delicate skin before fastening the Velcro tabs on the new diaper.

"I guess you didn't miss him much when he left," she remarked.

He lifted the baby, cradling her gently against his chest as he carried her over to the bed. "I certainly didn't miss being knocked around."

She felt her skin go cold. "Your stepfather hit you?"

"Only when he was drinking."

Which he'd just admitted the man spent most of his time doing.

"How did I not know any of this?" she wondered aloud, as she unfastened her top to put the baby to her breast.

He shrugged again and turned away, as if to give her privacy.

If the topic of their conversation hadn't been so serious, Regan might have laughed at the idea of preserving even a shred of modesty with a man who'd watched the same baby now suckling at her breast come into the world between her widely spread legs.

"It's not something I like to talk about," he said, facing the closed blinds of the window.

"So why are you telling me now?" she asked curiously.

It was a good question, Connor acknowledged to himself.

He'd tried to bury that part of his past in the past. He didn't even like to think about those dark days when

Dwayne Parrish had lived in the rented, ramshackle bungalow with him and his brother and their mother. To Dwayne, ruling with an iron fist wasn't just an expression but a point of pride most often made at his stepson's expense.

He turned back around, silently acknowledging that if he was going to have this conversation with his wife, they needed to have it face-to-face.

"Because part of me worries that, after living with him for seven years, I might have picked up his short fuse," he finally confided.

Regan immediately shook her head. "You didn't."

"We've only been married for six months. How can you know?"

"Because I know *you*," she said. "You are gentle and generous and giving."

"I hit him back once," he revealed.

She didn't seem bothered or even surprised by the admission. "Only once?"

"I never thought to fight back."

As a kid, he'd believed he was being disciplined for misbehavior. By the time he was old enough to question what was happening, he was so accustomed to being smacked around, it was no more or less than he expected.

"Not until he backhanded Deacon," he confided.

His little brother had been about seven years old when he'd accidentally kicked over a bottle of beer on the floor by Dwayne's recliner, spilling half its contents. Deacon's father had responded with a string of curses and a swift backhand that knocked the child off his feet.

"You wouldn't stand up for yourself, but you stood up for your brother," she mused.

"Someone had to," he pointed out. "He was just a kid."

"And how old were you?"

"Fifteen."

"Still a kid yourself," she remarked. "What did he... How did your stepfather respond?"

"He was furious with me—that I dared to interfere." And he'd expressed his anger with his fists and his feet, while Deacon cowered in the corner, sobbing. "But I guess one of our neighbors heard the ruckus and called the sheriff."

Faith had arrived home at almost the same time as the lawman. Connor didn't know if his mother would have found the strength to ask her husband to leave if Jed Traynor hadn't been there with his badge and gun. But he was and she did, and Dwayne opted to pack up and take off rather than spend the night—or maybe several years—in lockup.

"He left that night and never came back," Connor said.

"Is that when you decided that you wanted to wear a badge someday?" Regan asked.

"It was," he confirmed. "I know it sounds cheesy, but I wanted to help those who couldn't help themselves."

She shook her head. "I don't think it sounds cheesy. And that's how I know you're going to be an amazing dad."

"Because I finally stood up to my stepfather?"

"Because you didn't hesitate to do what was necessary to protect someone you care about," she clarified.

"There isn't anything I wouldn't do for my brother," Connor acknowledged.

And apparently, that included lying to his wife about the reasons he'd married her.

Chapter 2

Aₛ Regan climbed the steps toward the front door of the modest two-story on Larrea Drive that had been her home since she married the deputy, she knew that she should be accustomed to surprises by now. Over the past eight months, her life had been a seemingly endless parade of unexpected news and events.

It had all started with the plus sign in the little window on the home pregnancy test. The second—and even bigger surprise—had come in the form of not one but two heartbeats on the screen at her ultrasound appointment. The third—and perhaps the biggest shock of all—Connor Neal's unexpected marriage proposal, followed by her equally unexpected yes.

She hadn't known him very well when they exchanged vows, and if she hadn't been pregnant, she never would have said yes to his proposal. Of course, if she hadn't been pregnant, he never would have proposed. And though marriage had required a lot of adjustments from both of them, Connor had proven himself to be a devoted husband.

He'd been attentive to her wants and needs, considerate of her roller-coaster emotions and indulgent of her various pregnancy cravings. He'd attended childbirth classes, painted the babies' room, assembled their furniture and diligently researched car seat safety. And in the eight days that she'd spent in the hospital since their babies were born, he'd barely left her side.

But when she finally stepped inside the house, after fussing over the dog, whose whole back end was wagging with excitement as if she'd finally returned from eight weeks rather than only eight days away, she found another surprise.

The living room was filled with flowers and balloons and streamers. There was even a banner that read: *Welcome Home Mommy, Piper & Poppy!*

She looked at him, stunned. "When did you—"

"It wasn't my doing," he said, as he set the babies' car seats down inside the doorway.

Baxter immediately came to investigate, which meant sniffing the tiny humans all over, but he dutifully backed off when Connor held up a hand.

"Then who…" The rest of her question was forgotten as Regan looked past the bouquets of pink and white balloons to see a familiar figure standing there. "Ohmygod… *Brie.*"

Her sister smiled through watery eyes. "Surprise!"

Before Regan could say anything else, Brielle's arms were around her, hugging her tight. She held on, overwhelmed by so many emotions she didn't know whether to laugh or cry; she only knew that she was so glad and grateful her sister was home.

"Nobody told me you were coming," she said, when she'd managed to clear her throat enough to speak. She looked at Connor then. "Why didn't you tell me she was coming?" And back at Brielle again. "Why didn't *you* tell me you were coming?"

"When I spoke to you on the phone, I wasn't sure I'd be able to get any time off. But I needed to see you and your babies, so I decided that if I had to quit my job, I would."

Regan gasped, horrified, because she knew how much her sister loved working as a kindergarten teacher at a prestigious private school in Brooklyn. "Tell me you didn't quit your job."

Brie laughed. "No need to worry. I'm due back in the classroom Monday morning."

Which meant that they had less than four days together before her sister had to return to New York City. Four days was a short time, but it was more time than they'd had together in the seven years that had passed since Brielle moved away, and Regan would treasure every minute of it.

"Well, you're here now," she said.

"I'm here now," her sister agreed. "And I asked the rest of the family, who have already seen the babies, to give us some one-on-one time—with your husband and Piper and Poppy, of course." She moved closer to peek at the sleeping babies. "If they ever wake up."

"They'll be awake soon enough," Connor said. "And you'll have lots of time with them."

"Promise?" Brie asked.

He chuckled. "Considering that neither of them has

slept for more than three consecutive hours since they were born, I feel confident making that promise. But for now, I'm going to take them upstairs so that you and your sister can relax and catch up."

Regan smiled her thanks as he exited the room with the babies, Baxter following closely on his heels, then she turned back to her sister. "When did you get in? Are you hungry? Thirsty?"

"I got in a few hours ago, I had a sandwich on the plane and, since you asked, I wouldn't mind a cup of tea to go with the cookies I picked up at The Daily Grind on the way from the airport, but I can make it."

"You stopped for cookies?"

"I made Spencer stop for cookies," Brie explained. "Because he picked me up from the airport. And because oatmeal chocolate chip are my favorite, too."

"Now I really want a cookie," Regan admitted. "But I no longer have the excuse of pregnancy cravings to indulge."

"Nursing moms need extra calories, too," her sister pointed out.

"In that case, what kind of tea do you want with your cookies?" she asked, already heading toward the kitchen.

Brie nudged her toward a chair at the table. "Your husband told you to relax."

"Making tea is hardly a strenuous task," Regan noted.

"Then it's one I should be able to handle." Her sister filled the electric kettle with water and plugged it in. "Where do you keep your mugs?"

"The cupboard beside the sink. Tea's on the shelf above the mugs."

Brie opened the cupboard and read the labels. "Spicy chai, pure peppermint, decaffeinated Earl Grey, honey lemon, country peach, blueberry burst, cranberry and orange, vanilla almond, apple and pear, and soothing chamomile." She glanced at her sister. "That's a lot of tea."

"I was a coffee addict," Regan confided. "The contents of that cupboard reflect my desperate effort to find something to take its place."

"Anything come close?" her sister wondered.

She shook her head. "But I'm thinking the vanilla almond would probably go well with the cookies."

"That works for me," Brie said, setting the box and two mugs on the counter.

Connor walked into the kitchen then, a baby monitor in hand. "Baxter missed his morning w-a-l-k so I'm going to take him out now, if you don't mind."

"Of course not," Regan assured him. "But why are you spelling?"

"Because you know how crazy he gets when I say the word."

Regan did know. In fact, Connor didn't even have to say the word; he only had to reach for the leash that hung on a hook by the door and Baxter went nuts—spinning in circles and yipping his excitement. But today the dog was nowhere to be found.

Brielle took a couple of steps back and peered up the staircase her brother-in-law had descended. "Is that first door the babies' room?"

"It's the master bedroom," Connor said, following her gaze. "But we've got the babies' bassinets set up in there for now."

"He's stretched out on the floor in front of the door," Brie said to Regan, so that her sister didn't have to get up to see what everyone else was seeing.

"And you were worried that he might be jealous of the babies," Regan remarked to her husband.

"He was abandoned when I found him," Connor explained. "So I had no idea if he'd ever been around kids or how he'd behaved with them if he had."

"What kind of dog is he?" Brie asked.

"A mutt," Connor said.

"A puggle," Regan clarified. "Though Connor refuses to acknowledge he has a designer dog."

"He has no papers, which makes him a mutt," her husband insisted.

"A puggle is part pug, part…beagle?" Brie guessed. Her sister nodded.

"That might explain why he's already so protective of the babies," Brie said. "Beagles are pack animals, and Piper and Poppy are now part of his pack."

"Say that five times fast," Regan teased. "And since when do you know so much about dogs?"

"I don't," her sister said. "But for a few months last year, I dated a vet who had a beagle. And a dachshund and a Great Dane."

"That's an eclectic assortment," Connor noted.

"He had three cats, too."

"Wait a minute," Regan said. "I'm still stuck on the fact that you dated this guy for a few months and I never heard anything about him until right now."

"Because there was nothing to tell," her sister said.

"Baxter," Connor called, obviously preferring to walk rather than hear about his sister-in-law's dating exploits.

The dog obediently trotted down the stairs, though he hesitated at the bottom. His tail wagged when Connor held up the leash, but he turned his head to glance back at where the babies were sleeping.

"Piper and Poppy will be fine," Connor promised. "Their mommy and Auntie Brie will be here if they need anything while we're out."

Of course, the dog probably didn't understand what his master was saying, but he seemed reassured enough to let Connor hook the leash onto his collar.

"I won't be too long," Connor said, then reached across the counter to flip the switch on the kettle.

Brie looked at her sister. "How long were you going to let me wait for the water to boil before telling me that there was a switch?"

"Only a little while longer."

Connor chuckled as he led Baxter to the door.

"So tell me when and how you met the hunky deputy," Brie said, as she poured the finally boiling water into the mugs.

"I've known Connor since high school. He was a year ahead of me, but we were in the same math class because I accelerated through some of my courses."

"I remember now," Brie said. "He was a scrawny guy with a surly attitude who you tutored in calculus."

She was grateful her sister didn't refer to him as the bastard kid of "Faithless Faith"—a cruel nickname that had followed Connor's mother to her grave. Regan had never met Faith Neal—later Faith Parrish—but she knew of her reputation.

In her later years, Faith had been a hardworking single mom devoted to her two sons, but people still remembered her as a wild teenager who'd snuck out after curfew, hung with a bad crowd and smoked cigarettes and more.

Some people believed she was desperately looking for the love she'd never known at home. Others were less charitable in their assessment and made her the punchline to a joke. If a man suffered any kind of setback, such as the loss of a job or the breakup of a relationship, others would encourage him to "Have Faith." That advice was usually followed by raucous laughter and the rejoinder: "Everyone else in town has had her."

"He sure did fill out nicely," Brie remarked now. "Was it those broad shoulders that caught your eye? Or the sexy dent in his square chin? Because I'm guessing it wasn't his kitchen decor."

Regan reached into the bakery box for a cookie. "This room is an eyesore, isn't it?"

"Or are white melamine cupboards with red plastic handles retro-chic?"

"Connor's saving up to renovate."

"Saving up?" Brie echoed, sounding amused. "I guess that means he didn't marry you for your money."

"He married me because I was pregnant," Regan told her. Because when a bride gave birth six months after the ring was put on her finger, what was the point in pretending otherwise?

"Well, if you had to get knocked up, at least it was by a guy who was willing to do the right thing."

"Hmm," Regan murmured in apparent agreement.

Brie broke off a piece of cookie. "I would have come home for your wedding, if you'd asked."

"We eloped in Reno," Regan told her.

"Doesn't that count as a wedding?"

She shook her head. "Weddings take time to plan, and I didn't want to be waddling down the aisle."

"I'm sure you didn't waddle," her sister said loyally.

"I showed you my belly when we Facetimed, so you know I was huge. I was waddling before the end of my fifth month."

"Well, you were carrying two babies," Brie acknowledged. She chewed on another bite of cookie before she asked, "What did the folks think about your elopement?"

"They were surprisingly supportive. Or maybe just grateful that their second and third grandchildren wouldn't be born out of wedlock."

Their first was Spencer's daughter, but he hadn't even known about Dani's existence until her mother was killed in an accident. He'd given up his career on the rodeo circuit to assume custody, then moved back to Haven with his little girl and fallen in love with Kenzie Atkins, who had been Brielle's BFF in high school.

"They were a lot less happy to learn that I was pregnant," Regan confided to her sister now. " Dad's exact words were, 'And you were supposed to be the smart one.'"

Brie winced. "That's harsh. Although it's true that you're the smart one."

"They don't let dummies into Columbia," Regan pointed out.

"True," her sister said again. "But no one I met at Columbia is as smart as you." She selected another cookie from the box. "What did Mom say?"

"You know Mom," Regan said. "Always practical and looking for the solution to a problem."

Brie's expression darkened. "Because a baby is a problem to be solved and not a miracle to be celebrated."

"I like to think they were happy about the babies but concerned about my status in town as an unwed mother," Regan said, though even she wasn't convinced it was true. "You know how people here like to gossip."

"And then Connor stepped up to ensure the legitimacy of his babies and all was right in the world?" Brie asked, her tone dubious.

"Well, Dad was happy that Connor had done the right thing—at least, from his perspective. Mom made no secret of the fact that she thinks Connor and I aren't well-suited."

"How about *you*?" Brie asked. "Are you happy with the way everything turned out?"

"I never thought I could be this happy," Regan responded sincerely. Not that her marriage was perfect, but she was confident that she'd made the right choice for her babies—and hopeful that it would prove to be the right choice for her and her husband, too.

"I'm glad."

It was the tone rather than the words that tripped Regan's radar. "So why don't you sound glad?" she asked her sister.

Brie shrugged. "I guess I'm just thinking about the fact that everyone around me seems to be having babies," she explained. "Two of my colleagues are off on mat leave right now, a third is due at the end of the summer and another just announced that she's expecting."

"That's a lot of babies. But still, you're a little young for your biological clock to be ticking already," Regan noted.

"I'm not in any rush," Brie said. "But I do hope that someday I'll have everything you've got—a husband who loves me and the babies we've made together. Although I'd be happier if they came one at a time."

Regan managed a smile, despite the tug of longing in her own heart—and the twinge of guilt that she wasn't being completely honest with her sister. "I have no doubt that your time will come."

"Maybe. But until then, I'll be happy to dote on your beautiful babies."

"You'd be able to dote a lot more if you didn't live twenty-five hundred miles away," she felt compelled to point out.

"I know," her sister acknowledged. "I love New York, my job, my coworkers and all the kids. And I have a great apartment that I share with wonderful friends. But there are times when I miss being here. When I miss you and Kenzie and—well, I miss you and Kenzie."

Regan's smile came more easily this time. "So come home," she urged.

Brie shook her head. "There's one elementary school in Haven and it already has a kindergarten teacher."

"That's what's holding you back?" Regan asked skeptically. "A lack of job opportunities?"

"It's a valid consideration," her sister said. Then, when she heard a sound emanate from the monitor, "Is that one of my nieces that I hear now?"

Regan chuckled, even as her breasts instinctively responded to the sound of the infant stirring. "You know, most people don't celebrate the sound of a baby crying," she remarked.

"But doting aunts are always happy to help with snuggles and cuddles."

"And diaper changes?"

"Whatever you need," Brie promised.

Chapter 3

As soon as Connor and Baxter stepped outside, the dog put his nose to the ground and set off, eager to explore all the sights and smells. They had a specific route that they walked in the mornings and a different, longer route they usually followed later in the day. At the end of the street, Baxter instinctively turned east, to follow the longer route.

"We're doing the short route this afternoon," he said. Although he enjoyed their twice-daily walks almost as much as the dog, he didn't want to leave Regan for too long on her first day back from the hospital.

He knew it was silly, especially considering that her sister was there to help with anything she might need help with. But Connor was the one who'd been with her through every minute of twenty-two hours of labor and for most of the eight days since, and he was feeling protective of the new mom and babies—and maybe a little proprietary.

Baxter gave him a look that, on a human, might have been disapproving, but the dog obediently turned in the opposite direction.

Connor started to jog, hoping to compensate for the abbreviated course with more intense exercise. Baxter trotted beside him, tongue hanging out of his mouth, tail wagging.

He lifted a hand in response to Cal Thompson's wave and nodded to Sherry Witmer, who was carrying an armload of groceries into her house. It had taken some time, but he was finally beginning to feel as if he was part of the community he'd moved into three years earlier.

There were still some residents who pretended they didn't see him when he walked by. People like Joyce Cline, the retired music teacher whose disapproval of "that no-good Neal boy" went back to his days in high school. And Rick Beamer, whose daughter Connor had gone out with exactly twice, more than a dozen years earlier.

But he was pleased to note that the Joyce Clines and Rick Beamers were outnumbered in the neighborhood. The day that Connor moved in, he'd barely started to unpack when Darlene and Ron Grassley were at his door to introduce themselves—and to give him a tray of stuffed peppers. An hour later, Lois Barkowsky had stopped by with a plate of homemade brownies—assuring him that they weren't the "funny kind," even though recreational marijuana use was now legal in Nevada. He told her that he was aware of the law and thanked her for the goodies.

Over the next few weeks, he'd gotten to know most of the residents of Larrea Street. When he'd taken in Baxter and started walking on a regular basis, he'd met several more who lived in the surrounding area.

Estela Lopez was one of those people, and as he and Baxter turned onto Chaparral Street, they saw the older woman coming toward them. At seventy-nine years of age, she kept herself active, walking every morning before breakfast and every evening after supper—and apparently also at other times in between.

"Oh, this is a treat," she said, clearly delighted to see them.

In response to the word *treat*, Baxter immediately assumed the "sit" position and waited expectantly. She chuckled and reached into the pocket of her coat for one of the many biscuits she always had on hand. Baxter gobbled up the offering.

An avid dog lover who'd had to say goodbye to her seventeen-year-old Jack Russell the previous winter, Estela worried that she wasn't able-bodied enough to take on the responsibility of another animal. Instead, she gave her love and doggy biscuits to the neighborhood canines who wandered by.

"How are you doing, Mrs. Lopez?" Connor asked her.

"I'm eager to see pictures of your girls," the old woman told him.

Connor dutifully pulled out his phone. "They came home today."

"Eight days later." She shook her head. "I remember when they kicked you out of the hospital after only a day or two. Of course, most people couldn't afford to stay any longer than that."

Which they both knew wasn't a concern for his wife, whose family had not only paid the hospital bill but made a significant donation to the maternity ward as a thank you to the staff for their care of Regan and the twins.

He opened the screen and scrolled through numerous images of Piper and Poppy—a few individual snaps of each girl, others of them together and a couple with their mom.

"Oh, my, they are so precious," Estela proclaimed. "And Regan doesn't look like she labored for twenty-something hours."

"Twenty-two," Connor said. "And she did. And she was a trouper."

"You're a lucky man, Deputy Neal."

"I know it," he assured her.

Baxter nudged her leg with his nose, as if to remind her of his presence. She obligingly reached down and scratched behind his ears.

"I heard your sister-in-law made a surprise visit from New York City."

"Well, there's obviously nothing wrong with your hearing," Connor teased.

"I was at The Daily Grind, having coffee with Dolores Lorenzo, when she stopped in to pick up a dozen oatmeal chocolate chip cookies," Estela confided.

"Regan's favorite."

"I almost didn't recognize her—Brielle, I mean," Estela clarified. "Of course, she's only been back a few times since she moved out East—it's gotta be about seven years ago, I'd guess. And even when she came back for Spencer and Kenzie's wedding, she only stayed a couple of days."

"She's only here for a few days now, too," Connor noted.

"Is she staying with you or at that fancy house up on the hill?"

That fancy house up on the hill was the description frequently ascribed to the three-story stone-and-brick mansion owned by his in-laws. The street was called Miners' Pass, and it was the most exclusive—and priciest—address in town.

"With us," he said. "She wants to spend as much time as possible with Regan and the twins."

"Of course she does," Estela agreed. "I can't wait to take a peek at the little darlings myself, but I'll give your wife some time to settle in first. Although my kids are all grown-up now—and most of my grandkids, too—I remember how stressful it was in those early days, trying to respond to all the new demands of motherhood—and I only had to deal with one baby at a time."

"Regan would love to see you," Connor said. "Especially after she's had a chance to catch up on her rest."

"Well, I'm not waiting until the twins' second birthday," she told him, sneaking another biscuit out of her pocket for Baxter.

"Please don't tell me it's going to be that long before Piper and Poppy sleep through the night."

"Probably not," she acknowledged. "But dealing with the needs of infants requires a special kind of endurance—which I don't have anymore, so I'm going to get these weary bones of mine inside where it's warm."

"You do that," he said.

She started up the drive toward her house, then paused to turn back. "But don't let those babies exhaust all your energy—" she cautioned, with a playful wink "—because new moms have needs that require attention, too."

"I'll keep that in mind," Connor promised, then he waited to ensure his old neighbor was safely inside before heading on his way again.

But the truth was, if his wife had any such needs, Connor would likely be the last to know. Although he and Regan presented themselves as happy newlyweds whenever they were in public together, they mostly lived separate lives behind closed doors. Sure, it was an unorthodox arrangement for expectant parents, but it had worked for them.

Until his brother came home for the Christmas holidays.

Because, of course, Deacon expected to sleep in his own room. He had no reason to suspect that his brother's marriage wasn't a love match—although he was undoubtedly smart enough to realize that his sister-in-law's rapidly expanding belly was the reason they'd married in such a hurry—and Connor didn't ever want him to know the truth.

So for the sixteen days—and fifteen nights—that his brother was home, Connor moved his belongings back into the master bedroom to maintain the charade that his and Regan's marriage was a normal one.

The days hadn't really been a problem—especially as Regan continued to work her usual long hours in the finance department at Blake Mining. But the nights, when Connor was forced to share a bed with his wife, were torture.

He made a valiant effort to stay on his side of the mattress, to ignore the fragrant scent of her hair spread out over the pillow next to his own, and the soft, even

sound of breath moving in and out of her lungs, caus-
ing her breasts to rise and fall in a steady rhythm. But
it was impossible to pretend she wasn't there, especially
when she tossed and turned so frequently.

She apologized to him for her restlessness, acknowl-
edging that it was becoming more and more difficult to
find a comfortable position as her belly grew rounder.
Connor knew she was self-conscious about her "babies
bump," but he honestly thought she looked amazing. He
knew it was a common belief that all pregnant women
were beautiful, though he'd never paid much attention
to expectant mothers before he married Regan. But
he couldn't deny that his pregnant wife was stunning.

Of course, he'd always believed she was beauti-
ful—and maybe a little intimidating in her perfection.
In addition to the inches on her waistline, pregnancy
had added a natural glow to her cheeks and warmth to
her smile, making her look softer and more approach-
able. And as the weeks turned into months, Connor re-
alized that he was in danger of falling for the woman
he'd married.

During one of those endlessly long nights that his
brother was home, Connor pretended to be asleep so
that Regan would relax and sleep, too. But he froze
when he heard her breath catch, then slowly release.

"Are you okay?" he asked, breaking the silence as
he rolled over to face her.

"I'm fine," she said. Then she took his hand and
pressed it against the curve of her belly.

He was so startled by the impulsive gesture, he
nearly pulled his hand away. But then he felt it—a sub-
tle nudge against his palm. Then another nudge.

His other hand automatically came up so that he had

both on her belly as his heart filled with joy and won-der. "Is that...your babies?"

"Our babies," she correctly quickly. "Or at least one of them." Then she moved his second hand. "That's the other one."

"Oh, wow." He couldn't help but smile at this proof that there were tiny human beings growing inside her. Sure, he'd seen them on the ultrasound, but feeling tangible evidence of their movements was totally different than watching them on a screen. "Apparently, they've decided that Mommy's bedtime is their play-time," he noted.

"According to the baby books, it's not uncommon for an expectant mother to be more aware of her baby's movements at night," she told him.

"Or for babies to be more active at night, as their mother's movements during the day rock them to sleep," he remarked.

"You've been reading the books, too," she realized.

"I can't wait to meet your—our—" he corrected himself this time "—little ones."

"I'm not sure how little they are anymore," Regan said. "I know that I'm certainly not."

"You're beautiful," he said sincerely.

"You don't have to placate me. I know I look like I swallowed a beach ball."

"You look like you're pregnant—and you're beau-tiful."

She looked at him then, and their gazes held for a long, lingering moment in the darkness of the night.

Afterward, he couldn't have said who made the first move. He only knew that she was suddenly in his arms, and her lips were locked with his in a kiss that was so much hotter than he'd imagined.

Because yes, there had been occasions since they'd exchanged vows that he'd found himself wondering what it might be like if their marriage was more than a piece of paper. There had been times when their eyes had locked, and he'd thought that maybe she wouldn't mind if he breached the distance between them to kiss her, that maybe she even wished he would.

But he'd always held back, because he knew that if he was wrong and the attraction he felt was not *reciprocated, their living arrangement would become so much more awkward.*

Neither of them was holding back now.

She wriggled closer—as close as her belly would allow. He cupped her breasts through the soft cotton nightshirt. His thumbs brushed over the peaks of her already taut nipples, and she gasped. "Oh, yes." She whispered the words of encouragement against his lips. "Touch me, please."

He couldn't respond, because she was kissing him again.

And he was *touching her, tracing the luscious contours of her body, learning what she liked and what she* really *liked by the way she arched and sighed.*

Their lips clung as their hands eagerly searched and explored. The encounter was as hot and passionate as it was surprising—and it might have led to more if he hadn't suddenly remembered that theirs wasn't a real marriage and recalled that all the baby books he'd been reading talked about how the hormonal changes a woman went through during pregnancy could increase or decrease her sexual appetites. Add to that the forced proximity of their sleeping arrangements and the excitement of the holidays, and he had to wonder how much those factors were influencing her reactions right now.

But did it matter what was motivating her sudden desire?

Or did it only matter that she wanted him—as he wanted her?

Unfortunately, his body and his brain were in disagreement on the answers to those questions.

And his conscience—reminding him of the deal he'd made with her father—won out.

Because even if making love was her choice, it couldn't be an informed choice so long as there were secrets between them. And there was a very big secret between them.

For the remainder of the holidays, he'd stayed up late every night to ensure Regan was asleep before he slid between the sheets of their shared bed. Thankfully, Deacon returned to Columbia early in the New Year, allowing his brother and sister-in-law to once again retreat to their respective corners. But there was no "back to normal" for Connor, because there was no way he could forget the passionate kiss they'd shared. Or stop wondering what their marriage might be like now if he hadn't put on the brakes that night.

And with her sister visiting, he would be forced to share his wife's bed again.

Of course, there was no question of anything happening between them only eight days after she'd given birth. But he suspected that knowledge wouldn't prevent his body from responding to her nearness, and he prepared himself for the sleepless nights ahead that had nothing to do with the demands of their newborn babies.

* * *

Regan and Brielle were on the sofa in the living room, each with a baby in her arms, when Connor and Baxter returned from their walk.

"You weren't gone very long," Regan remarked.

"We did the short route," Connor said, unhooking the dog's leash to hang it up again.

Baxter immediately ran to his bowl for a drink of water.

"Did you see Mrs. Lopez?" she asked.

He nodded. "And Baxter got two treats."

"Spoiled dog," she said affectionately. "What about you?" she asked her husband. "Did you get any treats?"

He shook his head.

"Well, then it's lucky you did the short route," she told him. "Because there are still a couple of cookies left in the bakery box on the counter."

"Only a couple out of the dozen that Brie picked up at The Daily Grind?" he teased.

"How did you know where I got the cookies? And how many?" Brie wondered.

"Mrs. Lopez was in the café when you stopped by," he admitted.

"You've been away so long you've forgotten the many joys of small-town living," Regan remarked sardonically.

"Because having everyone know your business is a joy?" her sister asked skeptically.

"Having a freezer full of casseroles courtesy of neighbors who want you to be able to focus on your babies is a joy."

"I'll reserve judgment on that—until after dinner," Brie said. "Just don't expect me to eat anything called tuna surprise, because I'm not a fan of tuna and I don't think anyone should ingest something with *surprise* in the name."

"No tuna surprise tonight," Connor promised. "Celeste dropped off a tray of lasagna, a loaf of garlic bread and a bowl of green salad."

Brie gave her sister a sidelong glance. "Now who's spoiled?"

Regan just grinned.

Over dinner Brielle entertained them with stories about her job and her life in New York. Though Regan was in regular contact with her sister via telephone and email, she'd missed this in-person connection. Connor seemed content to listen to their spirited conversation while he rubbed Baxter's belly with his foot beneath the table.

It seemed a strange coincidence to Regan that her sister and his brother were both currently living in the Big Apple. If their circumstances had been different— and they didn't have two newborn babies—she might have suggested that they take a trip to New York to visit their respective siblings. But their circumstances weren't different, and she didn't envision any joint travel plans anywhere in their immediate future.

"There's an Italian restaurant near our place—Nonna's Kitchen—that my roommate Grace would swear has the best lasagna she's ever tasted." Brie dug her fork into her pasta again. "I told her that she only thought it was the best because she's never had Celeste's lasagna, but even I'd forgotten how good this really is."

"Her chicken cacciatore is even better," Connor noted.

"Apples and oranges," Brie said. "Though I would say they're both equally delicious."

By the time they'd finished eating, Piper was awake and wanting her dinner, so Regan and Brie went to deal with the babies while Connor washed the dishes and tidied the kitchen. He walked into the living room as Regan lifted a hand to her mouth, attempting to stifle a yawn.

"I'm sorry," she said to her sister.

"I should be the one to apologize," Brielle said. "You just got home from the hospital after giving birth barely more than a week ago—it's a wonder you're still awake."

"And since the babies are sleeping…" Connor began.

"I should be, too," his wife said, finishing the recitation of the advice all the doctors and nurses had given to her. "And I will, as soon as I make up the bed in the spare room—"

"Already done," he said.

"You didn't have to go to any trouble," Brielle protested. "I would have been happy camping on the sofa with a blanket and pillow."

"It wasn't any trouble at all," Connor assured her.

She hugged him then. "You are, without a doubt, my absolute favorite brother-in-law."

"I'm your only brother-in-law," he remarked dryly.

Brielle grinned. "And that's why you're my favorite."

Regan couldn't help but smile, too, as she listened to the banter between them. She was pleased that Brie had so readily accepted Connor as part of the family, especially because she knew he hadn't been welcomed with open arms by her mom and dad.

But she wasn't worried about his relationship with her parents right now—a bigger and more immediate concern was the fact that she had to share a bed with her husband tonight.

Chapter 4

"Does your sister have everything she needs?" Connor asked, when Regan entered the master bedroom a few minutes later.

"I think so." She paused at the bassinet to check on the babies. "I still can't believe that she's here."

"You're surprised that your sister wanted to see you and meet her nieces?"

"No," she admitted. "But I am surprised that the wanting was stronger than her determination to stay away."

"I'm obviously missing something," he realized.

She nodded. "Brie moved to New York seven years ago and she's only been home twice since. The first was for my grandmother's funeral, the second—four years later—for Spencer and Kenzie's wedding."

"What's the story?" he wondered.

"I'm not sure I know all of it," his wife said. "But even if I did, it's not my story to tell."

"Well, whatever her reasons for staying away for so long, she's here now."

"And I'm grateful," Regan told him. "But I wouldn't have minded if she'd chosen to stay at our parents' place, where she would have had her pick of half a dozen empty guest rooms."

"Here she can maximize her time with you and Piper and Poppy."

"I know," she agreed, lowering her voice. "I just feel bad, because I could hardly tell her that she's kicking you out of your room."

Actually, it was his brother's room, but Connor had been sleeping in it since his wife had moved in at the beginning of October—save for the two endlessly long weeks that Deacon was home over the Christmas holidays.

"It's only for a few nights," he said philosophically.

"You're right," she agreed, pulling open a dresser drawer to retrieve a nightgown.

But Regan knew that her brother-in-law would be home again at the beginning of May—and not just for a couple of weeks but the whole summer this time. And she had to wonder how long she and Connor would be able to maintain a physical distance while they were sharing a bed—or even if they'd want to.

Because even now, when her body was still aching and exhausted from the experience of childbirth, it was also hyper-aware of his nearness, stirring with desire.

In defense against this unexpected yearning, she went into the bathroom to change and brush her teeth, and when she came back, she saw that Connor had pulled on an old T-shirt and a pair of sleep pants. The clothes covered most of her husband's body but couldn't disguise his size or strength.

She estimated his height at six feet four inches, because even when she added heels to her five-foot-eight-inch frame, he stood several inches above her. His shoulders were broad, his pecs sculpted, his arms strong. He had a long-legged stride and moved with purpose—a man who knew where he was going and inevitably drew glances of female admiration along the way.

He had an attractive face on top of those broad shoulders. Lean and angular with a square jaw, straight brows and a slightly crooked nose. His lips, though exquisitely shaped, were usually compressed in a thin line. Many people attributed his serious demeanor to his serious job in law enforcement, but Regan had known him since high school, so she knew that his somber outlook predated his employment. The little he'd told her about his youth confirmed that he hadn't had much to smile about while he was growing up. Yet despite his often stern and imposing expression, his eyes—the color of dark, melted chocolate—were invariably kind.

Her husband was a good man. She had no doubts about that. It was their future together that was a whole series of questions without answers—none of which she was going to get tonight so she might as well climb into bed and get some sleep.

But first, she checked on the babies one more time. They were sleeping peacefully for the moment, each with one arm stretched out toward the other, so that their fingertips were touching.

"I want to believe that they'll be the best of friends someday, but I think they already are," she said quietly.

"Like you and your sister?"

"We weren't always so close," she admitted. "Of course, there are four years between us, and only fourteen minutes between Piper and Poppy."

He moved so that he was standing directly behind Regan to peer down at the sleeping babies. "Not to mention that they were roommates in your womb for thirty-six weeks."

"We probably didn't need two bassinets," she acknowledged. "By the time they're too big to share this one, they'll be ready for a crib."

"So we'll put the other one downstairs," he suggested.

"That's a good idea."

"I have one every once in a while."

She tipped her head back against his shoulder and looked up at him. "Was getting married a good idea?"

"One of my best," he assured her.

"We'll see if you still think so when they wake you up several times in the night."

"In order to be woken up, we first have to go to sleep."

She nodded and, with a last glance at her babies, tiptoed to "her" side of the bed. The queen-size mattress had been plenty big enough when she was the only one sleeping in it, but it seemed to have shrunk to less than half its usual size now that Connor would be sharing it.

For the past six and a half months, he'd been a strong and steady presence by her side—if not in her bed. And she was sincerely grateful for everything he'd done and continued to do.

She'd always prided herself on being a strong, independent woman. She'd never balked at a challenge or let any obstacles deter her; she didn't need anyone to hold her hand or bolster her courage. Not until that plus sign appeared in the little window of her home pregnancy test.

Somehow, that tiny symbol changed everything. She suddenly felt scared and vulnerable and alone, unprepared and ill-equipped for the future.

Then Connor had shown up at her ultrasound appointment and changed everything again—but in a good way this time.

She remembered taking a quick look around the waiting room of the maternal health clinic and noting that many of the seats were already taken by couples sitting with their heads close. No doubt they were whispering their thoughts about the journey into parenthood they were taking together. And that was great for them, she'd acknowledged. But she didn't need a husband or boyfriend or partner. She could do this on her own.

So she'd stepped up to the counter and given her name to the receptionist, then taken a seat as directed— a single woman in the midst of countless happy couples.

But that was okay because she was excited enough for two people, because this was her first ultrasound. A first look at her baby. There were still some days that she wondered if her pregnancy was real or just a dream. As shocked and scared as she'd felt when she'd seen the result of the home pregnancy test, her brain didn't seem able to connect that little plus sign with the concept of a baby.

Even after Dr. Amaro had confirmed the results of that test, Regan still had trouble accepting that a tiny life was taking shape in her womb. The queasiness and sore breasts that came a few days later were more tangible evidence, but still not irrefutable proof.

Or maybe she'd just been lingering in denial because the prospects of childbirth and parenthood—especially as a single mom—were so damn scary.

She hadn't had the first clue about being a mother. Numbers and balance sheets and cost flow statements were second nature, but babies were a completely foreign entity. Her sister had always wanted to get married and have a houseful of kids. Regan's lifelong dream had been to work at Blake Mining. She didn't *not* want kids, she just hadn't given the idea much thought. And, whenever she *had* thought about it, she'd always assumed it would happen after she'd fallen in love and married the father of her future children.

But there was a saying about life happening while you were making other plans, and the tiny life growing inside of her was proof of that.

So while being a single mom was never part of her plan, she'd vowed to give it her best effort. And she would do it alone, because she had no other choice.

As a defense against the threat of tears, she'd grabbed a magazine from the table beside her. She opened the cover and began to flip through the pages, not paying any attention to the photos or articles, unable to focus on any of the words on the page where she paused.

"'Preparing Your Child for Kindergarten',' a familiar voice read from over her shoulder. *"I know there's an old adage about planning ahead, but don't you think you should focus on getting ready for the birth before you worry about your baby's first day of school?"*

She closed the cover of the magazine as Connor low-

ered himself into the vacant seat beside her. *"What are you doing here?"*

"I didn't want you to be alone for this."

"But how did you even know I'd be here?"

"You mentioned the appointment when our paths crossed at The Trading Post."

"And you remembered?" she asked incredulously.

"Well, you looked like you were ready to have a meltdown in the frozen food aisle, and I realized you were overwhelmed by the idea of doing this alone, so I noted the date in my calendar app."

That he'd done so and made the trip to Battle Mountain to be with her was a surprise—and her eyes filled with tears of relief and gratitude.

Because right now, at least in this moment, she wasn't alone.

"I should probably tell you to go, that I don't need someone to hold my hand," she said. *"But... I'm so glad to see you."*

He reached for her hand and linked their fingers together. *"Everything's going to be okay."*

It was a ridiculous thing to say—the words a promise she knew he shouldn't make and couldn't keep. And yet, she already felt so much better just because he was there. Connor Neal—former bad boy turned sheriff's deputy— so strong and steady, an unexpected rock to cling to in the storm of emotion that threatened to consume her.

"Regan Channing."

She rose to her feet, her heart knocking against her ribs.

Connor stood with her and gave her hand a reassuring squeeze.

"Are you going to come in?" she asked.

"Do you want me to come in?"

She nodded, surprised to realize that she did.

The technician had introduced herself as Lissa and led them to an exam room.

She'd explained that they were there to take a first look at the baby, reassuring Regan that Dr. Amaro didn't have any specific concerns, so the primary purpose of the scan was to take some measurements to get an accurate estimate of her due date.

When Regan had stretched out on the table and lifted her shirt, Lissa squirted gel onto her belly and spread it around with a wand-like device she'd called a transducer, explaining that the sound waves would be converted into black and white images on the screen and provide an image of the baby.

Regan had reached for Connor's hand again, and squeezed it a little tighter, as both anticipation and apprehension swelled inside her.

"Now I really have to pee," she said, as Lissa pressed the transducer against her belly and began to move it around.

"Sorry," the technician said. *"The full bladder can be uncomfortable for the expectant mom, but it does allow us to get a better picture of the uterus and baby."*

She continued to move the device—and press on Regan's bladder—as she made notes of measurements.

"The baby's heartbeat is strong and steady," Lissa said.

Regan tried to focus on the screen, but it was hard to see through the tears that blurred her eyes. Again. *Since she'd taken that pregnancy test, she'd been quick to tears no matter what she was feeling. Happy. Scared. Angry. Sad.*

"*Actually...both heartbeats are strong and steady,*" Lissa remarked.

Regan blinked. "*I'm sorry... What?*"

The technician smiled. "*Yeah, that's the usual reaction I get when I tell an expectant mother she's going to have twins.*"

"*Twins?*" Regan echoed, uncomprehending.

Lissa moved the wand over her patient's abdomen with one hand and pointed at the monitor with the other. "*There's one...and there's the other one.*"

"*Ohmygod.*" Regan looked at Connor—as if he might somehow be able to make sense at what she was seeing, because her brain refused to do so. "*There are two babies in there.*"

"*I can see that,*" he acknowledged, sounding as stunned as she felt.

"*I can't have two babies,*" she protested. "*I don't know what to do with one.*"

"*You'll figure it out,*" he assured her.

As Regan's eyes drifted shut now, she finally believed that she would figure it out—so long as Connor was by her side.

Lying next to his wife in bed, Connor found himself also recalling the fateful day that he'd made the trip to Battle Mountain for Regan's ultrasound appointment.

She'd asked him why he'd shown up at the clinic, and the answer might have been as simple as that he knew she was feeling a little scared and overwhelmed and he wanted to be there for her—as she'd been there for him when he'd been struggling in twelfth grade calculus. Or maybe he hadn't completely gotten over the crush he'd had on her when she tutored him in high school.

Regardless of his reasons, seeing how freaked out she was at the sight of those two tiny little blobs on the screen—twins!—he'd been doubly (Ha! Ha!) glad that he'd cleared his schedule for the morning.

"You still look a little shell-shocked," he'd noted, as they walked out of the clinic.

"Only a little?"

He'd smiled at that. "Let's take a walk. There's an ice cream shop just down the street."

"I don't think a scoop of chocolate chip cookie dough is the answer."

"Considering the circumstances, I was going to suggest two scoops," he told her.

Her eyes had filled with tears then. "That's not funny."

"You're right. I'm sorry." He'd pulled a tissue out of his pocket and offered it to her. "But I have to admit—it was pretty cool to see those two little hearts beating on the screen."

"Sure," she'd agreed. "If cool is another word for terrifying."

"What are you afraid of?"

"Everything."

"C'mon." He slid his arm across her shoulders and steered her down the street.

She hadn't protested. She hadn't even asked where they were going—a sure sign to Connor that she was preoccupied with her own thoughts. At least until he'd stopped in front of Scoops Ice Cream Shoppe.

"You don't have to do this," she said, when he'd opened the door for her to enter. "I'm not one of those women who tries to drown my worries with copious amounts of chocolate."

"Well, I *am* one of those guys who believes that ice cream is essential for any celebration."

"What are we celebrating?"

"I would have thought that was obvious," he'd said. "But since you're feeling a little overwhelmed by the prospect of impending motherhood right now, we can focus on something else."

"Such as?"

He'd gestured to the sky outside. "The sun is shining."

"Do you celebrate every sunny day with ice cream?"

"I might, if we had a Scoops in Haven," he told her.

Regan had managed a smile as she moved closer to view the offerings in the glass freezer case.

She'd opted for a single scoop of chocolate chip cookie dough in a cup. He'd topped a scoop of rocky road with another of chocolate in a waffle cone. And they'd sat across from each other on red vinyl padded benches with a Formica table between them.

He'd enjoyed his ice cream in silence for several minutes, giving her some time to sort out whatever thoughts were creating the furrow between her brows.

"You're not eating your ice cream," he'd commented, as she continued to mush the frozen concoction with her spoon.

She lifted the utensil to her lips. "I was just starting to get my head around the fact that I was going to have a baby, only to find out that I'm going to have *two*," she'd finally shared.

"All the more reason to tell your family sooner rather than later," he'd pointed out. Because he knew that he was the only person she'd confided in about her pregnancy so far.

She'd nodded and swallowed another mouthful of ice

cream. "I know you're right. I just can't imagine how they're going to react." Then she shook her head. "No, that's not true. I'm pretty sure my dad's going to flip."

Her comment had prompted him to ask, "Does your father have a temper?"

"Not that most people would know," she'd said. "Because it takes a lot to make him lose his cool, but I suspect my big news will do the trick."

He'd frowned at that. Even in a relatively quiet town like Haven, he'd responded to his share of domestic violence calls—and he knew, better than anyone, that some of the worst abusers presented a completely benevolent persona to the outside world.

"Would he… Has he ever…hit you?" he'd asked cautiously.

Regan's eyes had gone round with shock. "Ohmygod—no! He would never… I didn't mean… No," she'd said again.

Her automatic and emphatic denial rang true, which had been an enormous relief to Connor.

"When I said that he had a temper, I only meant that he'll probably yell a little," she'd confided. "Or a lot. But far worse than the yelling is that he'll be disappointed in me."

"And your mom?" he'd wondered aloud.

"She tends to be a little more practical—the 'no sense crying over spilled milk' type," Regan had told him. "She'll want to start interviewing nannies right away, so that I can get back to work as soon as possible, because nothing is as important to her as Blake Mining. And then we'll probably argue about that, because I may not know a lot about parenting, but I know I don't want a stranger raising my babies. I mean, I don't plan to be a stay-at-home mom forever, but I don't want my children to have to visit my office if they want to see me."

Which he'd guessed, from her tone, had been her experience. "Well, that's your decision to make, isn't it?"

"You'd think so," she'd said, a little dubiously.

He'd popped the last bite of cone into his mouth. "Are you ready to head back?"

She'd nodded and picked up her mostly empty ice cream container to drop it into the trash on their way out.

He'd walked her to her car, parked only a few spots away from his truck.

"I know you're not looking forward to the fallout, but you should tell your family," he'd encouraged her. "With two babies on the way, you're going to need not just their support but their help."

"You're right," she'd acknowledged. "I just wish…"

"What?"

She'd sighed and shaken her head. "Nothing."

"You shouldn't waste a wish on nothing," he'd chided gently.

And her lips had curved, just a little.

"What do you wish?" he'd asked again.

"You've already done so much for me," she'd said.

"Tell me what you need. I'll help you if I can."

Because he was apparently a sucker for a damsel in distress—or maybe it was just that he hated to see *this* damsel in distress, as he seemed unable to refuse her anything.

"Will you go with me…to tell my parents?"

Of course, he'd said "yes."

And ten days later, he'd said, "I do."

Chapter 5

He didn't feel any different. But as Connor drove back to Haven, the platinum band on the third finger of his left hand was visible evidence of his newly married status—and proof that everything was about to change.

"You've hardly spoken since we left the chapel," he remarked, with a glance at his wife, sitting silently beside him, her hands folded in her lap. "Having second thoughts already?"

"Are you having them, too?" Regan asked, sounding worried.

"Actually, I'm not. I mean, there were a few moments during the drive when I wondered if we were making a mistake—or at least being too hasty," he acknowledged.

But there were time constraints to their situation that had required quick action—not just because a twin pregnancy would likely show sooner than a single pregnancy but because of the deal he'd made with his now father-in-law.

He'd experienced a moment of hesitation after the legalities were done and the officiant invited Connor to kiss his bride. But it was just a simple kiss. Except that her soft lips had trembled as he brushed them with his own, and her breath had caught in her throat as her eyes lifted to meet his. In that moment, something had passed between them.

Or maybe Connor had just imagined it.

In any event, that moment was gone.

"But I have no doubt that we've done the right thing for your babies," he said to her then.

"What about us?" she'd wondered aloud.

"We'll make it work," he promised.

She twisted her rings around on her finger. "I never even asked if you had a girlfriend."

"Not anymore."

She gasped. "Ohmygod—"

"I'm kidding," he said.

"Oh." She blew out a breath. "For the record, not funny."

"Sorry."

"So..." she began, after another minute had passed in silence. "Why don't you have a girlfriend?"

"I'm not sure my wife would approve," he remarked dryly.

"Also not funny," she told him.

"I've had girlfriends," he'd assured her. "In fact, I dated Courtney Morgan on and off for several months earlier this year."

"What caused the off?"

He shrugged. "We had some good times together,

but I think we both knew it was never going to be anything more than that."

"How do you think she'll react to the news of your marriage?" Regan wondered.

"Probably with disbelief, because I told her right from the beginning that I wasn't in any hurry to settle down." And that had been the honest truth at the time, but a lot of things had changed since his first date with Courtney Morgan.

"I think people will be less surprised by the news of our wedding when they realize I'm pregnant," she acknowledged, splaying a hand over her belly. "And with two babies in there, that probably won't be too long."

"There's going to be a lot of gossip," he acknowledged, reaching across the console to take her hand. "But we'll face it together."

But first they had to face her parents.

"I feel a little guilty," he'd admitted, when he pulled his truck into the stamped concrete drive of 1202 Miners' Pass.

"Why?"

"Because you're leaving all of this to come and live with me in a house that's only a fraction of its size."

"Your house is more than adequate," she said. "Although I wouldn't object if you wanted to update the kitchen. In fact, I encourage you to do so."

He opened the passenger-side door and offered his hand to her. "When you start cooking, I'll start thinking about renovating," he said teasingly.

"Just because I don't cook doesn't mean that I can't," she warned. "Celeste taught all of us to make a few basic dishes."

"Suddenly married life is looking a whole lot brighter."

She smiled, but the way she clutched his hand as they made their way to the door told him that she was uneasy anticipating her parents' reactions to the news of their impromptu nuptials.

He wished he could have reassured her that her father, at least, wouldn't object to their marriage. But before he'd exchanged vows with his bride, he'd made a promise to Ben Channing, and he knew that reneging on that promise could jeopardize everything.

As Connor listened to the quiet even breaths of his wife beside him, he knew that was as true now as it had been the day they'd married.

But now, he had so much more to lose.

Regan hadn't been asleep for long when soft plaintive cries penetrated the hazy fog of her slumber.

Immediately, she felt a tightness in her breasts that she'd started to recognize as the letdown reflex, readying her milk for the babies—because when one was awake and hungry, the other was soon to follow. She sat up, swinging her legs over the side of the mattress and reaching for the hungry infant.

Connor had plugged a night-light into the wall so that she wouldn't have to stumble around in the dark, and as she reached into the bassinet, her heart plummeted to discover there was only one swaddled baby inside.

She gasped and turned her head, searching for her husband in the dimly lit room.

"I'm right here," Connor said. His tone was quiet and reassuring, though the words emanated not from the bed but the rocking chair in the corner. "And Poppy's here, too."

She exhaled a shuddery sigh of relief as she reached into the hidden opening of her nursing gown to unhook the cup of her bra and set Piper to her breast. The baby, hungry and intent, immediately latched on to her nipple and began to suckle. Regan tried not to wince as she settled back on the mattress with the infant tucked in the crook of her arm.

"What are you doing up?" she asked. "Did Poppy wake you?"

"I wasn't really sleeping," he said. "So when she started fussing, I decided to change her diaper and sit with her for a little while in the hope that you'd be able to get a few more minutes' sleep."

"Did I?" she wondered.

"A very few," he told her.

But she was grateful for his effort. "What did I do to deserve a guy like you?" she teased in a whisper.

He rose from the chair and returned to the bed, sitting on top of the covers beside his wife, with Poppy still in his arms. "I'm the lucky one," he said. "I've got a beautiful wife and two gorgeous daughters."

She smiled to lighten the mood, because his tone—and words—had been more serious than she'd expected. "You mean a hormonal wife and two demanding babies?"

He tipped her chin up, forcing her to meet his gaze. "I say what I mean."

"No regrets?" she asked, then held her breath, waiting for his reply.

"Not for me," he immediately replied. "You?"

She shook her head. "Fears, worries and concerns— yes. Regrets—no."

Poppy started to squirm and fuss then, and he shifted her in his arms, offering his finger for her to suck on. That satisfied the infant for all of about ten seconds— until she realized no sustenance was coming out of the digit.

"I guess she's hungry, too," Regan remarked.

"She can wait a few minutes until her sister's finished. Or I could go downstairs and make up a bottle," Connor offered.

She shook her head again as she eased Piper's mouth from her breast and lifted the baby to her shoulder. "Switching back and forth between breast and bottle can cause nipple confusion."

"*Can* doesn't mean *will*," he pointed out.

Piper let out a surprisingly loud burp, then sighed and laid her head down on her mother's shoulder, her eyes already starting to drift shut.

Regan touched her lips to the infant's forehead, then exchanged babies with Connor.

He carried Piper to the dresser and laid her down on the change pad. There was an actual change table in the twins' bedroom, but while they were sleeping in here, it made sense to change them in here, too.

"Everybody talks about how natural breastfeeding is," she said, as she unfastened the other cup of her nursing bra for Poppy. "But that doesn't mean it's easy."

"It's also a personal choice," Connor said. "So you don't have to continue with it if you don't want to."

"I want to," she insisted. "I just worry that I'm not going to be any good at it."

"The lactation consultant at the hospital said you were doing just fine," he reminded her.

"But they seem to be eating all the time," she lamented. "They're eating all the time, and it's only day eight and…"

"And what?" he prompted.

A single tear slid down her cheek. "What if I can't do this?"

Regan's voice was barely a whisper in the quiet room, as if she was afraid to say the words aloud because that might make them true.

"Do what?" Connor asked gently.

Over the past few months, he'd learned that her fears and insecurities, though not unique, were real, and he tried to offer sincere support rather than empty platitudes.

"Feed my babies," she admitted. "What if my body doesn't make enough milk?"

She was his wife. He shouldn't feel uncomfortable having this kind of conversation with her. But theirs wasn't a traditional relationship in which they'd fallen in love after dating for a while. In fact, they'd never been on a date and had only married because she was pregnant and didn't want her babies to grow up without a father, so he didn't think any of the usual rules applied.

He plucked a tissue from the box beside the bed and gently blotted the moisture on her cheek. "The more they take, the more you'll make," he said, echoing the doctor's words. "But if you don't think they're getting enough, it's okay to supplement with formula."

"But Dr. Amaro said that breast is best."

He wished they were talking about something— *anything*—else.

Yes, breastfeeding was natural and normal, and maybe most guys could watch their wives nurse their babies and view it as a simple biological function, but Connor wasn't one of those guys.

He averted his gaze from the creamy swell of her breast and cleared his throat. "And nursing Piper at midnight while Poppy has a bottle is okay, because you'll nurse Poppy at three a.m. and give Piper a bottle then," he suggested reasonably.

"I'd feel like a failure," she admitted.

"You're not a failure," he assured her.

Another tear slid down her cheek. "My nipples hurt."

He really did *not* want to be thinking about her nipples. Or any other part of her anatomy that identified her as female, because his body, too long deprived of sex, couldn't help but respond to her nearness.

Maybe it was inappropriate, but it was undeniable.

He cleared his throat and tried to clear his mind. "Did you try the cream they gave you at the hospital?"

She shook her head.

"Why not?"

"Because—" she sniffled "—I forgot."

He laid the now-sleeping Piper down in her bassinet and rummaged through the various pockets of the diaper bag until he found the sample size tube of pure lanolin that the doctor had assured them was safe for both mom and babies.

He set it on the bedside table, then picked up her empty water glass. "Do you want a refill?"

"If you don't mind," she said.

He took the glass, grateful for the excuse to escape the room so that he didn't have to attempt to avert his gaze while she rubbed cream on her breasts.

He stepped through the door—and muttered a curse under his breath as he nearly tripped over Baxter.

"What are you doing up here?" he demanded in a whisper.

The dog lifted his head and thumped his tail a few times.

Connor sighed and squatted down to rub the animal's head. "Yes, you're a good boy," he said. "But you're supposed to sleep on *your* bed in the living room, not outside *my* bedroom."

Baxter rose slowly to his feet and stretched.

"Living room," he said again, and pointed toward the stairs.

The dog looked at the stairs, then back to the bedroom again.

"The babies are fine," he promised.

Apparently Baxter was persuaded, because as Connor headed to the kitchen, the dog trotted down the stairs beside him.

"Can I help you find something?" Connor asked, when he returned from his morning walk with Baxter to see his sister-in-law digging through the cupboards in the kitchen.

"Coffee?" Brielle said hopefully.

He pointed to the half-full carafe on the warmer.

She shook her head. "No, I mean *real* coffee."

"Sorry," he said. "I switched to decaf when Regan did."

His sister-in-law frowned. "She doesn't like decaf."

"And therefore isn't tempted to sneak an extra cup," he pointed out.

"I couldn't finish a first cup," she said. "How do you

survive on that?" She immediately realized the answer to her own question. "You get the real stuff at the sheriff's office, don't you?"

"Of course," he agreed. "You want to come in for a cup?"

"Desperately," she said, as she plugged in the kettle—and remembered to flip the switch this time. "But I'll settle for herbal tea and try to pretend my body isn't going through serious caffeine withdrawal."

"Have a cookie," he said, nudging the bakery box toward her.

She opened the lid and frowned. "There's only one left—I can't take the last one."

"I took two up to Regan earlier," he said.

"In that case—" she snatched up the cookie and bit into it. "It's not a cup of freshly brewed dark roast, but the sugar rush might give my system a boost."

"Did the babies wake you up in the night?" Connor asked, as he refilled his own mug.

Brie shook her head. "No, I'm a pretty heavy sleeper. But my body's still on Eastern Standard Time, so I've been up since three o'clock."

He'd been up at 3 a.m., too, but then he'd crashed again—at least for a little while. He'd never realized he could enjoy sharing a bed with someone solely for the purpose of sleep, but when he'd managed to tamp down on his inappropriate desire for his wife, he'd found himself comforted by her presence. If their circumstances had been different, he might have shifted closer and wrapped his arms around her. But their circumstances weren't different, so he'd stayed on his own side and only dreamed of breaching the distance between them.

"And by the time you get used to the time change,

you'll be heading back to New York," he remarked to his sister-in-law now.

"Most likely," she agreed, as she poured the boiling water into her mug.

Regan wandered into the kitchen then, tightening the belt of her robe around her waist, and her sister pulled another mug out of the cupboard, dropped a tea bag inside, and filled it with water, too.

Brie pushed the mug across the counter. "Are the babies still sleeping?" she asked.

"Not still, just," Regan said, reaching for the tea. "They just went down for a nap. Hopefully, a long one." She lifted a hand to stifle a yawn. "You didn't hear them in the night?"

Brie shook her head. "How many times were they up?"

Regan looked at Connor.

He shrugged. "I lost count."

"Me, too," she admitted. "But I'm pretty sure one or the other was up...almost constantly."

"That sounds about right," he agreed. "And that's why you should go back to bed."

She looked him over, noting the uniform he wore. "I should go back to bed but you're going in to work?"

"I'd be going back to bed, too, if I had the option."

"Which is why you shouldn't have been up with me, every single time, in the night," she pointed out to him.

"I'm fine," he said. "And everyone else will be, too, so long as I don't have to pull out my weapon today."

"You're kidding—I hope."

He chuckled softly. "I'm kidding. And I'm going to pick up dinner on the way home, so you don't have to worry about anything but taking care of the babies and hanging out with your sister today."

"Didn't you say the freezer is full of casseroles from friends and neighbors?" Regan asked.

"It is," he confirmed. "But you mentioned that you've been craving Jo's Pizza."

"I did." She closed her eyes, as if picturing a pie with golden crust and melted cheese, and hummed approvingly. "And I am."

"Then Jo's Pizza it is." He bent down to give Baxter a scratch and started toward the door, then paused and turned back to kiss the top of Regan's head and wave to his sister-in-law before heading out.

"That's a good man you've got there," Brielle said to her sister when Connor had gone.

"He is," Regan agreed, lifting her mug to her lips.

"And yet…" Brie let the words trail off.

She sipped her tea, refusing to take the bait.

Her sister popped the last bite of cookie into her mouth and chewed.

Regan lasted another half a minute before she let out an exasperated sigh and finally asked, "And yet *what*?"

"That's what I'm trying to figure out," Brielle admitted.

"Well, let me know when you do."

"I know I've been gone a long time," Brie acknowledged. "But I know you, Regan. I know how you respond to men you like, and to men you *really* like. And I know there's more—or maybe less—going on here than you want everyone to believe."

"What are you talking about?" she asked.

"I'm talking about your relationship with your husband."

"Connor's amazing," Regan said. Because it was true—but it wasn't the whole truth, and she felt a little guilty that she wasn't being completely honest with her sister. "Since I told him that I was pregnant, he's been there for me. He rearranged his schedule to be at my first ultrasound appointment, and he even went with me to tell Mom and Dad that I was pregnant."

Brie's brows lifted. "*Before* he put a ring on your finger? He's even braver than I would have guessed. But I'm still missing something," she decided. "I'm adding two plus two and somehow only coming up with three."

"You were never particularly good at math," she teased her sister.

"That's why I'm the kindergarten teacher and you're the accountant," Brie agreed. "But as a teacher, I've become adept at knowing when one of my students is hiding something from me, and I know you're hiding something now."

"You're right," Regan acknowledged, almost relieved to say the words aloud, to confide in her sister. "There's something I haven't told you. Something nobody knows."

Brie laid a hand on her sister's arm, a silent gesture of support and encouragement.

"Connor married me because I was pregnant…but he didn't get me pregnant."

Chapter 6

Connor could empathize with his sister-in-law's craving for caffeine, and the always-fresh pot of coffee was his prime target when he arrived at the sheriff's office a short while later.

"I want to see pictures," Judy Talon, the sheriff's administrative assistant, demanded as soon as he walked through the door.

"I've got pictures," he promised. "But I want coffee first."

"Black?" Judy asked, rising from her chair.

When Connor had first been hired, the older woman had clearly and unequivocally stated that she was nobody's secretary or servant. While she had no objection to making coffee, she wasn't going to serve it to anyone else. And in four years, this was the first time she'd ever offered to pour him a cup.

He nodded gratefully. "That would be perfect. Thanks."

Along with the mug of steaming coffee, she brought him a glazed twist from the box of donuts that Deputy Holly Kowalski habitually brought in on Friday mornings.

"Thanks," Connor said again.

"You look like you've had a long day already and it's not yet nine a.m.," she noted.

"Long night," he clarified.

"One of the joys of being a new parent," Judy remarked.

"But these are the real joys," he said, unlocking the screen of his phone to show her the promised photos.

"Oh, they are precious," she agreed, leaning closer for a better look. "And so tiny."

He pointed to the baby with a striped pink cap on her head. "Piper was born at 3:08 a.m., weighing five pounds, eight ounces and measuring eighteen and a half inches." His finger shifted to indicate the baby wearing the dotted pink cap. "Poppy followed fourteen minutes later at five pounds, ten ounces and eighteen inches."

"Piper and Poppy are rather unusual names," Judy remarked.

"Unique," Connor agreed. "Although we did opt for more traditional middle names. Piper's is Faith and Poppy's is Margaret."

"Oh." Judy's lips curved as she glanced down at the phone again. "Your mom would be tickled pink to know that you shared her name with your firstborn."

The sheriff's admin had known his mom "way back when." They hadn't been friends, but Judy had been friendly to Faith, which was more than could be said about a lot of other women in town. They'd attended the same church—that is, his mom had attended when she wasn't required to work on a Sunday morning—and Connor knew there had been occasions when Judy had encouraged Faith to take her kids and leave her dead-beat husband. But Faith Parrish always replied that she'd promised to stick by Dwayne "for better or for worse," and she intended to honor those vows.

"She'd also be so proud of the man you've become," Judy told him now.

"Look at this one," he said, swiping the screen to show the next photo—hopefully making it clear that he didn't want to talk about his mom.

Faith had been gone for almost five years now. The doctors had ruled her death an accidental overdose, sug-gesting that her mind had been muddled by the tumor growing on her brain, which resulted in her taking too many pills. Connor had a different theory. He'd over-heard his mom talking to a neighbor about her grim prognosis and confiding that she didn't want her sons to watch her waste away. Six weeks later—ten days after Deacon's high school graduation—she was gone.

Connor still missed her every day. He missed her gentle smile and her wise counsel. No doubt she would have something to say about the predicament he'd got-ten himself into, but he couldn't begin to imagine what that *something* might be.

Judy continued to *ooh* and *ahh* as she scrolled through the pictures. "Is that Regan—in the hospital?"

He glanced at the screen. "Yeah."

"She looks like someone who just went for a leisurely walk in the park, not someone who just gave birth to two babies."

"She was a trouper," Connor said, flexing the hand that had been clamped by her iron grip with each contraction. "But it was not a walk in the park."

"Says the man whose most strenuous task was probably cutting the cords," Judy said.

"I did cut the cords," he confirmed.

He'd been surprised when Regan asked him if he wanted to perform the task—and even more surprised to discover that he did. And still, he hadn't been prepared for the significance of the moment or how severing the tangible link between mother and child somehow seemed to forge a stronger bond connecting all of them.

"My husband did it when our son was born," Judy told him. "But he was in Afghanistan when our daughter was born. She's twenty-four now and regularly gripes that she's still waiting for him to cut the cord."

"Or maybe it's just hard for dads to let go of their little girls—even when they're not so little anymore," Connor said.

"That's probably true, too," she acknowledged. "And lucky for you that you have a badge and gun, because if those girls grow up to be as pretty as their mama, you're going to need both to keep the boys at bay."

"Don't I know it," he agreed.

"Hey, look who's back," Holly said, coming up from the evidence storage locker downstairs. "Congratulations, Deputy Daddy." She went to her desk to retrieve an oversize gift bag, then set it on top of his.

"What's this?" He eyed the package suspiciously.

She chuckled. "It's going to be fun watching you raise two little girls if just the sight of pink tissue makes you cower with fear."

"I'm not afraid," he denied. "I'm just…surprised."

"Surprised that I'd give a gift to my coworker's new babies?" she prompted, sounding hurt.

"Yes. I mean, no. I—"

"Why don't you shut up and open the gift?" Judy suggested.

Deciding that was good advice, Connor pulled out the tissue that was stuffed in the top of the bag and then two neatly folded blankets. He opened up the first, noted the patchwork of pale pinks and soft purples. The second blanket was a different pattern in the same colors. "Thanks, Kowalski. We can definitely use more blankets."

Judy shook her head despairingly. "Those aren't baby blankets. They're handmade quilts. That one—" she nodded to the one that Connor was holding "—I recognize as a pinwheel pattern. But this one—" she traced a fingertip over a line of tiny stitches and glanced questioningly at Holly.

"That's a fractured star," she said.

"It's beautiful," the admin told her. "They both are. I especially love how you used the same fabrics in the different patterns so that the quilts coordinate."

Connor frowned and turned his attention back to the deputy. "You *made* these?"

"Kowalski's more than just a deadeye with her service pistol," Sheriff Reid Davidson remarked, as he entered the bullpen.

"Apparently," Connor agreed.

"Tessa won't go to sleep without the one you made for her," Reid told Holly.

She actually blushed in response to his praise. "I'm glad she likes it."

The sheriff shifted his gaze to encompass the other

deputy and his admin. "And if you were going to have a baby shower in the office, you should have invited the boss."

"Your invitation must have gotten lost in the mail," Judy retorted.

"I'm sure it did," he remarked, his tone dry.

Connor folded the blankets—*quilts*—and put them back in the bag.

"You could have taken a few more days, Neal," Reid said.

"Regan's got her sister helping her out today, so I figured I'd come in and try to catch up on some paperwork."

The sheriff nodded as he filled his mug with coffee. "Are you ready for your Stranger Danger presentation at the elementary school, Kowalski?"

"Is that today?" The female deputy feigned surprise. "Because I have a dentist appoint—"

"You don't have a dentist appointment," her boss interrupted. "Or if you do, you're going to cancel it, because this has been on your calendar since the beginning of the month."

She sighed. "Maybe you should send Neal," she suggested. "You don't want to depend on a sleep-deprived new dad to back you up if you have to take down a strung-out junkie."

The sheriff shook his head. "You're the only person I know who'd rather face a strung-out junkie than a room full of second-graders."

"Because no one would fault me for shooting the junkie," she pointed out.

"Stoney Ridge Elementary School. Eleven o'clock," Reid said. "And Kowalski?"

"Yes, sir?"

"Lock up your weapon before you go."

Connor coughed to cover up his laugh.

The sheriff lifted the lid of the donut box. "Dammit—who took my glazed twist?"

Kowalski didn't even try to disguise her snicker.

Regan held her breath in anticipation of Brie's response to her confession about the paternity of her twin babies.

"Wait a minute." Her sister held up a hand, apparently needing another moment to process the startling revelation. "Are you telling me that your husband isn't Piper and Poppy's father?"

"He's their father in every way that counts," Regan insisted. "They just don't share his DNA."

"Does he know?" Brie asked cautiously.

"Of course he knows," she said.

Her sister seemed relieved by her response, albeit still a little puzzled. "But if he's not the father and he *knows* he's not the father—biologically," she hastened to clarify, "why did he marry you?"

"Because I was a damsel in distress and he has a white knight complex?" Regan suggested.

Brie immediately shook her head. "I've never known a woman more capable of rescuing herself from any situation than you."

"I appreciate the vote of confidence, but you weren't here when I took the home pregnancy test," Regan reminded her. "Or when I finally told Mom and Dad."

But Connor had been—at least on the latter occasion—and she'd repaid his kindness by metaphorically throwing him to the wolves.

She'd taken his advice and told her parents the truth about the pregnancy. Except for one, tiny detail…

"What just happened in there?" he demanded when they left the house on Miners' Pass. "Why did you let your parents think I was the father of your babies?"

"Because if they hadn't assumed you were the father, they would have asked a hundred questions about him and our relationship."

"Questions you didn't want to answer," he realized.

"Questions I can't answer." She buried her face in her hands. "Not without admitting that I had an affair with a married man."

"You didn't know he was married," he said, repeating what she'd previously told him.

"But maybe I should have known. Maybe I didn't ask enough questions."

"All of that's academic now," he pointed out.

"I'll tell them the truth," she promised.

"When?" he demanded.

"Soon. I just need some time to figure out what to say."

"Here's a suggestion— 'Connor Neal isn't the father of my babies.'"

But then, before she'd had a chance to right the wrong, he'd apparently had a change of heart. Instead of distancing himself from the mess she'd made of her life, he'd offered to marry her—putting himself squarely in the middle of it.

"I was completely freaking out," Regan confided to her sister now. "I hated lying to Mom and Dad. I was having a really hard time processing the news that I was having twins! And although I wanted to believe that I could be a single mom, Connor's proposal gave me another option. A better option for my babies."

"Still, marriage is a pretty big step to take without any previous investment in the relationship," Brie noted.

Regan nodded. "But Connor grew up without a father—excluding the few years he lived with an abusive stepfather—and he didn't want Piper and Poppy to be subjected to whispers and speculation about their paternity."

"That's admirable," her sister said. "But it implies that he would have offered a ring to any unmarried woman who got knocked up."

"I wasn't any unmarried woman," she pointed out. "I was one who could bolster his standing in the community."

Brie frowned at that. "You're not seriously suggesting that he married you because our mother was a Blake?"

"It was a factor," Regan acknowledged. "Marrying into one of the town's founding families seemed like a surefire way for a man from the wrong side of the tracks to elevate his status in the community."

"He told you that?"

She nodded.

"That seems rather calculating," her sister noted. "On the other hand, it also makes a little more sense to me—a marriage of convenience for both of you."

"Except that it doesn't always feel convenient," Regan confided.

"Because you have feelings for him?" Brie guessed.

"Yes. No." She sighed. "I don't know."

"Well, as long as you're sure," her sister remarked dryly.

"I have all kinds of feelings," she said. "But I don't know if they're feelings *for* Connor or if the overwhelming love I feel for my babies is spilling over in his direction. Or maybe I'm just so grateful to him for everything he's done that I'm making something out of nothing."

"You could also be transferring your feelings for the biological father to the man who stepped up to take his place," her sister suggested as another alternative.

This time Regan shook her head. "I wasn't in love with Bo Larsen."

"So how did you end up in bed with him?" Brie wondered.

"He was handsome and charming, and it had been a really long time since a handsome and charming man showed any interest in me."

"Does he know...that you had his babies?"

"No," she admitted. "I mean, I told him that I was pregnant, because I thought that was the right thing to do."

"How did he respond?"

"He gave me money for an abortion."

Brie responded to that with a single word that questioned *his* paternity, and the fierceness of her response made Regan smile.

"I haven't seen or spoken to him since," she said.

"I assume that means he isn't from Haven?"

"No, he's not," she confirmed. "He was in town for a few months on a business contract, and when the contract ended he went back to Logan City—and his wife."

Brie's eyes went wide. "He was *married*?"

Regan felt her cheeks burn with a hot combination of guilt and remorse. "*Is* married," she corrected. "Though I had no idea, when we were together, that he had a wife." She swallowed. "And...two daughters."

"Wow."

She nodded, her face flaming with the memory of their confrontation—and her shame upon hearing his revelation.

"When did you find out?" her sister asked.

"When I told him that I was pregnant. Until then... I had no idea *I* was the other woman."

"Oh, honey." Brie wrapped warm, comforting arms around her. "I'm so sorry."

"I was such a fool," Regan noted.

"We all make mistakes when it comes to matters of the heart," her sister said. "And occasionally an over-load of hormones."

She managed to smile through her tears. "You're the only one, besides Connor, who knows the whole truth."

"My lips are sealed," her sister promised. "But I have to admit, I'm curious about something."

"What's that?"

"Your platonic relationship with your husband."

The comment blipped on Regan's radar. She knew Brielle too well to assume this was an innocent question. "Why is that curious?" she asked, unwilling to admit that she was less-than-thrilled that Connor seemed determined not to stray beyond the friend zone. She should focus on what they had rather than wishing for more.

"Because it's obvious to me that there's some real chemistry between the two of you—and equally obvious that you're both pretending to be unaware of it."

"The only thing obvious to me is that your romantic heart is looking for a happy ending where one doesn't exist," Regan said.

But there was a part of her that wished her sister was right—and a happy ending wasn't outside the realm of possibility.

Chapter 7

Connor hadn't thought to ask Brielle what she liked on her pizza, so he ordered two pies: one with bacon, pineapple and black olives—Regan's favorite, and one with only pepperoni. Of course, when he went into Jo's to pick up the order, he had to pull out his phone again and show pictures of the babies to everyone gathered around the counter.

Not that he minded—especially when Jo refused to take his money "just this once," suggesting that he should put it into a college fund for his daughters, because it was never too early to start saving. He knew that she was speaking the truth. He also knew that, even if he started saving right now, the spare pennies from a deputy's salary wouldn't add up to enough.

Thankfully, Piper and Poppy's maternal grandparents had expressed their intention to set up education funds for both of them, as they'd already done for their other granddaughter. He wanted to resent all the ways that the Channings threw their money around, but that would be rather hypocritical considering how he'd already benefited from their generosity.

When he finally got home, he found his wife and her sister snuggling with the babies in the living room. Baxter usually raced to the door whenever he heard Connor's truck pull into the driveway, but today the dog didn't move from his sentry position on the floor in front of the sofa.

"So much for man's best friend," he lamented, though he didn't really object to the dog's allegiance to the newest members of the family.

Baxter lifted his head to sniff the air—or, more likely, the pizza—then gave a soft *woof.*

He set the flat boxes on the coffee table and the dog rose to his feet, his nose twitching.

"Not for you."

Baxter looked at his master, pleading in his big brown eyes.

"He's had his dinner," Regan said. "So don't let him tell you any differently."

The animal swung his head to look at her, a wordless reproach.

"Well, you have," Regan said to him, as she rose to her feet to lay Poppy down in the playpen. "And you're not allowed people food, anyway."

Baxter let out a sound remarkably like a sigh and dropped to the floor again, his chin on top of his paws.

Connor went to the kitchen to get plates and napkins. When he returned, he saw that his sister-in-law hadn't moved from her position on the sofa.

"It will be easier to hold a plate without a baby in your arms," he remarked.

"Probably," Brielle agreed. "But I don't think I'm ready to let this little one go."

"Your nieces will still be here long after the pizza is gone," Regan pointed out, as she lifted a gooey slice covered with bacon, pineapple and olives onto her plate.

"A valid point," her sister acknowledged, and laid Piper down beside her twin.

"By the way, you can probably skip the w-a-l-k to-night," Regan said to Connor, as he loaded up his plate.

"Why's that?" he asked.

"We took him—and the babies—out this afternoon."

He frowned. "The wind was a little brisk this afternoon."

"It didn't seem to bother him," his wife remarked.

"I was thinking about Piper and Poppy," he clarified.

"They were wearing hats and mitts and tucked under a blanket in their stroller—even Mrs. Lopez approved," Regan assured him.

"I'll bet she was thrilled to get a peek at them."

"And Baxter was in doggy heaven because she kept slipping him treats while we were chatting."

"So you did the long route," he realized.

"And then some," Regan agreed. "Brie didn't believe me that the old Stagecoach Inn had reopened, so we went by there, too."

"It's been open a few months now, I think," Connor said.

"Since Valentine's Day, according to the brochure I picked up and which promises the ultimate romantic experience any day of the year," his sister-in-law noted.

"Well, Liam Gilmore's investment certainly seems

to be paying off, because there are always cars in the parking lot."

Brie went still, then slowly turned and looked at her sister. "You didn't mention that Liam Gilmore owned the hotel."

"I didn't think it mattered," Regan said.

"It doesn't," Brie said, but the sudden flatness in her tone suggested otherwise.

Connor knew about the acrimonious history between the Blakes and the Gilmores, of course, but he sensed that his sister-in-law's reaction was based on something more recent.

"People rave about The Home Station restaurant, too," he said, in an effort to defuse the sudden tension.

"Have you eaten there?" Brie asked him.

He shook his head. "It's impossible to get a table without a reservation, and reservations aren't easy to get."

"That's hardly surprising. When I lived here, the only place you could go for a decent meal in this town was Diggers'. Or Jo's, if you wanted pizza," she added. "Which, by the way, was delicious."

"And now, instead of going to Battle Mountain for a special occasion, people from Battle Mountain are coming here to celebrate," Regan told her.

"And I thought nothing had changed in the seven years I was gone," Brie remarked lightly.

"For six of those years, nothing did," her sister agreed.

"But now I have a brother-in-law and two adorable nieces—and a pedicure appointment at Serenity Spa with my sister tomorrow afternoon."

"Really?" Regan was obviously surprised by this announcement.

"Two o'clock," Brie confirmed.

His wife sighed happily. "I haven't had a pedicure in…a very long time. Then again, for a very long time, I couldn't even see my feet, so pampering them seemed unnecessary."

"Pampering isn't ever necessary but it's always fun," her sister said. "And after our treatments, I'm going to take a closer look at the hotel, because it looks like the perfect place for a romantic getaway for new parents who never had a honeymoon."

It didn't require much reading between the lines to realize that Brie was thinking about her sister and brother-in-law.

Connor exchanged an uneasy glance with his wife before she looked away again, her cheeks flushed with color. Because she didn't want to imagine a romantic getaway with her husband? he wondered.

Or because she did?

They had their pedicures Saturday afternoon, then Brielle insisted on cooking dinner for her sister and brother-in-law Saturday night. The chicken simmered in a white wine sauce was tender and delicious—one of Celeste's recipes, Brie confided. After dinner the sisters stayed up late talking, trying to squeeze every possible minute out of a visit that was soon coming to an end.

On Sunday they went to Regan's parents' house for brunch, so that the whole family could celebrate the twins' birth together before Brie headed back to New York City.

Connor wouldn't have minded skipping the event. He

always felt a little out of step around his in-laws—or maybe it was just that he didn't have a lot of experience with such family get-togethers. But he wanted Piper and Poppy to grow up with a strong sense of family and the security of belonging, so he tamped down on his own discomfort and carried the babies' car seats out to the truck.

It would be a tight squeeze for Brie in the backseat between the two babies, but it wasn't a long drive. Of course, nothing in Haven was too far from anything else, although the town was starting to expand and push out its long-established boundaries. The Channings' house—three towering stories of stone and brick—was an architectural masterpiece in the newest residential development. To a man who'd grown up in very modest circumstances, it was more than impressive—it was intimidating.

Connor pulled into the concrete drive behind a truck that he recognized as belonging to Regan's younger brother Spencer, a former bull rider turned horse trainer. The truck parked in front of Spencer's had the Adventure Village logo painted on the driver's side door, confirming that it belonged to Regan's older brother Jason, who owned the family-friendly recreational facilities. Jason was married to Alyssa—a West Coast native who, for reasons that no one could fathom, had willingly traded in the sun and surf of Southern California for the arid mountains of Northern Nevada.

"Looks like everyone's here," Brie remarked, sounding relieved as she lifted the twins' diaper bag onto her shoulder.

"I don't see Gramps's truck," Regan noted.

"Maybe he decided to stay at the ranch to watch over the cows."

Again, Connor suspected there was a deeper meaning to her words. Although Jesse Blake continued to supervise operations at Crooked Creek Ranch, the modest herd was more of a hobby than a livelihood now that the family's focus had shifted to mining.

Though Regan had lived in the fancy house on Miners' Pass prior to her marriage to Connor, she rang the bell and waited for the door to be opened rather than just walking in. And while he'd become accustomed to the formality—unheard of at his mother's house—it still gave him a start when the door was opened by a uniformed housekeeper.

Apparently it wasn't hard to find good help if you were able to pay for it, he mused, as Greta took their coats. And Ben and Margaret could definitely afford it.

If the Channings hadn't been filthy rich, they likely would have been viewed as neglectful parents. Because they owned and operated the mines that kept half the town employed, excuses were readily made for the parents who were simply too busy to attend teacher conferences, holiday plays, awards ceremonies and—in Spencer's case—even high school graduation.

If Ben and Margaret harbored any regrets about the milestone events they'd missed sharing with Jason, Regan, Spencer and Brielle, they never said as much. But it appeared to Connor that his in-laws were making a distinct effort to be involved in the lives of their grandchildren more than they'd ever done for their children.

They'd surprised Dani with the gift of a pony for her fourth birthday—and surprised Dani's father even more by actually attending the party rather than just sending the gift with their regrets. When Piper and Poppy were born, the maternal grandparents weren't the first visitors to the hospital—Alyssa and Jason took that honor—but they did show up on the first day. And now they'd cleared their schedules—because yes, even on a Sunday, their time was in demand—to host a family gathering where everyone could coo over and cuddle the newest additions to the family. (Though Connor noticed that his mother-in-law seemed more comfortable with cooing than cuddling.)

Of course, it was Celeste who'd done the real work. The Channings' longtime housekeeper and cook— solely responsible for planning and preparing meals since her employers had moved into a much bigger house—had prepared a veritable feast for the occasion, with breakfast items such as eggs benedict, bacon, sausage and pancakes. She'd also baked a ham, made cheesy scalloped potatoes, a green bean casserole and cornbread. An apparent new offering on the menu— fruit salad with mini-marshmallows—was a big hit with Dani, though Connor noted that his wife took a second scoop of the salad, too, after she'd polished off her first serving.

She'd frequently lamented the extra twelve pounds she still carried after giving birth—and that she was always hungry. The doctor had assured her that was normal for a nursing mom—and she was nursing two babies!

Connor didn't know how to reassure her that she looked great, because he didn't want to focus on how great she looked. He didn't want to acknowledge that he was wildly attracted to his wife or that he thought those new curves looked really good on her. Or maybe it was motherhood that added a softness to her features and a glow to her cheeks.

Conversation during the meal touched on numerous and various topics: Jason and Alyssa's recent trip to California over the spring break; the surprise visit of a famous actor to Crooked Creek with a request for Spencer to train his horses; excited recitations of Dani's riding lessons; a discussion of Brie's options for summer employment—because she couldn't imagine doing nothing for the ten weeks of her summer break.

Regan's maternal grandfather—known as Gramps—was in attendance, having driven over from Crooked Creek with Spencer's family, who now lived in the main house on the ranch. Connor noticed that the old man didn't contribute much to the various conversations that took place during the meal, but he kept a close eye on the little girl seated beside him, helping to fill Dani's plate with the foods she wanted, even cutting her pancakes and pouring the maple syrup. Though he hadn't been part of the family for very long, Connor had heard murmurs about a rift between Gramps and his granddaughter visiting from New York City. The lack of any direct interaction between them gave credence to those murmurs.

"I can't believe you're going back to New York already," Jason said to Brielle, as he dug his fork into his lemon pie. "It seems like you just got here."

"Because she did," Spencer agreed.

"I've been here four days," Brie reminded them.

"Four whole days?" her oldest brother echoed. "You've definitely overstayed your welcome."

"And," she continued, ignoring his sarcasm, "I've got fifteen six-year-olds who will be waiting for me at eight thirty Monday morning."

"Because some people have real jobs," Alyssa teased her husband.

"Just because I don't punch a clock doesn't mean I don't work hard," he replied, a little defensively.

"I know, " she said soothingly.

"On the bright side, I think I've almost convinced Brie to come back in June, for Piper and Poppy's baptism," Regan announced.

"Really?" Margaret looked at her youngest daughter, her expression equal parts surprised and hopeful.

"So long as it's later in June, after school's finished," Brie said.

"We'll make it late June," Regan promised.

"And by then it will be time to look at flights for Thanksgiving," Kenzie said. "Because they tend to book up fast."

Brie shook her head. "I won't be coming back again in November."

"But you have to," her friend and sister-in-law said. "You set a precedent by coming home to meet Piper and Poppy, so it's only fair that you do the same for your next niece or nephew."

The silence that fell around the table was broken by Spencer's four-and-a-half-year-old daughter. "Can I say it now?" Dani asked. "Can I?"

Spencer put a finger to his lips, urging her to shush. "We're going to give Auntie Brie—and everyone else— another minute to figure it out."

The little girl crossed her arms over her chest, clearly unhappy with this decision. "But you said that *I* could tell everyone about our baby," she reminded him, obviously in protest of the change of plans.

"And you just did," Gramps remarked, evidently amused enough by the exchange to speak up.

At the same time Brie put the pieces together and said to Kenzie, "You're pregnant?"

Spencer's wife nodded, the wide smile that spread across her face further confirmation of the happy news. "Our family will be growing by one in early November."

"Or maybe we can have two babies, like Auntie Regan," Dani chimed in hopefully.

Connor and Regan shared a look, silently communicating amusement that anyone would wish for the double duty that came with twin babies—and a wordless acknowledgment that they'd been doubly blessed by the arrival of Piper and Poppy.

"We're *not* having two babies," her stepmother said firmly.

"Not this time, anyway," Spencer said, with a conspiratorial wink for his daughter.

Dani sighed. "Well, can we at least have a girl baby, then?"

"We won't know if we're having a girl or a boy until the baby's born," Kenzie cautioned.

"But the news of another baby—girl *or* boy—is cause for celebration," Ben said.

"And that means we're going to need a bottle of champagne," his wife decided.

"A great idea," Regan remarked dryly. "Let's celebrate Kenzie's pregnancy with alcohol that she can't drink."

"Well, we'll open a bottle of nonalcoholic champagne, too," Margaret said.

Celeste brought in the bottles of bubbly, along with

enough champagne glasses for everyone. Corks were popped as best wishes and embraces were shared around the table.

Spencer, in charge of pouring the nonalcoholic bubbly, distributed glasses to his expectant wife, his young daughter and his sister—the nursing mom.

"I'll have a glass of that, please," Alyssa said, gesturing to the bottle in his hand.

"Why? Are you pregnant, too?" Spencer teased his brother's wife.

"Can't a woman decline alcohol without everyone assuming she's pregnant?" Alyssa countered.

"Of course," Regan spoke up in her sister-in-law's defense. "But it's interesting that you avoided answering his question by asking one of your own."

Alyssa, her cheeks flushed, turned to look helplessly at her husband.

"We were planning to wait awhile longer before sharing our news," Jason said. "But yes, we're going to have a baby before the end of this year, too."

"When?" Kenzie immediately wanted to know.

"Late November," Alyssa confided.

Of course, this news was followed by more hugs and congratulations as the rest of the glasses were passed around the table.

"Champagne?" Margaret asked, offering her youngest daughter a glass.

"I definitely want alcohol," Brie replied. "Because I'm beginning to suspect that there's something in the water in this town, and I'm not taking any chances."

Chapter 8

It was harder than Regan expected to say goodbye to her sister. For the past seven years, she'd had regular if not frequent contact with Brielle via text, email and FaceTime, but visits had been few and far between.

She'd gone to New York a couple of times, but it was different there. Brielle had been pleased to have Regan stay with her and her roommates hadn't voiced any objections—they were happy to include her in all their plans. But that was the problem: they always seemed to have plans, which meant that Regan had little one-on-one time with her sister.

Regan didn't begrudge her sister these friendships. In fact, she genuinely liked Lily and Grace, and she had other friends of her own, too. But none that she was particularly close with or would confide her deepest secrets to.

Had she ever shared that kind of kinship with anyone other than Brielle? Maybe, when she was younger. But once she'd set upon her career path, she'd focused on that to the exclusion of all else. And anyway, there were some secrets that she didn't feel she could entrust to anyone outside the family—such as the truth about Piper and Poppy's paternity.

When Ben and Margaret left to take Brielle to the airport, the rest of the siblings said their goodbyes to one another and went their separate ways. Celeste had packed up various leftovers for each family, instinctively knowing who would want what. Which was why Dani happily skipped out the door with a Tupperware container of marshmallow fruit salad in her hands.

Regan and Connor were the last to leave, taking longer than everyone else who wasn't carting around twin babies. For the new parents, the cook had prepared plates of baked ham, scalloped potatoes and beans that could be easily reheated in the microwave for their dinner.

"Are you sure you don't want to come home with us?" Connor asked as he accepted the plates.

"Don't think I'm not tempted," she told him, her wistful gaze shifting to the twins securely buckled into their matching car seats. "But I promise, anytime you want to bring those babies for a visit, you won't leave here hungry."

Celeste gave an extra hug to the new mom before she left. "You used to spend so much time working, I was afraid you'd never meet and fall in love with a wonderful man," she said quietly, her words for Regan alone. "I'm so glad to see that I was wrong. And so happy to know that he loves you, too."

Regan hugged her back, saying only, "Thank you for everything today."

Because while there was no denying that Connor was a wonderful man, their marriage wasn't the love match that Celeste obviously believed it to be—and that Regan found herself starting to wish it *could* be.

Baxter was waiting at the door, fairly dancing with excitement as he greeted them upon their return. He didn't wait for Connor to put the car seats down, but walked all the way around them, sniffing, his tail wagging happily because his favorite little humans were finally home. When the sleeping babies were transferred from their car seats to the bassinet in the master bedroom, Baxter immediately settled down beside it.

The parents retreated to the living room, where Regan dropped onto the sofa and stretched her legs out in front of her.

"What are your plans for the rest of the day?" Connor asked her.

"To do as little as possible," she admitted.

"Do you mind if I join you?"

She patted the empty space beside her.

"Are you up for a movie?" he asked, reaching for the television remote.

"Put on whatever you want," she said. "Because there's no guarantee I'll stay awake to watch anything."

He grinned. "That means I don't have to worry about picking something you'll like."

She smiled back, grateful and relieved for the easy camaraderie they shared. Maybe this wasn't quite how she'd imagined marriage would be, but she had no cause for complaint.

It had taken some time for them to become comfortable with one another and their new living arrangement, and adjustments had been made on both sides. They shared some common interests, including a love of dogs, action movies, baseball games and Jo's pizza. And they respected their differences with regard to musical preferences, literary genres and art appreciation. Most important, they talked and laughed together, and she knew that he loved Piper and Poppy as much as she did.

And—except for that one time, during the Christmas holiday three months earlier—he seemed completely oblivious to the fact that she was female. Which maybe wasn't something she should complain about, she acknowledged, recalling a conversation she'd overheard between two of her coworkers.

The women had been complaining about the unrealistic expectations of their respective husbands. As if, after working at an office all day and then running around after the kids at home, the wives wanted nothing more than to indulge the sexual fantasies of their partners.

"I might feel a little more energetic in the bedroom if he put a load of laundry in the washing machine while I was making dinner," Becky had said.

Sandra nodded. "Or pulled out the vacuum every once in a while instead of waiting for me to do it."

Regan had listened to their chatter with sympathy but she had nothing to add. Because the truth was, Connor probably did twice as much laundry as she did. He even hung up her delicates, as recommended by the labels, instead of tossing them into the dryer. And if he spilled crumbs on the floor, it was likely that Baxter would clean them up before the vacuum could be plugged in. But when it came to other household chores, he was more than willing to do his share, if not more.

No, she had no cause for complaint, she reminded herself.

Except…wasn't it unusual for a man not to express an interest in sex? Even if there was a lot about their marriage that wasn't usual.

They hadn't specifically discussed sleeping arrangements before their impromptu wedding ceremony, but he'd vacated his bed for her, confirming that physical intimacy wasn't part of their bargain—and maybe not even desired. But if "separate rooms" was a marriage of convenience "rule," she was starting to think they should throw out the rule book.

Of course, she'd already been pregnant when they got married, and maybe Connor was turned off by the idea of making love with a woman who was carrying another man's baby. Or maybe he just wasn't attracted to her at all—although the passionate kiss they'd shared in December certainly suggested otherwise.

She tipped her head back and closed her eyes as the memory of that kiss played out in her mind and stirred her body.

"You might be more comfortable upstairs, if you want to take a nap," he suggested.

And the tantalizing memory slipped away, leaving only the remnants of an unsatisfied hunger.

Regan held back a regretful sigh as she shook her head. "If I go upstairs, the babies might wake up. It's almost as if they can sense when their food supply is in close proximity."

"You nursed them before we left your parents' place, though, so they should be okay for a while, I'd think."

She held up her hand, showing her fingers were crossed.

And though she tried to hold back a wistful sigh, she must have made some sound because Connor asked, "Are you okay?"

"Yeah," she said, albeit not very convincingly.

"I know you're going to miss your sister, but she's going to come back in a couple of months for the baptism, and probably again in November, after Spencer and Kenzie's baby is born. Or maybe at Christmas, to meet Alyssa and Jason's baby at the same time."

Regan nodded. "I'm sure you're right. And I am going to miss Brie, but…it's more than that," she admitted.

He shifted on the sofa, so that he was facing her, and took her hands in his. "What's more than that?"

Her eyes filled with tears. "Everyone was so happy to hear the news about Spencer and Kenzie's baby—and then Jason and Alyssa's baby."

"You mean, unlike your parents' reactions when you told them about your pregnancy," he guessed.

She nodded again. "Obviously my situation was different," she acknowledged. "And although I wouldn't change anything that happened, because we've got Piper and Poppy now, I sometimes wish I'd been able to savor the joy of discovering that I was going to be a mother. Instead, I was too busy being worried that I was going to have to do everything on my own."

Connor squeezed her hands gently. "You're not on your own now."

Regan smiled. "I know. And thanks to you, I was able to relax and prepare for the babies during the last five months of my pregnancy."

His brows lifted. "When were you relaxed? Was I out of town that day?"

She elbowed him in the ribs.

He chuckled.

"Seriously, though, I hope you know how grateful I am to you. For everything."

"We entered into a mutually beneficial arrangement," he reminded her.

"It sounds so romantic when you phrase it like that," she said dryly.

He shrugged. "Romance isn't really my thing."

"It was never mine, either." She lifted her head to meet his gaze. "But lately I've found myself wondering if that could change."

Then, before she could think about all the reasons it might be a mistake, she leaned forward and pressed her lips to his.

It wasn't the first, or even the second, time they'd kissed, but somehow Connor had managed to forget how potent her flavor was. Now her sweet taste raced through his veins like a drug, making his heart hammer and his blood pound. And like an addict coming down from that first euphoric rush, he wanted more.

She sensed his desire, and willingly gave more. She didn't hold anything back. When he touched his tongue to her lip—testing, teasing, she sighed softly and opened for him—readily, eagerly. Her hands slid over his shoulders to link behind his head, her fingers tangling in the hair that brushed the collar of his shirt. The gentle scrape of her nails against his scalp had all the blood draining out of his head and into his lap.

His arms banded around her, pulling her closer. Her breasts, full and plump, were crushed against his chest.

Their tongues touched, retreated. Once. Twice. More. The rhythmic dance mimicked the sensual act of love-making and somehow made him impossibly harder.

He wanted her—more than he could ever remember wanting another woman. But she wasn't another woman; she was his wife. And not even two weeks had passed since she'd given birth to their twin baby girls. Maybe he didn't share any of their DNA, but his name was in the "father" box on their birth registration. That status not only gave him certain rights and responsibilities, it was a gift that he was trying to prove himself worthy of.

With a muttered curse and sincere regret, he eased his mouth from hers.

Regan exhaled, slowly and a little unsteadily, before lifting her gaze to his. "What's wrong?"

"We got married so that your babies would have a father," he reminded her. "I didn't—*don't*—expect anything more."

He saw a flicker of something—disappointment? hurt?—in her eyes before she looked away. "Are you seeing someone else?"

"What?" He was shocked that she would even consider such a possibility. "No! Of course not."

"So you're being faithful to a wife you're not even sleeping with?"

"We exchanged vows," he reminded her. "And I don't make promises lightly."

She considered his words for a moment. "I can appreciate that," she said. "But what I really want to know is—are you at all attracted to me?"

Connor was baffled by the question.

How was it possible that she couldn't know how much he wanted her?

But apparently she didn't, and he decided that admitting the truth and intensity of his desire for her might do more harm than good at this point.

"Regardless of my feelings, there are times when it's smarter to ignore an attraction than give in to it," he said.

"Maybe—if you're attracted to your best friend's sister or another man's girlfriend," she allowed. "But I don't think there's any danger in acting on feelings for your own wife."

"Honey, you are the most dangerous woman I've ever known," he assured her. "Not to mention that anything we start here is doomed to remain unfinished."

"There are various ways to finish," she pointed out. Then, in case he needed more convincing, she leaned forward to nibble playfully on his lower lip.

"There are," he agreed hoarsely, and his body was more than ready to accept any variation that she wanted to offer.

This time he reached for her. His hand slid beneath the curtain of her hair to cradle the back of her head, holding her in place while his mouth moved over hers. His kiss was hot and hungry. Desperate and demanding.

Somehow she found herself in his lap, where she could feel the solid evidence of his arousal pressed hard against her, stoking the embers of her own desire. His hands were on her breasts now, gently kneading, his thumbs brushing over her peaked nipples. Even through the lightly padded cups of her nursing bra, she was hyperaware of his touch, as arrows of sensation shot from the tips of her breasts to her core, stirring an unexpectedly urgent hunger.

She arched into him, wanting, *needing*, more. More of his touch. More of his taste. More everything.

She reached between their bodies to unfasten his belt, then released the button of his jeans. The zipper required more effort and attention as the fabric was stretched taut over his straining erection, but she finally succeeded and rewarded herself by sliding her hand beneath the band of his briefs to take hold of her prize.

As her fingers wrapped around him, his groan of approval reverberated through her, encouraging and emboldening her. In the far recesses of her mind, she thought she heard something—maybe a sound coming from the baby monitor? But it was a vague inkling that failed to draw her attention away from her task.

Then Baxter woofed—a sound not so vague or distant.

Regan tried to ignore the dog and concentrate on the task in hand, but Baxter, apparently displeased that she wasn't already racing up the stairs in response to the sounds of a baby stirring, put his paws up on the edge of the sofa and nudged her arm with his nose.

She couldn't help it—she giggled. Her husband cursed.

The dog nudged her again, more insistently this time.

Connor put his hand over hers, halting her motions.

"You better go check on the babies," he said. "Because Baxter isn't going to give us any peace until you do."

She knew he was right, and she appreciated the animal's diligence—although not as much as she resented the interruption right now. "I'll be quick," she promised.

But the twins conspired to thwart her efforts.

When she reached the bedroom, Poppy was wide awake and demanding attention. Regan changed the baby's diaper, then settled into the rocking chair with the hungry infant at her breast.

Of course, by the time Poppy was sated, Piper was awake, so Regan had to go through the whole routine again. She was fastening a fresh diaper around the infant's middle when Connor popped his head into the room.

"Everything okay?" he asked.

"Yeah, but the girls both decided it was dinner time—again, and I'm just getting started with Piper."

"In that case, I might as well take Baxter out," he said. "He's pacing by the door, eager for his w-a-l-k."

She nodded and returned to the rocking chair to feed her firstborn daughter. When Piper was finished nursing, Regan laid the now-sleepy baby down in the bassinet beside her twin.

Then she stretched out on the bed to eagerly wait for her husband's return…and was fast asleep only minutes later.

Chapter 9

Connor wasn't surprised to find his wife completely out when he returned home. To be honest, he might even have been relieved to discover that Regan had succumbed to her obvious exhaustion. After all, wasn't that one of the reasons he'd decided to treat Baxter to an extra-long walk?

Well, that, and to give himself the necessary time and distance to cool the heat that pulsed in his veins. Because while she'd given every indication that she craved physical intimacy as much as he did, he worried that he'd taken advantage of her vulnerable state.

She'd been through a lot over the past couple of weeks, and giving birth to Piper and Poppy was only the beginning of it. In addition to the physical toll of the experience, her emotions had ebbed and flowed like the tide. Except that suggested a predictable and almost gentle rhythm, whereas her moods had been anything but. Perhaps a more appropriate analogy would be the heart-pounding climbs and breath-stealing plunges of a roller coaster—like Space Mountain, completely in the dark.

Not that any of that dampened his desire for her. He only had to look at her to want her again. In fact, his body was already stirring, urging him to stretch out beside her and pick up where they'd left off.

Instead, he picked up the blanket that was neatly folded at the foot of the bed and gently draped it over her sleeping form, accepting his own unfulfilled desire as the price he had to pay for the bargain he'd struck. Because he knew that getting tangled up in a physical relationship with his wife would only make it that much harder for both of them when she eventually decided that she wanted to extricate herself from their marriage.

Because he'd been convinced, when they exchanged their vows, that the arrangement was only a temporary one. Not that she'd suggested any particular time frame, but he felt certain the day would come when she no longer wanted to be tied down to a man who was so wholly unsuitable. When she was more comfortable with and confident in her role as a mother and accepted that the difficulties of raising twin daughters on her own was less of a trial than staying with a man she didn't love.

Maybe, lately, he'd started to let himself imagine that they could make their marriage work—and admit to himself that he wanted to. Since sharing his home with Regan—and now their babies—he'd realized how empty his life had been before, without her in it. But Regan had given him no indication that the vows they'd exchanged meant anything more to her than a means to an end.

As Connor made his way back down the stairs, leaving his exhausted wife sleeping, he silently cursed Ben Channing for forcing him into this impossible situation.

Except that no one had forced him to do anything, his conscience reminded him. He'd taken the easy way. He'd sold out.

His conscience was right.

He should have spoken up and corrected the assumption that he was the father of Regan's babies when she first told her parents about the pregnancy. He should have made the truth known, loudly and clearly, because even when he'd acceded to her wordless request, he'd suspected his silence in that moment was going to come back to bite him.

As he passed the laundry room, he noticed an empty basket beside the dryer—a telltale sign that there was a load in need of folding. Diaper shirts and sleepers, he guessed. Because there always seemed to be a load of diaper shirts and sleepers in the laundry.

He transferred the contents of the dryer to the basket and carried it into the living room. He found a baseball game on TV and listened to the play-by-play as he folded the tiny garments—and a couple of even tinier pairs of bikini panties that obviously belonged to his wife.

He didn't know how to fold women's underwear—or even if they should be folded—so he simply made a neat pile of the panties and tried not to notice the silkiness of the fabric and peekaboo lace details. Because being in a marriage of convenience with a woman he wanted more than any other was painful enough without thinking about the sexy garments that hugged her feminine curves.

The fact that she wanted him, too—as she'd made abundantly clear before Baxter's interruption—only made their situation more difficult. While the sharing of physical intimacy would satisfy certain needs, Connor knew that the secret he continued to keep prevented them from developing a real and honest relationship.

A secret that dated back to the day after Regan's ultrasound, when Connor looked up from the report he was writing to see her father striding toward his desk. He'd been pretty sure he could guess why the man was there—but at least he wasn't carrying a shotgun.

The sheriff had offered his office for a more private conversation, and Connor had braced himself as he closed the door.

Regan's father had surprised him then by asking how his brother was doing at Columbia and commiserating with the deputy about the outrageous costs of a college education—especially a top-notch law school like Columbia. And just when he'd started to think that he might have been mistaken about the reason for this visit, the other man asked if Deacon knew that Connor had put a second mortgage on his house to pay his brother's tuition.

Connor had admitted that he didn't and that he'd prefer to keep it that way. He hadn't bothered to ask how Regan's father knew about his financial situation. Ben Channing was a major shareholder in the local bank and his signature was required for most mortgages and loans.

The other man had acknowledged his request with a nod before unnecessarily pointing out that there wasn't enough equity in the property to finance a second year at Columbia.

And then he'd spoken the words that changed everything.

"Blake Mining is always looking for ways to give back to the community," Ben said. "And I'm confident that a scholarship fund to help with your brother's education would be a good use of our resources."

Connor had been intrigued by the idea—and more than a little wary. "Do you really think your company would be willing to give Deacon a scholarship?"

"If you help me, I'll help him."

Said the spider to the fly, Connor mused.

But still, he had to know: "What is it you think I can do for you?"

"Marry my daughter," Ben said.

Connor had, of course, anticipated this demand. And if the man had shown up with a shotgun in hand, he would have refused, for a lot of valid reasons. Instead, Regan's father had come armed with something much more dangerous.

"How do you think your daughter would feel if she knew you were here trying to buy her a husband?" Connor had asked him.

"I don't imagine she'd be too happy," Ben admitted. "Which is why I'd appreciate your discretion."

"The situation isn't as black-and-white as you seem to think," he cautioned.

"I'm aware of the many shades of gray," the other man assured him. "And I'm not nearly as oblivious to what goes on in my daughter's life as she thinks. Thankfully, no one else knows about the short-term romantic relationship she ended a few months back.

"So when news of her pregnancy spreads, there's going to be talk and speculation about the father. If you put a ring on her finger, people will assume that the two of you did a remarkable job of keeping your relationship discreet."

"Why me?" Connor asked.

"Aside from what I said earlier about each of us being able to help the other, it occurred to me that you must care about Regan if you were willing to let her drag you into our home to announce her pregnancy, and then not correct our mistaken assumption that you were responsible."

"I didn't want to be there," Connor admitted. "But your daughter can be rather persuasive."

"Now it's your turn to persuade her that marrying you would be the best thing for her unborn children."

"How am I supposed to do that?"

"I don't think it will be too difficult," Ben said. "For all her courage and conviction, Regan's very much a traditional girl at heart. Given the choice, she'll want her babies to have both a mother and a father. A family."

Then he reached into his pocket and pulled out a check in an amount that made Connor's brows lift.

"I'm on my way to the bank now, to give the manager this. It only represents about half the costs of your brother's first year of law school," Ben acknowledged. "Consider it a sign of good faith. As soon as Regan's wearing your ring on her finger, your brother will get the other half. Just remember—she can't know that we had this conversation."

"You want me to lie to my prospective bride—your daughter—about my reasons for proposing to her? *If*

I decide to go along with this plan," he hastened to clarify.

"I want you to make a case in favor of a legal union that will give her and her babies the security of a family and that will give you legitimacy in the eyes of the community."

And there it was—the acknowledgment that no matter how hard Connor had worked to turn his life around, to most of the residents of Haven, he was still just Faithless Faith's bastard son.

"I'm surprised you'd want your daughter to marry a man of questionable reputation," he'd remarked.

"I put more stock in character than reputation," Ben told him.

"A man of strong character wouldn't let himself be bought," Connor noted.

And before Ben Channing had pulled out that check, he would have said that he wasn't for sale. He was ashamed to acknowledge now that his assertion would have been wrong.

"Every man can be bought for the right currency."

For Connor, that currency had been his brother's education. Because Ben Channing was right—he'd had no idea how he would manage to pay for Deacon's second year of law school when he'd barely been scraping by after helping to finance his first semester.

And maybe, selfishly, he did crave the legitimacy that he knew marriage to Regan would bring.

So he'd taken the last of his meager savings and bought a ring.

He'd sold out.

He'd convinced himself that he was doing Regan a favor. That he was being noble and self-sacrificing.

But the truth was, his actions had been selfish and self-serving. And yet, he'd been rewarded with a beautiful wife and two adorable babies.

He'd been fascinated by the twins since that very first ultrasound, and he'd become more and more enchanted as their growth and development was reflected in the changes to Regan's body. And when Piper and Poppy were finally born, the rush of emotion filled his heart to overflowing. He truly did love those baby girls as if they were his own. And watching his wife with their babies, he realized that he was developing some pretty deep feelings for Regan, too.

And that was before she'd kissed him tonight, tempting him with possibilities that he hadn't let himself even dream about.

There were days when he wondered how he'd let himself get caught up in the drama of her life and what his life would be like if he'd never made the trip to Battle Mountain for her ultrasound. But he couldn't imagine not having been there every day over the past several months.

And maybe that had been his punishment: being married to a warm, sexy woman that he couldn't touch.

Until today, when she'd suddenly changed all the rules.

When she'd turned his whole world upside down with a kiss.

Just thinking about those soft, sweet lips against his was enough to have the blood in his head migrating south. He didn't dare remember the press of her body against his, the glorious weight of those plump breasts filling his palms, the tantalizing rhythm of her pelvis rocking against his. The not remembering required so much effort that perspiration beaded on his brow.

As she'd pointed out to him earlier, there were different ways to finish, and he was going to have to utilize the old standby of teenage boys if he hoped to get any sleep tonight. But there would be no pretending that his callused hand could replicate her soft, tempting touch.

And that was probably for the best.

By her own admission, Regan had been feeling a little out of sorts after the family gathering at her parents' house. Maybe she wanted to pretend—at least for a while—that she had a real marriage like each of her brothers with their respective wives. The important thing for Connor to remember was that whatever she was feeling, it wasn't about him.

It had never been about him.

Theirs was just a marriage of convenience that was becoming more and more inconvenient with every day that passed.

Chapter 10

Connor was up early after a restless night. As he moved down the hall past the master bedroom, he heard no sound from inside, suggesting that Regan and the twins were still asleep. He'd heard the babies in the wee hours and had felt a little guilty for leaving Regan to respond to their demands on her own. But apparently his self-preservation instincts were stronger than his sense of responsibility, because he hadn't gotten up to help. Because he didn't trust himself to walk away from her again if she invited him to share her bed.

He poured water into the coffeemaker, measured the grounds into the filter, then retrieved Baxter's leash from the hook by the door. The dog trotted happily along with his tongue hanging out of his mouth and his tail wagging.

As they made their way down Elderberry Lane, Connor noted an unfamiliar red Toyota pull into Bruce Ackerman's driveway. A slender woman with long blond hair got out of the driver's side and moved around to the back of the vehicle.

As she lifted a bucket of cleaning supplies out of the trunk, Connor thought there was something familiar about her. A gust of wind swept through the air, and she lifted a hand to tuck an errant strand of hair behind her ear.

The movement afforded him a clearer view of her profile and revealed why she seemed familiar. Mallory Stillwell had lived across the street and two doors down from Connor while they were growing up. Though she was two years younger than he, they'd frequently hung out together and even dated for a brief while.

He'd lost touch with her after high school. The last he'd heard, she'd taken off for Vegas in the hopes of making a fortune—or at least a better life for herself. He didn't know if she'd found what she was looking for, but she was obviously back in Haven now.

"Mallory." He called out her name as he made his way down the street.

She didn't hear him.

Or maybe she was ignoring him, because she slammed the lid of the trunk and hurried toward the front of the house with the bucket in hand.

"Mallory," he called again, jogging to catch up with her.

Baxter barked happily, always eager to run.

She'd ignored Connor—twice, but the bark seemed to give her pause, reminding him that she'd always had a soft spot for animals.

In fact, she'd volunteered at the local animal shelter

twice a week throughout high school. Of course, she'd said that anything was better than hanging around at home, deliberately downplaying the value of her efforts. He'd stopped by the shelter a couple of times to see her and noticed that she had tremendous empathy for all the animals, especially those that exhibited obvious signs of abuse.

She wasn't looking at him now, but at his canine companion. "Rusty?" she said, her voice hesitant.

Baxter barked and wagged his tail.

"Ohmygod…it *is* you." She dropped to her knees on the driveway to embrace him, tears sliding down her cheeks.

"How do you know my dog?" Connor asked cautiously.

She wiped the backs of her hands over her tear-streaked cheeks before finally looking up at him. "He used to be my dog," she admitted. "Where did you find him? *When* did you find him?"

"Last April," he said. "Out at the train yard."

"Oh, Rusty," she said, her eyes filling with fresh tears.

"His name's Baxter now," Connor told her.

"Baxter," she echoed, and nodded. "It's a good name. He's a good dog."

"The best," Connor said. "So…how did he end up at the train yard?"

Her gaze skittered away. "I don't know."

"But you have a theory," he guessed.

"Evan said he ran away." She shrugged her narrow shoulders. "I suspected he left the door open on purpose, so that Rusty could do just that."

"Evan?" he prompted.

"My husband."

He glanced at her left hand, noted there was a thin gold band encircling her third finger.

"He was tied to a fence post," Connor told her. "Shivering. Starving."

She flinched, as if each word was a physical blow. "Evan never wanted a dog," she admitted, stroking her hands over Baxter's glossy coat as she spoke. "I picked Rusty—*Baxter*," she immediately corrected herself, "out of a litter of puppies that I helped take care of at the SPCA in Vegas, where we were living at the time. Evan was driving a rig and sometimes gone for weeks at a time, and I thought a dog would be good company for me and my daughter."

"I didn't know you had a child," he admitted.

Mallory nodded, her expression brightening slightly. "Chloe's almost six and the light of my life. When Rus—*Baxter* went missing, we were out all night looking for him. And again the next day, and the day after that."

She tipped her head forward, so that her face was curtained by her hair. "I thought Evan—" her voice broke and she shook her head, as if unable to complete the thought. "I'm so glad he's got a good home now." She looked up at him then and managed a tentative smile. "Good people."

"He does," Connor agreed. Then, "So what brought you back to Haven?"

"My mom died and left the house to me and my sisters, but they have better places to live. Madison's in Houston and Miranda's in Battle Mountain, so now I'm paying them rent to live in a house I didn't ever want to come back to." This time her shrug was one of resignation. "But Evan didn't grow up in Haven, and he figured that if we missed one or two rent payments here, my sisters wouldn't evict us."

"Is he still driving a rig?"

She shook her head. "His CDL was yanked for DUI. He's applied for a few jobs around town, but there aren't many."

They both knew the town's biggest employer was Blake Mining and that his wife was a Blake, so Connor had to give her credit for not attempting to leverage their shared history into a job for her husband.

"You've done good for yourself, though," Mallory noted, in an obvious effort to shift the conversation. "Working in the sheriff's office now, living in a house on the right side of town, married with children. Of course, no one was more surprised than me to hear that the Channing ice princess went slumming and got herself knocked up by my first boyfriend."

"Regan's a good person," he told her. "And a wonderful mother."

"Maybe, but those names—" she rolled her eyes "—Piper and Poppy? What were you thinking?"

"Piper's full name is Piper Faith Neal."

"Oh." Her sneer immediately faded. "For your mom. That's nice."

"It was Regan's idea."

"So maybe she's not all bad," Mallory allowed.

"She's amazing," Connor said.

She tilted her head to look at him. "Huh."

"What's that supposed to mean?"

"I guess I just assumed that you'd married her because she was pregnant. I never considered that you might actually have feelings for her."

Before he could respond to that, the front door opened and Mr. Ackerman poked his head out. "Everything okay, Mallory?"

"Just catching up with an old friend," she told him.

"I'm not paying you to chitchat, you know."

"I also know that you pay me by the job not the hour," she retorted. "So it doesn't really matter when I get started as long as the job gets done."

"Cheeky girl," the old man grumbled, with a twinkle in his eye.

"But I probably should get started," Mallory said, when Mr. Ackerman had disappeared back inside. "This is only the first of three houses I have to do today."

Connor nodded. "It was good to see you, Mallory."

"You, too." She looked at the dog at his feet and gave his head a quick rub. "And especially you, Baxter."

As Connor headed toward home, Mallory's comment about his feelings for Regan continued to echo in the back of his mind.

Of course he had feelings for Regan—but he wasn't inclined to put a label on those feelings.

He cared about her and enjoyed spending time with her. And why wouldn't he? She was beautiful and smart, with a generally sunny disposition and good sense of humor. She was also sexy as hell, and his attraction to her often felt like more of a curse than a blessing.

But for the better part of seven months, he'd managed to ignore the attraction. He'd ruthlessly shoved it aside, reminding himself that she'd married him not because she wanted a husband but because she wanted a father for her babies.

Their hasty vows had offered her a degree of protection when she could no longer hide her pregnancy.

Sure, there was plenty of gossip as residents pretended to be shocked when they counted the months between the wedding and the birth of her babies and came up with a number less than nine. But the revelation that Regan Channing *had to* marry Connor Neal was scandalous enough that they didn't suspect there was more to the story.

Connor knew the whole truth, and that was a burden he carried alone. Regan had shared her deepest secrets with him, trusting that he would keep them safe. But he couldn't do the same, because his secrets—if revealed—could tear apart the fragile foundation of their family.

Maybe that foundation would be stronger if he'd been honest with her from the beginning. Instead, they'd built their marriage on secrets and lies. It was ironic, because he'd urged her to tell the truth to her parents, and when she'd stopped by to tell him that she was going to do just that, he was the one who backtracked from his own advice.

Twenty-four hours after Ben Channing's visit to the sheriff's office, Connor had been mulling over the man's proposition when Regan showed up at his door.

She'd offered him two containers of ice cream and a tempting smile. "Rocky road and chocolate."

"What's the occasion?" he'd asked.

"I've decided to tell my parents the truth tonight," she told him.

Baxter had been out in the backyard taking care of business, but he came through the doggy door then, and sensing—or maybe scenting—they had a visitor, raced to the front entrance as Regan stepped inside.

Before Connor could caution her or restrain the dog,

Regan had dropped to her knees to fuss over the excited canine.

"Oh, aren't you just the cutest thing?" she'd said, clearly talking to the dog and not him. "And friendly," she noted with a chuckle, as she rubbed the back of her hand over her cheek to wipe away his slobbery doggy kisses.

"Baxter, sit."

The dog plopped his butt on the floor, but his tail continued to wag.

"He's very well trained," she'd remarked, rising to her feet.

"If he was well trained, you wouldn't have dog hair all over you," he'd noted.

Regan had glanced down and, with a dismissive shrug, brushed her hands over the thighs of her pants.

It might have been that moment, Connor realized now, when he really started to fall for her. Because who wouldn't fall for a beautiful, sexy woman who showed up at his door with ice cream and didn't mind his canine companion shedding all over her clothes?

His own hands had started to go numb from the cold, reminding him of the ice cream he was holding.

"What kind do you want?" he'd asked, leading the way to the kitchen.

"Can I have a scoop of each?"

He took two bowls out of the cupboard. "I thought you weren't one of those women who drowns her worries with copious amounts of chocolate."

"If I wanted to do that, I would have stayed home with both containers and a spoon," she'd said.

He'd chuckled at her remark as he pried the lid off the first container and dipped the scoop inside.

"So why today?" he'd asked, when he handed her the bowl full of ice cream and a spoon.

"I figured, after three days, my father's blood pressure should have come down to something approximating normal. And I know you're anxious for me to rectify their misunderstanding."

Of course, he'd urged her to do exactly that—but that was before Ben Channing had shown up at the sheriff's office with his intriguing proposition.

"So tell me," she said, apparently wanting to discuss something other than the impending visit with her parents. "Was this circa 1980 kitchen a deliberate design choice?"

"Actually, I think it's circa 1972, because that's when the house was built."

She glanced around. "You're not interested in updating the look?"

"It's functional," he said, well aware that the space was in desperate need of a major overhaul. But right now, Connor could hardly afford a can of paint, never mind a more substantial renovation.

Except that Deacon had called him that afternoon, practically bursting with excitement over the news that he'd been awarded another scholarship—confirming that Ben Channing had honored at least the first part of his promise. Deacon wanted to send the money back to his brother, to repay him for his first-term tuition. But Connor had suggested that he hold on to the funds for second term, because he knew it might be the last "Aim Higher" check he ever saw.

Of course, that scholarship depended on Connor more than Deacon. All he had to do was convince

Regan to marry him, and her father would ensure that Blake Mining continued to fund the scholarship.

Sure, he had qualms about proposing for mercenary reasons. Truthfully, he had qualms about marriage in general. And a lot of reservations about his ability to fulfill the responsibilities of parenthood. Because what did he know about being a father? His biological father had never been part of his life and his stepfather had been an abusive drunk, ensuring he had no role models he'd want to emulate.

But something had happened when he'd seen Regan's babies on the ultrasound monitor. He'd felt an unexpected swell of emotion, a desire to help and protect both the mom and her babies. Maybe he didn't know anything about being a dad, but he knew that if he was ever entrusted with the care of a child—or children, he would do everything in his power to be the best dad that he could be.

"Did you stop by to critique my decor?" he'd asked Regan, picking up the thread of their conversation.

"No." She'd sighed. "My visit was solely for the purposes of procrastination—and ice cream."

"You're not eager to tell your parents the truth," he'd guessed.

"Definitely not," she agreed. "When my dad hears that you're not the father of my baby, he's going to demand to know who is, so that he can force me to marry him."

"You don't want to marry the father?"

"Not an option," she said bluntly.

"Why not?" he wondered.

"Because bigamy's illegal in Nevada."

And he'd thought nothing could have surprised him more than her pregnancy. "He's married?"

She'd nodded slowly. "I didn't know he was married when we were together," she explained. "But maybe I should have suspected something was up.

"He was an environmental consultant in town on a contractual assignment, and because he was only going to be in town for a short while, he wanted to be discreet. To protect my reputation, he said, because he understood how gossip worked in small towns and he didn't want people talking about me.

"In retrospect, it was obvious that he didn't want people talking about *us*, because some people did know that he was married."

"When did you find out?" Connor asked her.

"When I told him that I was pregnant," she admitted. "Our relationship was already over, but when I realized I was going to have his baby, I went to see him."

She shoveled another spoonful of ice cream into her mouth. "I didn't want or expect anything from him—not that I was willing to admit, anyway—but I felt I had an obligation to tell him that he was going to be a father." She swirled her spoon inside the bowl. "Turned out he didn't just have a wife but two kids—and he didn't want any more. And he definitely didn't want me causing any trouble for his perfect little family.

"He used me," she said quietly. "And I was foolish enough to let him."

He'd never seen her like this—so vulnerable and insecure. Even when she'd been throwing up outside of Diggers', she'd given the impression of a woman in control of her life—if not her morning sickness. Even at the clinic for her ultrasound, she'd seemed appreciative of his support but not in need of it. And her sudden openness and uncertainty now brought out every protective instinct he had, urging him to help her in any way that he could.

She dropped her gaze to the remnants of the ice cream, then pushed the bowl away, her craving sated— or maybe her appetite lost.

"I just wish there was a way to be sure he couldn't ever make a claim to my babies."

"Do you have any reason to suspect that he would?"

"No," she admitted. "He was pretty adamant that he wanted nothing to do with another child. I just hate to imagine what might happen if he ever changed his mind."

And Connor hated that she'd just given him leverage to push his own agenda, but that didn't prevent him from using it. "I'm not a lawyer, but I know there's something called a presumption of paternity," he'd told her. "If a man is married to a woman when she gives birth, he is presumed, in the eyes of the law, to be the father. If you want to be sure this guy can't make a claim to your babies, you could marry someone else before they're born and put your husband's name on their birth certificates."

Regan had seemed intrigued by the idea at first, but after another moment of consideration, she'd shaken her head. "I don't think I could trick some hapless guy into marrying me."

"You don't have to trick anyone," Connor had assured her then. "You could marry *me*."

Chapter 11

"I was starting to worry that you might have gotten lost," Regan said to Connor, when he returned from his walk the next morning.

Baxter raced over to her chair for the pat on the head that he figured was his due. Then he raced into the living room, no doubt looking for the twins, and upstairs to the master bedroom, where he dropped to the floor to stand guard in his usual position outside the door after finding them.

Connor washed his hands at the sink, then retrieved a mug from the cupboard and filled it with coffee. "I ran into an old friend from high school."

She didn't ask if it was anyone she knew, because there had been little—if any—overlap between their social circles when they were teenagers.

"Do you want me to make you some breakfast?" she asked.

"Mmm…" He sounded intrigued by the offer. "Belgian waffles with fresh berries and powdered sugar would be good."

"You had Belgian waffles at brunch yesterday," she reminded him. "How about scrambled eggs and toast?"

"Eggs and toast sound good, too," he agreed. "But I'll make them."

"I know how to break eggs," she remarked dryly.

"You're also going to be up and down with the twins all day, so why don't you sit for ten minutes and let me take care of breakfast?"

It sounded perfectly reasonable—considerate, even. And yet, she couldn't help but wonder if this was another example of her husband attempting to ensure that they didn't fall into any kind of usual married couple routines.

"I'm not fragile, Connor."

"I know."

"And I don't need you to take care of me."

"Maybe I want to," he said. "It seems only fair, since you spend so much time taking care of Piper and Poppy."

She shrugged. "In that case, I like my eggs with Tabasco mixed in and cheese melted on top."

He set a frying pan on the stove to heat, then retrieved the necessary ingredients from the fridge.

"I'm sorry about last night," she said, as he whisked the eggs. "Not about what happened—or almost happened—but about the interruption."

"There's no need to apologize." He shook a few drops of Tabasco into the egg mixture and continued whisking. "And anyway, it was probably best that we didn't take things too far."

She frowned at that. "How's that best?"

"Getting intimate would only complicate our situation," he explained, as he dropped bread into the slots of the toaster.

"We're married. Isn't physical intimacy usually a key component of that situation?"

"Except that ours isn't a usual marriage," he reminded her.

"I'll concede that sex usually comes before marriage and children," she said.

He poured the egg mixture into the hot pan. "And you only gave birth two weeks ago," he reminded her.

"What does that have to do with anything?"

"Pregnancy and childbirth take a toll on your body, not just physically but emotionally, and it's going to take some time for your hormone levels to recalibrate and—"

"You're not seriously trying to explain postpartum physiology to me, are you?" she asked, cutting him off.

"Of course not," he denied, as he pushed the eggs around in the pan with the spatula. "I just want you to know that I understand what happened last night wasn't really about us as much as it was a reaction to the emotional stresses of the day."

"Have you been reading my pregnancy and child-care books again?"

"I thought you wanted me to read them."

"To learn about the growth and development of the babies—not about what exercises help strengthen pelvic floor muscles or how long it takes for a uterus to shrink back to its normal size," she told him.

"Kegels, and about a month," he said, as he grated cheese over the eggs.

She huffed out a breath. "Okay, you get a gold star for that. But the implication that what happened last night was about nothing more than hormones is insulting to both of us.

"Maybe I was an idiot for wanting to feel close to my husband," she continued. "But you don't need to worry—it's not likely a mistake I'll make again."

She pushed back her chair as the toast popped up.

Connor transferred the eggs to a plate. "Your breakfast is ready," he said.

"I'm not hungry," she snapped, as she moved past him toward the stairs.

Which, of course, only proved that he was right.

Regan was just sliding Estela Lopez's chicken pot pie into the oven when her husband got home from work. She'd moved the babies' bassinet into the kitchen so that she could keep an eye on them while she peeled potatoes—which meant that Baxter was close by, too.

Connor offered her a smile when he entered the kitchen, then set a cylindrical tube on the table as he bent to give Baxter a scratch.

He'd made the first overture, and she knew that the next step needed to be hers.

"I'm sorry," she said.

He rose to his full height again and turned to face her, tucking his hands into his front pockets. "Isn't this how our conversation started this morning?" he asked warily.

She poked at the potatoes with a fork, checking them for doneness. "That's why I'm apologizing."

"Should I tell you again that it's not necessary?"

"But it is," she insisted, setting the fork down again and moving away from the heat of the stove. "Once I had some time to calm down and think about what you were saying, I realized that you were trying to be considerate of my feelings—physically and emotionally."

He nodded slowly.

"So I apologize for overreacting and storming out of the room," she said. And though she knew she should leave it at that, she couldn't resist adding, "But I'm still annoyed that you didn't give me credit for knowing my own feelings."

"Then I will apologize for that," he told her. "And, since we're clearing the air…"

She looked up, waiting for him to continue.

But instead of saying anything else, he pulled her close and kissed her.

It happened so fast—or maybe the move was just so completely unexpected—that she wasn't sure how to respond.

The touch of his mouth, warm and firm, wiped all thought from her mind. Desire tightened in her belly, then slowly unfurled like a ribbon, spreading from her center to the tips of her fingers and toes and every part in between. Just as she started to melt against him, he lifted his mouth from hers and took a deliberate step back.

She caught her bottom lip, still tingling from his kiss, in her teeth and lifted her gaze to his.

"What—" She cleared her throat. "What was that about?"

"I didn't want there to be any doubt about my attraction to you."

"Point taken," she told him.

He nodded. "Good. Also—" he picked up the tube again "—I have a peace offering."

"It doesn't look like flowers or jewelry," she noted, trying to match his casual tone though her insides were all tangled up from his kiss.

"I think it's something you'll like much better."

"Now my curiosity is definitely piqued."

He lifted the cap off the tube and pulled out—

"The blueprints for the kitchen?" she guessed.

He nodded.

He'd shown her the plans a few months earlier, when she'd lamented the sorry state of the kitchen cabinets after one of the doors almost came off its hinges in her hand. Apparently he did aspire to a cooking and eating space that was more than functional, but the price tag of a major renovation had forced him to delay implementing his plans.

"But…you said you couldn't afford to make any big changes right now," she said, hating to remind him of the fact.

"Because I couldn't, but Deacon paid me back for his tuition when his scholarship came through, and now I can."

"I'd say that scholarship was a stroke of luck, but I have no doubt Deacon earned it through hard work rather than good fortune."

Connor busied himself unrolling the papers. "He's always been a good student—diligent and conscientious."

"And it paid off," she said.

"So it would seem," he agreed.

"I know I've said it before, but I'd be happy to—"

"No," he interrupted.

"But I could easily—"

"No," he cut her off again.

Regan huffed out a breath. "Why are you being so bullheaded about this?"

"Because I don't want you to think that I married you for your money."

"The prenup you insisted on made that perfectly clear."

"Good." He nodded again, indicating that the subject was closed. "But there is one other thing we need to discuss."

"What's that?" She dumped the potatoes into a colander to drain the water, then returned them to the pot and added butter and milk.

"If we're going to move ahead with the renovations, you can't stay here," he told her.

She frowned as he retrieved the masher from the utensil holder and took the pot from her to finish the potatoes.

"Why not?"

"Because it's not healthy for you and the babies to be living in a construction zone."

"Where are we supposed to go?" she asked.

"The easiest solution would probably be Miners' Pass." He added salt and pepper to the pot.

"You want me to take Piper and Poppy and move back to my parents' place?"

"Only temporarily," he said.

"Now I have to wonder if your impulsive decision to renovate is about updating the kitchen or putting some distance between us."

"Maybe both," he acknowledged.

"Well, at least you're honest."

Maybe he was right. Maybe the forced proximity during Brielle's visit had stirred up something that would have been better left alone. And maybe a couple of weeks apart would be good for them—with the added benefit that she would come home to a new kitchen.

"So which plan are you going with?" she asked. "The one with the walk-in pantry or the one with the island?"

"Which one do you want?"

"You're letting me choose?"

"It's your kitchen, too," he reminded her.

"I want the island," she immediately responded. Then reconsidered. "But the walk-in pantry is a really nice feature, too."

"I thought you'd say that." He gestured to the blueprints, encouraging her to look at them again.

It was then that she noticed there were now *three* sets of plans.

"I asked Kevin to come up with a new design that incorporated all of the elements you seemed to like best from the first two plans."

She moved for a closer look. "Oh, Connor...this is perfect!"

"And now you know my decision to renovate wasn't as impulsive as you think. In fact, the cabinets should be ready next week, which means these ones need to be ripped out this weekend so the tile people can come on Monday."

She threw her arms around him. "Okay. I'll take the babies to my parents' house," she agreed, because she definitely didn't want their newborn lungs breathing in construction dust and paint fumes. "But I want to help. What can I do?"

"You can pick out the paint."

She was tempted to roll her eyes but managed to restrain herself, because she did like the idea of choosing the color for the walls. And they'd need a new covering for the window—maybe a California-style shutter to replace the roll-up bamboo shade that she suspected had been put in place by the original owners.

The plans called for slate-colored floor tiles, glossy white cabinets with stainless-steel handles and countertops of dark gray granite with blue flecks. She could already picture the finished room with cobalt blue and sunny yellow accents.

"And maybe I can get new dishes for the new kitchen," she said.

"What's wrong with my dishes?"

"Aside from the fact that they're *your* dishes, I don't think there are any two plates or bowls that match."

"Who cares if they match?" He immediately read her response to that question in her expression. "Okay, if you want new dishes for your new kitchen, you can buy new dishes."

"And glasses and cutlery?"

"And glasses and cutlery," he confirmed.

She narrowed her gaze. "Why are you suddenly letting me do this?"

"Because you're right—everything in this kitchen, in this house, was here before you moved in, when it was *my* house. Now it's *our* house, and I want you to do whatever you need to do to feel as if it's your home, too."

"That makes me feel a little bit better about the fact that you're kicking me out of *our* house for the next couple of weeks," she said.

"You wanted the new kitchen," he reminded her.

"Then I guess the lesson to be learned from this is that I shouldn't give up hope of getting what I want." She leaned across the counter and brushed her lips over his. "A lesson I will definitely keep in mind."

With a light step and smug smile, she moved away to take the casserole out of the oven, making Connor suspect that she wasn't only thinking about the kitchen renovation.

It felt strange to be back in her parents' house again.

Though she'd lived there for three years prior to marrying Connor and moving in with him, the mansion had never felt like home. It was an impressive structure built with meticulous attention by reputable craftsmen, the interior professionally finished and elaborately decorated with no expense spared. The result was a stunning presentation suitable to a spread in *Architectural Digest* but lacking any sense of history or feeling of warmth.

She'd set up the portable playpen in the great room, close enough to the fire to ensure the babies wouldn't catch a chill, while she brought in the rest of their things. The housekeeper had helped unload the cases from her trunk and promised to move them upstairs as soon as she had Regan's bed made up. Ordinarily Regan would have insisted on carrying them herself, but as the babies were starting to fuss for their dinner, she was grateful for Greta's help.

She'd finished nursing and had settled them down again when she heard the door from the garage open and the voices of her parents as they came in. From the sound of it, she was the topic of their conversation.

"—she was coming?" Ben asked.

"No," his wife replied. "If I'd known she was coming, I would have told you."

"Maybe it's not her car."

Margaret huffed out a breath. "Of course it's her car."

"Hi, Mom. Hi, Dad," she called out.

Her mother's heels clicked on the marble tile as she drew nearer.

Margaret stopped abruptly and pivoted to look at her husband. "I told you this would happen."

"Let's not jump to conclusions," Ben cautioned.

"What do you think happened?" Regan asked curiously.

Her mother waved a hand at the pile of bags and baby paraphernalia beside the door—the size of which had already been reduced by half by the diligent efforts of the housekeeper.

"Obviously you've left your husband. Not that I'm surprised, really, except maybe by the fact that the marriage lasted a whole six months."

"Please, Mom. Don't hold back—tell me what you really think."

"I'm sorry," Margaret said, not sounding sorry at all. "But if you'd bothered to talk to me before running off and getting married, I would have told you that you were making a mistake and you wouldn't be in this mess right now."

"I didn't leave my husband, and I'm not in a mess," Regan told her, speaking slowly and carefully so as not to reveal the hurt and disappointment elicited by her mother's assumptions. "The only mess is going to be in our kitchen, while Connor oversees the renovations. He suggested that I bring Piper and Poppy here for a couple of weeks so that we're not living in a construction zone."

There was a moment of stilted silence as her parents digested the information.

"Well, what was I supposed to think?" Margaret demanded without apology.

"I don't know," Regan admitted. "But I didn't expect you would immediately jump to the conclusion that my marriage had fallen apart."

"You might have called first to let someone know your plans," Ben suggested, his effort to smooth over the tension clearly placing the blame at Regan's feet.

"I did," she said. "I talked to Celeste."

"Has Greta made up your room?" Margaret asked.

"She said that she would," Regan replied. "But I can probably stay at Crooked Creek with Spencer and Kenzie, if you'd prefer."

"Don't be silly," her mother chided. "You don't want to be out in the middle of nowhere. Not to mention that we've got a lot more room for you and the twins here."

Regan nodded, because the latter statement at least was true. As for being out in the middle of nowhere— right now she wanted to be anywhere but here, but she wasn't foolish enough to bundle up her babies and pack up all their stuff again just because her feelings were hurt.

"I'll let Celeste know she can put dinner on the table," Margaret said now.

"She didn't mean anything by it," Ben said, when his wife had gone.

Regan just shook her head. "I don't understand. I thought you were happy that I married Connor."

"Under the circumstances, it seemed the best course of action," he said.

The circumstances being that she was pregnant, and they'd assumed—because she'd let them—that Connor was the father of her babies.

"He's a good man," Regan said now. "And I wouldn't have married him if I didn't believe we could make our marriage work."

He nodded. "I'm glad to hear it."

"And he's a wonderful father."

"Anyone who's ever seen him with your babies would agree with that," Ben assured her.

It was only later, when she was alone upstairs in her bed, that she wondered about his reference to Piper and Poppy as "her" babies.

Was it possible that her father knew more about her relationship with Connor than she'd told him?

"Damn, the house is quiet."

Connor didn't realize he'd spoken aloud until Baxter lifted his head off his paws and whined in agreement. He didn't believe the dog actually understood what he was saying, but he suspected his canine companion was responding to the regret in his tone.

"Maybe I didn't think this through enough," he acknowledged with a sigh. "I wanted to get the kitchen done because it seemed to mean a lot to Regan, but I also figured it would be easier to keep my hands off her if she was out of the house." He shook his head. "I just didn't expect it to feel so empty without her."

Baxter belly-shuffled closer, so that he was at his master's feet. Connor reached down and patted the dog's head.

Baxter immediately rolled over, exposing his belly for a rub.

Connor laughed and obliged. "Just like old times, huh? Just you and me?"

The dog whined again.

"It wasn't so bad back then, was it? At least we got to sleep through the night without being awakened by babies wanting to be fed or changed."

The dog looked at him with soulful eyes, clearly unconvinced.

"Okay, yeah. Maybe it didn't seem so bad back then because we didn't know anything different."

Baxter lowered his chin onto the top of Connor's foot.

"I'll get to work on the kitchen first thing in the morning," he promised. "Because the sooner I get started, the sooner I can finish, and Regan and Piper and Poppy can come home."

Chapter 12

Connor had just poured his first cup of coffee—not decaf but the real stuff, which he'd snuck into the house after a string of sleep-deprived nights made it almost impossible to keep his eyes open during the day—when there was a knock at the door.

"We've got an early-morning visitor," he said to Baxter, who was already jumping up at the front door.

"None of that," he said, giving the hand signal for sit.

The dog sat, though his body fairly vibrated with suppressed energy.

Connor unlocked and pulled open the door, surprised to see his boss on the other side of the threshold. "Good morning, Sheriff."

"Reid," he said, confirming that he wasn't at the door for any kind of official business. "I heard you talking to Kowalski about a demolition project you're tackling this weekend and thought maybe you could use a hand."

"Your wife doesn't have a list of chores for you at home?" Connor asked, opening the door wider to let him in.

"There's always a list," Reid said, and grinned at the dog sitting but not at all patiently inside the foyer.

He offered his hand for the dog to sniff, which Baxter did and gave his approval with a lick. The sheriff chuckled and scratched him under the chin.

"But Katelyn took Tessa out to the Circle G for a visit," Reid explained. "So she's not home today to remind me about all the things on the list."

Connor led the way to the kitchen. "So you came here to help with my list instead?"

"Tearing things apart is always more fun than putting them back together," Reid noted. "Although I have to say, it seems like an odd time to be tackling kitchen renovations—barely three weeks after the birth of twin daughters."

"Yeah," Connor agreed. He found another coffee mug in one of the boxes that he'd used to empty the cabinets and held it up, a silent question.

Reid nodded.

"But Regan would argue that updating the space is twenty years overdue," Connor continued, as he filled the second mug. "Notwithstanding the fact that I've only owned the house for three."

"Katelyn wouldn't move into our new place until all the work we wanted to do had been done. Thankfully, most of it was cosmetic."

"This is going to be a complete overhaul," Connor told him.

"You want to salvage the cabinets?" Reid asked.

He shook his head. "Not worth salvaging. Everything's going in the Dumpster."

"That will speed things up considerably," Reid said.

What also sped things up considerably was having an extra body pitching in. By the time they broke for lunch—Connor popped out to pick up Jo's Pizza—all of the top cabinets and half of the bottom had been removed and hauled out to the Dumpster.

As Connor closed the lid on the empty pizza box, the sheriff's phone chimed to indicate a message.

"Kate texted me a picture of Tessa with Ava, Max and Sam," Reid said, turning his phone around so Connor could see the screen. "Tessa absolutely adores the triplets and is constantly asking to go see the babies. In fact, I think her favorite word now is *babies*. Although her first word was *Da-da*," he added, with a grin.

"Does it make you think about giving her a brother or sister?" Connor wondered.

"Sure," Reid agreed, as he tucked his phone away again. "But Katelyn's not yet on board with that plan. In all fairness, that might be because she tackles most of the childcare responsibilities. I've been encouraging her to check out the new daycare, but she insists that Tessa's too young to be left with strangers."

"A valid consideration," Connor noted, tugging his work gloves on again. "Though not a choice all parents can make."

Reid nodded. "But getting back to your question, yeah, I think Tessa would benefit from having a sibling."

"It is a unique bond," Connor noted. "Though I'll be the first to admit, I was a little panicked about the prospect of twins—"

"Especially twin girls, I'd bet," the sheriff interjected.

"You'd be right," Connor agreed. "But now I can

appreciate how lucky Piper and Poppy are to have one another."

"They are lucky," Reid remarked. "I was an only child, so I didn't grow up with the benefit of knowing there was someone else who would always have my back. Of course, Katelyn had a sister and two brothers, so she wished sometimes that she was an only child."

Connor chuckled at that. "Well, there were eight years between me and Deacon, so that likely helped minimize any sibling rivalry."

"Speaking of—is your brother coming home for the summer?"

He nodded. "He was hoping to land a job in New York, something in the legal field for experience to add to his résumé, but nothing panned out."

"Katelyn's practice is growing like crazy, and she's been talking about wanting to hire a junior lawyer to help with research and case prep," Reid said. His wife was widely regarded as one of the top attorneys in the area and, as a result, her services were in great demand. "You should tell him to send his résumé to her."

"Deacon's hardly a junior lawyer," Connor pointed out. "He's only just finishing his first year of law school."

"First year at Columbia," his boss clarified. "That seems to me a pretty good recommendation right there."

"Well, he's obviously smarter than me, or I would have waited to tackle this renovation until he was home to help."

"On the other hand, there are certain therapeutic benefits of physical labor, which I'm sure you can appreciate right now."

Connor paused with the sledgehammer on his shoulder. "You're not really asking about my sex life, are you?"

"I don't need to ask," Reid told him. "I've been there. And I swear, those six weeks postpartum while we waited for the doctor to give us the green light were the longest six weeks of my life."

Six weeks?

Connor and Regan had been married for more than *six months* and hadn't even consummated their marriage—not that he had any intention of admitting that to his boss.

Instead, he responded by lifting the sledgehammer off his shoulder and heaving it at the wall marked to come down.

The plaster cracked and the sheriff laughed.

By her third day at Miners' Pass, most of the sting of her mother's words had faded, allowing Regan to acknowledge that it wasn't a horrible place to wait out the renovations. She didn't see much of her parents, who always went to the office early and came home late, but Celeste and Greta were more than happy to help with anything she needed or even just spend some time cuddling with the babies when they had nothing else to do.

But Monday was Celeste's grocery shopping day, so Regan had decided to go into town, too. She'd only been back a little while when Greta escorted a visitor to the great room, where Regan spent most of her time hanging out during the day.

"What are you doing here?" she asked, as pleased as she was surprised to see her husband.

"I came by to see if you've picked a paint color yet."

"As a matter of fact, I have." She reached into the side pocket of the diaper bag that was always close at hand and pulled out an assortment of paint chips. "I finally tried out that twin baby carrier we got from Alyssa and Jason, and Piper and Poppy had a great time being carted around the hardware store." She fanned out the samples, looking for the one she'd marked, then plucked it out of the pile and offered it to him. "Are you prepping to paint already?"

"Not even close," he admitted.

She lifted a brow. "So why are you really here?"

He shoved the paint chip in his back pocket without even looking at it. "Because I missed you."

"Oh." She felt an unexpected little flutter in her belly.

"Even with all the hammering and banging going on, I find myself listening for the familiar sounds of Piper and Poppy waking up or growing restless," he told her.

"You miss the babies," she realized, as the flutter faded away.

"I miss all of you," he clarified. "I miss the scent of your shampoo in the bathroom in the morning, the sound of your humming in the kitchen and the way your smile shines in your eyes."

And the flutter was back.

But still, she felt compelled to point out: "I don't hum."

He smiled. "Yeah, you do."

"And if you miss me, it's your own fault," she said. "Because you sent me away."

"I didn't know how empty the house was going to feel without you."

"You still have Baxter."

"He misses you as much as I do," he told her. "And a moping dog isn't very good company."

"You could bring him with you for a visit sometime," she said.

He looked pointedly at the cream-colored suede furniture on the ivory carpet and shook his head. "I don't think so."

"Then maybe I'll bring Piper and Poppy to your place—"

"*Our* place," he reminded her.

"—and take him out for a walk one day."

"He'd love that," Connor said. "But are you sure you can manage two babies and a dog?"

"With the twin carrier, I can," she assured him. "And speaking of the twins, I'm guessing you'd like to see them."

He grinned. "Well, I have no intention of leaving until I do."

She took his hand and led him upstairs. "Not because I want you to leave," she assured him. Piper and Poppy were sharing her former bedroom, where she'd taken up temporary residence again, and were snuggled together in the bassinet near the head of her bed. On the other side of the room was a rocking chair that Greta had brought up for the new mom.

Connor stood for a long moment, just looking at the sleeping babies. "I swear they've grown in the past three days." Though he whispered the remark, Piper stirred as if she'd heard and recognized her daddy's voice.

"Considering how often they're eating, I wouldn't be surprised," Regan told him. "But they're sleeping a little bit longer now. Last night it was almost five hours."

"Have they been asleep for long now?" he asked.

"I think what you really want to know is, are they going to be waking up soon?"

"Are they?"

She lifted a shoulder. "New moms who have their

three-week-old babies on any kind of schedule are obviously better moms than me."

He shook his head. "There is no better mom than you."

"And that's why I'm going to risk breaking the rule about not disturbing a sleeping baby," she said, reaching down and gently lifting Piper out of the bassinet.

"But the books—"

"I'm going to hide those books from you," she said, gesturing toward the rocking chair.

He sat down and she transferred Piper to him, then went back to the bassinet for Poppy.

"They've had their baths already today," he noted.

"Maybe it's the scent of *their* shampoo that you remember," she teased.

"I can remember more than one scent," he told her. "Your shampoo smells like apples."

Poppy exhaled a quiet sigh and snuggled closer to her daddy's chest. Piper yawned.

"I think they missed you, too," Regan said quietly.

"I could sit here like this for hours," he said. "But that isn't going to get the new drywall taped and mudded."

"You're doing that yourself?"

He nodded. "It's not hard work, just messy, and it cuts down on the cost of labor."

"And you're going to tackle that tonight?"

"I'm going to get started anyway, as soon as I figure out what I'm doing for food."

"You could stay and have dinner with me," she suggested. "You know Celeste always makes enough for unexpected guests."

"I didn't come here to beg a meal," he assured her.

"But it would be nice to eat something that wasn't Wheaties."

"Your dinner plan was Wheaties?"

"No, but I probably would have ended up eating Wheaties because I didn't have a dinner plan. And because I don't have a stove," he said, reminding her that the appliances had been taken out of the kitchen along with everything else.

"Then this is your lucky day," Regan said. "Because Celeste has a box of Frosted Flakes in the cupboard."

"Frosted Flakes are more a dessert than a main course."

"Beggars can't be choosers," she said.

Connor knew she was only teasing in quoting the old proverb, but there was something about being in this house that made him feel like a beggar—though he suspected a vagrant would never get past the housekeeper at the front door.

His mother, a big admirer of Eleanor Roosevelt, would have pointed out that no one could make him feel unworthy without his consent. He knew it was true, that his insecurities said more about him than anyone else. And Regan had never said or done anything to indicate that she thought any less of him because he was "that no-good Neal boy" from "the wrong side of the tracks."

So he shook off the unease and carefully settled Piper and Poppy back in their bassinet, then followed his wife downstairs again and into the kitchen.

"Connor's going to stay for dinner," Regan said to the cook, who was drizzling caramel sauce over the top of a pie.

"And dessert," he added.

"You like pecan pie?" Celeste guessed.

"I like everything you make," he assured her.

She set the pie aside and reached into the cupboard for two plates. "It'll just take me a minute to set the table."

"The kitchen table is fine," Regan said, pulling open a drawer to retrieve cutlery.

"You know how your parents feel about eating in the kitchen," Celeste chided.

"I do, and since they're not going to be home for dinner, we'd like to eat in the kitchen—with you."

"You can eat wherever you like," the cook agreed. "But I'm having dinner in my room with *Top Chef.*"

"This is the first you've mentioned wanting to watch a cooking show tonight," Regan remarked.

"Because I didn't want you to have to eat your dinner alone. Since you now have the company of your handsome husband, you won't miss mine."

"Did you hear that?" Connor said to his wife. "She thinks I'm handsome."

"Just about handsome enough for my beautiful girl," Celeste confirmed.

"That's me," Regan told him.

The cook chuckled. "Now you two sit down and enjoy your dinner," she said, as she filled their plates with crispy honey garlic chicken, roasted potatoes and steamed broccoli.

Connor and Regan lingered over the meal, discussing all manner of topics.

"I'm doing all the talking," Connor realized, when his plate was half empty.

"Because your life is so much more interesting than mine right now," she told him. "You have an exciting job, a construction project underway and a faithful canine companion at home. My days are taken up by two admittedly adorable infants who eat, sleep, pee and poop—not necessarily in that order."

He chuckled, but then his expression turned serious. "Do you miss work?"

"Not yet," she said. "Right now I'm so tired out from keeping up with Piper and Poppy that the idea of going into the office and trying to make sense of numbers makes my head hurt."

She frowned as she lifted her glass of water to her lips. "But now that I think about it, there was a weird message on my voice mail the other day from one of the junior accountants at work. I haven't had a chance to call him back yet, but Travis's message said something about a scholarship fund."

The delicious chicken dinner suddenly felt like a lead weight in Connor's stomach. "He shouldn't be bothering you with trivial inquiries when you're on mat leave," he said. "Isn't there someone else who can answer his questions?"

"My father, probably," she said.

"Then you should let your father deal with it."

She nodded. "Yeah. When I get a chance to call Travis back, I'll tell him to talk to my dad."

"Or tell your dad about the call," he suggested. "And let him handle it."

"That's another option," she agreed.

He pushed his chair away from the table and stood up to clear away their plates.

"I suppose you want that pie now?" Regan asked.

"Actually, I didn't realize how late it was getting to be," he said. "If I want to make any progress with that drywall tonight, I should probably be heading out."

"You could take a slice with you," she offered. "We won't call it a doggy bag, so you won't feel obligated to share it with Baxter."

"I'd love to," he said. "It'll be my reward for getting the first layer of mud done."

She found a knife and cut a thick wedge of pie, which she slid into a plastic container. Just as she snapped the lid on, a soft, plaintive cry came through the baby monitor on the table.

"Well, we actually got through a meal without interruption," she said.

"It was a great meal," he said. "Thanks for asking me to stay."

"Thanks for stopping by." She started to walk with him to the door, but even he could tell that the cries were growing louder and more insistent. She folded an arm across her chest, her cheeks suddenly turning pink. "Letdown."

And because he'd read the books, he knew what that meant. "You better go see to the babies."

She nodded and turned to hurry up the stairs.

Connor was admittedly sorry that he hadn't had the chance to steal a goodbye kiss, but at the moment he had more pressing concerns. And a call to his father-in-law was at the top of the list.

When the two men had struck their deal, Connor hadn't given any thought to the possibility that Regan—Blake Mining's CFO—might question why a check written by her father from a company account had been deposited into an account with her husband's brother's name on it. So he hoped like hell Ben Channing had given the matter some thought—and had a credible explanation ready for his daughter if one was required.

Chapter 13

Detouring to Miners' Pass became part of Connor's routine over the next couple of weeks. He never stayed long, as he was anxious to get back to work on the kitchen so that Regan and the twins could come home. But it was always worth the trip, just to spend a few minutes with them—with the added benefit of a fabulous meal that beat any kind of takeout.

He was usually gone before Regan's parents got home from the office. It seemed a shame to him that they'd spent so much money to build a beautiful home that was empty most of the time, but he got the impression that the display of wealth was almost more important to Margaret than the enjoyment of it.

In any event, he didn't mind not crossing paths with Ben and Margaret—no doubt at least in part because of his own guilt with respect to the secret he was keeping from his wife. No matter how many times Connor tried to reassure himself that the money Ben Channing had put up for Deacon's scholarship had nothing to do with his relationship with Regan, he knew it wasn't really true.

There would have been no scholarship if he hadn't convinced Regan to marry him, and lately, he'd found himself wishing that he'd never entered into any sort of agreement with his now father-in-law. He didn't regret his marriage to Regan. He just wished the exchange of vows had happened for different reasons.

"You're rather introspective tonight," she noted.

"Sorry," he said. "I was just making a mental list of a few last things that I need to pick up at the hardware store on the way home."

"Does *a few last things* mean that the renovation is almost complete?"

He nodded. "Fingers crossed, you'll be able to see the completed project on Saturday."

"You've made a lot of progress in two weeks, then," she said.

"I had a powerful incentive."

Regan smiled. "I can't wait to see it."

"You really haven't checked on the progress at all?"

He found it hard to believe that she hadn't even peeked when she'd come by the house, as she'd done a few times, to take Baxter for walks in the middle of the day. He had all entrances to the kitchen area blocked off with plastic to keep the dust and debris contained, but it would be easy enough to pull back the plastic and take a look. He'd taken pictures to document the progress, but she'd insisted that she didn't want to see those, either, until after.

She shook her head now in response to his question. "I was tempted," she admitted. "But I decided I'd rather wait."

"Well, I think you're going to be pleased. And Baxter is going to be so excited when you come home—the house has been so empty without you."

"Remember you said that," Regan teased. "Because we'll all likely be tripping over one another when your brother comes home."

"It won't be so bad," Connor said. "Especially as he has a full-time job for the summer."

"Where's he going to be working?"

"At Katelyn Davidson's law office."

"That's great," she said.

Her enthusiasm seemed genuine, prompting him to ask, "You don't mind that he's going to be spending his days with your archenemy."

"Archenemy?" she echoed, amused. "Am I a comic book character now?"

"Hmm...now that you mention it, I wouldn't mind seeing you in a spandex jumpsuit."

"Not going to happen," she assured him.

"Disappointing," he said. "But I was only referring to the history between the Blakes and the Gilmores."

"There's some bad blood there, as a result of which I can't imagine ever being best friends with a Gilmore," Regan acknowledged. "But it has nothing to do with me or Katelyn, even if she was a Gilmore before she married the sheriff."

"What about your sister and Liam?" he asked.

She seemed taken aback by the question. "Why would you ask that?"

"The way she reacted to the mention of his name

when you were talking about the inn, I got the impression there might be some history there."

"No." She shook her head. "There's no history between Brie and Liam."

"Brie and Caleb, then," he guessed.

"So when is Deacon coming home?" she asked.

It was hardly a subtle effort to shift the topic of conversation, but Connor obliged. "His last exam is May ninth, and he flies back on the tenth."

"I'm sure he's eager to get home."

"And excited to meet his nieces," Connor told her.

"I'm glad you think so," Regan said. "Because I was hoping we could ask him to be Piper and Poppy's godfather."

"Really?"

She nodded. "Brie was the obvious choice for godmother, because she's my only sister, and since Deacon is your only brother, well, it just made sense to me. What do you think?"

"I think it's a great idea," he agreed.

"Then the next order of business is to actually schedule a date for the baptism."

"You can work that out with your sister," he said. "Just tell me when and where."

She nodded. "And you should be forewarned—my parents have already said they'd like to have a party here after the event."

"You say that as if you expect me to object," he noted.

"I just thought we should do something for our daughters at our house."

"Which I wouldn't object to, either," he assured her.

"But your parents have a lot more space—especially if the party had to be moved indoors."

"They also have Celeste," she realized.

"Well, yeah."

"I think she's the real reason you want to have the party here, because you know she'll be in charge of the food."

"That might have been a consideration," he allowed.

She grinned. "In which case I will say, you're a very smart man, Connor Neal."

"What's going on here?" Regan asked, sidling between a vacant stool at the bar and the one upon which her husband was seated.

It was Friday—the day before the big unveiling he'd promised—so she'd been understandably surprised to get the call from the owner of Diggers' Bar & Grill revealing that Connor was at the bar. Duke had asked if she could pick up her husband because he was in no condition to drive home and he didn't trust the deputy would be able to find his way if he walked.

"We're shelebrating."

She looked pointedly from the empty stool on her side to the trio of vacant seats on his other side. "We?"

"Well, everyone elsh is gone now."

Duke carried a steaming carafe of coffee over to top up the cup on the bar in front of Connor.

"He didn't have a lot to drink," the bartender said, shaking his head. "I've never known a grown man who was such a lightweight."

"How much isn't a lot?" she asked.

"Two beers, and then a couple of shots. It was the shots that seemed to do him in."

"Well, you said it," agreed Regan. "He's not much of a drinker."

And knowing that he grew up with a stepfather who got angry and belligerent when he was drunk, she understood why.

She turned her attention back to her husband. "What were you celebrating?"

"Kowalshki's gettin' married."

"That's happy news—and a good reason to celebrate," Regan acknowledged.

"Everyone was goin' for drinks," he explained. "I couldn't say no."

"Of course not," she agreed. "Though next time you might want to say no to the shots."

"Damn Shack Daniels."

She bit back a smile and looked at the bartender again. "Has he paid his tab?"

"Sheriff took care of it," Duke said.

She nodded and nudged her hip against Connor's thigh. "Let's get you home."

He put his feet on the ground, then reached out to grasp the edge of the bar to steady himself.

"You are a lightweight, aren't you?" she mused.

"Tired," he said. "Didn't sleep mush last night. Wanted to get the kitshen done."

She took his arm to guide him to the door. "Is it done?"

He nodded. "Celeste gave me a reshipee so I could make dinner for you tomorrow."

"A nice idea," she said, touched that he would want

to cook the first meal for her in the new kitchen. "But maybe we should wait and see how hungover you are in the morning before we make any plans."

"You can come home now," he said.

"I'm taking you home right now," she promised, opening the passenger-side door of her SUV for him.

He folded himself into the seat, then turned to look behind him. "Where's the girls?"

"At my parents' place."

"Your parents are lookin' after them?"

She snorted. "I'd have to be drunker than you are to let that happen."

He frowned, clearly not understanding.

"Celeste is looking after them."

"Ahh." He nodded. "Celeste took care of you when you were a baby."

"Celeste still takes care of me—of all of us," Regan said.

"I wish we had a Celeste."

"My parents offered to pay her salary and have her help us out for a year," she reminded him.

"Your father thinks he can buy anything…or anyone."

She frowned at the bitter edge underlying the muttered words. "What are you talking about?"

"Nothin'."

"It sounded like something to me."

But he'd closed his eyes, and he didn't say anything else until they were almost home. "I have a 'feshun to make."

She turned into the driveway. "Is it something you're going to regret telling me when you're sober?" she wondered.

"I didn't jus' marry you to give your babies a father," he confided.

She turned off the ignition. "So why did you marry me?"

"I've hadda crush on you sinch high shcool."

"High school?" she echoed, surprised. "We barely knew each other in high school."

"You don't remember." He slapped a hand against his chest. "I'm wounded."

"I have no doubt your head is going to feel wounded in the morning," she told him. "But what is it you think I don't remember?"

"Twelfth grade calculus."

She got out of the car and went around to the passenger side to help him do the same. "I remember," she assured him. "I tutored you during lunch period on Tuesdays and Thursdays, and sometimes after school on Wednesdays."

"I got an A. Well, an A-minus, acshally, but I figured it counted."

"I know. You offered to take me out for ice cream to celebrate."

He nodded, paying careful attention to the steps as he climbed them. "But you had plans with Brett Tanner. Goin' to see 'Bill & Ted's Exshellent Avenshure.'"

She paused with her key in the lock. "How could you possibly remember such a trivial detail after so many years?"

"I hated Brett Tanner," he said. "Or maybe I jus' hated that you liked him."

She opened the door and hit the light switch inside. Baxter, waiting—as always—on the other side of the door, gave a happy bark and danced around them in circles.

Regan fussed over the dog for a minute while Connor struggled to take off his boots. When he'd finally accomplished that task, she followed him up the stairs.

Apparently he'd resumed sleeping in the master bedroom after she'd gone, because he headed in that direction and collapsed on top of the mattress.

"Don't fall asleep just yet," she warned.

"'kay."

She went across the hall to the bathroom, returning with a cup of water and a couple of Tylenol. "Sit up and take these."

He eased himself into sitting position against the headboard. She dropped the tablets in his hand, then gave him the cup. He tossed back the pills and drank down the water.

She took the empty cup back to the bathroom and refilled it, then set it on the table beside the bed.

"Are you going to get under those covers or sleep on top of them?" she asked.

"You sleep with me?"

"Not tonight," she said. "I need to get back to our babies."

"Pretty babies," he said. "Jus' like their mama."

"You're talkative when you're drunk," she mused. "I'll have to remember that."

"I don't get drunk," he denied. "No more'n two beers—" he held up two fingers and squinted at them as if he wasn't quite sure it was the right number "—ever."

"You should have told that to your pal Shack Daniels."

He shook his head. "Not my pal."

She really did need to get back to Piper and Poppy, but she was curious about something he'd said earlier. She perched on the edge of the mattress and said, "What does your high school crush have to do with your proposal?"

"I finally got the mos' pop'lar girl in shcool to go out with me."

"I wasn't the most popular girl," she denied. "In fact, I hardly dated in high school." Because even as a teenager, she'd been focused on getting into a good college and earning a degree so that she could go to work with her parents at Blake Mining.

"You were tight with Brett Tanner."

"Not as tight as he wanted people to think," she confided.

"It doesn' matter. You lived in one of the biggest houses in town…an' I was a loser from the wrong shide of the tracks."

"You were never a loser," she said, shocked that he could ever have thought so little of himself. "And that expression—the wrong side of the tracks—never made any sense to me. Especially considering that the trains stopped running through Haven more than fifty years ago."

"But people still 'member where they ran."

"For what it's worth, I thought you were kind of cute back in high school," she confided.

"Cute?" he echoed.

"All my friends did, too," she told him.

"Cute?" he said again, as if the word was somehow distasteful.

"But in an edgy kind of way," she said. "Of course, bad boys have always been the downfall of good girls."

"An' you were the goodest of the good girls, weren't you?"

"I was a rule follower," she acknowledged. "Most of the time, anyway."

"When have you not followed the rules?" he wondered.

"My first date with you."

His brow furrowed, as if he was struggling to remember. "The wedding chapel in Reno?"

She nodded. "Getting married was the craziest thing I'd ever done on a first date."

"Prob'ly mine, too."

"Only probably?"

"I'm a bad boy, 'member?"

She took the throw from the rocking chair and draped it over him. "You keep telling yourself that."

"But it was defin'ly—" his eyes drifted shut "—my best first date ever."

She waited until she was sure he was asleep, then she leaned over and touched her lips to his forehead. "Mine, too."

"You don't look any the worse for wear," Regan remarked when Connor came outside to greet her the next day.

"I figured it was too much to hope that you'd let me forget about last night."

"Actually, I'm curious to know how much you remember."

"All of it." He opened the back door of her SUV and reached inside to unclip Piper's car seat, then he went around to the other side and did the same to Poppy's. "I think. After a handful of Tylenol and a gallon of water this morning, my head stopped pounding enough for the memories to become clearer."

She hefted the diaper bag onto her shoulder and followed him into the house.

Baxter could barely contain his excitement when Connor took the babies into the house. Although Regan had brought the twins with her when she came to take him for his walks, he seemed to sense that this time was different—that they were finally home—and he was in doggy heaven.

"But thank you," Connor said to her now. "Although I'm fairly confident I could have found my own way home last night, I appreciate you coming to get me."

"It was my pleasure," she said.

His gaze narrowed. "And now I'm wondering if there are some gaps in my memory."

"Maybe I'm just happy to be home," she told him. "And eager to see the new kitchen."

"Then I won't make you wait any longer," he said, leading the way.

She'd seen the plans, of course, so she had a general idea of what to expect. She'd approved of the floor tile and cabinet style and granite he'd chosen, but the mental image she'd pieced together in her mind didn't do justice to the final result.

"This is incredible," she said, gliding her fingertips along the beveled edge of the countertop. She opened a cupboard, appreciating the smooth movement of the hinge, and smiled when she saw that the new dishes she'd ordered were stacked neatly inside.

But not all of them.

Two place settings had been set out on the island, with the shiny new cutlery set on top of sunny-yellow napkins. A bouquet of daffodils was stuffed into a clear vase in the corner.

"You do good work, Deputy."

He looked pleased with the compliment.

"And—do I smell something cooking?"

He nodded. "Chicken with roasted potatoes. Celeste promised it was a foolproof recipe, so if it doesn't taste as good as hers, I'm blaming the new oven."

"Don't you mean she promised it was a foolproof reshipee?" she teased.

He shook his head. "Are you ever going to let me forget about last night?"

"I won't say another word."

But truthfully, she didn't want to forget about last night—or at least not about the revelation he'd made. Because if it was true that he'd had a crush on her in high school, maybe it wasn't outside the realm of possibility that he might develop real feelings for her now. As she'd developed real feelings for him.

And then maybe, someday, their marriage of convenience would become something more.

Chapter 14

Every detail of The Stagecoach Inn reflected elegance and indulgence, and excited butterflies winged around inside Regan's belly as she checked in at the double pedestal desk. After the formalities were taken care of, she'd been invited to a wine and cheese reception for guests in the library, but she'd opted to explore the main lobby on her own while she waited for her husband to arrive.

She glanced at her watch. 5:58.

Connor was supposed to meet her at six o'clock, but because she'd gotten there early, she'd spent the last twelve minutes pretending she wasn't watching the time. She thought about taking a leisurely stroll down the street, to distract herself for a few minutes, but she didn't trust Connor to wait if he showed up at six o'clock and she wasn't there.

Instead she perched on the edge of a butter leather

sofa facing the stone fireplace and pulled her phone out of her pocket to send a brief text message to her sister.

Maybe this was a bad idea.

Brie immediately replied:

Don't u dare chicken out!

I'm not chi

That was as far as she got in typing her reply before Connor stepped through the front door.

She tucked the phone back into her pocket and stood up.

"Hey." He smiled when he saw her, and the curve of his lips somehow managed to reassure her while also releasing a kaleidoscope of butterflies in her belly.

"What's going on?" he asked. "Where are Piper and Poppy?"

"They're at home with the babysitters."

His brows lifted. "We have babysitters?"

She nodded. "Alyssa and Jason thought looking after the twins would give them a crash course in parenting, to help prepare them for the arrival of their own baby."

"Okay, but why are we here?"

"Because it's our anniversary."

He frowned at that. "We got married in September."

"The twenty-sixth," she confirmed. "Which makes today our seven-month anniversary."

"I didn't know that was a thing," he said, sounding worried. "Was I supposed to get you a card? Send flowers?"

She shook her head. "I didn't get you anything, either. This—" she held up an antique key "—is a belated-wedding-slash-early-anniversary gift from my sister."

He swallowed. "She got us a hotel room?"

"The luxury suite," Regan clarified, taking his hand and leading him up the stairs toward their accommodations on the top floor.

"It's a nice idea," he acknowledged, his steps slowing as they approached the second-floor landing. "But..."

She nodded, understanding everything that was implied by that single word. But theirs wasn't a traditional marriage. It wasn't even a *real* marriage. Although she knew that Brie had booked the suite for them in an effort to change that.

"Just come and see the room," she urged.

She'd already checked in and been escorted to the suite by Liam Gilmore, the hotel's owner doing double-duty as bellhop. He'd given her a brief history of the hotel as they climbed to the upper level, a scripted speech that filled what would likely have been an awkward silence otherwise.

She might have made some appropriate comment when he was done, but then he opened the door of the suite and she'd been rendered speechless. The plaque on the wall beside the door identified Wild Bill's Getaway Suite, but everything inside the space screamed luxury and elegance.

The floor of the foyer was covered in an intricate pattern of mosaic tile; the walls were painted a pale shade of gold and set off by wide white trim. Beyond the foyer was a carpeted open-concept sitting area that Liam had called a parlor, with an antique-looking sofa and chaise lounge facing the white marble fireplace over which was mounted an enormous flat-screen TV.

Beyond the parlor was the bath, with more white marble, lots of glass and shiny chrome and even a crystal chandelier. On the other side of the bath was the bedroom, which boasted a second fireplace—this one with a dark marble surround, a king-size pediment poster bed flanked by matching end tables, a wide wardrobe and a makeup vanity set with padded stool.

"This is…impressive," Connor said. Then, his tone almost apologetic, he added, "But we can't stay."

"Do you want to explain why to my sister, who prepaid for two nights?" she asked.

"She knows you're nursing Piper and Poppy. It should be simple enough to explain that you can't be away from them for two days."

"She also knows I've got a pump. And there's enough breast milk in the freezer at home for a week." She'd finally overcome her opposition to occasional bottle feeding after a visit from Macy Clayton—a single mom of triplets—who wanted to reassure Regan that there were other "moms of multiples" out there who could be a great resource when she had questions or concerns about raising her twins. (Coincidentally, Macy was also the manager of the Stagecoach Inn—and dating Liam Gilmore.) Macy had urged Regan not to demand too much of herself and suggested that if her husband was willing to give a baby a bottle, she should let him—and not feel guilty but grateful.

"What about Baxter?"

"Jason promised to walk him twice a day. I even mapped out Baxter's usual route for him."

"But all I've got are the clothes on my back."

"I packed a bag for you," she said. "It's in the bedroom."

"I guess that shoots down all my arguments," Connor acknowledged, sounding more resigned than pleased at the prospect of being alone with his wife.

And Regan was suddenly assailed by doubts, too.

Being married was both easier and harder than she'd anticipated when she'd accepted the deputy's impulsive proposal.

It was easier because Connor had truly become her partner in parenting Piper and Poppy. He obviously adored the two little girls—and the feeling was mutual. Their faces lit up whenever he walked into a room and they happily snuggled against his broad chest to fall asleep, assuring Regan that she couldn't have chosen a better father for her children.

And it was harder because of the deep affection and growing attraction she felt for her husband. She'd agreed to marry Connor because she'd been alone and scared. She hadn't worried that she might fall in love with her husband. In fact, she would have scoffed at the very idea that she could.

But over the past seven months, her awareness had grown and her feelings had changed, and she was hoping that his had, too. However, if she'd harbored any illusions that Connor would be overcome by desire when he found himself in a romantic hotel suite with his wife, his lukewarm response quickly dispelled them.

"Maybe we should go out to grab a bite to eat," he suggested to her now.

"We could go down to The Home Station," she said. "Unless you'd rather have something sent up here?"

"I heard it's next to impossible to get a table in the restaurant."

"Mostly because priority is given to hotel guests,"

she explained. "When I checked in, they told me to call down to the desk if we wanted to make a reservation."

"Then we should take advantage of that," he decided.

"Or we could take advantage of this luxurious suite," she suggested. "Because the restaurant menu is also available through room service."

He didn't take the hint. "But the restaurant is closer to the kitchen, so the food will be hotter and fresher when it gets to a table down there."

It sounded like a reasonable argument. And it was possible that he wasn't deliberately being obtuse but was simply hungry. Wasn't it?

"In that case, why don't you call down to the desk for a reservation while I go freshen up?" she said.

"Okay," he agreed, sounding relieved.

While he reached for the phone, Regan retreated to the bedroom.

She opened up her suitcase, trying to remember if she'd packed something suitable for a fancy dinner. Truthfully, she hadn't worried too much about what she'd thrown into the case, optimistic that she wasn't going to need a lot of clothes over the next couple of days. She'd been more concerned about ensuring that she had all necessary personal items—including the box of condoms that she'd bought in hopeful anticipation of finally consummating their marriage.

Was she being too subtle? Or was Connor simply not interested? Over the past few weeks, he'd sent so many mixed signals she could hardly figure which way was up. One day he was kissing her senseless, the next he was moving her out of his house. While she was gone, he could hardly stay away from her, but since her return, he'd gone back to sleeping in his brother's room.

Of course, that escape wouldn't be available to him for much longer. Deacon was studying for his final exams now and would be on his way home soon. But that was little consolation to Regan, who didn't want Connor to share her bed out of necessity but choice, and she hated that he seemed to want an escape.

The television came on in the other room.

With a resigned sigh, Regan picked up her phone again and sent another text to her sister.

I'm about to chicken out.

She waited for Brie to reply—and nearly dropped the phone when it rang in her hand.

"Don't you dare," her sister said without preamble when Regan connected the call.

"It's just…maybe it's too soon."

"You've been married seven months," Brie reminded her. "Or do you mean too soon after the babies? Because I thought you said the doctor gave you the thumbs-up."

"She did," Regan confirmed.

"So what's your hesitation?"

"I'm not sure," she admitted. "It just seems like a big step."

"It *is* a big step," her sister agreed.

"And if we have sex…it's going to change everything."

"Don't you want things to change?"

"Some things," she acknowledged.

"Such as the fact that you're not having sex with your husband?"

She sighed. "Okay, yes. But we've actually got a pretty good relationship otherwise."

"Just think about how much better it will be when you add naked fun to the mix," her sister urged.

"Maybe that's the part that's holding me back," she said.

"You're opposed to having fun?" Brie teased.

"I meant the naked part," Regan clarified.

"Well, it's been a long time since I've had sex," her sister offered. "But as I recall, it's easier without clothes on."

"You seem to be forgetting that I had two babies four and a half weeks ago."

"I'm not forgetting anything. The whole point of getting you out of the house was to ensure that my adorable nieces wouldn't put a damper on your love life—at least not this weekend."

"The babies have hardly put a damper on our love life," Regan assured her.

"Only because you don't have one…yet."

"I guess that's what I get for telling you the truth," she muttered.

"Or at least part of the truth."

"What do you think I left out?"

"How much you care about your husband," Brie suggested.

"Of course I care about him," Regan said.

"And that you're seriously attracted to him," her sister added.

"He's a good man with a lot of attractive qualities," she admitted.

"And a smokin'-hot body," Brie noted.

That gave her pause. "You checked out my husband?"

"I needed to be sure he was worthy of my sister."

Regan sighed. "What am I going to do?"

"Your smokin'-hot husband?" her sister suggested.

She choked on a laugh. "If only it were that simple."

"It's only complicated because you're making it complicated," Brie insisted.

"We're in a seriously fancy hotel room and I'm on the phone with my sister while he's watching TV in another room."

"I'm sure, if you put your mind to it, you could make him forget about whatever was on the screen—even if he was a diehard football fan and it was Super Bowl Sunday," Brie said. "But if you need a little confidence boost, look inside the drawer of the bedside table."

Curious, she tugged open the drawer and found a lingerie-size box wrapped in pink-striped paper. The tag attached read:

For Regan (& Connor)—Enjoy! Love, Brie XO

"Is it sexy or slutty?" she asked.

Brie laughed. "A little of both. Now go put it on—and I don't want to hear from you again until the weekend's over."

With that, her sister disconnected.

Regan stared at the package for a long minute, debating.

Brie had gone to a lot of effort to make this weekend special for her sister and brother-in-law, so Regan decided that she could at least do her part.

Connor had thought the first seven months of his marriage to Regan—living in close proximity but not being able to touch her—had been torturous enough. He suspected the next forty-eight hours were going to make those seven months seem like a walk in the park.

While she was in the bedroom, he'd checked to see if the sofa in the sitting area folded out to a bed. It did. But even if it didn't, he figured that squeezing his six-foot-four-inch frame into a five-foot sofa would likely be easier than trying to keep his hands off Regan if they were sharing a bed.

But maybe she didn't expect him to keep his hands to himself. Maybe she wanted to celebrate their anniversary the way most other couples celebrated anniversaries—naked together. Certainly she hadn't seemed the least bit reluctant to show him around the suite—including the luxurious bedroom dominated by the fancy bed. She might have been a little apprehensive if she'd known it had taken more willpower than he'd thought he possessed not to throw her down on top of that enormous mattress and have his way with her. Because he'd imagined a lot of various and interesting ways over the past seven months.

But Piper and Poppy were barely four weeks old, which meant that it would be another two before her body would be recovered enough from the experience of childbirth to engage in intercourse.

The longest six weeks of my life, Reid had remarked, in apparent sympathy with his deputy.

Of course, there were a lot of ways to share physical intimacy and sexual pleasure aside from sex. But Connor also knew that six weeks was only a guideline, that some women required a lot more time than that before they experienced any sexual desire.

He'd turned on the TV in a desperate effort to distract himself from the tantalizing thought that they were alone in a hotel room—at least until they could escape to the restaurant for their eight o'clock dinner reservation.

"Connor?"

"Hmm?" he said, his gaze fixed on the TV as he feigned interest in the action on the screen, though he couldn't have said if it was a movie or a commercial or a public service announcement.

Regan stepped forward then, so that she was standing directly in front of him, and his jaw nearly hit the floor.

The remote did slip from his hand and fall to the soft carpet.

He didn't notice.

He didn't see anything but Regan.

She was wearing something that could only be described as a fantasy of white satin and sheer lace. The lace cups barely covered the swell of her luscious breasts; the short skirt skimmed the tops of her creamy thighs.

He lifted his gaze to her face and swallowed. "I thought you were getting ready to go out for dinner."

"I decided that I don't want to go out for dinner."

"That's good," he said. "Because you'd start a riot if you walked into the restaurant wearing that."

She tilted her head to study him. "I can't tell if that means you approve or disapprove."

"Do you want my approval?"

"I want to know if you want *me*."

"Only more than I want to breathe," he admitted hoarsely.

Her glossy pink lips curved as she moved closer. "That's just the right amount," she said, as she straddled his hips with her knees and lowered herself into his lap.

The position put her breasts, practically spilling out

of her top and rising and falling with every breath she took, right there at eye level. But he wanted to do more than just look.

He wanted to touch, taste, take.

Instead, he curled his fingers around the edge of the sofa cushion, desperately trying to hold on to the last vestiges of his self-control, but it was rapidly falling away like a slippery thread.

She leaned closer, so that her mouth was only a whisper from his, and he was about half a second from losing his mind.

But instead of touching her lips to his, she touched them to his cheek, then his jaw and his throat. Light brushes that teased and tempted.

His hands gripped the leather cushion tighter.

"Six weeks," he said hoarsely.

She lifted her head, her eyes dark with desire and sparkling with playfulness. "What?"

"It hasn't been six weeks."

She laughed softly and nipped at the lobe of his ear. "Six weeks is only a guideline, not a rule," she told him.

"You're sure?" he asked.

Please be sure.

She nodded. "I saw Dr. Amaro on Tuesday."

He exhaled an audible sigh of relief. "Thank you, Dr. Amaro."

"Your sentiment is noted," she said. "But I'd prefer you to focus on me right now."

"I can do that," he promised.

And in one abrupt and agile motion, Connor rose to his feet, taking her with him.

Chapter 15

Regan yelped in surprise; Connor responded with a chuckle. One of his arms was banded around her waist while the opposite hand cupped her bottom, and though she didn't think she was in any danger of falling, she wrapped her arms and legs around him like a pretzel and held on.

He carried her to the bedroom and tumbled with her onto the mattress, pinning her beneath his lean, hard body. Her heart hammered against her ribs, not with fear but desire. Desperate, achy desire.

He eased back to hook his fingers in the satin straps of her baby doll, pulling them down her arms so that her breasts spilled free of their constraint. But then he captured them in his hands, exploring their shape and texture with his callused palms and clever fingers. His thumbs traced lazy circles around her already taut nipples, making everything inside her clench in eager anticipation.

"It's been torture, sleeping next to you night after night, not being able to touch you like this," he said.

"No one said you couldn't touch me like this," she pointed out.

"Well, it seemed to be implied that there were… boundaries…to our relationship."

"Tonight, let's forget about the boundaries," she suggested.

"That sounds good to me," he said.

And then he was too busy kissing her to say anything more.

He was a really good kisser: his mouth was firm but not hard; his tongue bold but not aggressive. At another time, she thought she could happily spend hours kissing and being kissed by him. But after so many months of wanting and waiting, it wasn't enough. She wanted more.

As if sensing her impatience, he eased his mouth from hers, skimming it over her jaw, down her throat. He traced the line of her collarbone with his tongue, then nuzzled the hollow between her breasts. His shadowed jaw rasped against her tender flesh, like the strike of a match. Then his mouth found her nipple, and the shocking contrast of his hot mouth on her cool skin turned the spark to flame. He licked and suckled, making her gasp and yearn.

Oh, how she yearned.

As his mouth continued to taste and tease, his hands slid under the hem of her nightie to tug her panties over her hips and down her legs. He tossed the scrap of lace aside and nudged her thighs apart. His thumbs glided over the slick flesh at her core, parting the folds, zeroing in on the center of her feminine pleasure.

Was it post-childbirth hormones running rampant through her system that were responsible for the escalation in her desire, the intensity of her response? Or was it finally being with Connor as she'd so often dreamed of being with him?

Had he dreamed of her, too? Had he imagined touching her the way he was touching her now? Or did he just instinctively know where and how to use his hands so that she couldn't help but sigh with exquisite pleasure?

She should have guessed that he'd approach lovemaking the same way he did everything else—thoroughly and with great attention to detail. But she wanted to touch him, too, so she yanked his shirt out of his pants and made quick work of the buttons.

She finally managed to shove the garment aside and put her hands on him. The taut muscles of his belly quivered as she trailed her fingers over his torso; a low groan emanated from his throat as she scraped her nails lightly down his back. When she reached for his belt, he pulled away to assist with the task—quickly discarding his pants, briefs and socks in a pile on the floor.

"Condom," she said, when he rejoined her on the bed.

It was widely accepted that nursing moms couldn't get pregnant, but with four-and-a-half-week-old twins at home, she didn't want to take any chances.

He reached for the square packet she'd set on top of the bedside table in anticipation of this moment, and quickly sheathed himself.

His eyes were dark and intently focused as he rose over her again.

"I feel as if I've been waiting for this moment forever," he confided. "I don't want to rush it now."

"And I don't want to wait a second longer."

His lips curved as they brushed against hers. "Demanding, much?"

But he gave her what she wanted—what they both wanted. In one smooth stroke, he buried himself deep inside her.

She cried out at the shock and pleasure of the invasion as he filled her, as new waves of sensation began to ripple through her. He held her hands above her head, their fingers entwined, then lowered his head and captured her mouth. She wrapped her legs around him, so that they were linked from top to toe and everywhere in between. Two bodies joined together in pursuit of their mutual pleasure…and finding it.

Regan awoke in the night, her breasts full and aching.

A quick glance at the clock beside the bed confirmed that it was 4 a.m. Poppy habitually woke up around 3:30 and Piper about half an hour later. The staggered times meant that each twin got individual attention, but it also meant that their mom spent twice as much time nursing. Regan knew that it was possible to nurse two babies at the same time, but she couldn't imagine ever being that coordinated—or able to sync their schedules.

She slipped out of bed, leaving Connor sleeping, and retreated to the bathroom with her breast pump. Her initial concerns about not being able to produce enough milk to satisfy the twins had proved to be for naught, and she'd left a more than adequate supply for the weekend in the freezer and detailed instructions for Alyssa about how to prepare it.

Regan was genuinely happy that Jason and Alyssa were starting a family. And that Spencer and Kenzie were expanding theirs. It was apparent that both of her brothers had fallen in love with their perfect mates. Not that either of them had followed a short or easy path to happily-ever-after, but they got there eventually.

Love hadn't been anywhere on Regan's radar when she'd exchanged vows with Connor at the little chapel in Reno. She'd been alone and scared—terrified of being a single mom to two babies, drowning in doubts and insecurities when he tossed her a lifeline in the form of his proposal. She'd snatched it up desperately, gratefully, never hoping or even imagining that their marriage of convenience would ever become anything more.

But over the past seven and a half months, her feelings for her husband had changed and deepened so much so that she knew she was on the verge of falling in love with him.

Or maybe she'd already fallen.

There wasn't any one moment or factor she could pinpoint as the time or reason why, although she knew a big part of it was that she loved him for loving their babies. It took a special kind of man to step up and be a dad in the absence of any biological connection to the child, but Connor had never hesitated or wavered.

Regan knew he loved Piper and Poppy—the only question that remained was: could he ever love her?

The next time she awakened, sunlight was trying to peek around the edges of the curtain. Beneath her cheek, she could feel Connor's heart beating—a slow and steady rhythm. She idly wondered how long it would take her to get his heart racing again, like it had raced the night before.

Not long, was the answer, as he proved when he woke up only a few minutes later.

Regan had never been a big fan of morning sex, but as she'd begun to realize, everything was different with Connor.

Afterward, when she was snuggled close to him, she stroked a hand down the arm that was wrapped around her, following the contours of taut muscles. It amazed her that a man so physically strong could be so tender and gentle, as he'd proved last night and again only a short while ago.

"What happened here?" she asked, her fingers skimming over the vertical line of puckered skin that ran down his forearm.

He glanced at the jagged scar, almost as if he'd forgotten it was there. "Broken glass."

"What'd you do? Put your arm through a window?"

"No."

"Did it happen on the job?" she prompted, when he offered no further explanation.

"No," he said again, adding a shake of his head this time. "It was a long time ago."

"How long?" she asked curiously.

"Ten…maybe twelve…years ago."

She was surprised and dismayed by the result of the quick mental calculation. "When you were a teenager?"

"Yeah."

Another single syllable response, but she refused to be dissuaded. "I know we're both adjusting to the new parameters of our marriage, but I believe communication is key to the success of any relationship."

"Words aren't the only means of communication," he said, with a suggestive wiggle of his brows.

"Yes, and you've proven that you're quite adept at other forms of communication," she assured him. "So if you don't want to talk about it, just say so."

"And you'll let it go?" he asked dubiously.

"Probably not," she admitted. "I can be like Baxter with a juicy T-bone when I want to know something."

He chuckled. "Yeah, that's what I figured." His expression grew serious as he looked at the scar on his arm again. "Do you know Mallory Stillwell?"

"The name sounds vaguely familiar," she admitted, already second-guessing her decision to push for an explanation. She'd thought she wanted to know everything about him, but she hadn't anticipated that his answer might involve another woman.

"She grew up in my neighborhood," he explained. "Across the street and two doors down."

"You took her to prom," Regan suddenly remembered.

"Only because Dale Shillington ditched her two days before the event and she was devastated about not being able to go—especially after she'd worked three weekends of overtime shifts at Jo's to buy a new dress."

"Dale Shillington always was a dick."

"I won't argue with that," Connor said.

"So you stepped in to help out a…friend?" she asked, blatantly fishing for more information about the nature of her husband's relationship with the girl-almost-next-door.

"We were friends," he confirmed. "And, for a while, we were more."

"You can spare me those details," she said quickly.

"I wasn't planning on sharing them."

Which she should have realized. Connor had never been the type to kiss and tell—which only made her that much more curious.

"And you went to prom with Brett Tanner that year," he noted.

"Because he asked."

"You wore a black dress," he said. "All the other girls were in shades of pink or purple or blue, heavy on the makeup and tottering around on too-high heels as if playing at being grown-up. Then you walked in—in your black dress with skinny straps and long skirt, and you were so straight-up sexy, you took my breath away."

"That's quite the memory," she remarked, embarrassed to admit that she couldn't summon an image of him at prom. She knew he'd been there, because she'd heard the stories that circulated, not just that night but for several weeks afterward, but it was possible she hadn't actually seen him.

"You made quite the impression," he assured her.

"And you got kicked out," she said, as her hazy memories slowly came into focus.

"What else would anyone expect from that no-good Neal boy?"

"Did you ever really do anything to earn that reputation?"

"I got kicked out of prom," he reminded her.

"What does any of this have to do with your scar?" she asked, in an effort to steer the conversation back on topic.

"Like my stepfather, Mallory's mom was a heavy drinker—and a mean drunk. And when she'd been drinking, she liked to knock her kids around. Mallory, being the oldest, usually took the brunt of the abuse."

Regan's fingers skimmed down his arm again, over the jagged scar, to link with his.

"One day she went at Mallory with a broken bottle and I stepped between them—and got thirty-four stitches for my efforts."

She winced, not wanting to imagine the bloody scene. "Was she arrested?"

He shook his head. "Mallory begged me to say that it was an accident."

"Why?"

"Because if her mother had gone to jail, family services would have come in and taken her sisters away."

"Considering their mother's violent abuse, that might have been better for them," she remarked.

"Says the girl born with a silver spoon in her mouth."

She nudged him away. "You're going to hold that against me?"

He shook his head. "No, I'm just pointing out why you can't understand the realities of life for those of us who grew up without the same privileges."

"You don't think Mallory and her sisters would have been better off in a different environment?"

"Maybe," he allowed. "Except that no one worried too much about separating siblings back then, and that might have been even more traumatic for all of them."

"I never thought about that," she admitted.

"And I don't want you thinking—and worrying—about it now," he said. "I just wanted to give you a complete picture."

"Got it."

"Good. Now can we stop talking about ex-girlfriends and high school and focus on the here and now?" he suggested, rolling over so that he was facing her.

"What, exactly, in the here and now do you want to focus on?"

"I'd like to start here," he said, and nibbled on her throat.

Her head dropped back and a sigh slipped between her lips. "That's a good place to start," she agreed.

"And here," he said, skimming his lips along the underside of her jaw.

"Another good place."

As his mouth continued to taste and tease, his hands moved lower. A quick tug unknotted the belt at her waist, and the silky robe fell open. She immediately tried to draw the sides together again, but he caught her wrists and held them in place.

"Why are you suddenly acting shy?"

"Because you opened the curtains and it's broad daylight."

"We're on the third floor. No one can see in," he told her.

"But you can see me," she protested.

"That was the point," he said. "I want to see and touch and taste every part of you."

"Some of those parts aren't as firm or smooth as they used to be."

"All of your parts are perfect." He brushed his lips over hers. "You're perfect."

She wasn't, of course. But it was nice of him to say so, and to sound as if he really believed it.

She'd had several boyfriends and a few lovers, but

she'd always been careful to keep them at an emotional distance. She enjoyed sex but was wary of messy emotional entanglements. She hadn't been able to keep Connor at a distance. Or maybe she hadn't wanted to.

"What are you thinking about?"

"I was just wondering…do you think we can make our marriage work?"

"I think we've been doing a pretty good job of it so far," he pointed out. "And that was without the added benefits of sex."

"I guess I just worry sometimes—"

"You worry all the time," he interjected.

She managed a small smile. "Well, sometimes I worry that you might wake up one day and regret marrying me."

He shook his head. "Never."

"How can you be so sure?"

"Because I love the life we have together," he said.

It wasn't a declaration of feelings for her, but she decided it was close enough—at least for now.

"I'm really glad you were there when I was puking in the bushes outside of Diggers'," she said softly.

He chuckled and brushed his lips over her temple. "Me, too."

Chapter 16

Two weeks after their weekend at The Stagecoach Inn—two weeks during which he'd continued to enjoy the many benefits of sharing a bed with his wife at home—Connor drove to the airport in Elko to pick up his brother. For a lot of years, it had been just him and Deacon, and it had been a big adjustment for both of them when his brother went away to school.

It wasn't just that Deacon was gone, but that he was so far away, and the cost of travel meant that he'd only been home once in the past eight months. And when he'd made that trip at Christmas, Connor hadn't been able to relax and enjoy his brother's company because Deacon's presence meant he had to move back into his own room, occupied by an incredibly sexy and far-too-tempting woman who just happened to be his wife.

This time there was no similar apprehension about

Deacon's homecoming, just anticipation for the chance to reconnect with his only sibling.

The first night, after Deacon had finally been introduced to his nieces and made a suitable fuss over "the cutest babies ever"—and then an equal fuss over Baxter, reassuring the dog that he was also loved and adored—they stayed up late talking. Regan lasted until ten o'clock, explaining to her brother-in-law that Piper and Poppy didn't just get up early but continued to wake a couple of times through the night.

"I didn't say it at Christmas, because I was still trying to wrap my head around the fact that you were married," Deacon said, after his brother's wife had gone upstairs. "But I'm really happy for you and Regan."

"Thanks," Connor said.

"And I think it's pretty cool that I'm an uncle—times two."

"With twins, everything is times two," Connor told him. "Twice as many feedings and dirty diapers and loads of laundry."

"Twice as much cuteness," his brother added. "Of course, that's only because they look so much like their mom."

"Lucky for them," Connor agreed.

And lucky for him, because if Piper and Poppy didn't look so much like Regan, people might start to wonder why they didn't look anything at all like their dad.

"Seriously, though, those kids are lucky they've got you for a dad," Deacon remarked.

"I'm the fortunate one," he said. "When I married Regan, I got everything I never knew I wanted."

"She seems pretty great," his brother acknowledged. "I have to admit, when I first got the letter about my scholarship, I didn't realize that it was my sister-in-law's family that was responsible for the fund."

"Blake Mining throws a ton of money around," Connor told him, attempting to downplay the familial connection. "Probably in the hope of some positive PR to combat the negative environmental impact of the business."

"So Regan didn't pull any strings to get me the scholarship?" Deacon asked, wanting to be sure.

"I promise that she didn't," Connor said.

Because Deacon returned to Haven in the middle of the week, he had a few days off before he was scheduled to start working at Katelyn Davidson's law office the following Monday. Unfortunately, Connor didn't have any of those days off. Not even the weekend, because it was his turn in the rotation.

"I know it sucks that it's your first week back and your brother's hardly been home," Regan said to him, after a leisurely breakfast Saturday morning.

"We'll have plenty of time to catch up over the summer," Deacon said. "And I've kind of enjoyed hanging out with you and Piper and Poppy. And Baxter," he added, with a glance at the dog sprawled by his feet.

"I was worried that you might feel uncomfortable, coming home to a place where so much has changed."

"You mean because I came back at Christmas and met my brother's wife? Then, four months later, when I finished the school term, there were two babies in the house?"

"Something like that," she agreed.

"There have been a lot of changes," he acknowledged. "But all for the better."

"I'm glad you think so."

"It's good to see Connor happy," Deacon said. "Not that he ever seemed unhappy, but he smiles a lot more now. Laughs more.

"I have to be honest, I wasn't sure he'd ever want to take on the roles of husband and father. It was pretty rough for him," he explained. "Growing up without a father."

"I doubt it was any rougher than you growing up with yours," Regan said gently.

He seemed startled by her remark. "He told you about Dwayne?"

She nodded.

"I don't really remember much about him. Or maybe I don't want to remember much, because what I do remember—" He cut himself off with a shake of his head.

"Anyway, it was Connor who mostly raised me," he continued. "Despite the fact that there's only eight years between us, he was the closest thing I had to a father. My own was useless on a good day, and our mom was always working.

"It was Connor who made sure I had clean clothes and a lunch packed for school. He filled out the trip forms and gave me milk money from his own savings."

"He never told me any of that," Regan admitted.

"He's always been the first one to step up to help someone else and the last one to want any credit for his actions," Deacon said.

She nodded, agreeing with his assessment.

"Do you know why I applied to Columbia?" Deacon asked.

"Because it's one of the top law schools in the country?" she suggested.

"Well, yeah," he acknowledged. "But I never actually planned to go there. Truthfully, I didn't even think I'd get in. But if I did, what an interesting story I'd have to tell the other lawyers in the barristers' lounge. Over single-malt scotch and imported cigars and conversations about our alma maters, I could casually mention that yes, I'd graduated from UNLV, but I could have gone to Columbia."

"You don't drink or smoke," she said, pointing out the obvious flaws in his story.

He chuckled. "In this futuristic scene of my imagination, I did. But Connor changed that futuristic scene for me. He changed that 'could have gone' to an 'am going.'"

"I know he's incredibly proud of you," she told him.

"And I'm incredibly grateful to him," Deacon said.

"How grateful?" Regan wondered.

"Uh-oh. That sounds like the prelude to a request for a big favor," he remarked.

"It is," she admitted. "Piper and Poppy's baptism is scheduled for June thirtieth and we'd like you to be a godparent."

A smile—quick and wide—spread across his face. "Me? No kidding?"

"No kidding," she assured him. "What do you say?"

"I'd be honored," he said. "But now I have a question for you."

"What is it?"

"What exactly is a godfather supposed to do —and does it include having to change stinky diapers?"

The middle of the following week, Piper and Poppy had their two-month checkup with their pediatrician in Battle Mountain.

"I appreciate the company on the drive," Regan said to Connor, when they headed back to the car with their healthy and happy baby girls after the appointment. "But you really don't have to come to every checkup with me."

"I know," he said. "But it's a long way for you to come on your own, especially if they start fussing. Plus, booking half a day off work gives me an excuse to take my wife out to lunch."

"Now that you mention it… I am kind of hungry."

"What are you in the mood for?"

"Pizza from Jo's," she decided.

"I thought you'd want to take advantage of the fact that we're in a town that offers a few more dining options than the Sunnyside Diner, Diggers' Bar and Grill, and Jo's Pizza."

"But if we pick up a pizza on the way home, I can take advantage of my husband before he has to go into work later."

He grinned. "I like the way you think."

By the time they got around to eating the pizza, it was cold, but neither of them complained. After lunch, Regan wrapped the leftover slices while Connor went upstairs to get dressed.

She was startled when the doorbell rang, because Baxter was out in the backyard and hadn't given her any warning that someone was approaching the house. Although it was unusual to get visitors in the middle of the day, she was more curious than concerned when she responded to the summons.

Until she opened the door and discovered Bo Larsen on the other side.

"Hello, Regan."

There were at least a dozen random questions spinning through her mind, and she blurted out the first one she latched on to: "What are you doing here?"

"I was in town and thought I'd stop by to congratulate the new mother," he said.

Though the words sounded pleasant enough, she remained wary. "Thank you."

"You don't want to know who told me?"

"It's a small town and hardly a big secret," she pointed out.

"True," he acknowledged. "And it wasn't really a surprise to me, either. At least, not after I received a tax receipt for my generous donation to The Battle Mountain Women's Health Center.

"You can imagine how awkward it was," he continued in a conversational tone, "trying to explain that to my wife."

"I can," she agreed. "But I have to say, I approve of your philanthropy."

"Don't you mean *your* philanthropy?" he asked. "You took the money I gave you and turned it over to the clinic."

She didn't deny it. "You wanted to pay for an abortion, and I wasn't interested in having one."

"You might have told me that."

"Why? You made it perfectly clear that you had no interest in my baby."

"Don't you mean babies?"

She swallowed. "What do you want, Bo?"

"I just wanted to make sure—" His words cut off as his gaze shifted to focus on something—or someone, she guessed—over her shoulder.

"Everything okay?" Connor asked, as he came down the stairs to take up position behind her.

"Everything's fine," Regan said, breathing a silent sigh of relief that her husband wasn't carrying one or both of their daughters. "And Bo was just leaving."

"I don't want to rush off without being properly introduced to…" He paused, obviously waiting for her to fill in the blank.

"My husband," Regan told him. "Connor is my husband."

"Husband," Bo echoed, sounding surprised. "When we…worked together, I didn't get the impression that you were looking for a long-term commitment. But I guess parenthood changes a lot of things."

"Meeting the right person changes everything," Regan said pointedly.

Bo nodded. "Apparently so."

Regan turned to her husband then. "This is Bo Larsen, a former colleague."

"Oh, we were more than colleagues," he chided.

Regan narrowed her gaze.

Of course, Connor knew exactly what she and Bo had been. When she'd told him about her pregnancy, she'd told him everything. What he didn't know, because she'd only recently realized it herself, was that her relationship with Bo had been a mistake from the beginning.

And yet, even if she could go back in time, she wouldn't change a thing, because Bo was the reason she had Piper and Poppy—and they were the reason Connor had married her.

"We were also friends," her ex continued.

"And now we're not," she said pointedly.

Bo nodded. "I'm glad I got to meet your husband." He looked at Connor then. "Congratulations on your wedding. And your new family."

"Thank you," Connor said.

As soon as Bo turned away, Regan closed the door and turned the lock.

Connor stood behind her, watching Regan as she watched, through the glass, her former lover drive away. He could see the tension in the rigid line of her shoulders and practically feel it emanating from her body.

Did she want to be sure that he was gone?

Or was she wishing that he'd stayed?

"Are you okay?"

She turned around quickly and nodded. "I'm fine." She added a smile. "And reassured."

"Reassured?" he echoed dubiously.

She nodded again. "I always suspected he'd show up someday. Now that day has passed, and I don't have to worry that he'll come back again."

"How can you be sure?" he wondered.

"Because I saw how relieved he was to learn that we were married."

Connor hoped she was right and they'd seen the last

of the other man. But even if it was true, that didn't eliminate the last of his concerns.

He hated to ask the question, but he needed to know: "Do you still have feelings for him?"

Regan shook her head. "Of course not. After the way he lied to me and used me? How could you even imagine that I would?"

"You said you knew he'd show up someday... I guess I just wondered if maybe that's why you made the donation to the women's health center in his name—to ensure that he would? To give him a reason to find you and force this confrontation?"

"No," she said again. "At the time, I was only thinking of getting rid of the money. Maybe I should have just torn up the check, but I was hurt and angry and obviously not thinking very clearly."

He wanted to believe it was as simple as that, but the other man's appearance at the door had shaken Connor more than he wanted to admit. He'd known about the relationship. She'd been honest with him about her former lover, but now that abstract persona had taken a specific form in a suit and tie, with a preppy haircut and neatly buffed nails.

Bo Larsen was exactly the type of guy he would have imagined Regan falling for—and a living reminder that, had her circumstances been different, she would never have chosen to get involved with a guy from the wrong side of the tracks.

Yet it was Connor she turned to in the night, not just willingly but eagerly. And when they came together, their passion was honest and real.

If that was all they ever had, he vowed it would be enough.

* * *

The next morning, as Connor made his way to the kitchen to start the coffee brewing, he found his brother in front of the mirror in the hall.

"You're up early today," he noted. "And all dressed up like a grown-up."

Deacon grinned into the mirror as he finished adjusting his tie. "What do you think?"

Connor, looking over his brother's shoulder, nodded. "I think you look like a lawyer."

"I'm a long way away from that, but I thought I should dress the part for my first day in court."

"I guess this is a pretty big opportunity, huh?"

"Huge," Deacon agreed. "And something else I owe to you."

"I didn't do anything except pass your résumé on to the sheriff, who gave it to his wife," Connor pointed out.

"That's the least of what you did," his brother said. "You always encouraged me to follow my dreams."

"I'm glad to see that you are."

"Actually, this is beyond my dreams." Deacon turned to face Connor now. "But you said that I could use the past to guide my future, but I should never let the past limit it."

"That sounds like pretty good advice," he said, lifting Baxter's leash off the hook by the door. "Here's some more—don't be late for your first day in court."

Deacon grinned in response to the not-so-subtle prompt. "I'm on my way."

When Connor and Baxter headed down Elderberry Lane, he saw a now-familiar red Toyota pulling into Bruce Ackerman's driveway.

"I haven't seen you around here in a while," he said, when he caught up to Mallory as she was lifting her bucket of cleaning supplies out of the trunk.

She didn't look at him when she responded. "I picked up a couple more jobs, so my schedule isn't as regular as it used it be."

Baxter barked, as if to ask why she was ignoring him.

She turned to scratch his head, but dropped her chin so that her hair fell forward to curtain her face.

The deliberate motion set off Connor's radar. He took a step closer and tipped her chin up, the muscle in his jaw tightening as he noted the faded bluish-green bruise on her cheekbone. "What happened?"

She shrugged. "I ran into a fist."

At least her flippant response was honest. Of course, she had to know that he'd never believe that she ran into a door. They'd both heard that lie too many times, and he was furious and frustrated and sorry and sad for the sweet girl he'd known.

"Your husband's?" he guessed.

"Yeah, but it's really not a big deal," she said. "I mean, it doesn't happen very often. Usually, he treats me pretty good."

Connor shook his head. "Are you hearing yourself, Mallory? Do you realize how much you sound like your mother? Do you remember how much you hated the way she always made excuses for the men who knocked her around? The same excuses she made when she knocked you around?"

"Well, I guess it's true what they say about the apple not falling far from the tree," she said, though the color in her cheeks suggested that she was more ashamed of succumbing to the cycle of abuse than she wanted to admit. "But anyway, I'm fine."

"You mentioned a daughter."

"What about her?"

"Is she fine?" he wondered. "How do you think she feels when she sees her mother get knocked around?"

"He's never hit me in front of Chloe."

"Yet."

"Save the lecture for someone who needs it, Deputy," she advised.

"I'm not lecturing, I just—" he cut himself off, realizing that he was about to do exactly that. Because she'd heard it all before, and there was nothing to be gained by putting her on the defensive now. "Just promise that you'll call me if you ever need anything."

He handed her a card with his cell phone number on it; she tucked it into her pocket without even looking at it.

"Sure," she agreed.

But they both knew she was lying.

Chapter 17

The day of the baptism dawned clear and bright.

The ceremony happened after the morning church service, by which time both Piper and Poppy were feeling a little restless and out of sorts. Everyone agreed the twins looked like perfect little angels in their matching christening gowns, but when it came time for the sprinkling with water, they screamed like little devils.

After the ritual had been completed, everyone gathered at the twins' grandparents' house on Miners' Pass. It was mostly a family event, although some of Regan's coworkers from Blake Mining and some of Connor's from the sheriff's office had been invited to attend. Holly Kowalski was there with her fiancé, and Regan was pleased to have the opportunity to thank her personally for the beautiful quilts she'd gifted to Piper and

Poppy—and to offer her congratulations on the deputy's recent engagement.

"Why do I feel as if I've lost something?" Regan asked her husband, when Connor returned with the glass of punch she'd requested.

"Probably because you don't currently have a baby attached to your body," he noted.

"That might be it," she acknowledged, scanning the crowd for their daughters.

They'd been passed around from one person to the next all day and had held up pretty well—after they'd gotten back to the house and had their empty bellies filled. She located them quickly enough. Piper was in Auntie Brie's arms and Poppy was being cuddled by her cousin Dani, under the watchful eye of Auntie Kenzie. No doubt the little girl was going to be a great big sister when Spencer and Kenzie's baby was born.

"You were thirsty," Connor noted, when she quickly drained the contents of her glass. "Want a refill?"

She shook her head. "No, but I'm going to head inside to the powder room." She pitched her voice to a whisper, so that no one could overhear. "I have to adjust my nursing bra."

"Do you want me to come with you?" he whispered back. "I've got some experience with your undergarments."

"Taking them off," she acknowledged. "And that will have to wait until later."

"Promises, promises."

She was smiling as she walked into the house. And why not? She had a wonderful life and she was grateful for every bit of it. Okay, maybe not the bulky bra, she mused, as she adjusted the garment. But everything else was pretty darn good.

She exited the powder room and caught a snippet of conversation from the great room.

"—personally thank you for funding the Aim Higher Education Scholarship."

Regan stopped in her tracks.

She immediately recognized Deacon's voice—but who was he talking to?

"Blake Mining believes in giving back to the community."

Her father?

"Well, I'm grateful for that," her brother-in-law said now. "The funds have been of tremendous assistance."

Regan took a step back, her mind spinning.

She knew about Deacon's scholarship, of course, but she'd had no idea that the money had been put up by Blake Mining.

Was it a coincidence?

She didn't think so.

Especially when she recalled part of a conversation that she'd had with her husband several weeks earlier.

"...there was a weird message on my voice mail the other day from one of the junior accountants at work," she'd told him. *"...something about a scholarship fund."*

"He shouldn't be bothering you with trivial inquiries when you're on mat leave...let your father deal with it."

Had Connor known?

And if so, why hadn't he told her?

Determined to get answers to those questions from her husband right now, she pivoted quickly and nearly bumped into him.

"Hey." He caught her arms to steady her. "Are you all right?"

She nodded, then shook her head. But she didn't want to have a private conversation in the middle of the foyer, so she took his hand and pulled him into the library, closing the door behind them.

"If you wanted to be alone with me, you only had to say so," he teased, smiling as he moved in to kiss her.

She put a hand on his chest, halting his progress. "I heard your brother talking to my father."

His smile faded, his gaze shuttered. "Is that a problem?"

"That's what I'm trying to figure out," she admitted, as the hollow feeling in her stomach grew. "Did you know that Blake Mining paid for Deacon's scholarship?"

To his credit, Connor hesitated only briefly before nodding. "Yes, I knew."

Maybe he deserved some credit for being honest, but his truthfulness didn't lessen her feelings of betrayal. "And yet, I didn't."

"You've had more important things to think about over the past several months," he said reasonably.

She couldn't deny that was true, but she still had questions that she wanted answered. The most important one being: "When did you know about it?"

"Your dad mentioned the possibility of a scholarship to me shortly after Deacon headed to New York for his first term," he admitted.

"In the fall, then?"

He nodded again.

"Before or after you asked me to marry you?" she wanted to know. *Needed* to know.

Except that, in her heart, she suspected that she already knew. But she fervently hoped his response would prove her instincts wrong.

"Does it matter?" he asked.

"Of course it matters," she said. "And I'm guessing, from your deliberate effort to sidestep the question, the answer is before."

She read the truth—and maybe regret—in his gaze before he responded.

"Yes," he acknowledged quietly. "It was before."

Now she nodded, even as her heart sank impossibly deeper inside her chest. "How much?"

"How much what?" he asked warily.

Her eyes stung; her throat ached. "How much did it cost my father to buy me a husband?"

"It wasn't like that, Regan," he denied, reaching for her.

She stepped back, away from him. "Or maybe he was more worried about the legitimacy of his grandchildren than his daughter's happiness?" she suggested as an alternative. Then she shook her head. "I can't believe I was such an idiot. That I actually believed you wanted to marry me and be a father to my babies, so they wouldn't grow up with unanswered questions about their paternity, like you did."

"I *did* want to marry you and I *am* their father," he said, sounding so earnest she wanted to believe him. "And even if you're upset that you didn't know about the scholarship, you have to know how much I love Piper and Poppy."

She nodded, because she did know. There was no denying that Connor loved their daughters. He'd also told her that he loved their life together, being a family.

But he didn't love *her*.

She hadn't expected happily-ever-after when they'd exchanged their vows. It wasn't part of their deal. Then again, she hadn't known he'd made a completely different deal with her father. And while they'd lived and worked together over the past eight and a half months— first preparing for the birth and then taking care of the twins—she'd been falling in love with him, and he'd been in it for the financial reward.

"You're right about the latter part," she acknowledged. "You are a wonderful father to Piper and Poppy. I just wish I'd known the real reasons you'd agreed to take on that role."

"I never lied to you, Regan." His tone was imploring, as if it really mattered to him that she believed him.

As if she could.

"Really? Is that how you justified the deception in your own mind? That you never actually lied?" she challenged. "Because you weren't completely honest with me, either."

"We each had our own reasons for wanting to get married," he reminded her. "And neither of us was under any illusions that it was for love."

"You're right again," she said.

"And everything I told you, all the reasons I gave for wanting to marry you, were true."

"But not the whole truth."

"You would never have agreed to marry me if you'd known the whole truth," he said.

"I guess we'll never know, will we?" she countered. "But one thing I do know is that I never would have assumed you were noble and honorable and—" She shook her head. "I was such an idiot. When I offered to pay for the kitchen renovation, you assured me you didn't marry me for my money. Because you married me for my father's money."

He flinched at the harshness of her words, but she refused to feel guilty for speaking the truth.

She swiped impatiently at the tears that spilled onto her cheeks. "If I'd known, I might still have married you," she decided. "I was so scared and desperate and alone, I might not have cared about your reasons. But at least then I would have gone into the marriage with my eyes wide open.

"And I wouldn't have been foolish enough to fall in love with you."

Before Connor could wrap his head around what she'd said, she was gone.

He was staring at the door through which she'd disappeared when her sister entered. "I came in to ask Regan where she put the diaper bag, and she walked right past without even seeing me," Brie remarked.

"Over there," he said, pointing to a chair in the corner.

His sister-in-law opened the top of the bag, took out a diaper and the package of wipes. "Why did she storm out of here?"

"Maybe you should ask your sister," Connor suggested.

"I'm asking you," she said.

He sighed wearily but knew there was no point in denying the truth. "I screwed up."

"Yeah, that was a given," she noted. "How badly?"

He just shook his head.

He should have ignored her father's directive and

told her the truth in the beginning. But he'd been afraid that she'd say no and he really wanted her to say yes. Not just because he'd needed the money for Deacon's education, but because he'd wanted a chance to be with Regan. Of course, he never would have admitted that was a factor at the time, because he hadn't been willing to acknowledge his feelings for her.

"Regan can forgive a lot of faults," Brie said to him now. "But she can't tolerate dishonesty. She was involved with a guy once who had a pretty big secret, and when it was finally uncovered, she was devastated—by the deception even more than the truth."

He guessed that she was referring to Bo—the ex-colleague, ex-lover, with the secret family. And he realized that it didn't matter how he'd managed to justify, in his own mind, keeping the truth about the scholarship from Regan. She'd trusted him with her deepest secrets, and he hadn't done the same.

"I screwed up really, really badly," he confessed.

"Then you better come up with a really, really good plan to fix it," she said. "Assuming you want to fix it because you're head over heels in love and can't imagine your life without her?"

"I am," he confirmed. He wasn't sure how or when it had happened, but he knew it was true.

"Then you might want to lead with that," Brie suggested.

When Connor got home, he found his brother in the living room with books spread out on the coffee table, a dog at his feet and a baseball game on TV. Deacon had left the party early to work on a pretrial memo that his boss had asked him to prepare, so he had no idea that his brief conversation with Regan's father had resulted in lasting fallout for his brother.

"Where's everyone else?" Deacon asked, noting that Connor was alone.

"They're staying at Miners' Pass tonight."

His brother hit the mute button on the TV to give Connor his full attention. "Why?"

"Because Regan's mad at me," he admitted.

"About?"

He shook his head. "It doesn't matter."

"Regan doesn't strike me as the type to go off in a tiff, so I'm guessing it was something that matters to her."

"Yeah." Connor scrubbed his hands over his face. "Maybe my mistake was in ever thinking we could make our marriage work."

Deacon frowned. "Why would you say something like that?"

"Because we're way too different."

"So?"

"So Regan's a Blake," he reminded his brother. "And that puts her way out of my league."

"Obviously Regan doesn't think so, or she would never have married you."

"She was pregnant and overwhelmed by the prospect of raising her babies alone."

"I don't have enough worldly experience to translate into words of wisdom," Deacon said. "So I'll suggest that you take your own advice."

"What advice is that?" he asked, a little warily.

"Let the past guide your future but don't let it put limits on it."

"I'm not sure that's really applicable to this situation."

"Well, it's all I've got," Deacon said. "Except to say that you owe it to yourself as much as Regan to fight for the family you've made together."

Regan was miserable.

She'd told Connor that she needed space and time to think about things, and he'd given it to her.

Idiot.

Why couldn't he know that what she really wanted was for him to fight for their marriage? To prove to her that she was worth fighting for. Or, if not her, at least Piper and Poppy.

Two days had passed since the party with no communication from him. On day three—Greta's day off—she responded to a knock on the door.

"Deacon, what are you doing here?"

"If the mountain won't come to Muhammad," he began.

She smiled at that. "Come in, Muhammad."

He stepped through the door and gave her a warm hug.

Inexplicably, her eyes filled with tears. Although she was mad at Connor and still feeling hurt and betrayed, she missed Deacon (and Baxter) and the rhythms and routines they'd established as a result of living together, and she really wanted to go home.

She'd only lived with her husband in the house on Larrea Drive for nine months, but it truly felt like home. And not only because Connor had renovated the kitchen in accordance with her preferences, but because being there with him—being his wife and a mother to their babies—she truly felt as if she was where she belonged.

It didn't seem to matter why or how they'd connected, all that mattered was that they were a family together.

Without him, she felt alone and incomplete.

But she pushed that thought aside for now to focus on her visitor. "Can I get you something to drink?" she offered. "Soda? Coffee? Beer?"

"I'm not thirsty," Deacon said. "I just wanted to come by to make sure you were okay."

The unexpected overture and genuine concern in his expression caused her throat to tighten. "I'm fine," she said, though her tone was less certain than her words.

"And to ask how long you intend to punish my brother," he added.

"Is that what you think I'm doing?" she asked, startled by the question—and perhaps his insight.

"Isn't it?" he prompted gently.

Regan sighed. "I don't know. I mean, it wasn't a conscious decision, but maybe I did want him to feel some of the hurt I was feeling."

"He knows he screwed up," her brother-in-law said.

"I screwed up, too," she admitted.

Growing up a Blake in Haven—because despite her last name being Channing, everyone knew Regan was a Blake—everything had come easily to her. So much so that she'd taken a lot of things for granted. She hadn't delved too deeply into Connor's reasons for marrying her because she'd wanted a husband for herself and father for her babies, and she usually got what she wanted.

She was spoiled and entitled, and she'd proven it by running away when Connor didn't respond to the shouted declaration of her feelings with an equally emotional outburst. She'd wanted him to fight for their marriage, but why would he when she hadn't fought to stay with him?

"Well, for what it's worth, he's miserable," Deacon told her now.

"That makes two of us," she confided.

"So come home," he urged. "It will be more fun to watch him grovel up close."

She managed a laugh. "I'll think about it. Now, that's enough about your brother—tell me about your job."

"Katelyn's got a ton of cases on the go, so I'm working my butt off—and loving every minute of it."

"That's great," she said sincerely.

"We're doing jury selection in court tomorrow."

"That sounds like fun—unless you're in the jury pool."

He chuckled. "Yeah, most people grumble about getting the summons. But it really is a fascinating way to see the legal system at work."

They chatted a little bit more about his work, until Regan lifted a hand to stifle a yawn.

Deacon immediately rose to his feet. "That's my cue."

"It wasn't a cue," she protested. "I'm a new mom of twins—I'm always tired."

"Another reason to come home," her brother-in-law said, with a conspiratorial wink. "Make the dad do his fair share."

Chapter 18

Connor was scowling at the coffeepot when Holly took the pot off the burner and filled a mug that she then pressed into his hands.

"You have to actually drink it for the caffeine to take effect," she told him.

He lifted the mug to his lips. "I didn't get much sleep last night."

"The twins keep you up?" she asked sympathetically.

He swallowed a mouthful of coffee. Missing the twins and their mother was what kept him up, though he didn't say as much. He didn't want anyone to know that his wife had left him because he was hoping it was a temporary situation soon to be rectified.

Regan had asked for time—but how much time was he supposed to give her? How much was enough and—

"Neal, Kowalski—you're with me," the sheriff said, striding briskly through the bullpen.

Connor put the mug down and automatically checked for his weapon and badge.

Holly did the same as she asked, "What's up?"

"Domestic," Reid said grimly.

"Damn," Connor muttered, falling into line behind his boss, who was already halfway out the door. "Who called it in?"

"Six-year-old kid hiding in the closet of her bedroom."

Connor swore again.

"It gets worse," Reid warned. "She claims her dad has a gun."

"Shotgun," Holly said.

Connor frowned as he reached for the passenger-door handle of the sheriff's SUV. "How do you know?"

"I don't." She nudged him aside with her hip. "I was claiming the front seat."

With a philosophical shrug, Connor moved to the rear door.

"Where are we going?" he asked, when the sheriff slid behind the wheel.

"Southside."

Connor's old neighborhood.

"Second Street."

He suddenly had a knot in his stomach the size of a fist. "Number?"

"Sixty-eight."

Mallory's house.

As the sheriff turned onto Second Street, Connor considered the possibility that the caller—the daughter Mallory had described as the light of her life—might be wrong about the gun. Sometimes kids had trouble separating fantasy from reality. And sometimes, he knew from personal experience, kids saw things that everyone else chose to ignore.

Either way, they were going to go in assuming the dad was armed—and hope like hell he didn't have more than one weapon.

Reid pulled the SUV over in front of number sixty-two so as not to tip off anyone inside number sixty-eight. He opened the back and handed out vests.

"The 911 operator said the kid was calling from her bedroom at the back of the house. Apparently there's a window accessible from the ground. Kowalski, go in and get the girl and let us know when she's safe.

"And no, I'm not keeping you out of harm's way," he said, before she could protest her assignment. "I'm sending you because the kid's terrified that her dad has a gun, so I don't want to send in another man with a gun."

Holly nodded. "Yes, sir."

"Neal, as soon as we get word that the kid's out of the house, you're going in the side door, I'm going in the front."

Though Haven was hardly a hotbed of criminal activity, bad things did occasionally happen in the town, and Connor had learned early on to trust his instincts when reading a situation. He was struggling to read this one. Although human nature was predictable, individuals often bucked the trends—especially when emotions were running high.

Evan Turcotte's emotions were running high, as evidenced by the pained expression on his face and the real tears in his eyes as he held his gun pointed at his wife. "You called the cops?" The gun shook in his hand. "How could you do that to me?"

"I didn't." Mallory's voice pleaded with him to believe her. "You know I didn't, Evan. I've been here with you the whole time."

Unable to argue with her logic, he shifted blame to the neighbors, using several choice adjectives to describe their interference in things that were none of their goddamned business.

"Do you have a daughter, Mr. Turcotte?" The sheriff spoke up now, attempting to engage the man and defuse the situation.

"Yeah," Turcotte admitted. "So what?"

"So maybe yelling at her mom and waving a gun around might have scared your little girl," Reid suggested.

Turcotte swore again and blinked hard, attempting to clear the moisture from his eyes. "Aww, man. Chloe called you?"

"She did," Reid confirmed. "Because she wants everyone to be safe."

"I've never laid a finger on Chloe," Turcotte said. "I wouldn't ever hurt my little girl."

"I'm sure it would be a lot easier for Chloe to believe that if you put the gun down," the sheriff continued in the same patient tone.

"Where is she?" Turcotte demanded. "Where's my daughter?"

"She's outside with Deputy Kowalski," Reid said.

"I want to see her."

"You put the gun down, and we'll make that happen," the sheriff promised.

"If I put this gun down, you're gonna put cuffs on

me and haul me off to jail," Turcotte said. "I know how this works—I'm not an idiot."

"You're obviously upset about something, Mr. Turcotte. Why don't we talk about what that is?"

"I only want to talk to Mallory," he said, his voice filled with despair. "I want you guys to go so I can talk to my wife."

"If you know how this works, you know we can't do that," Reid said. "This is what's considered an active threat situation."

"It's okay, Sheriff," Mallory said, but the trembling of her voice suggested otherwise. "You should go so me and Evan can talk."

Connor stepped out of the shelter of the doorway, hoping the sight of a familiar face would reassure her. "We're not going anywhere."

She shook her head. "Please, Connor. This isn't—"

"Connor?" Turcotte's interjection sounded pained. "Oh, this is just perfect. My cheating wife—" his voice broke a little as he swung the gun from Mallory to the deputy "—and her lover."

"I'm afraid you've been given some misinformation," Connor said calmly.

Unfortunately, Mallory didn't exhibit the same coolness. She threw her arms up in the air. "Ohmygod— where do you come up with this stuff?"

"I found his card on your dresser and I know you're sleeping with somebody," Turcotte snapped at her.

It was obvious to Connor that the man was at the end of his rope—desperate to hang on to his family and unable to see that his actions were pushing them away. So he took another step forward, attempting to draw the man's attention back to him.

"If you want to be mad at someone, Evan, be mad at me." He deliberately used the man's first name and a friendly tone, attempting to establish a rapport. To encourage him to look for a peaceful resolution to whatever conflict had driven him to this point.

But Mallory's husband wasn't interested in rapport. "I've got enough mad—and enough bullets—to go around," he promised grimly.

"Come on now," Connor said, in the same placating tone. "Put the gun down so that we can talk."

"I don't wanna talk to you."

"Well, you don't want to be making threats—especially against an officer of the law."

"I'm done making threats," Turcotte said, and pulled the trigger.

Ben and Margaret hadn't said anything when Regan told them that she was going to be staying at Miners' Pass with her babies again. Or maybe her parents had said plenty—just none of it to her. And for the first couple of days, she was happy to avoid any kind of confrontation with them. She just needed some time to sort through her own emotions—the most prominent of which were hurt and anger.

Although she was furious with Connor, she suspected that the marriage idea hadn't originated with him. Not that she intended to let him off the hook on that technicality when he'd proven only too willing to go along with the plan, but right now, her attention was focused in another direction.

"This is a surprise," Ben said, glancing to his wife for confirmation when Regan walked into his office four days after the baptism.

"We didn't have a meeting scheduled," Margaret assured him.

"No," Regan agreed. "But I needed to talk to you and I didn't want to wait until dinner."

"Talk to *me*?" her father asked, his tone wary.

She nodded. "But it's good that you're both here."

"What can we do for you?" her mother asked.

"I'm trying to understand—" she broke off, mortified to discover that her eyes were filling with tears. *Again.*

"Regan?" Margaret prompted gently.

She tried to focus on her father through her tears. "I need to know—was it your idea or his?"

"I've only ever wanted what's best for you," Ben said.

"Yours then," she realized.

Margaret frowned and turned to her husband. "What was your idea?"

Regan's brows lifted. "Mom doesn't know?"

Her father sighed. "No one was supposed to know."

"Know what?" Margaret demanded.

Ben seemed to be struggling to find the words to tell his wife what he'd done, so Regan explained, "Dad paid Connor to marry me."

Margaret gasped. "Is it true?"

"No," he immediately denied. "I never gave Connor any money."

"Not directly," Regan acknowledged. "But you wrote a hefty check to his brother."

"The Aim Higher Scholarship," Margaret murmured, putting the pieces together.

Regan nodded.

"You can't seriously be upset that your father wanted

to help your brother-in-law with his law school expenses," her mother chided.

"Except that Deacon wasn't my brother-in-law at the time and Dad didn't offer the money out of the goodness of his heart—he did it so Connor would marry me." She shifted her attention back to her father then. "But how did you know he'd go along with your plan?"

"I knew he'd put a mortgage on his house to pay Deacon's tuition," Ben confessed. "And I saw the way he looked at you, the day you told us you were pregnant, and I knew he'd do almost anything for you—even give his name to your babies."

There it was again, the reference to "your babies," as if her father knew—or at least suspected—that Connor wasn't their biological father.

"I don't understand," Regan said now. "For most of my life, you barely showed any interest in where I was or what I was doing, and now suddenly you're not only interested but interfering."

"We've always wanted what's best for you," Ben said again.

"Maybe you should have conferred with Mom first, because I don't think she believes Connor fits the bill."

"I'll admit I had some reservations when you first brought him home," Margaret said. "But only because he's not your usual type."

"What's my usual type?" Regan wondered.

"Well…" Her mother faltered a little. "You never really brought anyone home before."

"Or maybe you were just never there to meet the friends I did bring home."

"And if I had some reservations," Margaret continued, pointedly ignoring the truth of her daughter's remark, "well, the fact that you moved back home after only a few months proves they weren't unfounded."

"I didn't move," she denied. "I only needed some time to think about the fact that my husband had reasons for marrying me that I knew nothing about."

"How much time do you think you need?" her father asked. "Because you can't expect him to sit around waiting for you to stop being mad at him."

"I'm also mad at you," she pointed out.

"Do you want me to apologize?"

"Are you sorry?" she challenged.

"No," he admitted. "Because he's a good man—and a good husband to you and father to your babies."

She felt the sting of fresh tears. "He is a good husband and father."

"Do you love him?" her father asked gently.

She swiped at the tear that spilled onto her cheek. "Yes, but that doesn't make what you did okay."

"He loves you, too," he said. "Even if he hasn't told you so."

Another tear; another swipe. "How do you know?"

"Because your husband and I have more in common than you know."

"What do you have in common with Connor Neal?" Margaret asked.

Ben smiled at his wife. "For starters, we both fell in love with women who were way out of our league."

She smiled back. "It's true," she told their daughter now. "We've been together so long, I sometimes forget how socially awkward and financially challenged Benjamin was when we first met."

"That's your mother's way of saying I was a geek—and broke."

"But you were a cute broke geek," Margaret noted affectionately.

"And you were popular and beautiful and a Blake, and I fell head over heels the first time I saw you."

"And six months later, I finally agreed to go out with you—just so you'd stop asking," Margaret recalled fondly. "Then you kissed me good-night, and I was so glad I'd finally said yes."

Maybe it did warm Regan's heart to see the obvious and enduring affection between her parents, but she'd come into the office today to try to figure out what she was going to do about her own marriage.

"I need to go home," she suddenly realized.

"We'll see you at dinner then," Margaret responded, without looking away from her husband.

Regan shook her head. "No. I need to go home to Connor—to tell him that I want to make our marriage work."

"I think that's the right decision," Ben told her.

Before she could say anything else, her cell phone buzzed.

A quick glance at the screen revealed Connor's name on the display, and her heart skipped a beat.

"Are you going to answer it?" Margaret asked.

She nodded and swiped her finger across the screen. But when the call connected, it wasn't her husband on the other end of the line.

It was the sheriff.

"What's wrong?" Ben asked, when Regan disconnected.

She opened her mouth, then closed it again, unable to say the words.

"Regan?" her mother prompted, concern evident in her tone.

"He… Connor… He was shot."

"Shot?" Ben and Margaret echoed together.

Regan nodded. "He's okay," she told her parents, desperately clinging to that belief. "The sheriff said he was wearing a vest, but they took him to the hospital in Battle Mountain to be checked out, just as a precaution. I need to go there. To Battle Mountain."

"We'll all go," Margaret said.

Regan nodded again, but her feet remained glued to the floor while the upper part of her body seemed to be swaying.

"Sit down." Her mom nudged her into a chair. "I'm going to get you a glass of water."

Regan sat. She felt simultaneously hot and cold— empty inside and somehow full of churning emotions. But she didn't realize she was crying until her dad handed her a tissue as her mom returned with a glass of water.

"I wasn't done being mad at him," she said, dabbing at the wetness on her cheeks.

"So those are angry tears?" Margaret asked.

"I don't know why I'm crying," she admitted.

"Maybe they're tears of relief," Ben suggested. "Because you know he's okay."

"Maybe," she allowed.

"And maybe, somewhere deep beneath the hurt and anger, you're realizing that the phone call could have given you very different news," her dad said gently.

Fresh tears began to fall. "Ohmygod—he could have died."

"But he didn't," Margaret pointed out in a matter-of-fact tone. "And the sheriff said he's going to be fine."

But Regan knew she wouldn't believe it until she saw him for herself.

"I do love him," she sniffled.

"Then tell him that," Ben advised.

"I will," she vowed. "The first chance I get."

Connor didn't see why he needed to go to the hospital, but the sheriff had stood firm.

"You're going to get checked out," Reid insisted. "Then you're going to go home where your wife can fuss over your bruises."

Which didn't really sound so bad, except that Connor knew better than to count on Regan fussing over him. He was still trying to figure out how to convince her to come home.

"Knock knock."

He glanced over as the curtain was pulled back.

Mallory, a little girl he guessed was her six-year-old daughter, and another woman he vaguely recognized stepped into the exam area.

Though the effort made his chest hurt, he sat up on the table. "Hey," he said, not sure what else to say in the presence of the child.

"Hey," Mallory said back, and offered a wan smile. "You remember my sister Miranda?"

He nodded. "It's good to see you again."

"Same goes, Deputy," Miranda said.

"And this is my daughter, Chloe," Mallory said, brushing a hand over the little girl's hair.

"It's nice to meet you, Chloe."

The child watched him with wary eyes.

"The sheriff said you were okay," Mallory noted. "But we needed to see for ourselves."

"I'm okay," he confirmed.

Chloe didn't look convinced. "Daddy had a gun," she said quietly.

He nodded. "And you were very brave to call the police and tell them that."

"We learned about 911 at school," she said.

"Now you know why it's important to pay attention in class."

He caught the hint of a shy smile before she ducked her head again.

"Why don't we go see what they've got to eat in the cafeteria?" Miranda suggested to her niece.

"Mommy come, too," Chloe said, reluctant to let go of her mother's hand.

"You go with Aunt Mandy—I'll catch up with you in a few minutes," Mallory said, and pressed her lips to the top of her daughter's head.

"Promise?"

"Promise," Mallory said, and drew a cross over her heart with her finger.

The little girl finally let go of her mother's hand to take the one offered by her aunt.

"I'm glad you called your sister," Connor said.

Mallory nodded. "We're going to stay with her, here in Battle Mountain, for a few days. We can't go home until the sheriff's department clears the scene, anyway."

"And then what?" he asked her.

She shrugged. "Hopefully I'll figure that out over the next few days."

"How's your husband?" When Turcotte pulled the

trigger, the sheriff had responded—and Turcotte hadn't been wearing a vest.

"Still in surgery," she said.

"So…you finally told him you wanted a divorce?"

She nodded. "But I had no idea he had a gun. If I'd known…"

"If he makes it through the surgery, he'll be going to jail for a long time," Connor said, when her words faltered.

"I know." She brushed away the tears that spilled onto her cheeks. "I don't want him to die. He's the father of my child, but… I can't help thinking that she might be better off without a dad rather than have one who's in jail."

Her comment made Connor consider that never knowing his own father might not have been a detriment. It also reinforced his determination to be the best father he could be to Piper and Poppy—and any other kids he and Regan might have together, if he could convince her to give him a second chance.

Regan had planned to play it cool. For Connor's sake as much as her own. She understood that being a deputy wasn't just his job but an integral part of his identity, and she didn't want him to think she was going to get hysterical every time he had a little mishap on the job.

But this wasn't a minor mishap—this was a major event. Her husband had been face-to-face with an armed suspect, working to de-escalate a dangerous situation, and was rewarded with a bullet for his efforts. Someone had actually pointed a gun at him and pulled the trigger.

She couldn't envision the scene. She didn't want to. Every time she thought about Connor in that situation, she felt dizzy and nauseated and more terrified than she could ever remember feeling. But it was his job to put himself in exactly those types of situations and if she loved him—and she did!—she needed to accept that there were inherent risks to wearing a uniform and trust that he would take all necessary precautions to stay safe and come home to her and their daughters at the end of every shift.

Thankfully her parents had driven her to the hospital, so she didn't have to think about anything but Connor. Maybe they'd missed out on a lot when she was growing up, but they were here for her now and she was grateful for their support. She was also grateful that they opted to wait outside while she went in alone to see her husband.

Play it cool.

A reminder that she promptly forgot when she saw him sitting up on the examination table—alive and in one piece with no visible blood to be found. Unable to hold herself back, she flew into his arms.

He caught her close, enveloping her in the warmth and strength of his embrace. But she didn't miss the sharp hiss as he sucked in a breath.

She drew back, just far enough to see the pained expression on his face.

"What is it? What's wrong?"

"I'm a little sore," he admitted.

"The sheriff said that you were wearing a vest. That you weren't hurt."

"The Kevlar absorbed most of the impact," he conceded. "But a bullet still leaves a mark."

She pulled all the way out of his arms now to shove his T-shirt up, gasping when she saw the colorful bruise blooming in angry shades of red and purple against his skin. "Ohmygod."

"Are you going to kiss it better?" he asked.

"How can you make jokes about this?" she demanded, fighting to hold back a fresh onslaught of tears.

"It looks worse than it feels. Well, maybe not," he acknowledged. "But it's just a bruise."

"From a *bullet*," she said. "You could have been killed."

The devastating truth washed over her again, and she collapsed into sobs.

He tried to pull her back into his arms, but she held herself at a distance, explaining, "I don't want to hurt you."

"Having you here, being able to hold you, is the best possible medicine," he told her.

She wasn't sure she believed him, but she stopped resisting, because in his arms was where she wanted to be.

She sniffled. "I can't believe you were *shot*."

"It was pretty damn scary for me, too," he confided to her now. "And I did have a moment... My life didn't flash before my eyes...or maybe it did," he decided. "Because when I was staring at the gun, all I could think of was you.

"And I promised myself that if I made it out of there in one piece, I'd do whatever I had to do to make things right. Because you are my life. My everything."

He cradled her face in his hands, gently wiping the tears from her cheeks. "I love you, Regan. So much."

They were the words she'd wanted him to say, and hearing them now both filled and healed her heart.

"I love you, too," she told him.

He smiled then. "I kind of figured that out from what you said when you were yelling at me the other day."

"I was hurt and angry and—"

"And you had every right to be," he said. "I should have told you the truth from the beginning."

"Or at any other time over the past nine-and-a-half months," she suggested.

"You're right," he acknowledged. "But I was afraid that if I told you the truth, I'd lose you. And I didn't— don't ever—want to lose you."

"You're not going to lose me."

"Does that mean you'll come home?" he asked.

"I'd already decided to do just that when the sheriff called."

"Good," he said. "Because there's nothing I want more than a life with you and our daughters."

"I want that, too," she told him. "And…maybe another baby someday."

He brushed his lips over hers. "It's as if you read my mind."

Epilogue

"When my mom called to invite us for dinner, I didn't realize it was going to be a family affair," Regan remarked, as Connor pulled into the driveway where several other vehicles were already parked.

"Do you think they know it's our anniversary?" he asked.

"I wasn't sure *you* remembered it was our anniversary," she admitted.

"Of course I remembered. I even booked our suite at The Stagecoach Inn."

"*Our* suite?" she asked, amused.

"Well, I can't help but feel a little proprietary about the room where I first had the pleasure of making love with my beautiful wife," he confessed.

"I have very fond memories of that room, too," she

assured him. "And I'm eager to make more, so what do you say we skip this dinner and go straight to the hotel?"

"An undeniably tempting offer," he said. "But unless you want to take Piper and Poppy with us, we have to go inside."

"But we don't have to stay for dessert."

He chuckled as he opened the back door to retrieve the babies' car seats. "We won't stay for dessert," he agreed.

But their plans for a quick meal and quicker exit were thwarted by the discovery that Father Douglas had been invited to share the meal—and preside over a renewal of Connor and Regan's vows.

"We weren't there to share in the celebration of your wedding," Margaret explained. "So we were hoping you would exchange vows again today."

"You might have asked if this was something we wanted to do, rather than springing it on us," Regan noted.

"I want to do it," Connor said, before his mother-in-law had a chance to respond.

"Really?" His wife sounded dubious.

Margaret clapped her hands together excitedly. "Oh, this is wonderful."

"I haven't said *I* want to do it," Regan pointed out.

"I'll let you two discuss," her mother said, and slipped out of the room.

"For what it's worth, I think my parents set this up to show that they've accepted you as part of the family," she said, when they were alone.

"I only ever cared that I was accepted by you," he told her.

"Then you don't want to do the vow renewal?" she asked.

"No, I do want to do it," he said again. "My only regret, when we got married, was that I couldn't be completely honest with you about the reasons for my proposal. So today—" he dropped to one knee on the marble tile "—I'm asking you to marry me again, to take me as your husband and a father to your children, with no secrets between us, knowing that I love you with my whole heart and will continue to do so for all the days of our life together."

"And I actually thought I was starting to regain control of my emotions," Regan said, as her eyes filled with tears.

"Is that a yes or a no?" Connor asked.

"That's a very emphatic yes," she told him. "Because I love you with my whole heart, et cetera."

He lifted a brow. "Did you really just say 'et cetera' in response to my heartfelt declaration?"

"*After* I said that I loved you," she pointed out.

He grinned. "In that case, let's go get hitched so we can get to part two of our honeymoon."

And that's what they did.

* * * * *